THIS
PLACE

THIS PLACE

A novel by
Andrea Freud Loewenstein

P A N D O R A   P R E S S

Boston, London, Melbourne and Henley

First published in 1984
by Pandora Press
(Routledge & Kegan Paul plc)

9 Park Street, Boston, Mass. 02108, USA

14 Leicester Square, London WC2H 7PH, England

464 St Kilda Road, Melbourne,
Victoria 3004, Australia and

Broadway House, Newtown Road,
Henley-on-Thames, Oxon RG9 1EN, England

Photoset in Sabon, 10 on 12 pt
by Kelly Typsetting Ltd, Bradford-on-Avon, Wiltshire
and printed in Great Britain
by St Edmundsbury Press,
Bury St Edmunds, Suffolk

© Andrea Freud Loewenstein 1984

Library of Congress Cataloging in Publication Data

Loewenstein, Andrea Freud.

This place.
I. Title.
PS3562.04T4   1984   813'.54   84–11326

British Library CIP Data available

ISBN 0–86358–039–4

FOR MISTY

ACKNOWLEDGMENTS

A book which has taken so many years to finish and to see publication can only exist in its present form because of the support and caring I received from many people, too numerous to mention here. I thank them all. My mother, Sophie Freud Loewenstein, first showed me the power and joy in words, brought me up to believe that I could succeed, and has always implicitly believed in me and in this book. My father, Paul Loewenstein, was always there when I needed him. Sue Silvermarie tenderly and selflessly set me on the writer's path and helped me to take my writing seriously as an adult. Martha Spencer was my first muse. Ron Wallace was the first teacher who believed in my writing and told me to go on. Janice Irvine lovingly supported my work. Francine Rainone had faith in the book on its home stretch. Carolyn Stack and Amy Hoffman have supported me with their ongoing love and friendship. Michael Bronski's friendship gives me a sense of a family and a baseline trust which sustains me in my life and my writing. Jane Jacob's wisdom and warmth helped me finish this book, and will stay with me. Susan Saxe encouraged me to go on by always telling me this book was needed.

My publishers, at the Routledge offices in Boston and London, have been consistently warm, supportive, and helpful. I thank all those I have met and those behind the scenes who have put so much effort into the production and publication of *This Place*. Deirdre Doran's special dedication at home and Philippa Brewster's enthusiastic support from across the water have been inspiring during this year before publication.

Bernita Anderson typed the five or six 'final' versions of this book with speed and editorial understanding. Simone Reagor spent months and months of her time helping me edit. Her fine sensibility has done much to take this book from a rough to a finished work. Kate Dunn called me over the years, while this book was being turned down by publishers, reminding me of her belief. She was responsible for its publication, and provided the kind of editorial help that I am sure all authors fantasize about. Kate's ability to immerse herself in the book and its characters, her outstanding editorial skill, and her willingness to work closely with me have transformed *This Place* in a way I cannot be thankful enough for.

Finally I thank the women on the inside who shared their writing and their lives with me. Without them, this book could never have been written.

February, 1984

MONDAY, SEPTEMBER 14

TELECEA

This morning like this evening, night, aint no difference way I see it. In this place they torments you, vex you till you ready to curse the day you born. Even when you be sleeping send you them evil dreams can't even get no rest in here. Now she gone come bang my door, my head.

Unclean girl you, child of you father the Devil, seed of the Dulter Jezebel, gots to beat it out of you, beat that mark of Cain off you head, beat it out you soul.

Can't tell if I still dreaming or woke up. Tell me, Get up Telecea, get up out that bed right now. Wiggens-bitch aint got no right to come in on me when I still in the bed, in my dream.

I tell her, Watch out, don't be trying me this early in the morning, bitch, better keep off me with them stink sores on you, all that nasty filth.

She say, Telecea girl, this look to be one of your bad days well you better not lay a hand on me cause you know where you going if you does – Max.

Fool! Max aint no different than here. They both prison aint they? Just more quiet up there. Try me and try me one day they gone push too far. Then they see. He know. He been watching how they do me, gone send his Venger then they be sorry. I tell her. He be watching you bitch, you gone get yours.

She move back like all them do, talking all that Now don't you be starting with your threats now, girl, I aint got time this morning, got the others to wake up.

Tell her, Yeah? Well go wake up Billy Morris then. She don't never go in there, and I know why too. Cause that white ho' Jezebel be licking her ass, then at night she go in Billy room and I be hearing them with they filth and they no' bomination, moaning and ho'ing and Billy wif her dick out!

Know what happen to a girl think she a man and grow her one like that Billy done? He will cut it right off her that what and burn her up in the fire cause it a bomination in the eye of the Lord.

And Wiggins have the nerve to tell me, Go on up to Max, you can't stay down here Telecea, not less you act like a lady! Talkin' bout act like a lady with they ho'ing and they moaning, and she tell them, You two nice girls have a cup of coffee off of my hot plate. She better watch out Billy don't drop her dick on it. Ha ha, won't smell so nice then.

Time I gets in my shower everyone out but that old nasty thing, Billy. Girl want the shower to herself, tell me get out. Must think her dirt taste like candy. That her white bitch name, Candy. And when I do get in, oh Lord it be all nasty wif her bitch white pussy dirt and dick hairs on the soap. That aint right. That too much. So I smash that mirror in there and get me one of them nice long sliver for they ass. In case they try and stop me.

RUTH

Shivering in the cold morning, Ruth Foster reached for her clothes as quietly as she could, trying not to wake up Victor.

'It's OK Rooey, I'm awake. Look, the moon's still out, it's so early. Why don't you come on back, I'll warm you up.' He held out his arms and she could see how warm he was, the sleeping heat still radiating from him. She was tempted for a second, but it was her first morning back to work after vacation, and she wanted to be early.

'I can't, hon, I just washed.' She rubbed his wild curly hair. Then she pulled on her panty-hose, the feel of them strange after a month of sandals and sneakers, and the new light green suit she'd laid out the night before. She parted her hair neatly down the middle, combed it back and twisted it up, then checked herself in the mirror. Earrings, lipgloss, cologne. She slipped on her shoes and was ready. Victor lay still, enjoying watching her dress as he did every morning.

Ruth went through her briefcase carefully, checking to make sure she had everything. Victor was grinning at her. He thinks I'm cute, she thought, a cute little professional doll with a briefcase. A Barbie doll. She imagined the ad. 'Blond Barbie Social Worker in back-to-work fall outfit, with accessories, $5.50.' No, the price must have gone up since she was a child. She'd cost at least $9.95 now. With accessories. Barbie dolls had lasted a long time. She remembered reading that they'd altered them now, because people had complained that their breasts were too big. They'd reduced them to half the size. So now she'd fit right in. Only she was sure they hadn't added nipples. It was strange when you thought about it, those enormous breasts the old kind of Barbie doll had, without nipples. They made a black Barbie couple now of course, with matching Afros.

'Bye, hon,' she whispered, hoping that he'd gone back to sleep, but he held out his arms again, so she kissed him.

'Have a good day, Rooey,' he murmured sleepily into her hair.

'You too,' she said. She knew that the moment she left he'd go back to sleep. He loved to sleep, but always woke up for her. He liked her to wake him up if she had a bad dream at night, and she'd done it, especially when she'd first started working at Redburn Prison four

3

years ago, and was having prison nightmares every night. She was sure that it wouldn't really occur to him to think of her as a Barbie doll. Why was she being so unfair to him lately? He hadn't done anything to deserve it. She still had nightmares all the time, but he didn't know it, because she'd stopped waking him long ago.

She went to the bathroom again before leaving. The one at work was always filthy, and she'd seen roaches and silverfish crawling around on the floor. She got her sweater from the hall closet, and went out into the cool morning, glad the summer was finally over. The tree-lined street was still very quiet. Only the man from the next house, his face freshly shaven, his briefcase like hers but stiffer, smiled at her as he came out and unlocked his car door. Mary, one of the members of the lesbian couple next door, came out with her briefcase, wearing a pale blue pants suit. She taught at a nearby college, and walked to work every day, for the exercise.

'Good morning,' she and Ruth said to each other. 'Back to work again?' 'Nice day isn't it?' 'Cool.' It was a safe and friendly part of the city, and Ruth knew she was lucky to live there.

In the car, Ruth turned on the radio, and lit her first cigarette of the day. She was trying to cut down and didn't smoke at all while she was seeing clients, but allowed herself as many as she wanted on the drives in and out. During her vacation, she'd started to smoke too much. The truth was, she was relieved that it was over. She was really happiest working, she always had been. And it was hard to spend so much of one's time with one person, with any one person. That was all it was, there was nothing intrinsically wrong. The vacation was over anyway, and it was time to focus on work.

Her first appointment of the day was with Candy, and if she didn't manage to relax by then, Candy would pick it right up. She always did, just as Ruth always tuned into Candy's mood as soon as Candy came into the office. They'd been working together for two years now, and Ruth thought they were alike in some ways, although their lifestyles and backgrounds couldn't have been more different. Ruth began to make a list in her head of the ways that she and Candy were alike and different. They were both blond, of about the same height and weight, and both had the same slim figure and even regular features that made people call them pretty. Never beautiful or attractive, just pretty. Her features were sharper, her face more pointy than Candy's, her chin, cheekbones, and nose more pronounced. But, probably because Candy had been a junkie, her face

4

was older and more lined than Ruth's, even though she was four years younger. Partly because of their looks and partly because of a certain style they shared, both tended to be labeled as cold, cold pretty blondes. Neither of them was cold really, Ruth thought. Untrusting and secretive, yes. Closed up, often even to themselves. But not exactly cold. It would be good to see Candy again. The therapy with her had been really moving before Ruth left, and she'd missed Candy during her vacation.

Thinking about Candy as she pulled into the parking lot, Ruth reflected that most clinicians would find it surprising for a woman with a history of addiction, prostitution, and violence to have over-control as an issue, and it was true that most of the women she saw at Redburn had the opposite problem. They were much more overtly troubled, borderlines and character-disorders mostly, with a sprinkling of schizophrenics like Gladdy Dwight, whom she'd seen for three years, and finally terminated with before her vacation. And Telecea Jones, one of the institution's problems. Ruth had a reputation for being effective with the violent or acting-out women, which really meant that she was the only one on the mental health staff who wasn't terrified of them.

Slamming the car door, she wondered how Gladdy and Telecea were doing.

CANDY

Waking in Billy's arms in the still-dark, Candy felt that tenderness so fierce it was like a pain. It was maybe what other girls felt for their kids, though she'd never felt it for hers that she could remember, that little white-blond baby that would start in screaming just when her head would be hurting its worst, and it would already be ticking inside her, *get out on that street and make some money, girl.* If it had just been dark enough so Earl could of convinced hisself it was his, it might of been alright. Not real dark, he wouldn't of wanted a kid like that from his Silver Lady as he called her, but a cute little gold-coloured girl baby with curls, or, even better, a son. Maybe that could of added to her worth and not took off, but with her luck it had to of been a white trick got her pregnant. She even knew which motherfucker it was, cause she had took the fool off for four hundred, cash. Most of her tricks used to be either black or else Indian or Chinese or something, but there was this one ugly old white dude that was fool enough to come in the ghetto looking for pussy with all kinds of money sticking out his pocket, that didn't look like he had enough juice in him to make her a baby in the first place, but he had to of been the one, or the baby would of showed it someplace.

So Earl hated the kid, it was like a slap in the face to him. Like telling him he couldn't make her no baby. That not him or any brothers cum had been strong enough to slip in between the magic of them little pills. So an old white fart had to do it to her.

Course they hadn't been no magic about it. She got caught just like a lot of the girls did, by letting her habit get to where she worried and planned so hard about where the next high was coming from, she didn't have no time to be remembering did she take her pill that day. And after, she lost the edge she had from being his top white bitch. There wasn't no one to leave the baby with and she was dope-sick with a crying kid on her hands and she'd almost been relieved when they busted her a few months later, though it wasn't something you could say to no one. If only she knew they'd take and give her a hysterectomy a few years later, she would of done it different. But she didn't know.

They only kept her a couple weeks that time, just long enough for her to shake her habit, and when she got out the joint, wasn't no more little blond baby, not for her. Anyways, now she had Billy to love. She felt Billy move a little and moan in her sleep and knew she would not let her be stole or hurt by no one. Billy who acted so tough, the big bad butch around everyone but her, but that she had seen crying and held in her arms cause Billy trusted her that much.

Some of the butches would of been shocked at the idea of letting their women make love to them cause they felt it was giving up to them, like laying on your back and coming made you the bitch, but Billy wasn't like that. She mostly always wanted Candy to do it to her after she made Candy come, and when she did, Billy would moan out in the pillow in the way that gave Candy that sharp tender feeling. She guessed it was being in love, though the songs never made it sound so fierce, like knowing if anyone ever tried to hurt Billy she'd just step in between and kill them without even thinking twice, although she was not and had never been violent by nature, and had only hurt people when she'd had to sometimes, in self-defense. The black girls she knew would get up-tight if you said something bout their Mama or anyone else in their blood family, but to tell the truth, Candy didn't really give a shit about her blood. They could go on and say what they wanted about her dad that she hadn't seen since she was thirteen when he washed his hands of her as he put it, and she didn't even mind if they talked about her mom that had always did what he told her, like some fucking robot, and her brother and sister were strangers anyways, but when it came to Billy, they knew to keep their mouths shut. 'She's my people.' That's how she said it out loud.

She got up quiet as she could, and tucked the covers back around Billy and ran across the hall so it'd be her own room she'd come out of at wake-up. She didn't need no alarm now, just woke up automatic, but once she got back in her own bed she could never go back to sleep, and always ended up lying there worrying bout shit she would of just as soon forgot, like this about her kid. Usually smoking a little reefer and listening to her music would calm her nerves right down, but her and Billy had smoked up the last of it yesterday. Worrying always gave her big bags under her eyes that she had to cover up with makeup, unlike some of these bitches that just let themself go in here, got all fat and didn't do nothing with their hair or face and some even let their rooms get filthy which there wasn't no excuse for. They said it didn't matter cause it wasn't their real life. It wasn't hers either, that was for sure, but her and Billy was for real, even though this place wasn't. So she always kept up her appearance, plus their rooms. Even the sinks and the goddamn toilets were clean enough to eat off of, unlike the ones in the main building which you couldn't use without being afraid of catching something. She tried hard to give Billy and her both the respect they tried to take from you, but even so, being in here together was putting them through some very heavy changes, but she knew they'd be alright once they was out, which was getting close now. They had met on the inside, and had just been out together one time, on escape which didn't count, and anyway, that was another time she didn't like to think about too tough.

Anyways, they had worked it about as good as you could in here, with their rooms across from each other plus this arrangement with Wiggins that Candy had fixed by staying up one whole night listening to the poor bastard talk about her son that was trouble and her whole boring sick family. You could get over with almost anyone if you listened good enough, and she'd always knew how to do that. She got over in here cause she always volunteered for every halfass new group they thought up, showed up for her sucky state job on time, and listened to everyone on the staff when they came to rap to her about their asshole problems. But she never told them nothing about herself. It was a thin line between getting over and sucking ass, but she knew how to walk it and everyone knew she did. Some of the bitches in here, especially the white ones, thought the screws was on their side or something, and some would go as far as telling them other people's business which is when they found out what doing hard time was all about. But Candy had been around long enough to have it known she wasn't nobody to mess with and the few that had tried had been sorry after. They knew, too, that in one way she had to do twice as much to get over cause she was doing it for both of them. Billy didn't make no trouble, but she was considered sullen, the way she casted her eyes down and would refuse to even speak around any staff, let alone speak to them. They was always trying to speak to *her*, though, fine as she was. You couldn't help but notice Billy. But Billy hated all of them and let them know it. Candy thought of the way she acted around Miss Foster, which bothered her at times, cause she didn't want Foster to think Billy was ignorant.

Which reminded her – today was the day Foster was coming back from vacation. She didn't feel like seeing her, she was thinking about quitting anyway. Right before Foster left it had got so every time she saw her her stomach had went all tight like when she needed a fix, which she hadn't for more than a year now, and all those bad times had came flooding back.

'That it's started to make you feel that way isn't so bad,' Tight-Ass had the nerve to tell her. 'It shows that something is happening in here, that you're letting yourself feel things you need to feel about your life.' But what fucking right did that bitch have to tell Candy what she needed to feel? It wasn't her that had to live with those feelings, like dry heaves inside her afterwards, when she was off on her la-di-da vacation.

Fuck Foster anyways, who learned everything she knew from her shrink books and didn't even know what a real feeling, the kind she had with Billy, was. She was glad Billy acted ignorant to her. Candy thought of Foster as being dead inside. There was something so up-tight about her like she'd never in all her life let go and screamed or shouted or cried or came. That's why everyone called her tight-ass. She would of thought Foster was a goddamn virgin or something, even though she had to be at least thirty or so. But when Edie was out on escape this one time, she'd seen Foster downtown, walking with some big dude, hanging all over him, Edie said. So Candy guessed she must did get it somehow, but maybe it didn't do nothing for her. Probly she was funny and didn't know it, a closet case like half the staff, that was always looking at Billy that way. 'I don't care if she does have her shrink degree and a straight rich dude and a color TV set out in suburbia and probly getting ready to have three tightass little kids just like her,' Candy thought. She could of had all that herself if she wanted to, but she never did. She had Billy, and the life they'd have together and she wouldn't trade that for nothing. Even if it had to be inside this place for the time being.

The bell rung, and she heard Wiggins out in the hall grunt and start moving around. Loud as it was, the bell should of woke up anyone, but most of the girls was drugged, either on their own shit or on the shit that dickhead doctor-shrink loved to hand out, and no one, drugged or not, wanted to wake up all that much, cause what the fuck for – so Wiggins had to go from door to door shaking them awake like the little kids they would of liked to turn them all into.

Soon as she heard Wiggins, Candy moved. She had showered, turnt on Wiggins' hot plate, got dressed with her hair and make-up done, and made it to Billy's room with her coffee before most of the others was even up. Billy needed to get up slow, cause she had

9

nightmares and lots of times would wake up still down inside them. Today, with her eyes half-open, not tensed up yet, but all relaxed and soft, she leaned her arms out and took hold of Candy.

'Hey, Mama,' she said, and Candy could just picture her as the cute little girl in pigtails and pajamas she must of been, reaching out for her real Mama in the morning, not knowing if she'd be there. Cause Billy's Mama, that was too-too respectable now, use to be a hooker and wild, and wasn't around half the time when Billy was a kid. But now Billy had *her*, and she wasn't planning on going nowheres.

'Hey, baby,' she whispered. 'Your coffee's here waitin' for you and they've cleared out the shower by now. It's all yours.'

Billy started off for the shower, but then, over the noise of the radio and TV that had got turnt on for the day, Candy heard her run into Telecea Jones, who, from the sound of it, was about ready to go off again. Candy hoped she'd stay the fuck out of Billy's way, 'cause Billy was not too cool this early in the morning and that girl was one crazy bitch who when she went off and got confused, thinking you was her old grandma that used to beat on her or someone, would pull a fucking knife on you without thinking twice about it. A person like that didn't value her own life let alone someone else's, so Candy held her breath till she could hear Billy was safe in the shower.

As her and Billy walked into the main building to get breakfast, they ran into Foster first, and then that old bitch Hanson that was Director of Treatment.

'Candy dear, I want you to serve as tour-guide to the new art therapist who is starting today,' she said in her too-sweet voice. 'I know how good you are at orienting newcomers to our building, dear. She'll be down in Mental Health with your friend, Miss Foster, so why don't you just drop right in after your appointment and introduce yourself.'

'OK, Mrs Hanson,' Candy said. It was hard to be cool, with cuntface saying right in front of everyone that she was a sicky that went to therapy.

'Who knows, maybe you'd like to work with Miss Lehrman, too,' Hanson went right on. 'You're artistic, aren't you dear?'

After she walked off in that weird fake-leather shit she always wore, leaving her BO behind her, Billy gave Candy a disgusted look.

'Just what you need, huh baby?' she said. 'A little more therapy.'

Billy hated for her to go to Foster and she was mad now cause Foster was back. Candy thought maybe she'd switch from Ruthy Tight-Ass to this new one. Being artistic sounded easier than talking your guts out, and Billy wouldn't mind so much.

'I feel this type of therapy is more appropriate and helpful to me at this stage of the game,' she imagined herself saying to old cuntface, with her best sorry-looking smile.

SONYA

In her dream Sonya had been a kid back in the Bronx and now she stretched and looked around her new loft, orienting herself. She was not fourteen. She was an adult, an artist, starting a new career today. 'Art therapist, Redburn Prison for Women,' she said aloud solemnly, for the camera.

She got out of bed and went to turn on the bathwater, which came out in an irregular trickle. The tub was beautiful, though, with its pointy dragon feet, and she loved the way it was right there next to the stove. Her conception for the loft had been a great success, especially considering the short time she'd been working on it. It was both cozy and spacious, with the living area set off by three big hooked rugs she'd found in Goodwill and had cleaned, and the work area empty and pure looking, with its bare stripped down wood floor. She'd built a long, high work table all along one wall under the high windows, and had hung only one of her canvasses, the big nude self-portrait in three panels, on the back wall. Only the toilet area was enclosed, and that had already been done by the previous tenant. She'd dreamed of a loft like this for years, and now she had it. The only trouble was that she didn't have anyone to show it off to yet.

For a moment she missed Mira, who would have appreciated the loft. But when she thought of her, it was the accusing tearful Mira of their last days together who appeared. Sonya went to put on coffee, watching the people pass under the window on their way to work. It was good to be back in a real city neighbourhood again. Vermont had been alright in its own way, but she was a city girl at heart. And she was glad to be alone. Sometimes she wished she could take a wet sponge and wipe it right across her memory, like the chosen kid used to get to do to the blackboards at school. Which was a very nice image, when you thought about it.

She put cream and two sugars in her coffee and took it into the still only half-full, not very hot bathtub with her. The water situation was annoying, but still, it was a magic place. She half-believed she'd materialized it just by imagining it so well. It was too bad sculptures didn't happen like that, although of course they did, in a way. And the job had that same quality. The minute she'd heard about it, in Vermont, she'd known it was meant for her.

She decided that she'd start off her new life by losing weight. From now on she'd have nothing but coffee in the morning. She'd start jogging, and have so much more energy that even with this full-time job, she'd get more of her own work done than ever before. She'd come straight home and not even think about food, just start right in on her prison sculptures.

'Boxes,' she explained to the interviewer. 'Enclosures, cages, whatever you choose to call them. They just started coming when I began working at the prison.'

The bath water had cooled and Sonya shivered as she stood, dripping. They would laugh at her at the prison, they would see right through her with their cool practiced eyes, they would call her 'Fatty', imitate the way she walked, and trip her in the hallways like back in junior-high. No, they would do even worse than that. They would ignore her completely. No one would come to any of her classes, or even speak to her. She'd never make any friends here, and finally she would disappear.

She cut big pieces from the soft loaf she'd bought at the Portuguese bakery on the corner and ate it quickly because it was getting late, and she didn't even know what to wear, whom to dress as. Once she got thin it wouldn't matter at all. Then she'd look good in anything. Finally she put on her red embroidered smock top, the soft red and yellow striped pants, and gold hoop earrings. Then she brushed her hair hard, until it gave off sparks. She looked at herself critically in the mirror. She was OK. She looked like an artist.

She was late now, and so she ran for it, the movie camera shooting her progress. It was the opening scene, even before the credits had come on, and there was no dialogue yet, no music even, just a shot from the top of the stairs of the spiral and the smaller and smaller figure running gracefully down and out the door. And now the street noises would start, maybe the theme song, carried through naturally by a kid on a skateboard, with his transistor radio. A quick scene of her running through the neighbourhood, with just enough details to give an idea of it, and then down the subway steps and right onto the train which was now pulling in. The whole sequence hadn't taken more than five minutes.

'Not bad,' she thought. 'Not bad at all. *I'd* keep watching. If the character isn't your typical movie star type, at least she has her own style. And just look how all the people on the train are smiling at her.'

'No wonder,' Mira would say if she were here, 'the way you flirt.' But who could accuse her of flirting with this staid, mustached mother, who was taking her two little boys in ties to their Catholic school? They'd reached the last stop, the end of the line now, and she got off as she'd been instructed to do, and waited for the bus with five middle-aged black women carrying plastic shopping bags who must be maids going to their jobs in the suburbs. She tried smiling at them, but they looked straight ahead, ignoring her and talking in mono-syllables to each other.

'How long do you usually have to wait?' she asked the one closest to her, who shrugged.

'It all depends,' she said. When the bus finally came, Sonya was frantic. She was going to be late to work, on her first day, and make a terrible impression.

'Redburn?' the young driver said. 'You got quite a ride ahead of you. It's the last stop.' The bus crawled forward, letting off a passenger every few blocks. Finally Sonya was the only one left. There were long flat stretches of field here, and patches of woods with only a few houses. Sonya felt panicky, a party to some bad joke. Why was she the only passenger? Did no one else take the bus to work? Did the prison really exist? Finally the driver slowed down. 'Redburn,' he sneered. 'Last stop.'

Sonya got out on a winding, badly paved country road and watched the bus turn laboriously around and disappear. Next to her was a small parking lot with about twenty cars in it. Behind the parking lot, a wide field stretched invitingly in the sun. Two horses, restrained by a wire fence, grazed quietly. Across the street, a small embankment stretched for about 100 yards on either side of a large red brick building. As Sonya crossed to it, she saw that the building was surrounded by a barbed wire fence. It was higher than the horses' fence and ornamented almost decoratively on the top with a curling pattern of shaved knife-like wire which shone and sparkled in the sun. Signs on this fence read 'State Property – Keep Off.' Behind the large building Sonya could see part of a yard with smaller buildings and a few figures walking around. She was disappointed for a moment – she'd visualized the kind of solid wall prisoners tunneled under in the movies. But as she approached the solid brick building she saw the barred windows.

A thrill of excitement shot through her as she followed the sign that directed 'All Visiters' under the arch and through a large metal door. Shit yes, this was a prison alright. And now the movie camera was on again. Filming Sonya Lehrman, sculptor and art therapist, going through the prison gates for her first day of work.

MONDAY, SEPTEMBER 14

RUTH

Safe at her desk, Ruth let herself think of the camping trip to the mountains for the first time since their return. She thought it had been the worst time she and Victor had spent together yet. Maybe it had been even worse because it was so beautiful there, the same way more people commit suicide in Spring. She could hardly remember the beauty now – just the constant pressure, the unrelenting grating of Victor's presence.

One morning when they'd camped high up, just below the tree-line, she'd gotten up at dawn. The mountain tops were covered with mist, and she'd sat still on an overhanging rock and watched the whiteness roll off. Then she'd felt him standing behind her. That was the day the mountains began to feel like a weight they were carrying on their shoulders, and they had almost run all the way down, arriving at the foot of the trail after dark. Later he'd said, not trying to reproach her, simply stating a fact, 'You looked more relaxed than I've seen you look for months. I mean that morning you thought you were alone, before you saw me.'

There was a soft knock at the door and Ruth jumped and swore, caught in the unpleasant memory. Candy was never early. She wasn't ready to deal with Dave or one of the others yet. But when she opened the door a stranger stood there, a big woman with long black curly hair and a red smock, who didn't look like a new inmate.

'Ruth Foster?' The woman smiled and took a step forward. 'I'm Sonya Lehrman.' She paused, apparently waiting for recognition. When none came, her assured expression began to fade. 'I'm the new art therapist,' she said. 'You *are* Ruth Foster?'

'Yes, I am,' said Ruth, 'but I have no idea who you are. Apparently I should?' It was becoming increasingly clear that once again Hanson had taken advantage of her absence to go over her head.

'I guess I assumed you'd be expecting me,' the woman, whose name Ruth had forgotten, faltered. 'Mrs Hanson hired me two weeks ago. I'm supposed to start today.'

Ruth tried to contain her rising anger. After all, it wasn't the woman's fault that this place was run in such a way that no one bothered to inform the director of mental health that there was a new therapist. An art therapist, yet! Someone must have convinced Hanson that establishing a progressive program would look good on her record and help her up another step of the ladder of corrections when the time came, and she usually got what she wanted, since Tranden was almost never around. What made it even more infuriating was that Hanson had adamantly refused every desperately needed program Ruth had proposed in the past three years. And now here was this new art therapist – dressed for the part!

'I'd ask you to sit down,' Ruth said coldly, 'but I'm expecting a client any minute. If you could come back later maybe you wouldn't mind explaining all this to me, as I seem to be totally uninformed.' The woman clearly had no idea where to go, and Ruth heard the same bitchy tone in her voice that was there lately whenever she talked to Victor, but it was just too bad. She was damned if she was going to put off Candy to play welcoming committee to this one.

'If you'd come back in an hour . . . ,' she said firmly, and opened the door. The woman walked out, and Candy came in, staring. Ruth told herself it was alright. So the stranger would wander the halls for an hour. What could happen to her, really? She'd get a feel for the place, anyway. Then when 'the ladies' arrived, their usual half-hour or so late, they would take good care of her, would welcome her with sympathy and gossip and coffee. A new member for the coffee club, an artist. They'd be thrilled.

'What's the matter, Miss Foster?' asked Candy, sitting down and crossing her legs neatly. 'You sorry to be back? You don't like Miss Lehrman?'

'I just met her, Candy,' Ruth said as calmly as she could, wishing that Candy, who seemed to be a lot better informed than she was, had said the first name, too.

'I bet they didn't even tell you she was coming, huh? They sure don't tell you too much, do they, Miss Foster?'

'Whether they do or don't tell me things,' Ruth said gently, 'isn't the point. And neither is my opinion of Miss Lehrman, whom I just now met. I haven't seen *you* for a month, Candy. How are you? How have things been going?'

'You must of at least seen the broad.' Candy was talking very fast. 'Remember what I said to you about how you dress too nondescript? How you need some style to bring you out? Well that broad's good and ugly, aint no way she got your looks, but when she comes in the room, at least you see her. She's got style, she don't blend in the way you do.'

'This hour is for you, Candy,' Ruth said. She tried to remember what the woman, Lehrman, had looked like, but couldn't. 'It's not to talk about my style or lack of it.'

'Yeah, lack of it, that's it. I aint saying you're not nice-looking, cause you are. It's just that you could look a whole lot better than you do. You got the figure for it, and if you would just cut your hair nice and stylish to show off your face instead of twisting it back like that. I'll do it for you, I told you I would . . .'

Ruth said nothing this time, just sat there waiting.

'What you looking at me for' Candy asked shrilly. 'You know how I hate for people to stare at me. I'm not gonna do nothing like I did last time, if that's what you're waiting for.'

'Last time?'

'You know what I mean. Putting on a damn show for you. Crying and all that. Telling you stuff only me and Billy spose to know. How do I know what you're gonna do with it? You could write it down and show it when I come up for review next time for all I know! You wouldn't never let me see you cry, so why should I? I don't cry in front of no one. I don't even know why I keep coming in here!' She lit another cigarette, starting it before the last had burned down, but saving the ends. Her foot was tapping against the desk leg, punctuating her words. It looked small and white in the constricting plastic stacked heels.

'Candy, do you really think I would use what you say or do in here against you? After all this time?' Ruth looked at her, and, very slowly, Candy shook her head.

'But you make me say shit I don't want to.'

'I've told you before, you don't have to talk about anything you don't want to talk about,' Ruth said. These were old issues, but then, she had been gone a month. 'If you have some bad feelings from the last time we talked, then maybe that's what you'd like to talk about now.'

'OK.' And Candy told her about getting sick after last time, about her shame at having revealed too much, her conviction that anyone who saw her weakness would use it against her. And then Ruth had been gone for a month, and she'd been left to herself with all of it.

There was a kind of door inside Ruth when she was working.

That was how she thought of it; as a door which opened very quietly and smoothly inside her, and when it did open, as it usually did, she was a good therapist, and when it didn't she was a pretty good fake. It had opened now, for Candy, and Ruth, feeling this happen inside her after a whole month of not working, was relieved and glad to be back.

CANDY

Coming out from Foster, Candy didn't have to be nowhere. They wouldn't expect her back at the flag room, so she went and sat down in the sun next to the tree she thought of as her tree. Except for a few people with visits, everyone else was at work, so the yard was empty and quiet. Candy watched little Rosey and her old sugar daddy playing chess on a card table he always brought in, and Selina Roberts talking to her tired, squeezed out, yellow looking man that didn't have nothing better to do than to come out to Redburn every day and sit there without even saying nothing. Candy was feeling sad. Not sick, like last time after Foster, but just plain sad, like they was rain drip-dripping inside of her. Watching a few leaves fall off her tree it seemed to her like everything she looked at was about dying or going away or being locked up.

A few yards away, this pregnant white girl, Cathy, and her mother came out and sat down on one of the rusty old benches. The mother had her lipstick all smeared across her mouth, like some old bitches do, and that stiff dyed hair that was sort of a off blue color. She was doing all the talking, and you could tell she'd been drinking. Candy couldn't hear much, but from what she could make out it was all about their house, TV this and bedroom sets that and 'we had the basement all done over, you'll see,' and then real clear, 'Daddy says this time it's gonna be different, he made a vow to Father Thomas,' and then more about bedroom sets and ping pong and shit. Cathy just sat and nodded her little made-up doll face 'yeah Mom, yeah, uh-huh yeah' over her eight month pregnant belly.

'The fuck it is,' thought Candy. 'The fuck it is gonna be different.' They was both fools but they made her sad anyway, only she didn't know was it sad for Cathy, who she didn't even speak to on the compound cause she always kept to herself since some girls jumped her and took her shit when she first came in. Or for the old drunk bitch, or for that poor little kid that would have to live with all of them and Daddy when it got itself born. Or maybe even sad for her own self cause her name used to be Cathy too. It was what her mother knew her by, but her mother wouldn't even come see her in jail, not since the time her dad had forbid her to when she was in the first time. The truth was Candy didn't even know if her mom and dad lived at the same old address or if maybe he'd finally left her and her mom had turned into a drunk like that one with her lipstick smear.

Gladdy Dwight came walking through the yard, doing that old thorazine shuffle, like she'd just got up out of the bed and hadn't got it all together yet. Cathy's mother looked up with that 'so that's the kind of people they got my daughter in here with' look that visits always got when they first saw the nuts like Gladdy or Telecea, or some of the butchiest girls.

'Is she . . . violent?' she heard the old broad say. 'Honey, what's wrong with her?' If she hadn't been somebody's visit, Candy would of told her if they put *her* on half the shit they gave old Gladdy she would put on her skirt inside out and someone's old pajamas for a top too, plus how was Gladdy sposed to dress when didn't no one ever give her no clothes? At least Gladdy's breasts was covered up good today, which the visit's wasn't.

'Nah, Mom, she don't hurt no one,' was all Cathy said, which was the most words Candy had heard out her mouth yet.

Now Gladdy had came near Candy. She picked up a leaf that had just fell at Candy's feet. 'Leaf, you sposed to be still up in that tree,' she said. 'Aint time for you to be coming down yet.' Then she turned her head up to the sky.

'Leaves be coming down from the trees before they time, something wrong. Peoples gots to of done something bad to be punish this way.' She got down on her creaky knees in the grass, pointing out each of them that was out in the yard, one by one. 'Lord tell us what's wrong. All the mothers and the childs and the childs still in the bellies waiting to come out' (she patted her own belly here, she was always saying she was pregnant) 'and the old mans can't keep they hands to theyself aint playing no chess and the little girls should know better and the man think he live here but he don't. And me, Gladys M. Dwight, and the pretty little ho', Candy Cane, all of us we be praying to you right now asking you WHAT'S WRONG, WHAT'S WRONG LORD WHAT'S WRONG WHAT'S WRONG WHAT'S WRONG! She yelled this a couple of times at the top of her voice. Cathy and her mother went inside. Then Gladdy got up off her knees.

'Locks you up like some animal,' she said in a conversation type voice to Candy. 'Takes away one half you head. Takes you own kids that you suffered wif and born from your body. Puts you in a zoo to be look at. You gots to act just a little bit like one, don't you?'

21

'I hear you Gladdy,' Candy told her, and then turned away cause Gladdy had already got almost a whole pack off her last week and she didn't want to give up no more cigarettes. She thought none of them crazies was all that much gone if you took the time to think about some of the shit they said. Even Telecea Jones when she went off, talked some sense in between all that bible bullshit, if you listened real good.

It was like feeling sad, listening to crazy people talk. Out there on the street you had your crazies too, walking round talking their shit, and you might even give them some wine or something if you was in a good mood or just made some money. But you didn't never stop and listen to what they was saying, they just wasn't no time. And it was the same thing with being sad. On the street it was one hustle after another, you had to keep on moving all the time to survive. When you finally rested, it was by getting good and high or else if you passed out asleep. But never just sitting with time to be sad in. She could remember crying out there cause she was pissy drunk or cause her man had hit her, or if she'd got beat out of some blow or dope, but the feeling she had inside her now wasn't bout crying like that, like a kid would if someone took their toy away, it was a different crying. Only it wasn't crying for real, with tears, not yet. It was just drip drip dripping somewheres down in her belly, where no one else could see.

SONYA

When Ruth Foster slammed the door in her face, Sonya walked back through the heavy creaking iron door which separated the mental health corridor from the wide central hall which held the offices of Mrs Hanson and the social workers, as well as the beauty parlor and pool room. In this hall, women slouched against the institution-green walls. A few of those standing alone could have passed for inmates of the state mental hospital she'd worked at briefly in Vermont, but the others reminded her more of the angry out-of-work men who stood around or played cards outside the bodega in her neighborhood, and whistled or sneered at her when she passed.

They had been talking, but stopped at her approach. 'Hey lady, you got a cigarette?' someone asked her in a mocking voice. She had begun to shake her head, no, when another woman corrected the first. 'She mean do you got a *pack* of cigarettes?'

'She don't know what she saying,' said a third. 'She mean do you got a *carton*.'

'Sorry, I don't smoke,' Sonya managed, searching their faces for a break in the wall, a friendly instead of mocking grin. She noticed one young woman who was leaning neither on the wall nor on anyone else, but stood straight and still, a small distance apart. She was very black, and her eyes, which were intent on Sonya, stood out in a bizarre way in her bony face with its closely shaven head.

The others included both black and white women, Sonya saw now, as well as some couples: two women draped together with one exaggeratedly feminine and the other dressed as a man. It was a dense, frightening group, and its voice was not a friendly one.

'Don't smoke, huh? You one of them health freaks, huh?' It was the one who had first spoken, a heavy and commanding black woman. 'What are you anyway,' she continued. 'A new social worker?' It seemed to be a sincere question, and Sonya considered.

'No,' she said, 'I'm not a social worker. I'm an artist. An art teacher.' It was not quite the official introduction she had visualized, but she was pleased to be doing it herself, on her own terms.

'You sure you ain't no social worker, now?' Sonya had the uneasy feeling of being caught in a lie. Had Mrs Hanson already explained her presence to them by saying that an art therapist was a new kind of social worker? Sonya hated it when people thought of her as a social worker. As if to back this up, a tall strong-looking white woman with short dyed-black hair wearing a man's sleeveless T-shirt, spoke up in her behalf.

'The lady just *said* she ain't no social worker, Edie, Don't you believe no one?'

'No,' Edie answered her. 'Why should I?'

'Hey,' her champion went on, disregarding this. 'When's the last time you seen one a them social workers out in the hall? You heard the lady, she said she's an artist.'

'Could be a artist and a social worker both.'

'Mabe, you so ignorant I bet you don't even know what do a artist do.' This got a general laugh, and Sonya felt the atmosphere lightening a little in her favor.

'Today,' she recapitulated for the camera crew, who'd been discreetly filming the scene, 'today somebody asked me "What do a artist do." '

All of a sudden everyone had questions.

'You gonna bring us in some of them kits? To make jewelry?'

'Some yarn?'

'I need another crochet hook, somebody took mine.'

'Need some of them wires, you can make them flowers out of? Like Wanda made?'

'My friend, she made one of them tile things for her daughter, out of ceramics like, you bake it in one of them stoves?'

'Kills, you call them stoves kills, stupid.'

'Yeah, that's what I said, kills, and you bake it in this stove, and it come out real pretty and you can put hot shit on it, them hot pans.'

'One of them long crochet hooks, not the small kind.'

'The jewelry she make look like you buy it in a store.'

'Wrote her daughter name on it, and it came out real pretty, her sign on it too.'

'Aquarius.'

'Saggitarius.'

'Scorpio,' volunteered Sonya, hoping to turn the conversation firmly away from crochet hooks and kills.

'Scorpion, huh? Can't stand me no scorpions. Never could. Specially them white scorpions. They smiles in your face and stings

24

you in the back.' All the women turned to Edie and away from Sonya in the blast of laughter that followed. Thinking nervously about her own back, Sonya turned and walked in the direction she'd come from.

'Hey lady, never mind them.' She turned to see her original defender. 'They're just ignorant till they get to know you.'

'Thanks.' Sonya smiled at her. But it was the image of the other, strange one, who'd stood so still the entire time, that stayed with her. Sonya saw her clearly, with her new, blue high-top sneakers, and her closely shaven head with its scars and bumps.

Back in the mental health corridor, things were buzzing now. A plump blond woman who sat at a typewriter in a large office talking to two other young women greeted her with warm cooing noises.

'You must be Sonya Lehrman. I'm Lynda Wisen, the secretary, and this is Nan Brown and Cindy Hanvey, two of our therapists. Did you just now come in?' When Sonya told her that she'd been in for a while, Cindy, who was very thin and wore a lot of make-up, gave a little scream.

'Did you hear that? She came in and there was no one here. Don't tell me, I bet you walked down that hall and the girls did a number on you.' She and Lynda began talking about their first days, what the 'girls' had said to them in the hallway, and how they had each gone home and told their husband/boyfriend that they would never return.

'And here we all are,' said Lynda cheerily. 'So don't feel bad.' Sonya wanted to run again. The women in the hall had been scary but these were worse.

'I *don't* feel bad,' she told them. 'I was glad to meet the women alone.' There was a silence.

'Well, aren't you the brave one!' Cindy finally said. 'It must be because you're an artist.' She pronounced the word as if it were a highly contagious disease, and Lynda immediately began talking about her son who had a talent for art, they had told her so at his school. Nan, the dark somber one who hadn't said a word yet, just stared at Sonya until she began to wish that Ruth Foster, for all her bitchiness, would come in. She wondered what the story was there. Had she felt territorially threatened, afraid that Sonya would steal her clients? More likely, she'd reacted like that because she hadn't been told about Sonya in advance. Clearly she liked to be in control, to know what was coming. She probably hated going on vacation for just that reason. Anything could happen without her there to oversee it. At least she had taken a vacation. Some of these compulsive types couldn't bring themselves to go away at all.

Sonya imagined Ruth Foster, who was an extremely attractive woman in her cold WASPy way, apologizing to her for her behavior, tears coming to her eyes as she asked whether they might not be friends. Since someone had to supervise her she was just as glad it would be Ruth.

It was hot and uncomfortable in the office. The blasting music from the radio got on her nerves, and the smoke hurt her eyes. 'Have I been assigned an office yet?' she asked them.

'Oh no.' Lynda sounded a little reproving. 'You'll have to wait for Mrs Hanson for that. She handles office assignments, and she'll probably have you rove a little at first, to orientate you, you know.'

As Sonya reflected that anyone who used the word 'orientate' should be shot, a man entered the room noisily.

'And how are the ladies this Monday morning?' He gave her a quick look of assessment, and immediately changed his tone.

'You must be Sonya Lehrman. I'm Dave Thorne. Otherwise known as 'the shrink.' When you've had your coffee, why don't you come into my office and I'll fill you in a little. Then Mrs Hanson would like to see you, and Mr Tranden, the superintendent, should be making an appearance a little later too.' He gestured expansively down the hall. 'Good to see you here. I've been fighting for some of the expressive therapies programs for a long time now. We need you badly.' He was tall, dark, good-looking, condescending. She wondered how he and Ruth Foster got along as she followed him down the hall, hating him instantly and completely.

TELECEA

They may think they know who they got in here but don't no one
know. But the Truth gone come out one day. What they do not know
is every thing they do unto me go down. No thing they do pass free.
He see. Gone turn it all round break the pride of they power break
them all up and them fowls an them beasties gone eat them up, and
they kids too. Them big teefs gone crush them little white babies,
break they bones in pieces.

Just like they done Joseph. Put him in a pit without no water
take his pretty coat dip it all in the blood leave him for the beasties to
eat, sell his ass. Just like they done me. But it come round. Joseph be
king and they the ones die from thirst. Shrivel right up and them lions
eat they ass. Then they see how they like it livin in the land of they
enemies like they done me. And vext and torment all the time.

What you gots to do, you gots to be still, lissen good and then
you find out. In the hall they be talking to this white lady dress up like
a witch. It say don't suffer no witch to live but you gots to be sure
cause in here they all gots they disguise. Can't tell who who, just like
in this story I seen Little Red Goldilocks, it look just like somebody
Granny, but it a wolf drest in her skin, grab and eat up that little girl
that don't know no better cause she forgot to watch good.

Gots to keep your eyes open in here. Way they gots it hook up
you can't tell who who. Got your girls dress up as a boy and grow
them dicks so how you spose to tell? But I know. Then they gots it fix
so you can't tell who the real police here. Oh yes, they will try
anything to keep you confuse. They got some police that black and
some inmates that white and then they gone dress up some of them
police like they inmates and some inmates like police, so you always
got someone watching you all the time. That's why I don't hang wif
no one in here. I keeps to myself cause one day you could turn round
and this girl you been telling all you shit to turn out to be a police.

But what they don't know is I be watching all the time. If I stay
still and waits long enough, I know they gots to give theyself away.
This one name Ruth Foster, I be watching her every Wednesday and
Friday eleven oclock when she think she doing her therapy on me.
What I do, I say something and watch her real good. She think she

27

can hold her face all uptight but she aint. Tell the truth I aint yet figured out what her purpose is but I think maybe she a inmate they gots dresst up as a police. Cause sometime she know what I'm gone say before I say it and how she gone know that if she aint in here? Plus you don't see her hanging with any of them other police. I have check that room they got in her hall where they be making they evil plans and eating up all that nasty filth food and coffee wif cockroaches swim round in it. If I stand in the bathroom I can see who in that room, and Ruth Foster aint never in there. Make her own chocolate in her office and give me some. Plus, she look too much like that white ho' Candy that go wif Billy Morris and I know that gotta mean something.

Could be she a inmate but they aint told her. I think they don't always be knowing they own self.

This other one she got that long witch hair and say, I am a artist. I am a artist so don't call me no Social Worker. All the time she be talking with them others acting like she listening to they shit, bring me this and that. Ain't nothing but beggars got no pride, just wants to use someone. All that time she be looking right at me. Act like she listening to them but looking at me. Cause I a artist too, I been knowing that a long time. Just like how He send Joseph them dreams so he know what gone happen. Send him a vision. A picture, then make it come true. Like when he seen the man wif birds eating off his head and know that man head gonna hang on a tree and birds eat the flesh off. And it happen like that, too cause He make it happen. The Lord be sending *me* them pictures all the time and I know that what she here for. Pictures, that what she mean, not all that ceramic jewelry shit they be saying. So I be still and I waits and lissen. And I know she seen me good and seen I ain't like them bitches with they ho'in and thieving and begging, like she the welfare. She even seen my feets. They all ashame to wear state shoes, they rather beg they pretty little shoes from someone or ho' for them. But I ain't no ho', and I aint no beggar. I a artist, and I wears me my blue state tennis, and I know she seen.

WEDNESDAY, SEPTEMBER 16

RUTH

'What's happenin', SQ? Don't hide, I know you're in there.'

If she refused to answer, staying behind her closed door, Dave would keep it up for everyone to hear, including Telecea, her next client, who'd be coming down the hall any time now. Trapped, Ruth opened the door a crack.

'Get lost, will ya, Thorne?' She usually played along with him, not knowing what else to do. 'I've got a client coming.' Now he was inside her office.

'Aint no one here now, and don't tell me you aint prepared. I know you, SQ. Don't no one come in here without you prepared for them.'

'Will you stop with the dialect, Dave? At least until you master it?' She hoped he'd never try talking like that around anyone black. No, she hoped he would. He sat down in what would be Telecea's chair in a few minutes. She felt the violation, just as Telecea would.

'Actually, I'm doing you a favor. If you don't prepare up to the very last minute it'll add a little spontaneity. That's all you need to be perfect, SQ, my dear, a little spontaneity.' She struggled to keep her anger in check, to maintain her tone.

'All I need from you now, my dear, is to leave before my client comes in.'

'Ah-ha! Does Dr Thorne detect a note of panic? What if the precious schedule should get thrown off by one minute? Calamity! Or maybe I'm taking up precious listmaking time. God forbid. How would the Snow Queen function without her lists?' One time he'd sneaked in on her and grabbed the list she'd been making. She still didn't know for sure whether he'd seen the separate items. She thought she'd grabbed it back in time. There hadn't been anything private on it anyway. The shopping. Letters to write. Cases to review. People to call. Things she'd wanted to remind Victor about. The approximate amount of time these things would take. She knew that there were worse things than being compulsive, but she hated it that he should know this about her.

'Was I ever on one of your lists?' he asked now. 'Get Thorne off my back?'

'No, I only put important things in.'

'I bet. Important things. Like how to fill up the five free minutes between clients, huh?'

'Cut it out already, Dave. I have no trouble filling my free time, thank you.'

Now he switched to his professional colleague-to-colleague manner. 'So who's coming next, that you've got to prepare for so much?'

She couldn't quite get away with, 'It's none of your damn business, buddy,' and so said nothing, raising her eyebrows humorously instead.

'Tell me, so I can make myself scarce in case it's one of your dangerous ones. Wouldn't want to risk my life right before the weekend!' It was a joke, but not really, because once Telecea, walking out of Ruth's office and running into him in the corridor, had punched him in the face. Ruth remembered the blood from his nose running down over his blue and white striped shirt.

'Well, as it happens, it *is* Telecea, so you better make yourself scarce if you're going to.' It was a mistake, now he would have to stay to prove he wasn't scared.

'Uh-oh. TJ Jones the man killer. Not lethal alone, but when combined with SQ undefeatable. Brain and brawn together! One of them will freeze you with her eyes while the other moves in for the kill! The new miracle weapon!'

'Oh shut up, Dave, will you? Sometimes you make me really tired.' She'd done it now, allowed real hostility to show in her voice. He'd get her back somehow. If only she weren't so dependent on him professionally.

'Well, that's how it is with snow queens. Only a set quota of human contact allowed at one time. Too much and you might melt, huh?' She sat there wordless, trying to block him out. 'By the way, have you talked with Sonya much yet, Ruth? You should, it might do you some good. She'll be working with your friend Telecea too, did you know? They already seem to have quite a rapport going. Not bad in, what is it, two-three days? She made quite an impression on Tranden the other day, I hear.'

'You asshole, if you're going to be a bitch at least learn to do it with some finesse,' she told him. But not aloud. He'd strolled out of her office now, thank goodness, gone to pay his next call, on Sonya probably, to tell her what an uptight obsessive-compulsive Ruth was. They'd probably be best friends. He left her invaded with anger, and with Telecea about to come in.

'This fucking goddamn job! The staff is a million times worse than the prisoners,' she cursed. She wished they'd stick *them* all behind bars. Insipid, lazy Nan and Cindy, with their endless deadening chatter and the way they referred to their clients, when they ever had any, as girls. Bad girls. This new one, Sonya, an artsy-fartsy feminist, the one thing their little staff had lacked until now. And stupid Dave, who was so sure he knew all about her, but who was too stupid to know anything, not one thing. How she hated stupid people. Even Victor had been stupid lately. He played dumb on purpose. Sometimes she felt like she hated everyone in the world. It was worse in a way than being hated by everyone, to have it come from her. It was lonelier. Maybe Dave was right, maybe she was the frozen Snow Queen.

She heard Telecea's loud hollow voice, coming down the corridor. Dave must have hidden, as there were no insults to him, only a loud stopover at Lynda's office.

'Hey lady, aint you got no work to do? Why you always in here? You got some cigarettes? Gimme one of them doughnuts then.' She heard Cindy's voice, wavering in reply. Why did they all have to act so scared of Telecea? It was the worst thing for her, the very worst. She opened her door wide so that Telecea would see that she was expected, thinking with pleasure of the way the blood had dripped down Dave's shirt, and how he had stood holding onto his nose, looking as if he were about to cry.

Telecea came in and immediately threw the doughnut into the wastebasket. 'Aint no beggar,' she explained. 'Just wanted to find something out.' Then she stood posed in the door like a skinny naked fledgling ready to take off. 'They gone put me in Max. Aint spose to be in here.'

'Why are they sending you up to Max, Telecea? Anyway, they know and you know by now that therapy takes priority. Remember the meeting with Mrs Hanson where everyone agreed to that?'

'You tell Wiggin that,' Telecea grumbled. 'Put me up there for no reason.'

'I'll call Mrs Wiggins if you want me to,' Ruth agreed wearily. It had taken months of arguments and insistence on her part to establish that no matter where Telecea happened to be at eleven o'clock on Wednesdays and Fridays she would still be allowed to come to therapy. Only in the most extreme of circumstances, they had agreed, would Ruth go up to Max and conduct the therapy in Telecea's cell there. And under no circumstance whatsoever would therapy be interrupted. It was discouraging that Telecea had already forgotten this agreement.

'Never mind. It don't make me no difference, they both jail.' Seemingly reassured, Telecea moved into her chair, smelling it and changing its angle to the precisely right degree, mumbling as she did so. 'Who you been letting at my chair with they stink, switch it any old which way. Put they nasty sores on.' Then she said, 'I aint coming no more anyway,' and looked into Ruth's face.

Ruth sighed. Apparently the first meeting would consist of covering old ground for everyone. She knew the answer to this one by heart. 'You know you never break your word, Telecea. We both know that. And you decided you would keep coming. So it's all settled.'

'Yeah, but they a new lady, a artist, she say I can work wif her. Make my pictures I told you He be sending me.'

'That sounds good. I think you have time enough to do both.'

'I told her Wednesday and Friday eleven.'

'Then you can change those times.'

'You can't make me! You aint the Lord! I do what I wants to do.'

"OK, Telecea. But do you remember you agreed to tell me why, when you got angry at me?'

'You know why! Cause you been talking to that dirty nasty dick-doctor bout me. Bear false witness you spose to get you eyes pluck out!'

Ruth had long ago learned to disregard Telecea's biblical curses. 'Remember about explaining where you get your information, Telecea,' she said.

'Because! I come by here early and seen him in here kissing on you. Wif his big old dick out!'

'Dr Thorne was in here talking to me, yes. Talking, not kissing. And his dick wasn't sticking out.' (Not literally anyway), she added to herself.

'Lord say it shall be cut off. Right off. Make me sick. Seem like every place I go nowadays someone got they dick sticking out. Bomination in the eye of the Lord! Can't even walk down the hall no more without seeing some big fat old dick up in the air. Make me feel like I want to vomit. And make my head hurt.'

Ruth shook her head. 'I'm sorry you've been feeling so bad. How about when you're in the cottage? There aren't any men in there.'

'You don't understand, Ruth Foster!' Telecea had arrived at this as a suitable way to address her. Ruth liked it. 'That the worst of all. At night, in the cottage when them butches take out they dicks. Do it all night when I'm trying to sleep. And don't try to tell me it a dream, either, aint no dream keep me up every night this whole week!'

'So that's why your head's been hurting so much?'

'You try not sleeping one whole week and see how you head feel then, Ruth Foster. Like it gonna come out the top, like something gone bust, the way it building up in there. Lord say be His Venger!'

Ruth heard the danger signals. 'Telecea, listen. You know one reason you come in here is to take some of that pressure off. I've been gone a long time, so you haven't been able to talk about it. No wonder it feels all built up inside you. But now I'm back. So let's talk about those nights. Talk nice and slowly, so I can understand, so the pressure can come off slowly.'

Telecea was sitting up straight in her chair, stiff as a board, clutching the arms with taut hands. 'When I go to bed. Next door to me Billy and Candy you know them?'

'Yes, I know them.'

'Just want to see what you say. Well, they be talking bout they devil work, planning what they gone do to me. I lissens, try to find out what they gots on they mind. So I be prepared . . .'

'Yes . . .'

'And then it get so soft that I can't make out the words, and then they starts in on they moaning, and then Billy she take out her dick and they do it, you know but something wrong wif it, you know what I mean, it a bomination for two girls to do that, make me want to vomit.'

'So it's as if it's not bad enough in the day, now you have to think about this at night, too?'

'You right, Ruth Foster. But they din't do it before they found out.'

'Found out what?'

Telecea was clutching at her stomach now. 'Bout how it been on me all day long.'

'Slow down Telecea, please. Who found out what?'

'That Candy. Don't try and trick me! I know she come in here.'

'Yes, she does. Lots of women come in here beside you, Telecea. You know that.'

'Well, she found out. And that's why they been doin' it. And that's what you and that dick-face doctor been talking bout. Bearin false witness! Cause how else Candy gone know to do that to me at night?'

'Are you asking me if I told Candy what you said to me?'

'Yes!'

'Telecea, I have never told anyone else, not the doctor, not Candy, not anyone, what you tell me. What you tell me in here never goes any further. It stays right in here with me and with you.' Ruth spoke slowly, with all the force she could command. As she talked she watched Telecea unfreeze. Her hands loosened their grip, the muscles of her back changed from steel to flesh. Ruth even saw the beginning of a smile, and this effort moved her so deeply that she wanted to do what was forbidden between them, to reach out and touch. Instead, she switched on the hot plate for chocolate. It was their way of ending the sessions, their transition back.

'How about some chocolate?' she asked, and Telecea nodded gravely, as if at a new idea.

'That be real nice, you know.' Then another, unexpected gift.

'You know, in one way, I know you don't tell. Don't tell Candy nothing. But it seem like someone put that idea inside me and once it start it keep on and on, and even though I know it aint true, it just keep getting bigger.'

'I see.' Ruth handed her the hot chocolate, and poured her own. 'And I wasn't there, so there was no way to check it out.'

'Yeah, but when you say it, I knowed I knowed it all the time.'

Ruth nodded. 'Maybe you could try holding on real tight to the part of you that knows it's not true, that I don't tell anyone anything, maybe you could keep saying that part to yourself, in your head. And now, if something is bothering you, if you feel that pressure building up, you'll be able to tell me. On Wednesdays and Fridays like always. So you won't have to hit out at anyone. Or have those bad headaches.'

'Yeah, maybe I could even sleep sometime.' She laughed, and Ruth was filled with happiness. She'd thought at the beginning of the session that she might have to ask Dave to put Telecea back on medication. She was reluctant to do this, since the only observable effect medication seemed to have on Telecea was to strengthen her

34

conviction that she was being poisoned. Ruth doubted whether she actually swallowed it anyway.

'You know, I think you are going to sleep better this week,' she said.

As soon as Telecea left, Ruth's phone began to ring.

'Miss Foster!' It was Mrs Hanson. 'Has Telecea Jones just left you?'

'Yes, she has.'

'Well! I'm sorry to inform you that this morning Telecea threatened the officer on duty in her cottage with a piece of broken glass, which, incidentally, she destroyed state property to obtain! When the officer attempted to bring her up to Max, she resisted, claiming that she had an appointment with you and that you had told her to come no matter what! Now I remembered our agreement, dear, and I decided, somewhat against my better judgement, I'm afraid, to let her keep this one appointment. But we can't have her continuing to cause disturbances. I've sent a couple of officers down to the cafeteria right now to pick her up. And I'm sure you'll agree that letting her out again in the near future would be totally inappropriate under the circumstances. . . .'

'Mrs Hanson,' Ruth began. 'As you know, I've been away for a month, and it's been hard on Telecea. I think she'll be in better control now, after our session today. She came in for her appointment right on time. And we did agree that therapy takes priority. . . .'

Mrs Hanson cut her off. 'My dear young woman, no one can accuse me of being closed to new ideas. Up to now I've agreed to our, shall we say, liberal treatment plan for this case. But this latest incident makes it quite clear that a girl this sick simply cannot handle that kind of freedom. Telecea will feel a great deal safer in maximum security where there will be no glass for her to break and assault our staff with. And I'm afraid that I shall have to insist that during her stay in Max you do not see Telecea at all. She seems to be using you to justify her acting-out behavior, and I'm sure you don't want that, dear!'

Ruth began to protest, but Mrs Hanson interrupted her angrily.

'Now Miss Foster. You have nothing to complain of. We've given your, shall we say, unconventional treatment plan more than a fair chance, at considerable risk to our staff and the other girls. But this is a prison, my dear, not a day camp!' The phone was replaced with a bang.

Ruth put her head down on the desk. She wished she could afford to cry, or, better yet, to scream. You've just come back, she tried to remind herself. You forgot what it's like. But the feelings swept over her anyway, first anger, then a kind of deadening fatigue. She could hear them outside her door, talking about lunch. She didn't want to see them or even her other clients this afternoon. And most of all she didn't want to go home to Vic, to his sympathetic, 'Did you have a hard day at work, Rooey?', his big clumsy hands reaching out for her, his martyred tolerance of her coldness.

'Ruth . . .' It was Cindy, acting as their emissary, knocking on her door. 'Ya wanna come to the Steak Pit? Lynda lost ten pounds and we're celebrating.'

Ruth pulled herself together and opened the door. She turned on a smile, congratulated Lynda, and explained that she'd had a big breakfast that morning and wasn't hungry.

'Oh come on, SQ.' Dave had one hand on Cindy and the other on Lynda. 'You look pale. After your draining session with TJ Mankiller, you could use a good lunch.'

'God, you talk a line of bull!'

Ruth stared, amazed to hear someone else speak her thoughts. Sonya, who was standing behind Lynda, now turned away. 'I haven't done anything all morning anyway, I don't need a break,' she said. 'I think I'll go eat in the cafeteria with the women. See you all later.'

She walked off dramatically, and after a few moments, the others left too.

For the first time Ruth had really seen Sonya. She was a large, pleasingly curvy woman, a little shorter than Ruth, with masses of coarse wavy black hair falling over her shoulders and a wide expanse of forehead. She had a broad mouth with full lips, a fleshy nose, and big dark eyes. The woman had a wildness about her, a largeness which spoke of sensuality and of enjoyment, of eating with pleasure and without worry. She would never sit making lists. Ruth doubted whether Sonya would tolerate Hanson's plan for her first two weeks, to sit in on Cindy and Nan's almost non-existent appointments. And she didn't blame her. If I were a man, Ruth thought, that's the kind of woman I'd be interested in, not someone stiff and ordinary like me. She wondered for a moment what Sonya had meant about eating with the women, then decided that she surely had enough sense to stick to the staff dining room.

CANDY

'Then she say, 'Why don't you just do these while you're working, Mabel.' And the bitch have the nerve to slip in some of her nasty dirty sheets under my iron. Like I can't tell the difference or something, all bloodstained like they is. Bitch too lazy to wash her own sheets, now she gonna try and bring 'em in here, have me iron 'em.'

Mabe's loud voice was getting on Candy's nerves. She rubbed her leg against Billy's under the table and tried to pretend it was just the two of them sitting there.

Norma shook her head back and forth like a mother hen. 'I aint surprised,' she murmured. 'You know I used to work for them white ladies, I told you all that. And they is some nasty people! Used to make me sick.'

'Yeah well, that's alright for you. Me, I aint never been no domestic and I aint about to start now,' Mabe went on. 'I just told her to her face, I said, state pays me a dollar a day to wash and iron the institutional sheets, Mrs Riley. I aint your servant.'

'Better believe it,' Edie agreed. 'What she say then?'

'She turnt all red cause I found her out, you know the way they do,' Mabe laughed. 'She tell me, I'd advise you to do as you're told and press these sheets before I give you a D, Mabel. So I say, Alright, cool, if that's what you want, I'll press your sheets, Miz Riley. Then I take that big old iron, and I just lean it up against them sheets, put them all in a pile, you know?' Mabe showed how she did it. 'And pretty soon it start in smoking, and everyone smell it but her, you know the bitch can't smell shit, and we all book out the door cause it's legit quit time and them sheets was kicking ass! You know, I heard her screaming fire all the way up here. Hope the bitch burn up,' Mabe finished, satisfied.

'Girl, you fool! You coulda burn us all up,' Edie told her. 'Who you think gonna get left in here to fry if they have a real fire in this place? Don't be trying no shit like that no more!'

Mabe nodded, scared, and Candy thought of all of them burning up, maybe at night. They was one poor bastard in the cottage that was doing life for burning up her own kids in their beds and wasn't no reason she couldn't go off and do it again, as far as

37

Candy could see. She shivered and pushed aside the dead gray piece of meat on her plate. She didn't even like to think of no fire, cause of this one time in New York when she'd been living with some junkies and they'd gone out to cop leaving one girl, Mary Jane Spindella, passed out on the bed. She must of come to, lit up a cigarette and passed out again, cause by the time they got back the fire engines had came and gone and everyone was outside talking bout was someone in there or not. And later they asked Candy to come to the hospital to identify Mary J but when she saw her, even though she was still alive, she couldn't tell was it her or not, cause she looked like piece of burnt up meat.

She shivered again and pushed her tray as far away as she could.

'Hey, don't talk about no fire around Candy,' Billy told them. 'She can't eat if you do.'

Telecea Jones, who was sitting at a nearby table by herself listening to them like always, suddenly spoke up in her spooky voice, and Billy jumped.

'You said it, I aint. Fire gone burn you black, Candace Peters. Gone burn you white, Louisa Ann Morris. Cast in that burning lake and torment till you wish you could die. Think he don't see you, moaning and ho'ing all night, but he seen alright. Gone take and burn you up. Burn that dick up, and I be laughing.' Then she started in on her crazy laugh till Billy shouted for her to shut her fucking big mouth before she jammed a plate in it.

'Don't do no good to talk to that poor child like that, Billy Morris,' Norma scolded. 'More of that kind of attention she get the more she gonna aggravate you. Just leave her be, don't pay her no mind.' Then she called over to Telecea how she ought to be ashamed talking like that, and that was the reason why wouldn't nobody sit with her at meals. Norma was always trying to make peace, but it just made Billy madder.

'Fuck it,' she said. 'Wish they'd take and put her somewhere where I wouldn't have to listen to her. Someone gonna get hurt one of these days. Hey, get me a cup of coffee,' she told Candy. 'This place gives me a goddamn headache.'

When Candy went up to get it she saw that art therapist broad, Lehrman, that Foster had got a attitude about the other day, getting her lunch. She was dressed in mans pants today and looked kind of butch. After she got her tray she stood looking round like she didn't

38

know where the staff dining room was. Well, Candy wasn't gonna tell her.

When she got back with the coffee, they was all staring at Lehrman.

'That's the same one I told you about,' said Edie. 'That Scorpion, that was sucking up to us in the hall.'

'Well now, will you look at that!' said Billy, cause now Lehrman was walking into their dining room, looking for a place to sit. Finally she headed over to the one table that had a whole lot of room left at it, Telecea Jones's table.

'Hey, I hope y'all is watching now,' Edie laughed. 'This is gonna be fun.'

The broad, that didn't know no better, spoke right up to Telecea. 'Excuse me, do you mind if I sit here?' they heard her say. Next thing, they was both just sitting there quiet, talking and eating. Edie was disappointed. She flounced up to the table, with Mabe following right behind her.

'This room is for residents only, Miss,' she told Lehrman in her loud hateful voice.

'*And* they guests,' Telecea said right back. 'This lady wif me. And if you got something to say you can speak to me on it, Edie Sampson. And you too, Big-Mouth-Batelou, I see you there rolling them pig eyes at me.'

Like everyone else, they was scared of Telecea. Edie, who'd been mumbling shit about scorpions, shut right up and came back to the table. 'Well la-di-da,' Mabe said real quick, and she came back too. Candy thought to herself that she'd been right in what she'd been thinking bout crazy people. Telecea could act normal enough when she wanted. She had told Edie off as good as anybody could, and it served her right. Her and Mabe was always trying to stir something up just for a little excitement, but they was scared to fight when it came down to it.

Just then Moody, that big red-faced sadist, came hurrying in with two other screws behind him. Everyone got quiet and Candy knew Mabe was gonna git her excitement after all, cause they always used Moody when it was about jumping on someone to take them to Max or something.

'Hey now, Telecea, sweetheart, time to take a little trip up to Max,' said Moody all sarcastic and shitty. Next thing, Telecea had throwed her tray right at his face, he had grabbed her by the neck, and everyone was yelling and screaming.

'All right, Telecea!' shouted Mabe, switching sides. Candy watched Lehrman sit there, with meat and gravy all over her. 'Bet that's one bitch won't be back in here tomorrow,' she thought.

'C'mon baby, let's split before something else jumps off.' Billy took her by the hand. 'This place gonna git to me yet!'

SONYA

Sonya rode first the bus then the subway home at rush hour, swinging from a strap and trying to hold on to the pieces of her day. 'Pieces,' she thought, and saw the pieces of food and the maroon plastic tray flying at the big guard's head, then the intent, fragmented face of Telecea Jones, who had said to her, right before the guard arrived, as if she'd known what would happen, 'Be my witness.' The way she was hanging from the strap made her think of hanging sculptures and she thought she'd do Telecea's face, in pieces, as a mobile, intense staring brown eyes on two separate invisible threads, blown about by the wind, and another section of tender, scarred forehead. Telecea had not seemed surprised when Sonya had sat down with her. She'd told her that she, too, was an artist, and then, when those hateful women had hassled her, Telecea had made them leave Sonya alone. They'd been just sitting there, quietly talking about the process of art, of transferring one's vision into something concrete, when it had all exploded. There had been people screaming and shouting and laughing, and the tray flying and hitting, and then two more men had appeared to help the first one drag Telecea off. Sonya looked down at her black linen pants, which were still stained – the witness Telecea had demanded.

She looked around at the tired subway faces. She recognized some of them already, those maids whose hours were the same as hers. One of these sat with her skirt pushed up, grasping a large newspaper-wrapped package between her knees, unashamed, tired, and quite beautiful. The faces of the women she'd seen in the past three days swam in front of her eyes. Besides Telecea, the one who had struck her most was the very handsome black woman who was always with Candy, that pale one with the look of a store mannequin, whom she'd seen coming out of Ruth's office that first day. She'd do the beauty in gold wire – a long Giacometti-like piece, while Candy would have to be plaster, polished slick white plaster, the face and clothing painted on with bright, artificial looking china paint. She could hang the two figures across from each other on straps – it would be a Subway Sculpture! What if she made a whole lot more figures, of all different sizes, and then bought an old bus to set them up in, so people could actually walk through the sculpture to experience it! She rifled in her bag for her idea book, and made a quick sketch, trying to hold on to her balance and to this idea while others exploded in her head. She lost her footing for a moment, and a greasy man bumped her in the chest with his elbow.

She pulled in as much as she could within the small space, thinking suddenly and longingly of those long winter evenings in Vermont, with two or three or four women sitting by the fire, reading aloud or talking or sketching. She saw Mira on her cross-country skis, light as a bird skimming over the frozen field across from their house, saw herself on her own long solitary walks along the dirt road at night or early in the morning with the fine mist rising over the fields and the moon still hanging low in the sky. Often during these walks, a single sculpture or painting had begun to grow in her head, not the crazy flood of ideas she was having now, but a good slow birth, out of the quiet and the cold.

Now there were millions of sculptures springing up all around her, about to be lost. It was too much, a bombardment. Suddenly she could remember none of her reasons for having left Mira and Vermont, for being here, on this foreign smelly train coming back from a bunch of unfriendly criminals who had mocked her to strange empty rooms which would mock her too, which would grow fat furniture and turn on her, as all the rooms she had ever lived in had done. It was clear now that she had never deserved Mira; had gotten her only by trickery, and that in turning her back on her she had abandoned the one chance for happiness that she would ever have in her entire life.

Sonya's eyes filled with tears, and her whole body seemed to deflate like a balloon. She held tightly to her strap and tried to move away from the foul-smelling man who jostled her again, on purpose, she realized now. Turning, she met the contempt-filled eyes of the woman with the bundle between her legs, who seemed to hike her skirt up a little further to show tiny beads of sweat easing down her thighs. 'I'll give you something to stare at white girl,' she heard the woman thinking, but there was nowhere else to look. And now she could see that the smelly man, the angry woman might be ugly, but at least they were real people with real lives. Everyone but her was going back to children, lover, family – something. Only she was pretending, always pretending, living some unreal masquerade in which she recited strange lines which had nothing to do with her.

'It'll pass, it'll pass,' she kept telling herself, trying to call back the knowledge that her despair was not permanent, was something that followed her times of exaltation as surely as the ocean tide, and would just as surely wash through her and be gone. She tried to envision the ocean waves breaking gently, but they were building up like a giant tidal wave instead. She tried to think of work, imagined a sculpture to go with this feeling, but it became a nightmare, a trick sculpture in which everything reversed itself and the people she'd thought were her friends appeared in a sneering, laughing group, witnessing her shame, pointing their fingers at her in contempt. Ruth Foster was among them. Ruth Foster might in fact be on this subway for all she knew, and it was this possibility, and the absolute necessity not to fall apart in front of Ruth Foster, that held her together until her stop, and then all the way home through the three blocks of her neighborhood, which had now become a dangerous, hostile slum.

She held on past the men calling at her from the stoops, 'Hey big titty, give me some,' past the women peering out meanly from behind slits in their green plastic curtains, past the Sealytest Mattress building, with its painted advertisement of a leering blonde lounging on a mattress, and finally past the bodega, where one of the men drew his hand quickly out of his pocket and she knew it was a gun and that she would be shot. She gained her own building with tremendous relief. Once she started seeing guns it was time to lock her door, unplug the phone, get into bed, and let it pass.

On the stairs she felt a brief longing for Mira to be there, waiting to take her in her arms, but the truth was that whenever she'd let herself crawl into Mira's arms she'd ended up hating her for it afterwards. She closed the heavy door behind her and now she could let go, could lie on the unmade bed letting the loneliness and panic and self-hatred wash over her. She sobbed wildly, but at the same time part of her was conscious of a sharp, distinct relief – that there were no witnesses at all, that now, at least, she was alone.

TELECEA

At least up here don't no one bother me. Can't hear no moaning and ho'ing up here, how they be talking bout me all the time. Least up here they has to leave me alone. Down there you can't even eat nothing without them sitting there talking bout you. That ho' Candy all snake round Billy leg doing something wif her dick under the table and old nasty big mouf Mabe talking her shit bout blood and pus on the sheets. How they gone smoke me an burn me wif they hot irons. Ruth Foster she always say, Wait, Telecea don't do nothing, wait and just tell me on Friday, but sometime I can't wait no more. So I just turn round and tell them who gone burn. It aint me, that for sure. That bomination Billy start shaking and talking bout how she gone jam her plate in my mouf but you know she scared. They all scared of me, cause they know what they get. And Norma she tell them, No, no, child leave her be.

Then that artist lady come and ask can she sit wif me. Just like I knowed, she seen me and she know who I is, and so she come and ask my permission wif some respect the way people should act not like them others don't even be treating you like you a human being. Only Norma she the only one. We be talking bout pictures and how do you make them once you gots them in your head. Mabe and Edie come round trying to make trouble wif they ignorant self but I tell them once and they book.

So at least when they come and get me, take me up here, at least I do got me a Witness. And I know she seen.

FRIDAY, SEPTEMBER 18

RUTH

At the beginning of the staff meeting, Ruth told Sonya that Mrs Hanson had promised to assign her an office by Monday morning. Sonya immediately wanted to know what kind of an office it would be.

'I need a room with long tables, where I can have groups,' she explained in an aggrieved voice, as though Ruth could easily hand her such a room if she were in the mood. Ruth explained that she herself had nothing to do with room assignments, but that Mrs Hanson, who did, would be coming to the second part of their meeting. Sonya clearly had some disappointments coming, and Ruth began to feel sorry for her.

'I'm afraid you'll be lucky if you get the free office across from mine,' she tried to prepare her. 'Somehow I don't think Mrs Hanson will understand that an art therapist has different needs than anyone else. Good luck, though.' Cindy, who'd been listening, snickered, and Ruth realized that her speech had probably sounded sarcastic, although she hadn't meant it that way. 'I'll be glad to talk to her about it, I just don't have high hopes, Sonya,' she tried again. 'I've been trying to convince her to let me start a group here for years.' Sonya turned a stormy face to her, apparently convinced once and for all that Ruth was out to get her.

'Fine,' Ruth thought, exasperated. 'Let her find out what it's about here for herself.' The filth of Lynda's office was getting to her. Even the plants were half dead. And there was a banging noise above their heads which might have been the heating pipes or Telecea up in Max, banging her head on the floor. Ruth had sent a note up to her explaining her absence, and then, remembering at the last moment that Telecea couldn't read, had enclosed a note to Mary Proudy asking her to read it aloud to Telecea. For all she knew Mary hadn't bothered, and Telecea wouldn't get the message.

She felt sick at the memory of herself smugly assuring Telecea that 'they know and you know' that therapy wouldn't be interrupted, and was determined not to let Hanson out of the staff meeting until she'd lifted the ban. She'd even suffered through lunch with Dave at the Steak Pit in order to enlist his support.

Now she tried to ignore the pounding above her head and to concentrate on the main business of the first part of the meeting, which was the recurring problem of getting clients for Nan and Cindy. Gladdy Dwight, whom she'd left with Cindy, had already been in to ask why she'd given her away to a nasty bitch who laughed at her and didn't believe what she said. And now Cindy declared flatly that she wouldn't work with Edie Sampson any more because Edie was violent.

'What do you think this place is?' Ruth started, and then stopped herself as she heard echoes of Hanson in her voice and felt Sonya's judging eyes on her.

Then Dave came in, winking victory at Ruth over the top of Hanson's orange, slightly balding head. Feeling suddenly more hopeful, Ruth smiled, winked back, and turned quickly enough to catch Sonya's look of disgust. She felt torn between an impulse to take her aside after the meeting, maybe even ask her out for a drink, apologize for her initial rudeness, and fill her in a little, and an angry reluctance to justify herself. Why bother, anyway? For all she knew Sonya would tell her politely to go screw herself. She was probably another naïve fool who had come to rescue the strong but oppressed princesses from the mean witches in Castle Redburn. 'She'll last a month,' Ruth decided. 'I give her till Thanksgiving. At the latest.'

When the subject of Telecea finally came up, it was clear to Ruth that her lunch with Dave had paid off. Acting as though he'd come up with the idea on his own, he suggested that Telecea's latest episode of acting out was a somewhat delayed reaction to the disruption of her therapy, and that now that Ruth was back, her behavior might be expected to normalize.

'I'd like to try her back in the cottage with some supervision,' he suggested. 'Leave her in Max and she'll just decompensate right down the line.' Shaking her head and clicking her tongue, Hanson agreed to give it one more try, and Ruth breathed a sigh of relief.

As she left the meeting, she reflected that Sonya would probably hold her personally responsible if she didn't get the kind of room she wanted, as she most assuredly would not. Not that Ruth really cared what Sonya thought of her. She had managed to get Telecea out of Max within a week, that was what mattered.

CANDY

Candy sat in the old flag room upstairs that was so big that when you was sitting in your social worker's office or playing pool downstairs you could always hear the sound of the machines like a big bee buzzing over your head. 'Zi-p.' She sewed up one red stripe, turned it, sewed down the other end, and took out another stripe. Across from her, Delaney was fussing at a little new girl that had fucked her flag all up.

'You watch how Candy does it, watch that nice straight line she sews,' Delaney told her.

'Yeah, yeah sure lady,' the girl muttered, like she didn't know where she was. She coughed and sniffed and wiped her nose on her sleeve and Delaney walked off.

'Damn!' Frankie said on the other side. 'Sick as you are they should of kept you in the hospital, girl. Kid like you.'

Jammed as she was, the girl woke right up to the attention.

'Talk 'bout a straight line,' she grumbled. 'Got me flying so high on this shit I can't even see no straight line. Everything look fucking wavy to me.'

All of them in their section laughed at the mouth on her, until Delaney came back with the big scissors that no one was sposed to touch. She grabbed the girl's flag and tore out the seam. 'Now you can start all over and do it right.'

'Well, son of a bitch!' Frankie said, to no one in particular. Delaney ignored her and walked off. The girl just snuffed up more snot and Billy turnt her chair so she didn't have to look at her. Things like that, people that had bad personal habits, always bothered the hell out of her. Delaney had went back to her office to get her coffee or tranks or whatever she kept on going in there for, and Billy took out the book she'd been reading all morning, a paperback on Angela Davis. About two weeks ago, at supper, someone had this book with a picture of Angela Davis on it, and everybody agreed that Billy looked like her. Ever since then it hadn't been nothing but Angela, Angela, Angela, until Candy thought she'd scream if she heard that name one more time. Billy was even growing out her hair to look like her, though usually she had Candy cut it real close.

'But hey,' Frankie was telling the new kid. 'Aint that just what it's all about, huh? Sew it up, rip it up, and sew it up again. Could be the same flag all day.'

'Yeah,' the kid said. She might of been too young or too jammed to pick up that Frankie was after her little ass, but she wasn't too jammed to stop running her mouth. 'Motherfuckers gonna get their ass sued,' she grumbled out. 'Sending me in here so full of they medication I can't even see no straight line. What if I sewed my finger or something?'

'Listen,' Billy told Candy, ignoring the others. 'They got these interviews in here, of these girls that knew her in the joint she was in. You know, their impressions of her.'

'What?' Candy asked, like she could give a shit what their impression was. 'What'd they think?'

'Well, there's this one broad, she said she learned from her on the for real side, but not from nothing she actually said. Cause she was stone quiet in there, you know. Wouldn't suck no ass. Just from the way she carried herself, she commanded respect, you know. Wouldn't say nothing to the screws. No social workers, shrinks, therapists . . . none of them. Spent her whole fucking time in there without speaking to none of them.'

Candy didn't appreciate the dig about Foster, but she didn't say nothing. She wondered did Angela baby have someone in there to cover for her and sew her flags.

She reached over, stuck a half-done flag in Billy's machine, and put four of her own finished ones on Billy's table. Delaney never said nothing as long as Billy had at least four on her pile, even though she'd never saw her work the machine herself.

Candy went back to her seat and watched Billy sitting there, daydreaming about the time she'd make it to this big time leader of her people, and some reporter would come in here and ask the girls what was their impression of her. She'd known Billy for so long now she could usually tell what she was thinking. Even though she had it with the Angela Davis bit, there was something that was like a little kid about Billy when she daydreamed that made it hard not to go over and kiss the top of her head. 'I love you, you fool,' she thought. 'Shit, do I love you.'

Delaney came back, looking zonked out of her head. 'Zi-p.' Candy pushed the foot pedal down. If only Delaney let them have music in here like Lee did when she was on, it wouldn't be so bad.

When Delaney had took too much of what she took, and had to stay out, they put Lee in and then they all stayed high and dug the music for a while.

Delaney's phone rung. 'Candace Peters,' Delaney mimicked whoever had spoke to her. 'They want you down in mental health right now, to give a new lady a tour.'

'Lady! Shit! It must be that artist bitch, Lehrman,' she said to Billy. 'You know, the one that was in the cafeteria.'

'Well, go ahead and give the bitch a tour,' Billy told her. 'You know how to give the bitch a tour.'

Lehrman was standing outside Lynda's office in mental health, looking pissed off, probly cause she didn't have no place to be. 'No office yet, huh?' Candy asked her, real sympathetic.

'Uh-uh. I think they're watching me to see how well I wait!' she said.

Candy could tell from the I'm on your side, not theirs way she talked plus from the way she had came in the cafeteria the other day, and the way she dressed, that she must be one of those feminists. They came in on tours or to play ball or perform their white-girl music that was so bad it was embarrassing. They was your typical liberal types, except they was into rapping about women and was mostly funny. This Lehrman had long hair instead of that short, chopped-off kind, and wasn't as funky as those others, but she dressed weird, like she couldn't make up her mind was she butch or fem. Today she had on gauze navy blue pants with a drawstring and a light yellow blouse that made her sort of dark skin and eyes show, and she looked more on the fem side. She was the first feminist on the staff, so far as Candy knew, and as she started Lehrman off at the front door Candy hoped she'd be as easy a mark as some of them.

'I know you already seen the cafeteria and been up and down the main hall,' Candy started out, like she'd been paying a whole lot of attention to the bitch's moves. 'Up these stairs here you got the library and chapel and the schoolchildren but don't nobody much go in there. And the flag room's up there too, and they don't allow no visitors. You seen the mental health hallway and the stairs up from there don't go nowhere but Max. So why don't I take you out in the yard and show you the cottages? The hospital's out there too but you can't go in there either.'

'OK,' Lehrman said. 'Whatever you think I should see.'

'What you *should* see,' Candy told her, 'is Max, and the strip cells they got over in the hospital. But you know they aint gonna put that on my tour list.'

This was always a line that went over real big with the liberals and it did with this one, too. Lehrman asked Candy if she'd ever spent any time in Max, and by the time they got down to Four Corners Candy was into her doing hard time rap.

'You smoke reefer, don't you?' she asked, springing it real sudden, as they went out in the yard where no one could hear.

But unlike the others, that had looked real happy she asked, jumping all over theirself to tell about the 'drugs' they did, this one looked straight ahead and didn't say nothing.

'I don't need to hear you say it,' Candy told her real quick. 'I know you work here now and all, I can dig that. But shit, you and me aint that different. I aint been in here so long not to know what gir-I mean women – out there are doing. I mean the ones that's not living in the suburbs with their little hubby and their three kids and their pep pills. And I can tell you aint one of them.'

The bitch just nodded. She looked kind of like she might be laughing at her, but Candy went on with the rap seeing she had got this far into it.

'You know, there *are* a few things that can make a hard time a little easier in here,' she said, like she had just now thought of it. 'A few of the staff is pretty hip, you know. Has some understanding of what it would be like to be in here. Plus, there's no way you could get in trouble. They don't search the staff, and lots of places you can put reefer wouldn't nobody find it even if they did search you.'

Lehrman still didn't say nothing, so Candy thought maybe she better switch it up a little.

'If you're uptight about reefer, well I can understand that,' she said. 'From your point of view, I mean. But change you're allowed to bring in. For cigarettes or the soda machine or something. You're *sposed* to bring in change!'

They was at the door of Violet cottage now, and Candy opened up Sue Blakely's room that they always used for tours cause the girl had turned into a robot a long time ago that didn't mind who saw her private shit.

'You seen that officer that let us in?' she gestured back to the cottage door. 'She don't even think twice about it. Most of them officers, the ones that's on our side, you know, that's the way they feel about it.'

They was back out in the yard, and Candy stopped. She didn't like the way Lehrman had been letting her rap on, like for the amusement of hearing what crap she would come up with next. She got quiet too, playing the bitch's own game.

When Lehrman finally talked, it was in this real soft amused voice. 'By the way, Candy, is this a regular part of the tour?'

Candy froze. She was usually real good at psyching people out, but this time she'd fucked up. Now Lehrman would probly run and tell the nearest big-time staff – maybe Tranden hisself. The bitch hadn't said nothing about her personal life yet either, like most of them was so eager to do, so she didn't have nothing on her.

'You don't have to believe me, but the staff does it,' she said, disgusted at the begging sound of it.

'Hey, wait a minute, Candy. You don't have to worry, I won't go to anyone with this,' Lehrman said, like it was a real stupid thing to worry about in the first place. 'You may have got me wrong, but not that wrong.'

Candy could of hit her in the jibs, the just too cool way she talked, like she could read Candy's mind or something. She decided to stop the tour right where they was, out in the yard. 'Guess that just about wraps it up, Miss Lehrman,' she said. 'You know where to find me in case you change your mind.' But Lehrman was the type that always had to have the last word.

'I don't know how the grapevine works in here,' she said. 'I mean, I don't know if a lot of other people are gonna ask me what you just did, or if the word gets around fast. Just in case it does, the fact is there's no way I'm gonna bring in anything, dope or money or anything else, no matter who asks me. Because sooner or later someone does talk, and I plan to stay at this job until I'm ready to leave. By the way,' she added. 'I'm going by my first name in here – Sonya. I don't like calling people by their first names and having them call me 'Miss' back.'

'You can just call me Miss Peters then,' Candy wanted to say. 'Or better yet, bitch, don't speak to me at all!' Then she'd go on. 'Look bitch, if you like head games so much, I can play them a hell of a lot better than you. Just try me. And you may find it aint you that decides when's your leaving time, either. You think we can't put someone out of here inside of a day when we get ready to?'

But one thing you learnt in here was to keep your cool and not get these assholes on your case. This one might turn up sitting on her parole board or something in a few weeks so Candy smiled real sweet.

'I hear you, Sonya,' she said. 'I dig what you're saying.' Now she had to go back up and tell Billy no dice on this one. That she was a slippery bitch who they'd have to keep an eye on.

SONYA

Sonya had spent her morning sitting around waiting for the staff meeting, which turned out to be nothing to wait for, then taking a tour of the institution. The days of sitting doing nothing were beginning to get to her, and she had started to hate all three of them — Foster, Hanson, and Thorne. Her tour guide had been Candy, who'd looked at Sonya through the mask of her pale painted face and polished eyelids with disdain, and had immediately run a well-practiced line on her, designed to persuade her to bring in drugs, or, failing that, money. 'Shit, woman,' Sonya had felt like saying. 'If you want to run game on me you've got to do better than that. Don't you know enough to *pretend* to like me, at least?' Instead, she'd told Candy, as clearly as she could, that she wasn't playing. Candy had obviously been furious, but Sonya didn't know if the message had gotten through or not.

Now, since she was supposed to stay until five but there was nothing for her to do, she sat outside on a bench in the sunny compound with her sketch book. She figured that all the women must be up in the flag room or wherever they worked, because none of those she'd seen in the hall were out here. Except for a dour couple who must be a wife with her visiting husband, who were sitting silently on a nearby bench, the only people around were a few madwomen whom she supposed to be considered beyond the imperative of work assignments. Moving slowly and talking to themselves, they were much older than most of the other women she'd seen, who looked for the most part surprisingly young. She wondered whether these ghostlike creatures were the end-products — the way those younger women would turn out, if they lived long enough.

What would it be like to be in here herself, she wondered. Probably she'd make out alright. Persuade them to let her do her art all day. She'd try to get to know the beauty, Candy's lover, who looked sort of like a butchy Angela Davis. Sonya hoped that that one would sign up for art, but probably she was the type who was too cool to sign up for anything.

After a while, one of the wandering women came up to her

bench. 'Now she aint no inmate. And can't be no staff, they gots to sit in they office. Could be she someone's visit? Someone invisible?' Sonya laughed at this, and so did the woman, who must have been about sixty, although it was hard to tell, and was dark and heavy, in a ripped pink sun dress and an old pair of unlaced workboots. 'Someone invisible's visit want to squeeze Gladdy's breast?' she asked. 'Want to see the milk start up?' She pointed to her sagging belly. 'See that baby move in there?'

'No, thank you,' Sonya answered the question politely, as the camera recorded her sohisticated ease.

'Maybe she got a cigarette for Gladdy then?'

'Sorry, I don't smoke,' Sonya told her. 'My name's Sonya. I'm an art teacher. But I don't have a room yet.' She heard herself picking up Gladdy's pattern of speech.

'Art teacher got pretty hair,' Gladdy touched it. 'Got a pretty name. Gladdy may even name this new baby that pretty name the art teacher got. Sonya. They took all Gladdy's other babies away. William, Eleanor, Mahalia, Martin, John, Robert, Jesse. All gone.'

'I'm sorry.' Sonya felt at a loss for words. 'I hope you'll come in and do some art next week.'

'Maybe she will, maybe she will.' Gladdy nodded. 'Only God know the future.'

Left alone, Sonya made a few sketches of the women she'd talked with that day. Sketching Candy's sharp little features, she realized that, without all the make-up, she'd look a little like Ruth Foster. She decided to bring in a real sketch book from now on, and if they gave her nothing else to do she could make contact with the women by doing portraits. But hopefully, by Monday, she'd have worked it somehow to have her own room. As she planned her next strategy, it occurred to her, not for the first time, that she'd make an excellent whore.

TELECEA

That bitch that call herself working up here, Proudy, have the nerve to ask me, Can you read, Telecea? Try to insult somebody with that dicty voice of hers, shout it all loud from way down the hall so these other girls they gots up here from escape hear. I shout right back, Why don't you go ask your man up in Lincoln can *he* read? She do gots one up there, Wiggins tell Delaney one time, she say he got up there for doing it to they own daugther. They aint knowed I was there cause I was crouch down small, lissening. You gots to lissen and you gots to watch and be still, then you finds out!

That ho' get all quiet when I say that, then she come out with, Well, aint it too bad seeing how you can't read a word you don't take advantage of the education programs they got in here, of course it's not meant for the RETARDED, it's meant for people that know something, not for them that's so ignorant they can't even control themself.

The bitch ast for it now, so I tell her, Now you gone hear what He gots in mind for you, way you been ho'in with that bomination lockt up for doing it to his own baby! You gone eat the flesh of that child and then burn in the fire, you pus-color bomination, gots to be retarded you own self let someone do that to your child, so don't be calling me by you name!

She try to act like I aint bother her at all but her voice shaking bad like they always gets.

Oh you can read can you, that's good cause they's a letter for you here that this lady sent up and ast me to read it to you but as long as you can read it yourself then here, you crazy girl, and she push some paper under the door without putting her hand in. And don't be asking me for nothing either, cause we just run out of food and drink!

It supper time, too, but she can go on and starve me, I don't care, she gone get hers alright. Bet your baby couldn't eat none when that devil man got through wif her neither, I tell her. And you aint gone eat you own self when He get through wif you. Way He will do you, you gone wish you left that devil man alone! Now all the girls up here for escape be talking bout her just like the wind, Whooo—ee.

When she hear that, she get all upsetted. Girls, you know that one just too much, she has killed two people already and the mental wards won't even keep her, every word out of her mouth some kinda lie, that nut don't even know what she saying herself. But don't no one answer her. Ha! They knows what the ho' 'bout now.

This letter be laying on the floor of my cell. Open it up, and I can see writing in there. What I will do, I will ask Ruth Foster look at it for me when she come see me today, cause I aint got my reading glasses up here wif me. Cause Ruth Foster she tell me every Wednesday and Friday, say if I can't not get to her, like when I be up here, then she will come to me. So I will ask her take a look at this letter cause I think I know what it is. I just got a feeling it from that Sonya artist lady, tell me when we gone begin.

SUNDAY, SEPTEMBER 20

RUTH

Ruth and Victor sat at a small round table at the Cafe Francais with the Sunday *Times* between them, drinking cafe-au-lait. They had already had two croissants each. The place was a cellar really, and Ruth felt cold and damp. It was crowded with other youngish couples and singles, all reading their papers, and there was barely enough room for the two of them at the little table which would have to hold four when Bill and Lisa got there. Victor's bony knees bumped Ruth's under the table. She was reading an interview with Kate Millet, whose autobiography she'd read over the summer, and used in her fantasy life ever since.

'Millet, 42, separated from her Japanese 'wonderful friend', is a declared lesbian whose husband Fumio Yoshimura says she might enter into a male-female based sculpture. . . .'

Ruth realized that she was reading the column horizontally instead of vertically, the way it was written, but decided that it didn't really matter.

'You look beautiful this morning,' Victor interrupted his reading to tell her. She knew this couldn't be true, that she must look how she felt, tired and bored and washed out. She wore her weekend clothes, an old soft workshirt with her grey sweater over it and faded jeans. Her hair was in a ponytail. He had not shaved because it was Sunday morning. She thought how boring and predictable everything was. She wondered whether Kate Millet's life was as exciting now as it had been when she wrote the book.

'I wish it were still summer,' she told Victor.

'This is nice too,' he answered. 'I like our Sunday mornings.' Ruth tried to remember when she had liked them too. Lisa and Bill came in the door and they all exclaimed loudly. Lisa hugged Ruth and bumped her in the face with her glasses. She was small and dark and Jewish, with short curly hair and a manic intensity about her. Bill had a curiously unformed, permanently flushed face, as if he were blushing all the time, and always seemed a little vague. Ruth couldn't understand how the two of them got along. Last year Victor had done some counseling with them, which was something the therapists at Freeport were always doing for each other, but he'd never told her what it had been all about. She had always liked and quite admired Lisa, and had sometimes thought of asking her to get together without the men, until the time they'd all gotten high together, and Lisa had said, looking right at Ruth, that she'd always instinctively distrusted pretty blond WASP women.

Now Ruth sat with her back jammed against the whitewashed brick wall watching the window where the lower halves of strangers walked by, and trying to disassociate herself from the conversation about whether people having breakdowns should be treated at home.

'Support systems,' said Bill.

'Relief networks,' said Victor. 'Safety maps. Check-in-points.'

'Sometimes it can just aggravate the problem, though,' said Lisa. 'I mean leaving the person in the same system that caused the disturbance in the first place.' Ruth's eyes met hers, and she thought that they were both imagining having a breakdown and being nursed by Victor or Bill at home. She thought longingly of her fantasy mental hospital which was like one in a Bergmann film, with white starched sheets in a small clean white room. No clutter. No other people. Too bad it wasn't really like that.

'But of course with the present hospital systems . . .' Bill went on. 'And the jails . . .' He stopped vaguely in mid-sentence, waiting for Ruth, since jails were supposed to be her subject.

Ruth kept her face in the paper. She'd half-heartedly finished the Kate Millet article and had been letting her eyes drift over the words of an article about some architect.

Now she pushed the paper aside, bored to death. The three of them were talking about Mental Patients Liberation now. Ruth stared at the poster on the white wall showing a barge floating down the Seine. She tried to pretend she was there instead of here. At a table nearby, two women were talking loudly.

'I thought you were so big on non-monogamy!' one of them said.

'You never did understand the difference between intellectually and really,' the other told her. 'That's the one thing you consistently refuse to understand.' Then she got up, threw her *Times* on the floor with a clatter, and left.

'You know they're really men, of course,' Lisa whispered. 'The one who just left came in to Beacon a couple of months ago.' Ruth looked closely at the person remaining at the table, who was certainly a woman.

'Bullshit,' Bill said. 'That's a woman if I ever saw one!' They all stared, agreeing.

'Oh well,' Lisa shrugged. 'The other one wasn't.' Ruth wondered for a moment if Lisa, who counseled transsexuals and transvestites, was playing with them out of an angry boredom similar to her own, but Lisa was smiling to herself. It was impossible to tell.

'Is there something wrong, Rooey?' Victor asked her timidly, as they walked home. 'You were so . . . quiet. Don't you like them any more?'

'Sure,' she told him. 'As much as I like anyone.' He looked stricken.

'Oh Vic,' she moaned. 'Can't we *do* something today? Do we have to just sit around all day? Couldn't we go to the country or something? I wish it were still summer. It's going to be fall, and then it's going to be winter. . . .'

'Sure, let's go to the country right now,' he said. 'The leaves should be turning already, up in the mountains.' They were both silent then, thinking of their last time in the mountains.

Ruth knew she didn't want to go anywhere after all. She felt suddenly ashamed of how she'd been acting, whining like a three-year-old just because she knew he'd put up with it. She took his hand, and now she remembered when she too used to love their Sunday mornings.

'Rooey love,' he said, as they turned into their street. 'If I could, it would still be summer. We'd have it all over again, a better one.'

Ruth nodded. 'It's not your fault,' she told him gently.

CANDY

Candy sat with Billy's head clasped between her knees in the hot TV room, doing her hair. 'Can you fix breakfast all by yourself?' There was a furry puppet on the TV screen talking in a white fag voice. 'When Mommy and Daddy are still asleep, what if *you* had a surprise waiting for them when they got up?'

'Hey, one of y'all change the channel?' demanded Mabe, from her place on the floor. 'This stuff sucks.'

'Hold still!' Edie told her, waving her hot comb. She looked like a African queen in some cartoon herself, her big body all covered up by a red velvet robe with white rabbit fur on the collar that her visit had just brung in, and her head wrapped up in a stocking.

'You better stay still now,'' she told Mabe, 'or you gonna be minus them nice bushy eyebrows.'

'Cartoons!' Mabe snorted, but she stayed still.

Candy laughed. 'You rather keep your eyebrows and listen to some cartoons, right baby?' she asked.

'I don't even seen no cartoons yet,' Mabe answered. 'Call *that* a cartoon?'

'The first thing to remember,' the puppet was saying, 'is that hot stoves are very dangerous things! Wait for Mommy to use the stove. But just look what you can make with only your toaster and a few things from the refrigerator!' The puppet took a large white bottle of milk from an icebox.

With one hand, Candy reached over and turned off the sound, just as Norma, moving like she was 21 instead of 61, danced in the room with her radio. 'He's my bea-con in the storm,' she sang along. 'He's my ha-ven, he's my home. You-all needs some sounds in here,' she announced, 'and seeing that they got my gospel hour on here for me this morning, I will be so kind as to do you a favor and stay. Anyone else want they head done? I will do me just one head this morning.' Lou-Ann, the little girl that had been sick and mouthy in the flag room, got down between Norma's knees.

'Git that church music *out*-a-here,' Mabe said, but she said it real soft. 'Gonna shout shout shout,' sung the radio. 'Gonna tell everybody.'

'You all look like mother and daughter,' Mabe decided, pointing at Lou-Ann and Norma. Lou-Ann gave Mabe a nasty look.

'My Mama's back where I left her – Alabama,' she said in her tough little voice. 'She don't even know I'm down here.'

'You write and tell her today then,' Norma said. 'She got a right to know where you at, girl. I bet she worrying bout you right now.'

'She aint worried,' Lou-Ann answered. 'She told me she give me up. Told me the devil city done destroyed me and I better stay way from her.' Norma got a good grip on the girl with her strong knees. 'Gonna show them, what I found, in the Lord,' the lady on the radio sang out, and Norma rocked to the beat as she talked.

'Don't you believe it. Thems just words. Said when she in pain and couldn't help herself. She your mother. For all you know she sitting home right now, wishing she could take back them words. Sometime you got look at what lie *behind* words.'

'I done felt what lie behind,' Lou-Ann snorted. 'Felt it on my own behind.'

They all laughed. 'Listen to that little down-homey voice she got,' Edie said. 'Aint lost that, yet. You listen to Norma, Lil' Bit. Don't you know she got a girl bout the same age as you?'

Norma shifted Lou-Ann's shoulders inside her knee clasp so she could reach the other side of her head, and Candy saw how thin they was. Her little arms was needle marked and sorry looking. 'Have me some gold.' It was a man singing now in a real deep voice. 'Have me some silver. Diamonds too, when I git up there.'

'What I'm gone do?' asked Lou-Ann. 'Write and tell her I'm taking a little vacation? That my nine-to-five bossman said I was doing so good and steady he decided to send me to this fancy re-sort, get me some rest?'

'You tell her the truth, baby. Hold still, now. You tell her them streets done got to you, and that you tired, and need her now. She aint gonna tell you no.'

Candy snuck a look at Lou-Ann's face, to see was all this mother talk bothering her, but it was smooth and locked up tight. 'I bet she makes a real good little ho',' Candy thought. 'Lots of them like the real young-looking small ones the best anyways.'

She finished up the neat row of corn rolls down one side of Billy's head. 'We gonna have wings. We gonna be free,' she sung along, cause she liked that part. Her hand crept round and rested on Billy's cheek. 'You sure are quiet this morning,' she told her.

Billy stretched and yawned. 'It's alright in here this morning, you know?' she said. 'No fights or nothing. Nothing happenin', but it don't even matter.' Then she added, in a whisper, 'And I can smell you all round me, you know. Up there like that. Feel like I could just go *on* sitting here.' Candy felt happiness ease all through her bones.

The music switched back to R and B, and after a minute her and Billy's song came on, 'You're My Own Special Woman.' After a while she saw a cartoon come on the TV, but no one else noticed, so the sound stayed off. Then the puppet was back, in that icebox again. Out of the corner of her eyes, Candy saw Telecea Jones, that had just been let out of Max come in the room and lean inside the door watching the TV. Candy knew Billy couldn't see her the way her head was turnt, so she didn't say nothing. It was so rare for Billy to feel relaxed in a group like this, and Candy didn't want it spoiled too soon. But sure enough, Telecea had to start in on her crazy talk, at first real quiet, then louder. At first Candy couldn't tell what the hell she was going on about, but then she realized it was what she was seeing on the TV screen.

'You watch now, he gone drop that bottle,' she was saying. 'Crash! Broken glass all over the floor, what we gone do about it? Step on it, that's what, in our bare feets. Them long old slivers slide right in, easy. Ooo-no! Devil puppet done forgot about that toast sitting up there in the toaster. Reach in there with something metal, get hisself a shock. That devil puppet get itself stuck onto the toaster machine. Oooo – can't get loose. Stuck by the dick. Torment! Punisht! Got hisself a lectric shock in the dick!' she shouted out all loud, and Billy shifted real sharp outa Candy's knees. She never would keep her back turned to Telecea long.

'Girl, stop that retard talk!' she said. 'Can't even have no peace. Crazy bitch come in everywhere with her shit.' Candy saw Lou-Ann darting her eyes around, trying to figure out was something gone jump off, and Telecea started screaming at Billy, but Norma shut her up.

'Telecea Jones, we having a nice peaceful Sunday morning in here,' she told her, kinda strict, but still nice. 'It's the Lord's day, and I know right good an well that mean something to you, don't it, child?' Telecea nodded her head. 'Now you can come in here with us, but you gotta cut out that crazy talk and act like everyone else, you hear?' Telecea didn't say nothing but she did stop talking, and came and lay on the sofa near where Norma and Lou-Ann was. Billy reached and turnt on the sound on the TV.

'Just in case she do start in again,' she said. Now the TV and the radio was both playing so loud you couldn't really hear neither one, just a blare of noise. Billy shifted so she was facing Telecea, and Candy could tell by the stiffness of her shoulders that she was still all tensed up.

By now Telecea had fell asleep on the sofa, even with all that noise. She just lay there, snoring with her mouth open. 'Now you look at that, Billy Morris,' Norma said. 'Aint nothing but a tired child.'

'Everyone's a child to you,' Billy grumbled, but Candy could feel her shoulders go back to normal, and she turnt down the TV.

Wiggins came into the room then with her, 'Lunchtime, girls,' but they all decided not to go. Mabe said she had a can of sardines in her room, Edie had some chicken her visit had brung her, and Norma had some beans and rice. Candy and Billy said they would provide the reefer, and they fixed up a nice lunch right there, and put one plate on the side for Telecea.

After they had done eating Mabe turnt around and did Edie's hair, and Lou-Ann started in on Norma's. Billy's hair was finished, and looked real good, so her and Candy just sat close, and watched.

'This all-right!' said Lou-Ann. 'I never thought no prison be like this.'

'And you thought right, Lil' Bit,' Edie told her. 'Ninety-nine percent of the time you got your harassment, and your fighting, and whitey doing some fuckin' thing to you or other. When you get a little boring sit-around easy time, you gotta hold on to it.'

Candy didn't say nothing, but for once she agreed with Edie. She started to lay out a hand of cards so they would have something else to do when all the heads was done.

SONYA

Sonya was on the front steps of their house in Vermont. As she came in the door she saw a strange party going on, and now she remembered she didn't live here anymore. No one remembered her. She stood as flat as she could against the wall, watching Mira dance with a tall black woman. Then Mira gave her an angry look and led her firmly to the door. Sonya tried to protest, to tell her that this was her own house, but nothing would come out.

'I'm afraid I'm totally uninformed,' Mira said coldly. She had turned into Ruth Foster. 'You'll have to come back later and we'll see what we can do for you.' Now Sonya saw that everyone there but her was black and wore a ceremonial headdress. It was some kind of secret ritual that she'd spied on, by mistake.

'How did you get here?' the one who'd been dancing with Mira/Ruth asked her, in a perfectly emotionless voice. 'Now you will have to be killed.'

She woke up shaking. There was no one to tell it to, no one to hold her for a minute until it went away. It was Sunday morning, when people slept late and got the paper and had breakfast together. She put on water for coffee and wondered what Mira would say if she called her, in Marysbone, South Carolina, right now. She pictured Mira going to get the *Times*, wearing her old boy scout shorts and a white sleeveless boy's T-shirt, being mistaken by those who didn't know how to look, for a graceful teenage boy. When they'd been in New York together, she used to be approached occasionally by well-heeled and short-sighted older queens. But maybe in Marysbone Mira had to dress like a teacher all the time? And could she even get the *Times* there? She'd acted like a crazy woman, the way she'd telegrammed ahead accepting the offer from that tiny college in a town no one had ever heard of and then taking the first plane out, she was so eager to get away. No, Sonya wouldn't call. It wasn't Mira she wanted anyway, just someone.

She took her coffee and went to the work table. Through the window she could see families, walking close together on their way to church. She thought of her various sculpture ideas, but each of them seemed too ambitious to start on today. She needed materials, anyway, and the stores were closed. She'd probably never get any work done here.

She picked up a spool of thin gold wire that was on the table and listlessly began to play with it. The wire bent easily, and had to be looped around and around to hold a shape. It began to come alive in her hands, and suddenly there was a person, a small sad figure, with long dangling arms. She moved its legs so that it walked draggingly along. It was sexless, trailing a long umbilical cord of wire. She wound the cord around the figure, making a kind of bird's cage. Now when she tried to walk it in any direction, it hit up against the side of its cage. She stood back and looked at her work. It wasn't bad. Not bad at all.

She was ravenous now, and it was almost noon. She still had on the old Amelia Earhart T-shirt she'd worn to bed, and she put on jeans, stuffed her hair under her cap, and grabbed her old brown suede jacket. She stuck the little caged figure at the window where it could wait for her.

Outside the air was crisp and sweet. Sonya took long happy strides in her new city. The camera shot her progress – the sculptor, going for a walk after finishing a piece, living on her own with no one to account to but herself. She decided to walk to the Cafe Francais to have croissants. Last time she'd been there she'd seen a few attractive, stylish women sitting by themselves. She'd sit in a corner with her coffee and anything could happen.

But only a few blocks from the cafe, she saw Ruth Foster across the street, arm in arm with a tall curly-headed man. Sonya turned away, but Ruth was too engrossed in whatever he was saying to notice her anyway. Ruth looked much better than she did at work, in slim faded jeans, a grey sweater, everything understated, severe, and perfect. Sonya stopped and looked at herself in a store window which seemed to advertise S/M. Between the grimacing, emaciated, bald-headed mannequins, she made out her own wavy reflection, fat and messy, like a bag lady, or someone at a dress-up party. Relieved that Ruth hadn't seen her, Sonya decided to just get a bag of croissants and take them home on the subway. She didn't feel that much like being out in the world, really.

TELECEA

Fall to sleep on the couch in the TV room cause Norma she tell them leave me alone on the Lord's day so I know if they try something she be there to stop it. Couldn't even sleep last night in Max, my head be hurting so bad. Ruth Foster say she will come and aint even came. They likes to do that, makes you believe one thing, then turn it all round. Talk nice and sweet with they honey lips, and all the time be scheming how they gone trick and deceive you. Ruth Foster aint never came and no one tell me what do that letter say. Then in the morning they comes and moves me back down the cottage. Don't tell me nothing. When I seen Norma I gives my letter to her, ask her can she help me read it but she say she aint got her reading glasses neither.

Fall to sleep right on that couch and He send me a dream all about King Solomon how he tell them two ladies go ahead and pull that poor baby in two pieces cause they both say it belong to them. First they takes and pulls my liver in two and then they takes and tears up my soul.

When I wake up hear Norma talking to that ho' Candy about my letter that she aint had no business showing her in the first place. I hold my eyes shut like I still sleeping and lissen what can I hear.

Norma say, You mean to tell me this Ruth Foster lady write her this nice letter all the way up to Max just to let her know she can't git up there and see her?

Candy tell her yeah, that what the letter say alright.

Norma nod her head all up and down. So that why she came outa that hell hole so fast this time, cause she finely got someone in her corner. Well, thank the Lord, cause you know that poor child need someone of them that care what happen to her. Sometime I think them people would let that child rot up there just so long as they don't have to look at her. Sometime I think they don't have no human feelings at all.

Candy say that one of the qualifications for working here. Norma say who she really feel sorry for is they kids. Then she say, Well I sure hope she manage to act right round this lady and don't be talking all that crazy stuff round her.

That Candy ho' tell her, No, Norma, that's where you got it

wrong. That's one lady it's OK to talk shit to. That's the crazy lady, you sposed to act crazy round her, that's what they got her for.

The reason she say that is why I said, Ruth Foster the inmate, and that Candy ho' the police. Norma, she catch on something aint right too, and she tell her, No, Candy, don't you give me none of your smart white-girl talk now, telling me that poor child spose to act foolish round someone want to help her! It don't help her none the way they let her get away with all that crazy mess. Then once she go too far to please them they sends her up that hell hole again. Now you just tell me, Candy Peters, is this lady Ruth Foster good for real or not?

She could of ast me, I would of told her, She ain't no real police, you talking to the real police right in front of you now. But they think I sleeping so I stays still.

Then Candy laugh her devil laugh. She say, What do you mean is she good, I told you she the crazy lady. You go to her when you're crazy and she waves her magic wand and make it all better.

Talkin bout Ruth Foster like she one of them witches! Norma getting ready to go off on her now, so Candy say, You asking me does she really give a shit?

You *know* that what I'm asking, Norma say.

So Candy say, Yeah, I think she do, but what the fuck. If they find out she do, it just means they'll get rid of her sooner. And once she gone, what difference is it gonna make to Telecea that she used to care? Cause don't nobody care once they out. You think I'm gonna sit around and wonder is Telecea Jones still up in Max once they let me out of this place? *Hell* no. And neither will she.

Norma say, Candy, chile, when you gone stop trying to sound so old and bitter? You may fool some of them, but you aint never fool me. I seen you act real sweet to Gladdy and them when you think aint no one watching you. Now you tell me, you think this lady Ruth Foster would care for one of them little small afghans I make? And we put in a little note you write for me with your pretty handwriting you got? Say thank you for helping Telecea?

Candy tell her no, Foster might think someone trying to buy her off. Then she look over and catch me wif my eyes open. Norma, I tell you what. That poor innocent child of yours been awake this whole time listening to us.

Well, aint nothing wrong with that, Norma tell her right to her nasty lying ho' face. I hope she did hear what I have to say, you know

67

as well as I do Norma Lewis don't say nothing to your back she can't say to your face, and the child supper right here waiting for her when she do wake up.

MONDAY, SEPTEMBER 21

RUTH

Ruth was a fast and skillful driver, and she enjoyed her solitary trips to and from work. On her way in, she smoked, played the radio as loud as it would go, and allowed herself to reminisce or fantasize.

'Lucy in the sky, with diamonds,' sang the Beatles this morning, and she slipped immediately back to her college dorm, freshman year. She'd be in Martha's room, sitting on the floor, both of them listening to the stereo. Martha's long fingers would be playing with her hair, which she'd worn straight and long, down her back then. 'Lucy in the Sky' was supposed to be about an acid trip, everyone said so, but it always reminded Ruth of Martha, maybe because of the image of diamonds shining in the sky, and the 'girl with kaleidoscope eyes.' She remembered Martha's canvasses, huge multi-colored fields with light shining through. Everything she'd done that year, even the cup she'd given to Ruth had been full of that special scattered light.

She and Martha had taken Modern Poetry together, and had stayed up all one night on diet pills writing their term papers. When they'd both finished, in the early morning, light was pouring into the room, and they'd put on old Miracles and Temptations records and danced. Ruth remembered the weightlessness of it, different from anything she'd felt before or since. There had been a feeling, too, of being on the edge of things, a sense that something important was about to happen.

Not that it really had. The next year Martha had taken mostly museum courses and Ruth had stuck to English and Psych and had gotten involved with Rick. She and Martha had remained friends, but had never again been as close or, Ruth thought now, in her case anyway, quite as happy.

She thought of Martha living in San Francisco now, painting and spending a lot of time on some feminist newspaper. She'd always urged Ruth to go on with her writing. A lot of self-conscious imitation was how Ruth thought of it now. From time to time she still wrote Ruth charming letters, full of little sketches and their old phrases, but containing almost no real information about her life. Victor had been struck, when he read one, by Martha's lack of social consciousness. He had spent the years she and Martha played together protesting the war in Vietnam, and while he felt that Ruth had emerged at least partially from that cocoon of obliviousness, he claimed that Martha had stopped right there.

Ruth had agreed with him at the time, had seen that Martha had refused to grow up, while she'd gone on to the real world of a helping profession and a realistic, committed relationship. Still, driving the home stretch toward her realistic, committed job, Ruth sighed. She turned off the radio, which was now playing loud obnoxious music, and sang slowly to herself from that Temptations record.

'Like smoke from a cigarette, a dream you can soon forget, it fade away, fade away . . . You've changed, and it's showing, baby, where is your love going-going. . . .'

The image of Sonya Lehrman telling Dave that he talked a line of bull and then stalking away to be with 'the women' in the cafeteria flashed through her head. The well-staged, rather childish quality of it made her smile. Martha used to stage the same kinds of scenes sometimes, as if she were sitting back watching herself all the time. Sonya couldn't *look* more different than Martha, though. Pulling into the parking lot, Ruth decided that she would at least make an effort to get to know Sonya.

Now that she thought about it, she realized that she hadn't had a really close woman friend since Martha. She didn't know if she could count Ann Butler, whom she'd gotten close to in her first year of social work school. They'd even considered getting an apartment together, but then, in her second year, Ruth had gotten absorbed in the relationship with Victor, and had ended up moving in with him. Somehow, she and Ann had drifted apart. Ruth still ran into her from time to time because Ann had stayed in the area too, running a peer-counseling program for ex-cons and teaching in the Black Studies department of the state university.

Ruth hadn't met any women who interested her much since. Maybe that was at the bottom of the trouble she'd been having with Victor lately. Everyone knew it was bad to depend on one person to fill all your needs. No wonder she'd been feeling so boxed in. She just needed a friend.

CANDY

'Hey baby,' Billy told her. 'We aint in no jail. You know that.'

At first Candy didn't know what she meant, but then she did know. '*Hell*, no,' she said. 'We aint in no jail.'

They was outside on the steps of the cottage. Everyone else was at breakfast. Candy leant back against Billy's shoulders and Billy put her arm round her. 'Want to hold you tight,' Billy whispered. 'Don't ever want to let you go.'

Candy closed her eyes and listened to the sweet sound of Billy's voice. 'Tell me,' she said. 'Tell me bout when we get out.' The sun beat down on her bare legs. Billy's hand was in her hair and her fingers was warm against her face.

'First thing,' she said. 'You and me gonna be together. You know what together means baby?'

Candy nodded. 'Tell me though.'

'In one way,' Billy told her, 'don't matter *where* we go, cause wherever it is, that place is gonna be together. But I been thinking, and one place we *could* go to."

'Yeah,' Candy prompted. 'Go ahead.' Most of the time she talked more than Billy, but when they was good and wasted, like now, it was more often Billy that talked, with her listening.

'One place we could go to is California,' said Billy. 'You know how that man came here from the magazine and said you could make it as a model? Well, the place to do it is out there. We'll make them pay for just looking at you on the cover of some magazine. And I mean your face baby, not nothing below the neck. Then, when you get known, and they find out that you're a dancer and a singer both – well we'll be right on time, if you know what I'm talking bout. Right there in Hollywood, where it's happening. Won't be about no more streets, baby. Cause you is so far above them streets. And maybe I'll go back to school. They got some good schools out there. That's where Angela Davis is teaching at, California, in one of them Black Studies Departments. Well, that's what I'll take up. Study with her. Cop me a degree. Send Timmy to one of them hot shit private schools they got for Black kids out there. Teach him about his heritage. We'll just make us a little money on the side. Sell us a little nice blow, not no dope or nothing, no heavy scenes. And we could have one of them houses they got out there that's all glass on one side. And a pool. Won't have to deal with no winter there baby, no cold weather at all. Just be out in the sun together, and one day you gonna turn to me, and ask did we really meet in a jail. Cause it's all gonna seem like a dream, you know.'

'No,' said Candy. 'I'd rather have it that we remember. There's things I don't want to forget, even in California or nowhere.'

'Yeah, you got a point,' said Billy. 'Like the time I met you.'

'Tell me?' asked Candy.

Billy put her soft lips against Candy's neck. 'You always smell so good,' she said. Candy felt Billy's nose against her cheek, heard the wind whisper of Billy's words in her ear. 'Smell so sweet, baby. If they put me down somewhere in the middle of the California desert, I still would know your smell.'

Candy closed her eyes and she smelled the cut grass of the yard and Wiggins' coffee cooking inside and the warm clean salty smell of her lover. 'Tell me,' she said. 'Tell me bout when you met me.'

'Well, it was two years ago now. Two years and a little. Fall time, but later than this when you come in. I was just sitting in the cottage, playing cards, not thinking bout anything much, and then I hear this commotion behind me. Turnt around, and there's Mo Turner talking to this new skinny white bitch. Nothing special in that cause some new halfway decent girl come in you know Mo gotta check her out. But this girl don't want to be checked out. What she's doing instead, she's sticking her chin up in the air, flicking her little ass all around, telling Mo where to get off, and that's when I had to blink my eyes and look did I see right. Cause this girl starts talking to Mo, and this little white girl talks black!'

Here she imitated Candy's voice. ' "Tell you what honey. If I want to have me a conversation with you, I come looking for you". And this to what's sposed to be the biggest baddest butch in the joint at the time? I just sat there and looked. Wasn't my business, and I wasn't gonna get into it. All I thought was, Somebody better teach this bitch something before she git herself killed. And that's the only reason I started talking to you after Mo left. Aint even seen beyond that.'

Candy laughed. 'Well now aint that sweet,' she said in Norma's voice. 'Little Miss Larceny herself, trying to keep peace. You got a good heart in there if you would only let it show.'

Mabe came drifting by all dressed up for her visit that had got turnt away, though he had got near enough to pass in what he brought. It was her man, Clay, that she hadn't even seen once in the ten months she'd been in, that was starting to come round now she was getting out in a month or so.

'Man got hisself all dressed!' Mabe said. 'Gold leather coat and everything. Say he don't want me to forget I got me a pretty man out there waiting on me. Say next time he's gonna bring his lawyer with him and then they can try their shit, talking bout keeping him out! I didn't even get to touch him!'

'Look at it like this,' Billy told her. 'You seen him. And he did get over, you know. Looks like they couldn't keep him out after all.'

'Guess you're right,' Mabe agreed. 'I hadn't thought of it like that. That gold leather shined right through this fence!' Then she walked on, humming to herself.

Candy thought she looked pretty, but real horish with her tight little pants and pink shirt. Billy pulled her closer. 'She don't even want to know he's using her, long as he wears his gold coat and brings her some shit. That's enough for her. But not us, baby. I'm gonna take you on out of here, Candy,' she whispered. 'It don't have to be no California. Just some place where they aint got snow in the winter. You know I don't like no snow.'

Candy thought of the first time Billy had ever said she loved her. They was high, like now. All this snow had fell in the night and they was walking across the yard real early, before it had got tramped down. They both worked in the kitchen then, and they was going to fix breakfast. Candy had hold of Billy's hand. She hadn't been looking for Billy to say nothing to her. Holding her hand was enough. And then Billy had stopped dead, right in the yard in the middle of all that white shivery stuff and her face had got different.

'Wait a minute baby,' she said. 'Shit, I just realized something. I love you, Candy.' And then the snow hadn't seemed cold at all, it had seemed like a soft white blanket or something.

Billy was shaking her shoulder. 'Hey, baby,' she told her. 'What the fuck you doing out here nodding. You want to get us busted?'

'Don't holler at me,' Candy said. 'I was just thinking bout snow, that's all.'

'Aint hollering, baby. Just don't get us both busted, that's all. So close to our dates. Gots to be cool, you aint out on the street now.'

'I know that.'

73

It was right after that day in the snow they escaped. It seemed like the joint just couldn't hold the way they felt. Candy wanted to leave right away for out-of-state, but Billy wanted to at least see her mother and Timmy before leaving. So while Billy was with them, Candy had been out there working to make enough to fly out that cold city, cause it wasn't even about no dirty poor people's Greyhound. And it had been a cold city alright, and it kept on snowing, and even when it was falling and still clean the snow didn't seem soft no more but hard and freezing like ice and she felt like she was made of ice herself, standing out there on the corner with that wind blowing on her. And when it melted it got grey and ugly. Her tricks left puddles of it on the dirty hotel room floor. Seemed like they all had something wrong with them, crazy bastards that wanted to put on her panties and made her put on their nasty dirty ones. And them spanking and pissing-on-her dudes and them gonzo ones that had came back from Vietnam wrong in the head and would pull a gun on her and make her do it for free. Then that one she didn't even like to think of, cause it gave her nightmares. She had ended up by getting beat up bad, and had all their flying-out money took.

It was the day after that they got busted, right in their hotel room they couldn't pay for. Someone had to of dropped a dime on them, they didn't know who, and neither one of them had asked the other one too much about it.

Billy stuck her sharp elbow in her side again. 'I told you once about that nodding!'

'You're right, baby,' Candy told her. 'Let's do go someplace where it don't ever snow.'

SONYA

The guard at the front desk, whom Sonya remembered distinctly from last week, claimed she didn't know her. She said she'd have to check with Mrs Hanson before she could let Sonya in, and Mrs Hanson was in a meeting with the superintendent, Mr Tranden, and could not be disturbed. Sonya sat down on a bench with two visitors, men who were apparently also questionable enough to require official approval. The white one was nodding out, and had blood-shot eyes and clothes that looked and smelled as if they'd been slept in for weeks. The black one had processed hair, a shiny gold-colored full-length leather coat, and pointy black boots. When she tried to catch their eyes to acknowledge their common plight, both of them looked away.

After a while, she began to think that Mrs Hanson might send out a message that no, Sonya Lehrman was not a staff member, that in fact she had never even heard the name. Then she'd be free to leave. She'd go straight back to the airport and board the next plane for Paris. Or maybe the next plane for any foreign country, leaving it completely to chance. She realized she had no money, so she'd have to walk the streets for as long as it took her to earn the fare. She thought she could get it in two or three nights. Then she'd go to the airport with just the clothes she had on her back, without ever having gone back to that awful mistake of a loft, and she would never again even think about this exercise in futility they called a job. . . .

Ruth Foster startled her out of her reverie by coming through the inside door and stopping abruptly in front of her.

'I just heard they were holding you up here,' she scolded. 'It's typical of this place. Miss Murphy!' she called severely to the guard. 'This is one of our new therapists, Miss Lehrman. You should have been told, it's really too bad.'

'How was I supposed to know what to do when no one told me, Miss Foster,' and then, in a flash, Sonya was inside the magic set of doors, doomed to be an art therapist instead of a streetwalker.

Ruth Foster was all cool blond smiles as she led Sonya down the long front hall with its lounging women and through the door to the mental health corridor. She had on tailored beige slacks with a little row of pleats over her perfectly flat stomach, and one of those floppy-necked sweaters that had to be folded down in exactly the right way. Sonya knew a shirt like that would have made her look like her neck was in a cast, but it was just right on Ruth. Sonya remembered the man she'd seen Ruth with on Sunday. She'd only caught a flash of him, but that had been enough to take in his tall good looks.

'I really hope you get your office today,' Ruth said cheerily. 'I told Mrs Hanson this morning that it was inexcusable to make you wait around like this.' She seemed to be trying to make up for her rudeness of the first day, but once they arrived at her office she closed the door firmly behind her, leaving Sonya to the coffee room, where Lynda and Cindy were discussing the progress of Lynda's diet. It was not a topic of conversation Sonya felt like contributing to, and she was relieved when Mrs Hanson came barreling in, clothed today in an olive-drab crackling leather outfit which increased her marked resemblance to a rhino. She waved a perfunctory hand at the others, and seized on her.

'Sonya dear, you'll be glad to know I have an office for you this morning,' she announced, pausing for thanks. Sonya smiled, deciding to wait until she'd seen the office.

Mrs Hanson walked Sonya down the hall, guiding her with hard little shoves. 'I know you're very eager to begin work, even a wee bit impatient, dear. I've heard through our very efficient grapevine that you've begun mingling with our girls on their own grounds, shall we say, in the yard and the lunch room. Now that's all very well, but not quite as professional as we might hope for one of our mental health staff. These are very troubled girls you know dear, the security risks alone. . . . Well! I know you'll be most satisfied, we have a nice office for you right here in the corridor so you'll be included right away as part of our regular therapeutic staff, by association. Now that's a better way to break in with our girls. They won't even realize they're doing it but they'll associate you in their minds with something they respect. They're always watching us, you know, dear, we mustn't give them the impression that we want to be one of them.'

She had stopped at the office across from Ruth's and fumbled for the right key among her enormous bunch, then unlocked it. Like each of the other offices in the hall, this one had room enough for a large metal desk and three small chairs. With a little luck, Sonya thought despairingly, a few shelves might be inserted.

Mrs Hanson's tone was reproving now. 'You're very lucky, dear. Your office even has a window. Of course that adds distraction, not everyone prefers it, but a window does give that sense of openness, doesn't it, that cheerful note, it makes the girls feel freer and more relaxed, I always feel. As an artist I'm sure you've noticed the great importance of environment, my dear, though sometimes I fear we ordinary mortals tend to ignore such things. I'm so busy myself I'm afraid I often don't have the time to even notice whether there is a window in my little office or not. . . .'

The only way Sonya could interrupt the flow was to cut rudely into it. In the past few minutes, getting a decent room had become the most important and the least likely thing in her life, and she heard her voice tremble. 'I can't use this room, Mrs Hanson. It's just not big enough.'

'Well, really, my dear! I must admit I feel both surprised and disappointed in you. We've never had an art therapist here before, and I do hope I haven't acted hastily in hiring you so shall we say impulsively. I'm sure this size office has been perfectly satisfactory to all our staff, including our psychiatrist, Dr Thorne. . . .'

'It's just that I'm an *art* therapist.' This time Sonya didn't even attempt to keep the desperation out of her voice. 'I'll be working mostly with groups, not individuals. I'll need big tables to paint on, room to set up easels. . . .'

Mrs Hanson stood perfectly still against the door of the little office.

'I'm afraid I hadn't been informed that group therapy was one of your aims, my dear. You see, most of our girls have had so much 'group' therapy that they could probably lead a 'group' better than you could. These drug programs, you know. They go in for sob stories, and our girls certainly excel at that. A different life history every time you talk to them, and each one more heart-breaking than the next. No, as director of treatment I think we'll do quite well without any 'groups' here, thank you. Now, if you'd like to set up some paper and crayons, of course there is absolutely no reason why that can't be done right here on this desk.' Her tone signalled the end of the conversation, and she moved Sonya deftly out of the tiny space, into the hall. 'Of course, if you'd rather remain a 'rover,' that can be easily arranged too. I'm sure that one of our little social work students would be pleased as punch to have her own private office. With a window too,' she added.

Ruth's door opened, and she appeared, standing a little hesitantly in the hall. Sonya had noticed that even Mrs Hanson seemed to treat her with a little more respect, or perhaps caution, than she treated the others, with the exception of Dave.

'And how are you this fine morning, Miss Foster?' she asked now. 'Settling back to work now that we've resolved our little differences about your client?'

'I'm fine, Mrs Hanson. I was so pleased to hear that Telecea is already back in the cottage.' Ruth paused. 'I didn't mean to eavesdrop, but I couldn't help overhearing. I've been trying to think of any larger rooms here, and it occurred to me that there *is* that big empty room up on the second floor, right above us. Next to Max. I think it was the infirmary, before we got the hospital.'

Mrs Hanson looked ready to explode. Apparently Ruth was not *that* special. 'Miss Foster, have you been inside that room lately? It's the institutional garbage can! You know, girls, I always have one drawer in my desk I refer to as the garbage drawer. . . .'

Over Mrs Hanson's head, Ruth grinned at Sonya, lifting one elegant arched eyebrow, and Sonya knew she would get the room. There was no more question about it.

'And, in any case, this area's lack of security coverage makes it quite out of the question,' Mrs Hanson was concluding her speech. 'We do have our troublemakers, even in this institution, which we like to think does serve as a model for others all around the country as far as innovations in the rehabilitative treatment plan we've developed here for our girls. . . .'

'I realize that what I'm asking is highly unorthodox,' Sonya slipped in smoothly, at the next pause for air, 'but then, as you yourself pointed out, art therapy is a relatively new field, and the very fact that you hired me proves to me that you are committed to change, to true rehabilitation, as you say.'

Hanson nodded smugly, pleased.

'I'd like to ask you to take your commitment one step further,' Sonya continued, 'and to let me experiment with this large room, for a trial period only. If anything goes wrong, any security problems or anything at all, I'll gladly take this office with thanks. But for a real art therapy program, one that would serve as a rehabilitative model for other institutions. . . .'

Hanson was shaking her head back and forth. 'Impossible, girls,' she said. 'There is no point in this discussion. There just is not adequate coverage, and this is not a day camp, but a jail, as *you*,' she nodded to Ruth, 'ought to know by now, and as you, my dear, will soon learn. In any case, if you saw the state of the room. . . .'

'*Could* I see it?' Sonya was a little girl now, large-eyed and pleading. 'I'm sure you're right, but if I just saw it, I wouldn't keep thinking of it.'

Hanson must have realized that she was losing. 'I suppose so. Why don't you accompany us, Miss Foster.' She gave Ruth one of her little shoves. 'After all this was your rather unfortunate brainchild, I'm afraid you'll have to take some responsibility for it.'

The three of them walked down to the staircase just inside the iron door which was the entrance to the mental health corridor. Two women sat entwined a few steps up. As they approached, Sonya recognized her champion from the hall on the first day. Her companion was a fragile looking young woman, with long red hair of an improbable color. Sonya's champion had on the same sleeveless man's T-shirt, worn tight to reveal every detail of her large breasts. The arm she encircled the younger woman with was heavily needle marked and scarred. A clumsy heart was tattooed on her biceps, with the name Mary printed inside it. Sonya visualized a several panelled portrait, to be entitled Couple. She would do it in dark, heavy oil, in rather a mid-American, Hopperesque style, and the middle panel would show the two of them, a little dwarfed by the steps leading up to Max and the whole prison scene around them. The other panels would be close-ups, one of them a tattooed arm, one a close, almost cellular study of a section of dyed, teased red hair.

'Excuse *us*, girls,' trilled Mrs Hanson. 'Now who can tell me where you're supposed to be right now, Donnie?'

'Got a 'pointment with my social worker,' mumbled Donnie.

'Well! No one told *me* that Mrs Schofield had moved her office to these steps! I'll have to speak to her about that, won't I?' Mrs Hanson gave a gurgling laugh and put her face close to Donnie, who recoiled. 'Now why don't you just go on to work, dear, and I'll forget that I saw you and won't mark you out of place this time.' The women did not move or answer, barely shifting on the stairs to let them pass. Sonya heard the word 'cunts' behind them. 'Now you see,' Mrs Hanson continued serenely, 'some of our girls, Donna there is a good example (she prefers to be called Donnie you know, many of them will take on a male name) are quite hostile. They're just little girls, you see, with grown-up bodies. They don't want to act out, but

79

sometimes there just isn't the necessary control. Now you'll notice that our friend Donna didn't move when I asked her to, but she will have left for work by the time we come down. She had to save face, you see, it's a characteristic many of our girls share, and at times I allow them to do it, as I did in this case, although if we went strictly by the book, you see, that kind of disobedience would put her right in line for a D.'

Sonya wondered why Mrs Hanson was talking as though there had been only one woman on the stairs. Was it because if she'd admitted that there had been two she would also have had to admit that they'd been embracing? She must have noticed the other woman, who had been skinny but not invisible. She would have to ask Ruth just what the official attitude on lesbianism was here.

'The only other facility on this floor is our Maximum Security Unit,' Mrs Hanson said, pointing to the heaviest looking black iron door Sonya had seen yet. 'And so this area is *associated* with Max in the girls' minds, you see. I doubt whether any of them would care to come up here to do their art work.' A few steps down the hall from the large iron door, she took out her huge set of keys and opened the door, to reveal a large attic-like room, full of garbage and emitting a sour smell. Sonya saw stacks of old papers, piles of what looked like soiled clothing, and even trays of moldy food. She took in the strange, split angles of the five walls, which formed several different surfaces, the sloping low ceilings, and the large expanse of floor space.

'I'll clean it up. Mrs Hanson, I'll clean up every inch myself. This is perfect, it's exactly what I need.'

TELECEA

Now I'm out of Max, Schofield bring me round. I used to be cottage cleaner wif Norma but Wiggins she found out I hear what she tell that ho' Candy one all night long, when they aint knowed I was lissening. All about her son gone to the devil and her daughter have three babies wif three different daddies and aint none of them come out right. How she think them devil babies gone come out? Wif tails, that how and them little small horns and feets like ducks, like I seen on a baby one time. When Wiggins find out I know all about it, she tell Schofield, Oh no, I will not have that one in my hair all day, bad enough that someone don't have the good sense to keep her locked up there where she belongs instead of putting her in my decent cottage to upset my normal girls. When I hear who she calling normal I just laugh and laugh, and she say, Oh Dot, get her out of here will you, she just give me the creeps with that laugh of hers.

Soons we leave out the cottage Schofield have to start wif her, Give education a try, like she always do. Lady must think I'm crazy or something think I'm a go up that school so they can call someone retarded that just don't have her glasses wif her. She say, But Telecea, it's such a good opportunity for you, you wouldn't have to do one of those useless jobs that way and you've never given the school a chance.

Who she trying to say dint gave school a chance? I been there.

Where your mama, where your daddy, where you get them nasty clothes, out the Morgy box? Look at her, she stay wif that old lady beat her wif a big stick every night. My mama told me don't go near her stoop or that old lady gone get me and come at night if I bad! Yeah well, my mama say don't look at her or she give you the evil eye, put some roots on you. I shown them evil eye, shown them black and blue eye too, smack them in they lying moufs, try and call somebody Granny a witch.

Them teachers come and tell Granny don't bring me back to school no more and when they gone Granny beat me till the blood run down.

Talking to Him all the time. Please, Lord, help me wif this bad chile, help me save her soul from Hell where her mama done already

81

gone. Lord look down here and see me how I aint sparing no rod on this child born bad like her mother the Dulter and her Daddy seed of the Devil now they done told me she too bad to go to school now the whole world done seen the mark of Cain on her forehead. Well she aint goin' to no special school they gots for devil childrens.

Bitch have the nerve to tell me I aint gave school a chance. I been there. So then she take me up the flag room wif all them butch bominations they got up there and I tell them, Watch out now girls, gone catch you little dicks in them sewing machines. Butches start in wif what they gone do to me, and Delaney tell Schofield get her right out now Dot before I have a riot on my hands and don't bring her back here I don't care who told you.

Then we go down the basement to the laundry and Riley say, Dorothy Schofield, you know we had one fire in here already last week. While I have feet to walk off this job that one aint coming in here. Wouldn't work in no damned laundry noway, all that blood and pus they gots on them sheets.

Schofield take me out of there, say, Oh Telecea, what are we going to do with you? I give up for today, I have people waiting.

So I just be a wanderer like them childrens of Israel. Don't need none of they nasty unclean job, I walk round and lissens good and watches all the time and I got my dream pictures He send me. And I don't tell no one bout them cause you could get in trouble like Ruth Foster told me, You don't need to say all of what's in your mind, save it for Wednesday and Friday. And Norma she say so too. Cause or else they do me like they done Joseph when he told his dreams, they say, Behold this dreamer come, lets us kill him and throw him in a deep pit for the beasties to eat. What you gots to do you gots to save them for the person that meant to hear them. She just waiting for the right time to call me in.

TUESDAY, SEPTEMBER 22

RUTH

Alice Anderson came into Ruth's office trailing blood. 'Not again,' Ruth thought wearily. Her back ached as it always did right before she got her period, and she was ready to go home. Alice held one wrist tightly with her other hand. She wore the animated look which she had only at such moments, reminding Ruth of a dog that had just dragged a half-dead bird to its mistress for approval.

'How are you feeling today' she asked. Alice gestured impatiently at her wrist in answer. 'How are you feeling?' Ruth repeated.

'I think I'm OK. Now,' Alice answered. Ruth looked at her. Alice's lank light-brown hair hung in strands around her thin, acne-marked face. She wore a dirty pink rayon shirt with a torn collar, baggy plaid wool pants, now flecked with blood, and sneakers with dragging laces.

'I see that you've cut yourself,' Ruth said. 'And I also see that you look annoyed, and wide awake.' When Alice said nothing, she continued. 'The best way to let me know what you're thinking or feeling is to say it in words, Alice. Remember?'

'Mrs Hanson told me that the next time she hears I cut myself she's gonna send me straight up to Max.'

Ruth nodded again. 'Is that what you'd like?'

'No. They're gonna search my room,' she went on, 'but they won't find it. I hid it too good.' She paused, waiting, then continued as if Ruth had asked. 'I'm talking about the glass I cut myself with, Miss Foster. I hid it good so I can use it next time I want it!'

Ruth tried for kind firmness. 'I think you'd like me to ask where you hid the glass, Alice,' she said. 'But that's not what I'm here for. If you'd like to talk to me, I'd like very much to listen.' The bleeding had stopped. Ruth watched the blood turn brown and dry on the leather. It would certainly stain. She wondered if it might not be therapeutic to ask Alice to clean up her mess.

'You don't even care!' Alice spoke in a high pitched whine. 'At least the nurses over the hospital, they try and do something for me! Or when I was at State, they always asked me why I did it. They had real psychiatrists that helped you there!'

83

'I do care, Alice,' Ruth told her, wondering if she did. 'And that's why I'd like to help you find other ways of communicating than by cutting yourself.'

Alice had begun rocking back and forth on the end of the chair. 'I like it when it starts bleeding,' she said dreamily. 'It feels so good inside me.' She gestured vaguely between her legs. 'You're mad at me,' she added slyly. 'I can tell.'

Ruth's back ached. She hoped her own bleeding would wait until she got home. 'If I look mad, it's because I think you're wasting your time with me right now,' she said. 'You can go to almost anyone and show them your wrist, and they'll say, "poor Alice, you cut yourself again, what's the matter?" I think there are other things you can get from me.'

Alice looked bored. 'Can I go now?' she asked. 'I don't like staying in the same room with you when you're mad.'

Ruth swallowed her annoyance. 'Your hour isn't up, but you know you're free to leave any time,' she told her.

Alice began the slow process of detaching herself from the chair.

'I'll call the hospital and tell them you're on your way over there to have your wrist bandaged,' Ruth said. 'See you next week.' She listened to the dragging footsteps receding down the hall. 'Girl's been in too many damn institutions,' she thought, picking up the phone to call the hospital. 'I'm surprised she doesn't bore even herself.'

Miss Putnam, the nurse on duty, answered the call. 'That poor little girl.' she murmured. 'Of course, if anyone can help her, you can. You mean so much to these girls. Doesn't it show just how much, the way that poor little Alice came to see you even after she'd hurt herself! Now, some of the nurses over here don't like your attitude as far as your depriving the girls of their meds, but I've been meaning to tell you myself, I personally support you one hundred percent. It's the personal touch that helps, wouldn't you say, more than all the medication in the world. Now, I don't have your training psychologically speaking, Miss Foster, but I always said a little mothering never hurt anyone. . . .'

'You do a fine job, Miss Putnam.' Ruth tried not to let the irritation into her voice. 'And what I'd like for you to do for Alice is not to pay too much attention to her cutting. It's all she gets attention for, so she keeps on doing it. Try to mother her just for herself, not because she cut her wrist.'

Miss Putnam clucked on the other end. 'Isn't that just it, though,

84

Miss Foster! Mother her for herself. I'm going to tell Dr Thorne how you explained it to me. I was just telling Dot Proudy the other day, when she was criticizing you for the way you handle Telecea Jones, I just told her, Miss Foster doesn't rush you like the others do, Miss Foster *explains* things to you. . . .'

'Thank you, Miss Putnam. I'm afraid I *will* have to rush you now, I have a client waiting. Thanks again.'

She put down the phone feeling ready to throttle Miss Putman who was a perfectly well-meaning fool and genuinely good to the women. What if she did carry tales? It wasn't worth getting angry about. Maybe it was Alice. Of all of her clients, she was the only one Ruth found it genuinely impossible to like. It wasn't even Alice's constant cutting as much as her whining, sulky quality that really got to Ruth. If there'd been anyone else who could handle her she'd have transferred her months ago.

Now she had to clean up the damn blood. All she needed would be Telecea's reaction if she discovered it tomorrow on her chair.

As she walked down the hall to the bathroom, she saw Sonya and Telecea standing at the foot of the steps. They were both talking and gesturing at once, so intent that neither one noticed her. Ruth realized that it was the first time she'd seen Telecea actually having a conversation with anyone. Even more surprising, before she walked away she'd smiled, a perfectly sane smile. She looks peaceful with me sometimes, when we've resolved something, Ruth thought, but not happy like that.

'So what are you doing with Telecea, to make her look so happy?' she asked Sonya, who had come into the bathroom behind her. Sonya must have thought the room was empty, because she jumped and blushed. She had on a big white men's button-down shirt, like the kind Ruth had gotten from her father and brought in for art class as a child, and she was very dirty. She had pushed her long black hair behind her ears, but it stood out in damp ringlets around her face. She clearly hadn't been exaggerating when she'd told Mrs Hanson she'd clean out the room herself. Ruth wished she could take back the tone of the words she'd just spoken. It was the half-nasty, half-jokey tone she used with Dave and the others, and there was something about Sonya today that made her want to speak to her as she would to a child or to one of her clients, gently and without sarcasm.

'I'm sorry I startled you,' she said. 'Really, though, it was good to see Telecea looking like that.'

Sonya smiled. 'I was trying to convince her that it was a better idea for me to go home and come back tomorrow than to camp out here until we finish. She's been working me like a dog all day. Wouldn't even let me take a lunch break.'

Jealousy and admiration fought inside Ruth. 'I don't know if you're aware that most people on this staff wouldn't spend five minutes alone in a room with Telecea, let alone a whole day.'

Sonya laughed. 'I have to admit that I came out of there expecting to see dicks emerging from the most unlikely places.' Then she turned to Ruth. 'I'm so glad we ran into each other,' she said. 'I've been wanting to thank you for yesterday. I might have quit or something if you hadn't come along when you did.'

Ruth nodded. 'Mrs Hanson does have a way of making one feel that. She does it to me all the time. But don't quit yet. I'm very glad you're here, even though I did act like a shit that first day.'

The speech felt rehearsed and uncomfortable, but it was a relief to finally get it out. Ruth was suddenly aware that they'd been standing there talking in the filthy bathroom, which she never even entered if she could help it. She was about to say something about it, then stopped herself because she didn't want Sonya to think she was compulsive. She started for the door, feeling ridiculous.

'It looks like you're doing some cleaning, too.' Sonya pointed to the wet paper towels which she'd forgotten about but which still dangled from her arm.

'Oh yes,' she remembered. 'Somebody's been bleeding in my room, I have to clean up. Come on down, if you're not too busy.'

She'd thought it would be easier in her office, but she felt even more self-conscious and absurd scrubbing at the floor and the chair, with Sonya perched up on the desk.

'Did someone try to kill herself in here, or what?' she asked. 'You seem pretty calm about it.'

Ruth told her about Alice. 'She cuts herself at least twice a month. It's the thing she's known for here. They don't say 'Alice Anderson,' they say 'that girl who's always cutting on herself.' So I try to ignore the cutting and reinforce her for other things.'

'That makes sense.'

Ruth looked up to see Sonya stroking Martha's cup with one finger. 'It's nice here,' Sonya added. 'Like an island of sanity. Your things are beautiful, but there aren't too many of them. There's room for feelings.' It was exactly the effect Ruth had aimed at, and she blushed with pleasure. She felt even more irritated than usual when Dave knocked on the door, and came in without waiting for a response. At the sight of Sonya he stopped short, feigning amazement, and pointed a finger at her.

'Well, well, what do you know! A historic first.' He addressed Sonya confidentially, while Ruth scrambled to her feet. 'I hope you realize what a great honor is being conferred on you. SQ does not invite people into her office to socialize every day!' He turned back to Ruth. 'You better watch out. Before we could just say you were anti-social. Now we're going to have to take it more personally.'

Ruth's back ached. He got Telecea out of Max, she reminded herself, clamping her jaw down on her anger. 'Why don't you go run around the block, Dave?' she got out finally. 'Take a tranquilizer or something. Cool yourself down.'

'You heard that,' he appealed to Sonya. 'You're my witness, you see how she treats me. She has sympathy for all the most brutal female psychopaths in the state, but not for a poor lonely male psychiatrist.' Now he stood at attention, as if reporting to someone. 'Man-killer Telecea Jones must be let out of Max immediately! No medication. Never mind that she thinks she's God's personal instrument of revenge! SQ says let her out without medication! Who am I to question her orders? And then she wants to medicate *me*! Now would you call that fair?'

Sonya had moved to the window while he spoke, and had been standing there with her back to him, looking out. Now she turned. 'Were you speaking to me? I'm afraid I wasn't listening.'

Fifteen minutes later, Ruth and Sonya walked to the parking lot together. 'You shouldn't let him get to you,' Sonya advised. 'I find that when you treat them like invisible bugs, they tend to go away. What's that name he calls you, anyway?'

Ruth blushed again, feeling shy and stupid. 'SQ,' she admitted. 'For Snow Queen. From the Hans Christian Anderson story. He's such an ass.'

'Snow Queen.' Sonya looked at her, smiling. 'You don't strike me that way. Now now, anyway.'

Sonya lived only about ten minutes out of her way, and Ruth was ashamed that she'd never given her a ride home before. 'I could pick you up in the morning, if you want,' she offered. 'It seems silly for you have to take public transportation, when I drive out here every day. Anyway it's boring, driving alone.'

CANDY

Candy was in the TV room of the cottage watching her story, 'Stars of Life.' Even though it was just an ordinary Tuesday afternoon, Billy's mother had brought her little boy Timmy, and the three of them and Edie Sampson, that was from the same project, was all sitting outside eating fried chicken, potato salad, and homemade cake. Candy thought she would just stay in till they left. Mrs Morris made her sick the way she was all of a sudden coming round all the time now Billy was on her way out, when she hadn't even showed her face before. It was a pimpy way to act, just like Clay was doing Mabe. Maybe Mrs Morris was trying to convince herself she'd been a dynamite mother, just like she had Billy believing it now, both of them forgetting all the years when she went off and left her with some aunt or other that didn't want her. Really Candy had no interest in knowing the woman, it was just that Billy could of introduced her. And it hurt even worse about Timmy.

Billy was always talking all kinds of bullshit on the subject, saying the reason she didn't introduce Candy to her family was her mother would pick up right away on what kind of friends they really was. That she wanted to wait till they was on the outside and she could just bring Candy over to her mother's one day and say it right out, 'This is my woman, and from now on she's part of the family.' That as soon as the two of them had their place, they'd have Timmy come and live with them. But if all of that was for real, Candy didn't see why the fuck she wasn't good enough to meet the kid right now.

Lou-Ann, or Lil' Bit, like they'd all started calling her, was sitting on the floor watching the story, leaning up against Candy's knees.

'What's the matter, Can-Can?' she asked. 'You aint even look at your story.' Candy looked. Brenda was having a heart-to-heart talk with her daughter that was a doctor and married, only her marriage was in hot water.

'I just don't know what I'd do without you, Mom!' Dr Fran said. The two of them wiped the tears off of their eyes. Then it switched to Neil, that was Dr Fran's husband, talking to their teenage son Freddie, that was getting into trouble cause his parents was fighting.

'Where your mother and I sleep, young man, is none of your business!' Neil said.

'Damn right it aint!' said Lou. 'My baby know better than to ask me bout no sleeping arrangements, and he aint four yet.'

Candy was amazed. 'Lil' Bit, you aint old enough to have no baby!'

'What you mean?' said Lou-Ann. 'Got me two babies, Frankie and Jamael, and if they aint mine I like to know who had them? You shut up now, Candy, I want to hear me my story.' And she moved back, all huffed up like a little cat.

Now Fran was talking to Neil's mother, Edith, who was a patient at the same hospital that Fran was a doctor at. It was one of them small towns where they all bumped up against each other constantly. Edith got halfway out the bed and grabbed onto Fran's hand.

'Fran, dear, be patient with my boy,' she said. 'You know he's been under a lot of stress lately. Now that he knows the result of my exploratory I'm sure he'll be much easier to live with.'

Candy was getting bored with the stars and their stupid problems.

'Hey, I'm sorry I said you didn't have no kids, Lil' Bit,' she said. 'I was just surprised, that's all.'

'Hey, no beef Can-Can,' Lou said. 'You want me to go check is they still out there?' Candy nodded, and in a minute Lou was back. 'They gone,' she said. 'Billy must of walked them to the door.'

But when Candy went to her room to get her sweater, she heard voices from inside Billy's room.

'The reason I got permission for you to come in here where it's private,' Billy was saying, 'is I wanted you to be the first one to know, Mama. My social worker called me in yesterday, and it still aint official or nothing, but I got me a date! Spose to be out of here the first week in November.'

'Oh my baby,' said Mrs Morris and then they didn't say nothing and Candy thought they must be hugging and kissing like they thought they was in the damn story or something. And then Mrs Morris started in with 'I know you're going to make it this time,' and 'you just stay away from them good for nothing white bitches that always gets you in trouble' and 'you just do what that Mrs Schofield said, go to school and get you an education, she told you you got a good mind dint she?'

Billy was just eating it up. 'Yeah, well, she told me I scored the highest of anyone on them tests they gave us,' she said. 'Course the tests aint worth shit when you get out there.'

'Honey, you use them tests, that what they worth. That lady was telling me about some program these people got set up. For ex-offenders. All you gots to do is go to their meetings and they send you to school. Girl, you gotta use whitey, aint you learned that much by now? You takes what you can, you walks away.'

Candy went into her room and shut the door real quiet so they wouldn't know she was there. She'd heard enough.

SONYA

Ruth's car was an old grey MG with worn, soft upholstery. It was clean inside, but smelled of smoke.

'Can you get your seatbelt?' Ruth asked her from the driver's seat. 'They're sort of hard to figure out.' Sonya found two unmatching halves and fiddled helplessly. 'Here.' Ruth reached over her to do it, brushing Sonya with her small breasts. Her smell was unexpectedly sweet, and Sonya remembered a friend of her mother's, Rosie Stein, who used to smell like that. When she was a little girl, after Rosie had left their apartment, she used to press herself against the couch, intoxicated. A lady's smell, she'd called it. The seatbelt clicked, and Ruth moved back to her side, leaving her scent behind her.

As soon as they were on the road, Ruth lit a cigarette and inhaled hungrily. Her hands on the wheel didn't match the rest of her. They were elegantly long, but old and worn looking, covered with tiny lines. The nails were short and blunt, and flecked with white, like Sonya's own. She would have imagined Ruth's hands to be small and soft, with long glossy half-moon nails. They said you could tell a dyke by her short nails. Ruth was straight, of course. She lived with that man Sonya had seen. But she was worried about turning to ice. No, snow. She didn't want to be the snow queen any more.

Realizing that she'd been staring, Sonya looked out of the window. They were passing rows of houses, each with its tiny yard. Men were raking leaves, and children played neatly.

'I hope I wasn't too rude to Dave,' she led gently. Ruth took the bait eagerly, immediately launching into a long explanation of why she herself couldn't afford to be rude to Dave.

'Maybe,' Sonya thought, 'but don't tell me you have to flirt with him.' Instead she asked politely about the institution's policy on medication.

'That's all Dave does, really,' Ruth told her. 'And everyone knows it. The inmates, I mean.'

'What does one call them?' Sonya asked her. 'I've heard inmates, residents, prisoners, women. . . .'

'I've never been able to figure that out myself,' Ruth shrugged. They had reached the freeway entrance, and a ticket shot out of the machine. Ruth snapped it up without stopping. She was efficient and immaculate in a fawn-colored dress today, as if she had never been on the floor of a prison mopping up blood, as if she had no smell at all. She drove fast, zipping in and out of lanes, and yelling, 'Watch it, buddy!' out the window.

'Have you ever driven a cab?' Sonya asked her.

Ruth laughed, obviously pleased. 'No, but I've been asked that before.'

They were approaching their exit, where a large billboard showed a giant pair of red lips, wide open. Sonya didn't catch what product it was advertising. She wondered how Ruth would react if she began firing questions at her. *Are* you the Snow Queen? I know you live with that man, but are you in love with him? Have you ever slept with a woman? Do you want to? How old are you? As old as your hands or as old as your face?

'You look . . . inquisitive,' Ruth said. She was certainly not stupid. 'What are you wondering, or is it too personal?'

Sonya laughed. 'Let's see . . .' she hesitated. 'I was wondering about your hands. They look older than the rest of you. They're very nice.'

Ruth smiled. 'I fix the car,' she said, 'and do a little carpentry, stuff around the house. I've always done a lot with my hands. I'm thirty-two. How about you?'

'Thirty,' said Sonya, as Ruth pulled up in front of her building. The men in front of the bodega had stopped their card game. Ignoring Sonya today, they beckoned to Ruth, making smacking noises with their lips. Ruth appeared not to notice. 'Eight-thirty tomorrow?' she asked, and Sonya nodded.

She walked past the men, whose eyes were still riveted on the place the car had stood, and climbed the stairs. She was tired, and suddenly conscious of being dirty and sweaty from cleaning the room all day. She hoped she hadn't smelled, in the car. She thought of Ruth Foster, the lady in her fawn dress, holding out comforting arms to the hurt children at the prison. Then she thought of Ruth the mean taxi-driver, chain-smoking and cursing at other drivers. She preferred the second image, if she had to choose, but she thought she would use them both tonight, before she fell asleep.

TELECEA

All the rest of them with they fancy offices and you know what they give her? A room full of garbage. I have to help her clean it out. She new, how she gone know where to find what she need, who you gots to ask? They gots they dirty old food in there wif them white maggots crawling in it, green mold on top and who know what all. She say don't look too hard. And got old clothes in there wif lices crawling on it laying they filthy eggs and Oh Lord them white rubbers off they dicks got that old rotted up pussy come in it. Put all that in this room see can they chase her out that way cause they let her in here by mistake.

She say please Telecea do not tell her about no garbage unless I want her to be sick! Say, lets us just get it out of here and think how the room gone look after. She say a artist spose to have a nice clean room wif all them easleys and paint brushes and a sink right in the room, them clean wide-open space. And light pouring in. So that's what we making. And then you puts on your artist smock, she gonna bring me one, and either you paints or you makes sculpture-pictures.

That what Sonya be making most now. Sculpture-pictures. Things she see, or in a dream, don't matter, long as it in your head one whole day and overnight. That mean you got a vision and you spose to make it in a sculpture even if it seem like something bad, you spose to do it. For a painting, you just use them paints and brushes, but for a sculpture she say you can use anything, either clay or what you wants to, parts of clothes or something you found. Aint nothing wrong with it. She tell me she made this sculpture got a person in a cage like a birdcage! Ask her what she mean by person, boy or girl, and she tell me 'Oh well, neither one.' I aint asked nothing else, but I knowed. She mean one of them butch-bominations they got in here, girls in the light and grow they dicks at night. Ha ha ha you know who gonna laugh when one of them find her ass shut up in a birdcage and her dick too! Sonya got power.

I aint decided yet what my first one gone be, sculpture picture or painting. She say you could start with a dream or something you want or don't want.

She got power. They let her in by mistake. The way I can tell is sometimes when we be going up the stairs or she be telling me something she put out her hand and touch you. Don't none of them do that. Ruth Foster she aint allowed to, they don't be letting her. And them others they might do it for a reason, tryin' to get something from you or fuck wif you. When they do it you can feel that cold wind on your arm where they toucht, like them ghosts do you. But when Sonya do it, it feel real warm. It be cold up there in that garbage room, you know they aint gonna put no heat up in there for her. But when she put her hand on me it feel warm.

FRIDAY, SEPTEMBER 25

RUTH

Ruth and Candy were at a formal party. It was part of a plan to help Candy escape. Once outside, they had to run, but Ruth couldn't run well in her stacked heels and panty-hose. She took them off, leaving them in the street, and then they ran fast, hand in hand. It was raining. Ruth's bare feet felt wonderful, slapping the wet pavement. They could outrun anyone. They reached the car and Ruth leaned over to adjust Candy's seat-belt. She understood that they were safe now, that no one could capture them.

She woke in the middle of the night to the dark of the room. Victor was lying on his side watching her.

'Were you dreaming, love?' he asked her. 'I saw your lips moving.'

'I was dreaming I helped Candy escape,' she told him, and instantly felt guilty, as if she'd betrayed a real escape plan. She turned to the wall, shutting her eyes, and he said gently, 'Go back to sleep, Rooey, I love you.'

She could feel him lying there staring at her, wanting her. Then he moved against her, his penis hard against her ass. She willed herself not to move away in rejection, to wait at least a minute, but the force of his wanting was an assault. Finally, as if moving in her sleep, she pulled away, against the wall. Almost at once, she began swimming toward sleep, back to her lost dream.

They were driving, she and Martha. Martha had small holes in her black filmy dress, which kept getting bigger and bigger so that soon the dress was almost all holes. Martha's nipple poked through one of them. Ruth was afraid that they'd be stopped by the police and locked in Max for escaping.

'Can't you stop the holes?' she asked Martha. 'Don't you have something to put over your dress?'

Martha turned to her angrily, only it was Sonya, now. 'What's the matter with you?' she said. 'Why are you driving so fast? You're not a cab driver!'

It was true that Ruth was driving faster and faster, and now she

96

realized that the accelerator was stuck. There was no way to stop.
She lifted her foot all the way off but the car just kept going, faster
and faster and faster, as if it were about to take off like an airplane.
They would both be killed. She opened her mouth to scream and
nothing came out.

'Ruth, hon. Wake up, Rooey.' Victor's hands were on her. 'It's
alright, love. You're dreaming.' He was there next to her, large,
furry, warm, and known. She crept close to him, her belly against his,
pressed tightly to his warm hardness. He rocked her slowly, lovingly,
kissing her hair and eyes, her neck. 'It's alright now, love, it's alright,'
he kept on saying.

CANDY

Candy lay stiff in the bed. They had just been a beef in the cottage that Mabe and Edie had instigated as usual, by taking some poor bitch's shit, then calling her prejudice when she wanted it back. It wasn't Candy's beef so she stayed out of it, but it was hard to ignore all the noise. Her and Billy had slept separate ever since her mother had came, without even saying nothing to each other about it. She didn't want to tell Billy what she'd heard, and Billy wasn't telling her what she knew, so it was like they was both holding something back all the time they was together like this invisible curtain had came down between them.

They was a noise outside her door. Candy stiffed up cause you never knew who they was gonna try and involve in that shit, but then she heard Billy whisper her name, and she was at the door in a flash. Billy stood there in her pajamas, shivering even though it wasn't cold.

'You want me to come in with you, baby?' Candy whispered.

Billy nodded. 'I wake you up?' she asked, her voice all funny.

'No, baby,' Candy told her. 'I was lying in there thinking about you.' They tiptoed across the hall to Billy's room.

The bed was warm where Billy had been laying. Candy moved up against her, and it felt so good, like something hard was melting inside her. Billy reached out and held her tight in her arms. Candy knew they would talk later. For now she just wanted to lay there. Billy's head was up against her shoulder, and in a minute Candy felt something wet. Candy had only seen Billy cry about twice since she'd know her. She held on and whispered in Billy's ear.

'Hey baby, I know you're getting out before me, but it's OK. I aint mad. I know you gonna wait for me. I aint worried.' Then she just said. 'You cry. That's right. That's right.'

Billy held onto her shoulders real hard. After a few minutes she whispered, 'I was gonna tell you before anyone. Then, don't know why, just seems like I couldn't get the words out. Maybe I was scared it would change something between us, I don't know. And then I seen you in your room, and I realized you must of heard. And it was getting all built up between us. . . .'

'I know,' whispered Candy. 'I know.'

'Listen,' Billy told her, feeling better now, 'when I get out this time, I aint fucking around. Gonna do it right, not take no risks. Cause too much depends on it, you know? Get a nice little place, and by the time you come out, I'll have it all fixed up for us, I'll have it all ready for you, baby, I promise. And I'll be there just waiting for you. . . .'

'That'll be real nice,' Candy started to say. Then she stopped, feeling old and wise all of a sudden, like she had already lived through everything in the world. 'You don't need to make me no promises, lover,' she told Billy. 'No promises about nothing. You have a place, that's beautiful. You don't have one, I'll love you just the same.'

'I told you, I'm gonna have us a place.' Billy sounded a little angry.

'That's good,' Candy told her. 'That's real good. What I'm telling you is I don't care. Place or no place, if you straight or if you in trouble, I'm gonna be there. Aint goin nowhere, just gonna keep on loving you.' She whispered in Billy's ear, just saying whatever came to mind, cause wasn't no need to be careful or lie.

Then she kissed Billy's little ear and her neck and slid down to her breasts, and Billy took and lifted Candy's night gown off, took off her own pajamas, and told her, 'Come here.' But first Candy sat back a little and just looked cause they was plenty of light from outside, and it was Billy, the long creamy brown body of her, all lean and strong, and her smooth flat belly with the scar low down where they cut the baby from her, and her pointy little stand-up titties, the nipples all puckered and dark now, and her strong, long legs.

She came to Billy then, and dipped her head in the smell of Billy's soft neck. And she felt Billy's hands touching her all over in her secret wanting places, and the places she'd been hurt. She had scars too, only most of hers was the kind that didn't show, but every time Billy touched her they seemed to go away more and more. It was a loving of her that Billy's hands did, a healing and a loving.

Billy moved down on the bed so she could go down on her, and Candy turned over on her side so her mouth could reach Billy too, and Billy opened up her legs to let her in. Candy tasted the wet of Billy's cunt that was the best taste she knew, the best high of all, and at the same time she felt Billy's tongue down there teasing and tickling her and then, deep inside of her back and forth and now they was moving together until it wasn't even like her and Billy separate but like one blackwhite woman Candy Billy moving and loving and Billy was all in her and then out and all at once both until Candy Peters, the tough bitch who was so proud of never having came with a man in her whole life, was moaning out loud. And crying out and calling Billy's name until she came. And came. And came.

SONYA

Sonya sat on her big bed smoking a joint and rereading Mira's letter. Mira was a writer. She did badly arguing out loud, would blush or turn silent or suddenly leave the room, but on paper she was always fluent, her reproaches flowing so smoothly and logically they seemed irrefutable, her anger couched in the most elegant of language.

'It feels to me like reaching out to another land to write to you,' Mira wrote.

My life here is opening up. I've written about it to Barb and to Rainy and I talked to Barb on the phone the other day. It's so strange – it's you I lived with, you I loved, and we haven't even spoken. Is that what you want, Sonya, to cut things off that way? To me it feels crazy, like a denial that our life together ever existed, do you really want it to be wiped out like that? The anger isn't gone and there's no way I want to be with you again, but I don't want that year taken away from me either. It existed, you and I did, we were even happy for a while. And once I trust someone as much as I did you, once I love someone that much, it doesn't just disappear for me. How could it, unless there's something very wrong, very missing inside? Maybe your ideal is a life full of one lobotomy after another, but not mine. And so I want us to be in touch and I want to see you next time I come East. There are so many changes, so much to tell, but I can't write to a shadow. So let me know how you are, Sonya. I (almost) hope things are good with you, that you're happy. I feel sure that you have a lover, friends, there by now. That's always been so easy for you, it's the sustaining that's hard. So please write to me, even in anger.

Sonya ripped the letter up, violently shredding it in little pieces, but the guilt, which had gathered heavy and sick in her stomach the first time she read it, didn't go away. She saw herself lobotomized, empty, a fat and ugly robot, skipping from place to place, job to job, person to person, each new life wiping out the previous one. She would grow old, still alone, while everyone she knew, gay and straight alike, would long ago have settled into some kind of marriage. They would all be cozily flattened, taken care of, merged with one other person. 'No,' she shouted. 'They can all go ahead and do it, I won't.'

She wanted badly to eat, but she forced herself to get up and roll another joint instead. She turned the radio to jazz and took her joint back to the bed. She would forget that hateful letter. Instead, she'd think about Ruth Foster, who'd seemed awestruck, almost reverent when she'd come to see the loft and Sonya's work this afternoon.

The saxophone was deep and smooth. The bed was becoming an island of warmth and safety again. 'Mama's coming soon,' Sonya sang along, and spoke aloud to Ruth. 'It's alright, love,' she said softly. 'You don't have to be the snow queen. You can let yourself feel with me.'

The phone rang. She detached her fingers unwillingly, feeling her clitoris throb in disappointment, her vagina close back on its emptiness. She knew the call must be someone wanting her, in love with her. Could it be Ruth? Or maybe Mira, sorry about the letter, and telling her she'd be on the next plane. She picked up the phone, and walked with it, high and trance-like, back to her island, the bed. She lifted the receiver and spoke slowly, her voice low and sexy.

'Sonya madele, what's wrong? You sound so funny. You're asleep? Sleep, then, I call you in the morning. And don't work so hard.'

Sonya replaced the receiver gently, feeling a rush of longing for her mother who never reproached her for not getting married and settling down, but instead listened eagerly to her adventures. 'She works in a prison now, my daughter,' Sonya could picture her telling Olga from downstairs. 'Like a lion tamer she is with the criminals, my daughter.'

TELECEA

Covers all tuck in tight. Door to this room lockt. Door to the cottage. Can't no one get in. Norma say, How they gone get in, when it all lockt up? You safe. And when I fall to sleep, He send me a soft sweet dream.

Long time ago, Granny doin' my hair, holding me in her knees, tellin' me, I name you after your little aunt Telecea that die young and innocent without one sin on her soul not like your mother. And now you my little girl cause God told me hisself and I will watch over you and not let you come to no bad ways and you will grow up like your good aunt Telecea not like that no good ho'. Cause I protect you from evil.

She touchin' me so nice I know aint no beating coming this night. And close my eyes to feel it better the way Granny hand so soft on my cheek and neck and shoulders and then on my head where it be hurting, make it better and be talking in Sonya voice. Saying I got power, you know I got me some power, and I say this head aint never gonna hurt no more. Never no more.

SUNDAY, SEPTEMBER 27

RUTH

Ruth sat in her perfect kitchen, drinking French coffee and admiring the way the early sun fell on the rectangular section of brick she'd spent almost a week exposing this summer. Outside the open window, a pair of early joggers, the African man and his Radcliffe girlfriend, as she thought of them, ran by, bouncing seriously on the balls of their feet. They were the only ones up besides her. Victor would probably sleep for a couple of hours.

Ruth wondered if Sonya was still asleep, or if she might be sitting in her loft drinking coffee too. Now that she'd seen the loft she had somewhere to place Sonya when she thought about her at home working.

She tried to picture her painting the huge nude that hung over her work table. It was so big that it took up three separate long panels, and even then, the woman stretched right off the canvas. Ruth wished there had been room for all of her, for her fingers and toes too, 'Hands, fingers, toes,' she whispered to herself, liking the sound of it. The woman in the painting had been stretching, maybe just waking up in some sunny place, and the sun and shadow on her body made her all different colors, pink in some places, browner in others. Ruth thought of Sonya mixing these colors, Sonya knowing that a woman's body, lying in the sun, has more than one color.

Through the window she smelled the special autumn smell of the changing trees, the exhaust from passing cars, and a whiff of perfume or after shave from someone who'd just passed. She could even smell her own sun-warmed, still sleepy body. It smelled good to her, and she wondered if Sonya would think so. Maybe Sonya could even make a painting of smells. She'd have to ask her.

CANDY

'We still got about a whole month and a half,' Billy reminded Candy. 'Don't be treating me like I'm already gone, now.'

'And don't *you* be getting short-term-shitty on me!' Candy said, but she didn't put much feeling in it. It was Sunday anyway, and soon Billy's mother would come again, and they'd put their heads together and talk about the future, and *she'd* be invisible.

'Don't pay no attention to me right now,' she told Billy. 'You know how I be Sundays.' It was a nice warm fall day and they was sitting together on a blanket on the grass. Norma came by and introduced her grown-up daughter, a real pretty but conservative dressed girl called Edith, that was sposed to be a teacher or something. Candy noticed Telecea Jones following them, about ten steps behind like a wandering ghost. Billy looked embarrassed when Norma just introduced her daughter like that, cause it made it seem like such an easy thing to do. Candy wasn't dressed fit to be introduced to no one, in her old baggy jeans and a T-shirt that said 'Property of the Honolulu jails,' but Billy made up for it, all dressed up for her visit in the creased white pants that Candy had paid Donny Gitano to get for her on her furlough, and the white braided sweater that Candy had knitted her. She had combed her hair all out and looked better than that Angela Davis had ever looked. She was in a real lovey mood too, and had been ever since they made up.

'Tell you what baby,' she said suddenly. 'When my mama comes today, how about if you just kind of walk over and you-all meet? Like by accident, you know. Not no big heavy thing, just so it don't be too much of a surprise to her when we get our place together. Ease her into it gentle-like.' Candy looked at her hard to see did she really mean it. 'I told you I would introduce you,' Billy said. 'I just been waiting for the right time. When you gonna start believing me?'

Candy smiled all over and just then, 'Billy Morris,' Ginzer called from the cottage. 'Your visit's here.'

'Later, OK,' Billy said, sounding nervous as hell, but giving her a big kiss. Then she went up front to meet them, and Candy booked to the cottage to get dressed and see was there anything she could do with her hair real quick.

Half an hour later, when she came back out, Mrs Morris, Billy, Timmy, Edie, and a little girl Candy hadn't seen before was out on the lawn, sitting on some benches. Candy had put on some blue corduroy pants, a blue and white nylon blouse with flowers, and a white sweater. She had put up her hair and had on a little lipstick but no other make-up. *She* thought she looked like a real nice girl, that Mrs Morris might like even though she was white, and feel she'd be a good influence on her daughter.

But it didn't go like that. Just like Billy said, Mrs Morris picked it right up that something wasn't kosher, probably from the way Billy was acting, all nervous and jumpety.

'This one of your girlfriends?' she asked Billy, as soon as Billy said her name. 'How come I aint never seen her around here before?' She looked right over Candy at Billy, but Candy decided she might as well talk for herself.

'I mostly stay in the cottage,' she explained. Mrs Morris ignored her.

'What's the matter, aint she got no family to come see her?' she asked Billy.

'My family's out-a-state,' Candy said, biting her tongue not to tell the bitch off.

'Well, have some chicken, what did you say your name was, seeing that you aint got no one to bring you nothing.' Mrs Morris told her.

'No thanks,' Candy said, the shame of it rising up in her throat all hot and sick. She had started to walk off when Timmy came running up to her, butting his head at her waist.

'Hey lady, gimme some gum?' he asked. He was real wild and cute, and looked a whole lot like Billy, and Candy reached out to him.

Mrs Morris grabbed and yanked him real hard by the arm. 'How many times I got to tell you don't be asking no white peoples for nothing!' she said. She seemed like the queen with all of them her subjects. Even Billy looked all sorry, like a kid herself, and not a thirty-two year old woman with her own kid.

'Grandma, I got to use the bathroom!' the little girl whined. She was about the same size as Timmy, who was real big for five, and Candy thought she was maybe seven or eight.

No one paid no attention to the little girl until Timmy said, 'Ma, Teeny been saying she got to use the bathroom! You better do something, or she'll pee her pants again.'

The little girl hanged her head down and Mrs Morris started scolding, 'Child gotta pee every ten minutes! I wouldn't be surprised if she got a infection in there, the way her mother sent her up here all sick and dirty on that bus, like I aint got nothing better to do with my time than to cover up for her mistakes. Both of you all girls make me sick,' she turned on Billy now. 'You in here and Donna taking off like she done, move to Chicago, don't even know is she alive or dead and then she send me this one.'

Candy had meant to move right off but the little girl held her there, the way she just stood there and listened to her own grandma badmouth her, not saying it right to her face, but talking about her like she wasn't there, just like she'd did Candy. 'I'd be glad to take her to the bathroom,' she said. 'I'll bring her right back.'

Mrs Morris thought for a moment, then she must of decided that Candy was good enough to trust with this kid she didn't like cause she said to Billy, 'She can take her. Don't need to bring her no 'right back' neither, cause you and me got some family matters to discuss and this child Teeny got her some big ears.' Then she pointed at Candy, as rude as she could be. 'Ask her do she mind babysitting.'

Candy could feel Mrs Morris's eyes on her back till they got right inside the cottage. She thought the kid, Teeny, could too, cause she was walking all funny. But then she realized it was cause she'd started to pee her pants. Little drops was falling down her skinny legs. She stood still and started crying real soft like she was scared to make a noise.

'Never mind, Teeny,' Candy told her. 'Aint no one gonna see. I tell you what, we'll wash out your panties and dry them with my hair dryer and won't nobody even know. And then I'll give you something real pretty to wear like a grownup lady got, OK?'

The kid didn't stop crying or answer or nothing, just followed right behind her. When she got in Candy's room she just stood there with her wet panties down around her knees, and the tears coming down her face like she couldn't do nothing without being told.

Candy got the panties from her and washed them out. 'What's the matter?' she asked. 'You afraid your Grandma's gonna beat you cause you had a little accident? Cause she don't need to know.'

She still didn't answer, and even when Candy got out a cheap bracelet she had and told her she could keep it, the kid wouldn't take it, like she knowed it was a trick. Finally Candy just picked up her little limp self and held her on her lap with the hair dryer.

'See how you work this dryer,' she said. 'You gotta press this button and then you can dry out your own panties.' She was surprised that the kid started doing it. When the panties was dry Candy showed her how to use the little section for drying your nails. She was afraid to put polish on her in case Mrs Morris might freak over it, so she just told her, 'Pretend you're having a manicure. You're a grown up lady now.' It was getting to be a bet she made with herself, to see could she make the kid smile. She would of been a cute little yellow girl, if she hadn't been so pitiful looking. Candy blew the dryer on her fingers, and then down the neck of her little dress, and finally Teeny giggled.

'That tickle,' was the first thing she said.

Candy felt good. She picked up the bracelet and slipped it on the kid's wrist. 'You gotta wear it high up your arm,' she told her, 'till you grow a little more.'

The kid stared at it like she was waiting for Candy to take it back. 'Grandma say I took it,' she said, and Candy thought she was probly right. She thought of telling her to say it was Edie or somebody that gave it to her, but it wasn't right to ask her to lie.

Meantime, the kid had decided she was cool. 'My name aint really Teeny,' she said. 'It Tawanda.'

'OK, Tawanda,' Candy said. 'You remember my name?'

'Course,' the kid said. 'You name Candy.'

Then all of a sudden she started talking real fast gulping, for air, like she was making up for lost time.

'I come down here on the bus all by myself. All the way from Chicago. Cause my mama had to go to the hospital, go somewheres. She wanted take me with her but she couldn't. But she say if I be good she be back to get me. And take me to Disneyworld. And then Timmy gonna wish he could go, but we aint letting him. When you think she come to get me?' she asked Candy. 'Cause Granma don't like me. She say she got enough on her hands with Timmy. She let Timmy do anything. I hate Timmy.'

She just went right on talking, all cuddled in Candy's lap. How old are you, Tawanda?' Candy stopped her with the question she was almost afraid to ask. What she'd thought was true. Tawanda was seven, just the same age as her little girl.

'We better get back out there, honey,' she said. 'They gonna be wondering did I steal you.'

Teeny picked right up on it. 'Can I stay here with you till my mamma come for me?'

Candy hugged her, 'You can't stay here.' She tried to explain the best she could, just like the kid's mother must of when she got took away to jail or wherever it was she went. 'They's no children here,' she said. 'Just grown up ladies.'

She thought the kid understood but then, after she had gave her back to Mrs Morris who was ready to leave and had walked halfway back to the cottage, all of a sudden here she came, flying at Candy like she was shot out of a cannon. The poor little kid butted her head into Candy's stomach, locked her arms around her waist and screamed out, 'I aint goin', and no one could get her off.

By this time about twenty girls had came out the cottage to watch. Mrs Morris was doing her best to yank the kid back but not doing too swift cause she was trying to do it without touching Candy, and Timmy was dancing around the whole scene, singing out, 'Teeny gonna get a beating!'

Billy wasn't nowhere around. Finally Candy remembered the one thing that would work. 'You gotta stay with Grandma cause your Mama wouldn't never find you here,' she told Tawanda, and just like that the kid popped right off like a rubber band and went back to her limp crying self. The last Candy seen of her she was being drug off by the wrist with Mrs Morris telling her that no one had ever taught her how to behave and just wait till they got home.

When she got back in the cottage, Billy was holding up the bracelet that had fell on the ground. 'How come you gave her this, just to start some trouble?' she said. 'How you think it looked that her own grandchild didn't want to go home with Mama?'

'I didn't mean to, Billy, I was just trying to make her stop crying,' Candy said, cause she felt too worn out to get in a beef now.

Billy must of felt the same way, cause she right away got all sweet and started in about how when they had their own place it would be like Timmy would be half of her kid, to make up for her not being able to have none.

'Honey,' Candy said gently, 'you saw your mother wouldn't even speak to me. How you think she gonna let me bring up her grandchild?'

'Oh she'll come around, you'll see,' Billy started again.

But Candy didn't even listen. She was glad she was grown, not like Tawanda that didn't know no better than to believe that her mother was gonna turn up and take her to Disneyland. If she was good.

SONYA

Sonya sat at her table in the sun, eating breakfast and planning a portrait of Ruth. It would have to be multi-paneled, like the painting on the wall Ruth had admired so much when she'd come up on Friday, to include all her different sides. One would be Friday's Ruth, all soft lines and rosy cheeks, like a Renoir. Then there would be a glossy one, almost like a photograph from a fashion magazine, which she'd call 'American Blonde' and which would portray the Ruth men saw, which, come to think of it, was the way she sometimes saw her herself. She'd have to figure out another image for the force and tension of contained rage she sometimes felt in Ruth, maybe something full of concentric rays and electric lines, like a Van Gogh. Or else Ruth with a shaved head – a white Telecea done in a stark, German expressionist style. Sonya liked the ideas of doing the panels in totally different, maybe even exaggeratedly derivative styles. She made a quick sketch of the idea in her book, next to the similar sketch for the multi-paneled portrait of Donny and Linda on the stairs.

She leafed through the sketch book, feeling like a fake. On one page was an idea for the subway sculpture with Candy and Billy. Across from it was a sketch for the fragmented Telecea mobile, broken sections of forehead and eyes. So far, all she had to show for her time here was the little caged sculpture, which she'd done in about an hour. But she would do the others too.

When Ruth had seen her paintings she'd looked so awed. Now Sonya was an Artist to her – inspired, resplendent – a whole other species of human beings. She liked the image, but at the same time it felt strange. Of course she did the same thing to Ruth – treasured the hard tough image Ruth presented on the surface, and resented the other Ruth, as soft and malleable as rubber, as if any way you moved her she'd stay.

The image of a large bendable rubber woman grew in Sonya's mind and she spread her foam and wire on the work table. There were two large yellow foam half-circles which didn't even need to be cut, they were already perfect breasts.

She got out her huge bag of scraps to cover Rubber Woman

once she was constructed. A combination of velvet and very soft suede might be good. Sonya smiled. Suddenly she was full and pregnant with the work she was about to do. She turned the radio to a jazz station, picked up the marking chalk, and began.

TELECEA

I be lissening and watching. Norma she got her a daughter Edith,
dress and talk like a social worker. And Candy and Billy mama got
them this little girl, pus-color yellow. Tearing and pulling at that
poor child just like King Solomon he told them ladies do.

Her Granny get her, take that girl out of here tell her don't be
taking nothing from whitey bang her head on the floor teach her a
lesson. Lord be with me now, help me save this child. Beat her for her
own good save her for the Lord. They don't be beating on that boy
child he don't need no beating the Lord love him he a good child not
like you born wif the devil.

Norma daughter squinch up her eyes and say, Now, Mom don't
you worry bout anything, Bill and me we just told anyone that asked,
we said of course it was self-defense, you know she would not be
locked up if she was white. And Bill say as long as you can, you
know, forget the old life he would be all too pleased to have you
move in with us. Right in.

All the time she talking, she be watching Candy wif Billy mama
little girl. Everyone watching the way that child scream. Norma
daughter say, just listen to that poor child howl, can't stand to leave
her mother, isn't it a shame, my word, the father must be dark, oh the
poor child.

Then Norma go off on her. Tell her daughter, Shut up Edith
bout things you don't know nothing about. And you tell Bill he
can keep his home cause I don't want it. Talk about forget the old
life! Aint never been shamed yet and aint gone start now, and it
weren't to shame myself I sent you to that fancy-ass white girl
college, neither.

Edith she say back, You aint sent me nowhere, Ma, I sent my
own self, and stomp out.

Today Sunday. Visiting day. Tomorrow Sonya gone come back
in and start me on my wall. My wall I gots to paint on. Like when this
big hand come down from the sky and writ something on the wall.
Had to take Daniel right out that lion den so he can tell them what it
mean. Mean everything gone turn round, break the pride of they

power. Put that king in the lion den his own self let him feel them teefs chew him up and Daniel the king now. Cause it come round.

That wall get him his vengeance. And I gone get mine. Sonya she told me, This wall is yours, Telecea, you can paint whatever you want on it.

Gone paint me Heaven, Hell, and In Here. And then we see how it come round.

TUESDAY, SEPTEMBER 29

RUTH

'Look!' Alice Anderson held out a bloody hand this time. Ruth shook her head. 'See!' Alice sounded triumphant. 'You're just like all of them, you don't even give me a chance, you just believe the worse.'

'What are you talking about, Alice?' Ruth let her irritation show.

'You're the one that says always make sure before you come to a conclusion, then you just go and do the very same thing you tell me not to.' Ruth looked at Alice's hand. She saw that there was yellow and green there, as well as red.

'Paint?' she guessed.

'That's right, and you just automatically thought it was blood. See, that's why I keep on having problems,' Alice decided. 'Because nobody ever gives me a chance, they just want to see the worse.'

'Have you ever heard the story of the boy who cried wolf?' Ruth asked, and was immediately penitent. 'Where's the paint from?' she asked to make up for it. She knew perfectly well where it was from, but Alice deserved her story.

'Oh, it's just from my wall,' she said. 'My wall that I painted all by myself that's all mine, that's all. It was hard work,' she continued, 'because all the girls that's up there besides me is crazy, but Sonya and me, we were patient with them, and we got it done.' Ruth smiled, and nodded her approval.

'See, we each got a wall to express ourself with. Mine's good, too. Some of the others are all messy, you know how them girls are, but mine's neat, because I work very carefully.'

'That's really wonderful,' Ruth told her. 'Do I get to see your wall one of these days?'

'I was just getting to that part.' With a more genuine smile than Ruth had yet seen from her, Alice took a small piece of folded paper from her pocket.

'She said we could, you know, invite anyone we wanted of staff or the girls to come up and see it. And so I picked you, but then Telecea Jones, you know that real mean crazy colored girl that thinks she can see God and all that, she picked you, too, and she was gonna attack me until Sonya stopped her. Sonya said there wasn't no reason you couldn't get two invitations from two different people, but you should of heard that girl!' Alice's eyes bulged in horror and she shook her head. 'I wouldn't even want to repeat the language that girl used about you. I don't know why she got so upset, cause she sure don't like you. She called you a white you-know what! It got the word mother in it, though. And she said she was gonna do a witch-charm on me, put me in a picture and do something to it, you know, like what them Africans do, I seen it on TV. They'll stick a pin in this little doll they pretend is the person . . . But I know better than that. It's mostly the colored that believe in them superstitions, anyway.'

Finally Alice handed over the piece of paper. 'I wanted it typed out like they do, but Sonya said it's more personal-like if you make them yourself.' Alice had ruled the paper with straight smudged gray lines. In the border she had made a neat repeating pattern of hearts, autumn leaves, and pumpkins, all of them grey. In the middle she had neatly printed:

> Dear Miss Foster, Please come and attend the opening of our new ART ROOM. Come at 4 PM Friday afternoon, October 2. Refreshment's will be served. Sincerely Yours, your theripy patient, Alice Anderson.

As Alice talked on, Ruth listened with most of her attention. With the rest, she planned what she'd wear to the opening. Maybe she'd go shopping on her way home today, and get something new, something a little more adventurous than her usual style. And she could bring flowers. She thought of carrying them in, a huge pile. She could hear the sounds of a softball game starting outside and wondered whether Sonya might be out there, watching it. Maybe she'd go out and see, in a little while.

CANDY

'You Gladdy's friend, you pretty little Candy Cane?' Ever since Candy'd been listening to her a little more, Gladdy had stopped calling her a little white ho', and got so friendly it was a pain. Candy was sitting out in the yard on Norma's bedspread with Linda, Norma, and Lil'Bit, watching their softball team warm up, It was so warm and sunny they was all in their shirtsleeves, even so late in the afternoon, and Candy had brought out her radio.

'Sure, I'm your friend, Gladness,' Candy said. 'You know that. Why don't you have a seat and watch the game?'

'Gladdy can't sit down, Candy Cane. She too busy right now, gots to check these new folks in, get our team moving. Can't cut no corners.' Then Gladdy took a piece of paper out of the torn paper bag she always carried around. 'I got something for you, Peppermint,' she said, and gave it to Candy.

'You better watch out,' Lil'Bit said. 'Next time she gonna try and get her a lick!' The paper had INVITATION printed on it in big wobbly letters up top, and underneath was a real nice picture of a black lady, all dressed up in a matching blue and white summer outfit.

'You think she drawed that herself or did the art teacher help her?' Linda wondered.

'That's a picture of Gladdy!' Norma pointed out.

Candy read out what was printed on the bottom. 'Come to are art room to see wat we done. Friday 4 aclock.'

'Now aint that nice!' said Norma. 'That new art teacher is a nice lady you ask me, working with Gladdy and Telecea that aint got no one to help them. And that poor child Alice that always be cutting on herself.'

'Nice, shit,' mumbled Lil'Bit, who was talking even older and harder now she was Frankie's woman. 'She wish she could get someone but them crazies to go up there, but everyone else know better. She aint even got no shit for jewlery or nothing, just that kindergarten stuff. She one of them shrinks that after you do a picture she looks at it and finds out shit about you. Put it in your records.' Norma said she wasn't either about that, but Candy agreed with Lou. She didn't like to see that snotty bitch and Miss Foster getting tight.

'Turn up my song?' asked Linda, and she sang along with it, all dreamy eyed. 'You're my whole life, my reason for living. My sun and my moon, just want to keep on giving. You're my horizon, you're all I can see. You're superwoman, baby, to me. That's right,' Linda sighed, looking at Donny, on the pitcher's mound. Candy looked at Donny too, in her man's undershirt, with her weird black hair all greazed back on her head. Maybe she was superwoman, she sure didn't look like no ordinary woman, anyways.

'Will you look at that!' Edie pointed to the visiting team that was coming onto the field, with Gladdy out in front, and Telecea trotting along behind.

'There's some superwomen for you,' Candy said. They all looked about ten years behind the times with their bleached blond hair in beehives and shiny red hot-pants. Their shirts all had boys names on them, and Candy wondered why on earth did all these femmy broads have boys names.

'Hey, Jim!' called out Mabe from the field. 'Go on, Pete. Shake it, Ed.' Then, as they got closer, Candy saw that on top of the boys names, in smaller red letters was wrote Property Of. Telecea left them and zig-zagged over to drop a paper in Norma's lap, then run off again.

'I got me one of them invites too!' Norma said, all excited, like it was a real invitation to a party on the outside or something. Telecea had just got her head shaved again, and she looked like a hound dog sniffing the ground for something, with her big eyes and ears that stuck all out.

'She's smelling the perfume,' said Linda. It was true, the visiting team had left a trail of perfume that won, hands down, over the other smells, their own perfumes, the joint they had just smoked, and the new cut grass.

Then that bitch Sonya Lehrman came in and sat down on the grass way over the other side, which wasn't far enough as far as Candy was concerned. She wished to hell the screws would stay where they belonged, and not come messing in, like there wasn't no softball games to watch on the outside. Candy turned her back on the bitch. She looked at Billy move her long self onto the field, right under the ball, and snatch it out the air.

She looked just right in white shorts and a white shirt, unlike

Mabe and some of the others, who looked like they was ready to disco or something. It was nice herb and anyways softball as a game was boring to Candy so she didn't bother to follow the moves, just kept her eyes on Billy. Everything was cool for a while, and then Candy saw her run smack into Eds Property, on first, and the hair on her arm stood up like a cat's. She was pretty sure that short time as Billy had left, she'd lay down her glove and walk away if something started to jump off, but sometimes she could get proud.

Candy got up and started moving closer, just in case.

SONYA

When Sonya first drifted out to the yard, a woman was pushing a lawnmower up and down near the main building, handling it with a kind of stiff methodical grace and leaving the sweet smell of cut grass behind her. Further down, in the circle between the cottages, a softball game was beginning. It was an Indian Summer day, a phrase Sonya whispered to herself, rolling it on her tongue deliciously. It made her think of a lush country, full of Indian warpaint reds and oranges, hot and abundant even after its time. She remembered reading the phrase in a book as a child in the city, and now, wandering toward the game, she saw herself at eleven or twelve, standing on the edge of the vacant lot watching the kids playing softball without really noticing that she was there herself because that way no one else would have to notice her either, and it would be alright to remain, a dreamy, half-invisible fat girl.

Here, too, it seemed to be alright. For the first time at Redburn, she felt pleasantly invisible, and, sitting down on the grass at the far edge of the game, she was glad that she hadn't stopped for Ruth, as she'd half-considered doing. She wasn't the only staff spectator anyway. There were two officers sitting together on the steps of one of the cottages: the heavy, young white dyke she'd at first mistaken for an inmate, and a tall, also very young, black one in a silk shirt with her eyes made up as if for a night out. Sonya wondered what they were thinking, what their lives were like, and what their relationship to one another might be. She looked at the Redburn team and was pleased that she already recognized so many of the women. She picked out Donny at the pitcher's mound and Frankie at first, both wearing those outrageous sleeveless T-shirts, and Mabe at third, in a low-cut yellow nylon blouse which seemed designed to distinguish her from the butch women on the team. As she watched, Billy Morris scooped a high fly ball out of the air, as fluid and elegant as always. Sonya thought she smelled dope, and saw Candy and a small group of women sitting on a blanket and passing around a joint as though it were a perfectly safe thing to be doing in the yard of a prison. Maybe it was, because the two officers were sitting closer than she was, and they hadn't said anything. The visiting team, now up to bat, looked like a cartoon in some magazine. Sonya wondered where on earth they were from, and what had brought them here. Then she looked more closely at the batter, a bee-hived blonde with 'Property of Joe' written on her T-shirt, and was surprised to see strong, muscled arms. The visitors were tougher and more efficient than they looked, while the home team, fumbling, yelling at one another, and at the umpire, was rapidly falling apart.

'You gonna let them honkies do you like that?' Edie yelled from the sidelines, as one of the visitors hit what looked like a home run. Deciding that it was time to go home, Sonya got to her feet and saw Billy stick her foot in the path of the woman running to third, who tripped, fell to her knees, swore, and got up to run home. Immediately a wave of comments swelled from all sides.

'You hear what she say!' 'Say she punch Billy in the mouth.' 'Said, I'll punch that nigger in the mouth if she!' 'You hear? What she told Billy?' 'Peroxide say she gonna!' 'Billy, you hear what Bleachy say she gonna do, you hear?' Sonya noticed that the two officers had disappeared, and that Telecea was running frantic circles around the field, screaming something. Now Billy, walking with the precision of a cat getting ready to pounce, had approached her adversary.

'Got any insurance, Bleachy?' a voice shouted. 'Life insurance, that is?' On the field, the two women faced off, a few paces apart. Everyone else had frozen. Sonya, afraid to call attention to herself by moving, stayed where she was too. It was Candy who shattered the scene, bursting onto the field. Her loud shrill words broke the tension, as she grabbed Billy and led her off, dragging on her arm.

'Don't you let them get you in trouble over no bullshit game baby you know you bout to walk out of here in a few days don't you give them what they want you know they'd just love an excuse to keep you in here never mind what they say you let the bitch talk she don't belong to herself anyway it even say so on her shirt leave her be baby come on.'

As Sonya reached the door back into the main building, she saw a group of four or five male officers, headed by Moody, charging down the hall. She got out of their way, flattening herself against the wall, where Ruth found her.

'It was awful!' she heard herself babbling. 'Somebody could have been killed. Why didn't those two officers who were out there do anything? They could have called the men in sooner at least.'

Ruth smiled a little. 'They come when they're ready, which is always after whatever's going to happen already has. And then they just make things worse. You told me it was Candy who broke it up anyway, not them.' They walked together to the car in the warm early evening. Crickets and birds were singing, a horse moved out in the field, and the tall grass waved, but now everything seemed to Sonya to be full of a secret menace. She shivered violently so that Ruth, solicitous, moved closer to her and told her to get in the car, she'd turn on the heat.

TELECEA

Some of them already finisht they wall they messy self, well not me. I been painting on it two days now and it still aint done but Sonya she say don't worry, by Friday when they all coming in to see it and I sended my invitation out too, it be done. And anyway, even if it aint all dry, no one asking them to touch it, is they? It aint theirs.

Way I planned it first was to have three parts to it, Heaven, Hell, and In Here, but I aint had room for no heaven and don't know how it look anyway. So my wall just have two parts. The top part In Here and the bottom part Hell. And it have these slides and ladders and trap doors that show how they gone get down there. Whenever He get ready for them.

I standed up on a ladder to do the top part. Got them ho's up there, they insides all yellow wif them maggots and that pus. What I done, I show the inside and outside both, show they pretty little dresses and fancy shoes and how they all nasty and unclean underneath. Got some of them squeezed up next to they butch bominations with they dicks all curl up inside them trying to be a man. Got this one butch wif a beastie reaching up from the bottom part grab that dick of her in it teef, drag her down that way. Beastie got a body of a white horse, face of a man, teef like lions got and one of them tails wif stingers on.

Bottom part got some deep pits all black dark. And a big lake wif red and orange fire and she shown me how to paint them bubbles in it. Lake got one hand reaching, trying to pull itself out all tormented, been in there so long and still can't find no death.

What I been doing, I waits by the door till she come in and don't even stop painting till she leave. She say, 'Telecea you are amazing, are you sure you never painted before?'

Not to disbelieve me but meaning she can't not believe this my first time cause I already know how to do it so good. Gladdy she can paint pretty good too, but that fool Alice shouldn't of even got no wall to put her stupid straight lines she make wif a ruler and copying her pictures off something, everyone know that aint how no artist do it! But Sonya she gots to let them all have their wall cause that way won't no one know I got power.

Sonya got some too, that now she know bout mine. She say she almost afraid to look at my wall, it got so much power! And she right, too, cause already things have change and I aint even finish yet.

Out in the yard He have send these devils wif they red pants and a word wrote on they chest. Them bitches look too much like each other. Something funny alright. Talking bout they have come to play ball, and leave they devil smell behind them. Don't tell me they come to play no ball. Oh no, them devils got them bominations ready to jump at they throats like a mad dog. Just set on one another and destroy! But it aint time yet so He stop it before it jump off.

Seen Sonya there too. Watching and lissening just like me, but we gots to act like we don't know nothing. So I aint even spoke to her.

FRIDAY, OCTOBER 2

RUTH

Ruth met Candy in the downstairs hall on her way to the art room opening. She felt ridiculous in her new purple jumpsuit with her arms full of flowers, as if she'd been caught doing something shameful and embarrassing, like in a dream in which she realized too late that she'd forgotten to put clothes on.

'Let's see your invite.' Candy smiled at her kindly. She showed Ruth her own, from Gladdy, and concluded, 'Mine's prettier.' She looked much softer this morning, and Ruth realized that she'd never seen her without make-up before, and with her hair falling loose around her ears instead of pressed and set into its stiff shape.

Candy caught her look. 'I know, I look awful today,' she said. 'Would you believe I had forgot all about this and was in the bed taking a nap when Norma came to get me? I couldn't disappoint Gladdy, the poor bastard, so I just came like I was. But *you* look real nice today!'

'I was just about to say the same thing to you,' Ruth told her. 'I was going to say that you look very natural.'

Candy laughed.

'That's one word for it, I guess.'

Ruth felt the strangeness of meeting out of context like this, as if she, overdressed and overexcited, was the client whom Candy was talking down with her stream of polite chatter.

They stopped at the bottom of the stairs to listen to the commotion which had started on top. Ruth heard Telecea's voice.

'You aint bringing that ho' up here! You said it my wall, and now you gonna let that white bitch put her dirty unclean hands all over it!' There was an answering murmur, and Ruth and Candy looked at each other and hesitated.

'Shit,' Candy said. 'There I was, perfectly happy, taking my little nap. Well, you tell Gladdy from me I tried.' She was about to leave when Sonya and Telecea appeared on the stairs. Sonya was radiant in a red embroidered smock, her hair wild and electric. She had an arm through Telecea's and was talking to her intently. Telecea wore an orange version of Sonya's red smock. Her blue sneakers, which never seemed to get any more worn, shone proudly under the two inches of white sock exposed by her jeans, and her head was newly shaven. Finally she shrugged regally and spoke down to them.

'Guests don't belong to no one. They still theyself. So you my guest just as much as Alice's, Ruth Foster.' Then she looked at Candy. 'That one can come in too,' she said grudgingly. 'In case it get mix up and we be letting the wrong one in by mistake. But don't be touching on my wall.'

Ruth gasped when she entered the room. It was completely transformed. The strange angles of ceiling and wall were set off by glossy white paint, and colorful shocking murals decorated four of the five walls. A long table covered with an off-white oilcloth intersected the center of the room, and easels were set up at either end of it. Sonya had built several rows of shelves, already covered with bulging bags of material and jars of paint.

Ruth hadn't known what to do with the flowers, not wanting it to appear that she had brought them for Sonya, but sure that giving them to either Telecea or Alice would be asking for trouble. Now it was easiest to give them to Sonya after all. 'For the new art room,' she whispered. Sonya gave a little cry.

'They're so beautiful, Ruth, they're perfect,' she said, and Ruth felt her awkward, out-of-place offering transformed into the perfect touch, the only thing that had still been lacking. 'Look what Ruth has brought us.' Sonya's voice quieted everyone. 'Fall flowers for the new art room.'

They were chrysanthemums, yellow and orange and golden and white, and Sonya cradled them in her arms reverently, as she might hold an infant, then put most of them into empty milk cartons, breaking off a few stems. Rapidly, a white flower appeared at Alice's buttonhole, giving her the sedate look of a mother working a table at a PTA meeting or a church supper. A gold one at Telecea's throat added to the royal African effect, while Norma proudly arranged her own yellow flower at the lapel of her rusty blue dress. A white flower was princely on the collar of Donny's suit jacket, and another white one became a corsage for the senior prom Linda had never attended. Sonya paused a moment in front of Ruth, smiling a little, then her long warm fingers touched Ruth's neck as she threaded a gold flower through her buttonhole.

'We'll have a tour of the walls, now,' she said, and they all followed her, smiling and moving under her touch. Only Candy, who wore no flower, stood stiffly in a corner, tapping her foot and flicking ashes on the clean floor. So there was at least one person who had managed to resist the charm, Ruth thought.

'And look!' Sonya had completed the tour. 'There's one wall left! Isn't this a magic room?' At the word 'magic,' Ruth saw Telecea's eyes take on an expression that was too rapt for her taste. There was a quality about Telecea's involvement with her wall, and her weird almost hypnotized affect which made her uneasy anyway. She reminded herself to talk with Sonya again, especially about her word choice. The room did feel magic, though. Ruth found the unpainted wall restful in contrast to the others, and she was sorry to hear Sonya offering it up for grabs. Donny and Linda shook their heads in refusal. Norma too declined politely. Candy was not even there to refuse. She had edged quietly out of the room. Ruth, who'd been uncomfortably conscious of her disapproving eyes, was relieved. Now she heard herself begin to speak, without having planned to.

'If no one else wants it,' she said, 'I'll have it. But I'd want it white, just left blank. So you could look at it and see whatever you wanted to. Or see nothing, just rest your eyes if you felt like it. Would that be OK?'

'Of course! It's a wonderful idea. The wall stays blank, and it's yours.' And Sonya's fingers briefly squeezed Ruth's hand, in a kind of blessing.

'A-men,' chanted Gladdy, confirming this impression, and Ruth was glad all over again that Candy had left.

CANDY

When Candy saw Foster in the hall looking just like a starstruck kid on her first date she wished she could turn right around and go back to the cottage where she'd been all snuggled up nice and cozy with Billy when Norma had came in and reminded her about the stupid party or whatever it was sposed to be. At first she'd just snuggled closer and turnt her back on it, but then she kept on thinking about poor old Gladdy, till she got up and went just like she was, without even doing her face or fixing her hair. As soon as Telecea saw her she started going off. And now here was Foster, dressed in this hot little jumpsuit she must of bought special, and with her arms full of flowers, like she had lost her good sense and didn't know that anyone who saw her would know instantly what she was about.

She wished that her and Foster was both just people, so she could sit her down and tell her a few things. She could give her plenty of reasons for not messing with Lehrman without even going into her own personal feelings about the broad. Like she was on the staff, and girls was already talking about it, even though as far as she could tell hadn't nothing even jumped off yet.

'If you want to turn funny,' she'd tell Foster, 'go right ahead, I aint got nothing against it, obviously. But, Sweetheart, watch yourself. Like, not here, and not her!'

But then if Foster answered her that even if it did mean trouble, she really wanted this fat mess of an art teacher bad, Candy could of told her that she was going about it all wrong, with her new clothes and her flowers. Candy knew Lehrman's type, and she knew the only thing that would get to a bitch like that was being all cold and stand-offish, the way Foster used to act when they called her Tight-Ass. Shit, Candy thought, the name didn't hardly fit her no more. She hoped Foster had at least one good friend that could clue her in, since she couldn't do it herself, but come to think of it, it probly wouldn't make no difference. When it came to this love shit, you could talk till you were blue in the face, and the person would just go right on with what they had in mind in the first place.

Up in the room it was one weird scene alright, with Lehrman going around sticking Foster's flowers on everyone and getting in her little feel at the same time. Candy would of told her where to put her fat hands if she tried touching on her. Candy could tell that under the big smile she was laughing at them, pinning the flowers on them not to make them look good, but just to bring out the weirdness in them. She made the black girls look like wild Africans, the nuts even more off than usual, and poor Foster more starstruck and pitiful than ever. Candy had to admit though, it was nice the way the room was fixed up, and even though you could sort of tell by looking that most of the people that had worked in it was off, you couldn't really be sure because they was all kinds of art nowadays, and she knew that some of the messiest looking shit costed the most.

She looked at Gladdy's wall first, cause Gladdy had invited her. Just like the invitation, it was real pretty, and hard to believe that crazy Gladdy had did it. It was a country scene that had a long green river running through, a little house with smoke coming out the top, and a field with gold and blue flowers. There wasn't no people in it at all, and just looking at it made Candy want to be there.

Gladdy came over to her. 'You like it Candy-Cane?' she asked. 'Where I come up in Alabama? It look pretty to you?'

Next to Gladdy's wall was Alice's, that Candy thought was alright too, and a whole lot better than she would of expected. Alice had took the one big square of the wall and cut it down to about thirty little tiny squares that was marked off all even. Every little square had one thing in it, like a cross or a heart or a Santa Claus head and all the different things had a lot of red in them that, knowing Alice, was probly her own blood. That wall made Candy a little nervous to look at.

You could tell the next wall was Lehrman's cause a real artist had to of did it, it was so real looking. You could even tell who most of the girls in the picture was, sitting around a long table like the one in the room, painting and doing clay and shit. It was easy to tell which was Gladdy and Telecea and which was Lehrman herself, even though she made them a little better than they really looked, and made her own self even worse than real life, more wild and messed up. They was one blond-headed one that she thought was maybe Miss Foster but at the same time Foster, who was looking at it too, opened her mouth and asked, 'That one is Candy, right?' The girl in the picture had much shorter hair than either of them and was kind of butchy looking but pretty, with this loose green shirt on (you could even see the little nipples through the shirt) and blue jeans.

Candy wondered if maybe in a few days Foster would show up with her hair cut and in jeans. Gladdy looked at the two of them and the picture. 'Honey, you take the clothes off them two white girls and you got you some identical twins,' she said, which made everyone laugh. Candy snuck a look at Foster to see was they any truth to it, but she couldn't see the resemblance herself. The other girl sitting round the table in the picture anyone could tell was Billy, all in white like at the softball game, and Candy was so surprised that she almost said out loud, 'What the fuck you got Billy here for, I know she aint never come up here.' But in another way it was kind of alright to see Billy sitting there looking so fine, like the Queen of the table or something, so Candy kept her mouth shut.

You had to admit that Telecea's wall was the best of all, even though it was real crazy and sickening, like the shit that always came out of her mouth. They was a top part with all these people that was half animal and some that was male and female both at the same time and some that looked like they was twisted together having sex or something but not no nice sex, just real dirty and nasty like animals doing it. And the bottom part had a big pond with this hand reaching out. And all the people or animals or whatever they was sposed to be had these red eyes and animal heads and peoples bodies or the other way round, and when Candy saw that some of them was meant to be burning up she didn't look no more. She was just glad that Billy wasn't there to see it cause they was something about it that reminded her of voodoo and working roots and that shit that Billy always said Telecea was into.

Sonya started giving away the leftover wall like it was her own diamond or something that she was gonna be sweet enough to give up to whoever begged for it hardest, and Foster started to play right into it. The whole mess made Candy sick, and she left out so she wouldn't have to see the two of them acting a whole lot more childish even than the inmates.

Halfway down the stairs, she heard Telecea's voice, singing out, 'It worked, you all see that? She take one look at my wall and that ho' leave right out of here. I disappeared her, that's what I done.'

SONYA

Sonya believed in ritual, in the power of ceremony. Now, at the art room opening, she had the exultant feeling she got when she was in the middle of a successful sculpture. It was a very small event, but she wanted each of the women involved to feel the power of the room they'd built together. During the building process they'd become, in some sense, a family, and this was the statement she'd aimed for in the opening.

When Ruth and Candy came up the stairs together she was immediately struck by their resemblance. Each of the women noticed it too, Gladdy broadcasting her twin sister theory to the group, and Telecea possibly even confused as to which was which. The confusion worried Sonya for a moment, but then she realized that it was this very loosening of boundaries, this extreme sensitivity to connections, which made Telecea the fine artist she was. Her wall was truly spectacular, reminding Sonya a little of Bosch's nightmare world.

TELECEA

It start today. Things be turning theyself around. How I know for sure is when that ho' Candy take one look at my wall and start to shake and then she take her ass out.

I got me two visitors come up to see my wall. Norma and Ruth Foster too cause she even told me this morning she *my* visitor never mind if that nasty girl did give her one of them retard invitations she made wif all them straight lines and dirt from where she be picking her nose and putting it on the paper or picking at them sores she got. Oh, that one make me sick always whining and crying like some little child and aint even clean.

Aint none of them white peoples clean anyways like when they smells so bad and they hair get all limp and that oil run out like pus. Can't stand bein' near that Alice, and Ruth Foster feel the same way cause I be watching and when that girl leave her office I seen her scrub off that chair where she be sitting. Ruth Foster she like me, she don't like no filth, you can tell by how she do if a cigarette ash or something fall on the desk she scrub it right off and always got them very clean nails even though they bit off, if they clean is what count. Only if it be paint or something like Sonya sometimes have on her hands that's different, that a artist dirt and not no filth.

Me and Sonya we both got on our artist smock that no one else got, for a sign. She brung them in special, and mine orange the color of the setting sun and fire, that what she say.

Only thing go wrong today is all them switch-up mix-up tricks they up to. I had to let that ho' Candy up in my art room cause they got her all drest like Ruth Foster even they hair so you can't be sure which is which. They got Candy acting all stiff and froze up, and Ruth Foster acting like Candy when she round Billy, so how you spose to know? I has to tell her watch out, cause I seen one of them two wif her hands all out grabbing for Sonya, and then that Foster-Candy tell her, I want me a wall but leave it blank. Everyone know them walls is not to leave no blank white color on by no blank white ho'! No, you gots to do what we done, first you paint it white, then you paints over it, even Gladdy that aint got no sense or that unclean thing Alice knows that much!

Gots to tell Sonya a blank sheet got evil wrote all over it. She better watch out!

SATURDAY, OCTOBER 3

RUTH

Ruth sat at her kitchen table making a list. It was about Telecea, and Telecea's record, which she'd taken home to reread, was under the yellow legal pad she was writing on. The record told the same story it had the last time Ruth had read it. Telecea had been implicated in two deaths, both bizarre, still murky incidents which had never been completely cleared up.

In the first, which had taken place when Telecea was only seventeen, and still in reform school, an elderly social worker who'd taken a special interest in Telecea had fallen, or been pushed, down several flights of stairs. No one but Telecea had been around, and Telecea's psychotic condition after the event had made formal questioning impossible. The next death had been three years later, at the understaffed state hospital they'd shipped Telecea to. This time the victim had been one of the other patients on the violent ward, a woman who'd been friendly, if the word applied, with Telecea. There had been a kind of riot and the nurse on duty had panicked and left the scene. When the relief staff came in, they'd found the ward in chaos, and this woman dead, her head smashed in with a chair. Some of the other patients had implicated Telecea, but she'd never been popular, and they were certainly not the most reliable of witnesses. Telecea denied any memory of either death and had continued to deny it during the course of her therapy with Ruth.

Sonya had chosen not to look at any of the records, explaining that she preferred to start with each individual with a clean slate. Ruth had accepted this at the time, but now she wondered.

'Jealousy,' she added to her list. That much was clear – she felt jealous of the ease with which Sonya had managed to connect with Telecea in a way which seemed deeper and more significant than the relationship it had taken Ruth more than two years to establish with her. But her feelings weren't the issue here – as long as they didn't interfere with her judgment.

'Disintegration or disengagement,' she wrote. Again, it was hard to separate things out. She knew that Telecea was gradually withdrawing from the therapy with her, but she didn't know whether this meant trouble. Actually, given Telecea's borderline personality, it would have been highly surprising if she had been able to handle the emotional demands of two different therapists.

Ruth stared at her list with its neat headings and sub-headings, and crumpled it in disgust. No wonder Telecea preferred working with Sonya.

She remembered the two of them standing together in the hall, that first time she'd really talked to Sonya. Sonya had reached out and touched Telecea on the shoulder and Telecea had smiled. There was something about the memory of those two intent figures that made Ruth's own efforts with Telecea seem as stiff and ridiculous as the list she'd just thrown away.

She thought about how Sonya didn't hold back from touching Telecea, or some of the other more disturbed women. She herself had always been very strict about not touching. 'Establishing boundaries,' she'd called it in her head, when she'd refused that pull of physical need. Of course, it was true that touching could be dangerous because of the sexuality it opened up, but was this inevitable? Looking back, she could think of situations when a hand squeezed at the right moment, or even a hug, might not have been such a bad idea. But was she trying somehow to justify Sonya's unprofessional behavior? Or falling into the kind of touchy-feely liberalism that she always found so repugnant at Freeport? From what she'd gathered from her, Sonya's practice of art therapy served as an opening-up process – a way of giving the women access to their own feelings. While this was sometimes true of Ruth's work too, her effort with Telecea, and with others of her most disturbed clients, was in the opposite direction, toward containment.

Now she wondered whether she'd been justified. Had she been basing her treatment plan on her own neurotic inability to let go? Was the danger she saw in the opening-up process purely a projection?

Ruth remembered Telecea as she'd been at the art room opening, the tremendous force of energy she'd felt inside that tense body. Telecea reminded her of a tightly bound bundle of explosives that no one had bothered to label 'Handle with Care.' And maybe it was her knowledge of that part of herself that allowed her to see it in Telecea more clearly than Sonya, who was so open in her stance to the world, possibly could. Ruth smiled to herself, glad that the pieces seemed to fit. She decided she'd talk with Sonya about Telecea on Monday, on the drive in.

CANDY

Lou poked her head into Candy's room, where she was sitting on the bed, good and jammed, listening to some jazz on the radio.

'Can I come in?' she asked, careful cause she knew Candy was a in a pissy mood. They wasn't nobody on the entire compound, Candy thought, that didn't know it, and know why, too.

They was a new girl that had been sticking to Billy like a flea to a dog ever since she came in the cottage last night. A flea was the right word for the bitch, too, who was nothing but a ten-buck-a-shot street ho', with her skin-and-bones body and missing teeth from being strung out for years. Billy always played around from time to time, but at least she'd always had a good taste before this. But when Candy brought it to her Billy told her not to get uptight cause the bitch was doing a real short bit, and had a man on the outside that was some big-time dealer, so it wasn't nothing personal. And this after all that bullshit jive Billy had been running to her about going straight when she got out, which Candy had been asshole enough to halfway believe. . . .

'You thought any more about my plan?' Lou asked.

'I already told you, don't bother me with that shit,' Candy said. 'I'm too close to my date to get busted, and anyway I don't believe Frankie can get the key.'

'She can so!' Lou kicked up her skinny legs and stood on her head. 'Bet you didn't know I could do this,' she said from upside down, and started walking to the bed on her hands. She hit the bottom of the bed and crashed down.

'See what I gone through for you, Candy Cane,' she said. 'Now you got to at least consider my plan, or else at least give me a few drags on what you got there.'

'Shit, didn't nobody ever tell you you a pest?' But Candy handed her the tail end of her joint. 'What was you, in a circus or something when you lived down South?'

'No, but I could of been, huh Candy. I used to watch them, what do you call 'em, gymnastic ladies on TV, and do what I seen 'em do. And that's how I got my first job. That place in Memphis with all them young girls.'

'Yeah,' said Candy. You already told me about that place, Lou.'

'But I aint never told you about my number I did. See, I had one of them outfits like a Catholic school uniform, you know them little plaid skirts got all of them pleats? And had my hair plaited up real tight, like a little kid. See, I be walking across the stage with a skip-rope in one hand and sucking on a lollipop like this, and then all of a sudden I flips into this headstand, and start walking on my hands.' Lou acted out her story best as she could in the little space. 'And of course I aint had nothing on under. Them dudes used to go crazy, Candy, they come right up on stage and be grabbing on me, the bouncer had to pull them off.'

'I believe it. Probably went home and raped their daughters, too. Real cute job you had there.' Then Candy felt bad cause she'd done a whole lot weirder stuff than that herself. Lou sensed she was sorry and rubbed up against Candy's legs.

'Frankie do so got the key, and they don't never lock that main door no more,' she said. 'And I know that shrink gots to keep some nice stuff in his desk.' They was little balls of dust from the floor in her hair that half the perm had come out of, so it was sticking up all funny, and her shirt had come unbuttoned so Candy could see her breasts, that was just extra big nipples. She reminded Candy a little of that kid, Tawanda, that had came up with Billy's mother that time. She wondered did the kid's mother come and get her yet. She was pretty sure she didn't.

'How come you don't hardly hang with Norma no more, Lil' Bit?' she asked. 'Just cause you with Frankie now you still could. That'd be better than all that scheming shit you into. You keep up that shit and you gonna be here longer than you planned.'

Lou climbed up on the bed and started fiddling with the radio. When she spoke it was in a nasty play on Norma's voice. ' "Lil' Bit, you so much like my own little girl. Now do this, now do that. Pray to the Lord. Be good, now!" Fuck that! I didn't come to jail to be nobody's child.' Then she changed up and got all whiney. 'Anyways, Frankie and Norma both gone with the bible ladies. See, Candy, all the rest of you all got money and peoples that come and bring you shit. I aint got nothing and no one up here, and anyway, like I told you, they just aint no risk. You know that hall good, you go in there every week, and I promise you Frankie do got the key.'

'Stop that shit!' Candy told her. She was halfway fed-up, and halfway tickled at Lou, who reminded her of how she used to be at that age, manipulating everyone in sight to get what she wanted. 'You know damn well I don't get no visits either. If you dying for one so bad, why don't you go join Frankie and Norma and the bible ladies?' They both fell out laughing at the idea.

'You think they bring me some dope if I tell them I want to come to Jesus?' Lou asked. 'I could give them a real nice holy-holy show like they do down South. You want me to show you?'

'No!' Candy said. 'I know how they do, and anyway you already gave me enough of a show for one day. Leave me alone, and I'll think about the plan. I aint promised nothing, hear?'

'Sure, Candy!' Lou jumped off the bed. When she opened the door they could hear that as usual all kinds of shit was going down in the cottage. Ginzer was trying to bust into Telecea's room, speed-rapping at the top of her voice. Norma was trying to calm her down, telling her to leave Telecea to her. Candy rolled another joint. It wasn't none of her business, that was for damn sure.

SONYA

It was the beginning that was always so agonizing. Once Sonya started, it was usually alright. It was those first steps that she was avoiding now as she sat in her rocking chair, reading *Sita* and thinking about Ruth at the opening, glowing with warmth in her new purple jumpsuit, holding out the flowers. Now Sonya wondered why she hadn't pressed her luck then — it had been the perfect opportunity. But if Ruth turned her down it would have ruined the fantasy right there. Of course if she hadn't, that would have ruined it too, in a way. She had a pang of regret for the old tight-ass Foster, who seemed to have gone into permanent retirement, at least around her. Of course she might always return.

'OCTOBER 3' she wrote in large black letters in her book. 'What I do best of all is find excuses not to work. When I'm with someone she becomes the excuse, and when I'm alone, I fill it up with fantasy. FINISH RUBBER WOMAN TODAY!'

She'd worked on Rubber Woman again last night, after the opening, and now there wasn't too much more to do. Then there was the sculpture of Telecea's face, which she'd already started. Thinking of Telecea at the opening eased her over to the long table, where the almost completed wire skeleton lay.

TELECEA

Bad bad dream. Can't not get all the way woke up. My head hurting so bad and I know He be trying me this morning see am I strong enough. Gots to get that dream out, so I puts my head under the cold water but it still stick in.

Norma come in. What's the matter, baby, you trying to see can you get you a head cold this morning? Put a towel on that bare head of yours and why you shaking it like that?

I don't tell her that dream caught up in there cause Sonya, she know bout dreams but no one else know, and they try and stone a dreamer if you tells. Ruth Foster say don't tell everyone what be in my head, wait and tell her, but how can I tell her now? What if it turn out to be that ho' and not her?

Norma keep after me. Telecea baby, why you shaking your head?

Then that devil ho' Mabe have to start in. Norma Lewis, don't you know not to ask no nut why she do something. They don't know theyself. When I used to work in a home for mentals they be doing that shit all the time, shaking they heads like a dog do when it come out the water.

I was getting ready to smash her big ugly fat-lip ho'ish self, but I stop myself cause I gots to be in that art room Monday.

And Norma put her arm round me and say, That's right Telecea, don't pay no 'tention to them ignorant girls.

Mabe get up in her face, say, What's the matter, Norma, lost your other little girl to Frankie, now you just got the nut left?

Then two more come up in Mabe's face, say, Leave that woman be, what the matter wif you, girl, you talk to your own mother that way?

Mabe say No, to yours, and oh Lord my head feel like it bout to split right open and spill all them brains and gutses on the floor.

So I gets back in my room close the door put the bed up against it put the pillow on my head but I can still hear all them voices, way they be croucht down outside my door. Nut, crazy, mental, dog.

How you sposed to be strong when it don't never stop? Granny she used to say The Lord is my Shepherd when she be tormented.

Used to say it kept them devils off her that would come and bite at her arms. So I try now but it have that part bout the valley of temptation. That where they puts you if you born bad, wif the devil inside, puts you down there in that valley of the shadow of dicks, you can't even see what they doing in them shadows. Could put them big old dicks in you, or do something like what I dreamed last night. Dreamed that Sonya she turn into one of them bominations and be doing it to Ruth Foster up the art room.

That aint no dream-vision, that a devil dream He sended to see can he tempt me like He done Job, see can He trick me and make me give in, see am I strong enough. But I aint gave in. Now my head beating like it got a big drum in it, drum wif sharp kniveses and every time it beat them kniveses go right in. But I still aint gave in. Long as they leave me be.

Just lay there and tell myself. Do not hurt no one. Can not go up to Max cause the art room Monday. She say the art room Monday. Gots to be there make me my sculpture picture. When she come in. Monday morning. That dream aint nothing aint nothing aint nothing.

MONDAY, OCTOBER 5

RUTH

'I know she just does it to mess me round,' Candy said. 'That deep down she still does care for me. But every time she does it it seems like I just can't help getting all upset around it. Like the bottom just drops out and all of a sudden nothing makes no sense.'

Ruth nodded. She halfway wished that she were Candy's friend, instead of her therapist, so that she could stop being so noncommital, and advise her to break it off with immature, sadistic Billy Morris, who was standing right square in the way of Candy's getting her life together once she got out, and who would only hurt her in the end. She realized how absurd this was as she thought it. Whether from a friend or a therapist, advice was not particularly useful when one was in love. One was usually well aware of the risks, and took them anyway.

'What do you do,' Ruth asked, 'when you feel like that, as if the bottom had dropped out? Do you act upset? Do you let Billy know?'

'No!' said Candy quickly, angrily. Then she paused. 'At least I try not to. What I do, I try and act like when I was out on the street. See, they used to be able to look at me, and they'd say, That bitch may not be a fighter, but she don't give a fuck, so watch out for her. Them's the ones you got to watch out for, Miss Foster,' she explained. 'The ones that just don't care.'

'I see,' Ruth nodded. 'So when Billy hurts you like she did over the weekend you try hard to make it look like you don't care?'

'I can still do a pretty good imitation of it, I mean good enough to fool someone that don't know me. But it don't never fool her.' She smiled, realizing something. 'I guess in one way, I don't want to fool her. Don't want to have to. I'm sick of it, you know? And anyways, it's hard to do now. Maybe cause I aint turned no tricks for so long. Didn't never used to take no effort, it was just the way I was.'

Ruth looked at Candy, who was sitting in the same position she always took, the brown leather chair pushed a little back from the desk, her feet tapping on the floor, her eyes fixed on the blue mug. Smoke circled up from her cigarette in the ashtray, and the smell of it mingled with the smell Ruth associated with Candy, It was a synthetic smell, made up of make-up and perfume and hair-spray, but Ruth liked it because it was how Candy smelled.

'Miss Foster.' The tapping had momentarily stopped, and Candy was looking straight at her. 'What do you think, really? Is it good I can't do it anymore?'

'Do what?' Ruth stalled.

'You know, what I been saying. Turn off.'

'That's a good question,' Ruth said. 'What do you think yourself?'

'That's why I'm asking you, cause I don't know. When me and Billy was first together, I used to do it sometimes,' she remembered out loud, puzzled. 'Get all cold and standoffish like I'd gone away somewheres inside. Even when we was getting down. . . . She'd say to me, 'Don't you give me that look, girl, I aint one of your tricks.' But that aint happened for a while now. And what I've been thinking is, maybe that's one reason she keeps on disrespecting me so much lately. Cause she knows she got me, so it aint no challenge to it. So sometime I think it would of been better to stay cool, cause it's like that, you know? When you're all cool and don't careish is when people dig you the most. Then, once you show them you care, you may as well kiss them goodbye.' Candy stopped and took a deep breath. 'But I asked you what did you think, Miss Foster. You shouldn't just turn it around like all them shrinks do, you know.'

This was fair. The only trouble was that Ruth didn't know what she thought. And part of her didn't want to think about it anyway. The whole question made her a little sick.

'In one way, I think it's wonderful that you're learning to trust, that you're letting yourself feel,' she tried. 'But from what you've told me about Billy, I worry. I'm afraid you'll get hurt more by opening up than if you kept yourself shut off with her. Oh, I don't know,' she started over. 'Part of me thinks that even if you end up getting hurt, it's worth it, that allowing yourself to feel enough to get hurt in the first place is better than not letting yourself feel anything. I wish I could tell you to open up and watch out at the same time!' she heard her voice crack stupidly. 'But I know that's not much of an answer.'

Candy looked at her directly again, and gave her a small wry smile. 'I wasn't asking for no answer,' she said. 'I just wanted to know what did you think, not as a shrink, but you. And you told me. So hey, that's cool.'

Ruth returned the smile. But Candy had something else to say. 'I know it's none of my business,' she began, and Ruth tried to signal her to stop, because she knew she didn't want to hear it.

But Candy went doggedly on. 'See, sometimes it's easy for me to pretend you aint real. Like I'll say, Nothing bad ever happened to her, so how could she understand me, you know. When you used to say something I didn't want to hear, I could just say, Well, that's Tight-Ass Foster, she don't know nothing. But then other times, like when you talk to me like you been. . . .'

Ruth shifted uncomfortably and cleared her throat, trying to forestall what was coming. 'I'll shut up in a minute,' Candy said. 'I just wanted to tell you, remember that dude Earl I used to talk about? The one that turnt me out?' Ruth nodded. 'Well, there's something about that Sonya that reminds me of Earl. Calling you honey and all. Stroking you up with one hand, and the other one in your pocket all the time, ripping you off.'

CANDY

Sitting outside under her tree after seeing Foster, Candy wished she had kept her big mouth shut. She'd only been trying to say what a friend might of, but Foster had freaked. She was probably worried it would be all over the compound, which was fucked in itself when you thought about it, seeing that Candy had spent an hour a week for the past two years spilling her guts to the lady without worrying would she talk.

Maybe Billy was right about this therapy bit, it was just a set-up to get ripped off. Being the rip-off artist of the universe herself, Billy should know.

Candy wouldn't of said nothing in the first place, if Foster hadn't made her think it was cool by saying that shit about open up and watch out at the same time, like she was really talking about her own-self as much as Candy. Then when Candy went on with what she'd started, Foster pulled out. It wasn't fair. But like it or not, they was in the same position in a way, both hung up on bitches that wasn't no good for them.

'That aint true!' Candy almost said right out loud. 'Billy and me aint like that. I just feel that way now cause I'm mad.' But of course Foster could say the same thing in her own mind when that Lehrman gave her shit. That was how it worked.

SONYA

Magic seemed to slip in and out of Sonya's hands all day. Telecea appeared as soon as she came in the front door and drew wordlessly close to her, shivering as she usually did in the morning, although the place was always overheated. Sonya remembered learning the difference between warm and cold-blooded animals in high school earth science. The warm blooded ones maintained their own body heat, while the cold-blooded ones took on the temperature of their environment. Telecea must be more warm blooded than other humans, because her body temperature seemed to have little to do with her surroundings.

She seemed especially fragile this morning, and as they climbed the steps to the art room together, she took hold of the black cape Sonya had on.

'Witch-coat, magi-coat,' Sonya heard her mumble to herself. Once in the art room, she ran to get the orange smock. Inside it, like a bright bird, she circled the room, whispering to her wall, checking the materials on the shelves, and lighting finally at the long table, where the early morning sun gleamed whitely on the oilcloth.

'What you call them things aint got no water?' she asked.

'Which things?' They were sitting across the table from each other.

'Them things aint got no water, nothing but sand. Them cactuses.'

'Oh,' Sonya understood. 'A desert?'

'Yeah, that's it. Last night He send me a desert. All this sand. All them cactuses with them prickers, and them red flowers wif thorns.'

'Were there any people in the desert?'

'Nah!' Telecea was surprised at her ignorance. 'Don't you know can't be no peoples in a desert? Cause they aint no water to drink. Sometime you might think they is, but they aint. Just trick water.'

'Trick water?'

Telecea laughed to herself. 'Aint you seen it on TV? All them peoples be dragging theyself along almost dead wif thirst in all that sand . . . and then they see some water, mm-mm nice and green, so they gets right up to it, put they faces down in it and aint nothing there. Just that old hot sand.'

It was Sonya's turn to shiver. 'That's called a mirage,' she said.

'A mirage,' Telecea repeated. 'He send me a desert got a mirage in it. First we send they spirits there.'

'Who?' Sonya was getting out of her depth. 'Whose spirits?'

'I told you! All them people be tormenting me all the time. I aint slept all this weekend! Almost have to hurt someone but I know I have to be here this morning.' Sonya wished that Ruth, who had been full of advice and warnings about Telecea on the drive in, could have witnessed this evidence of her good influence.

'I'm glad you made it here today,' she told Telecea. 'You did really well. Are you going to make a desert sculpture, like in the dream?'

Telecea nodded, pleased. 'Make me a desert and send they spirits to it,' she said. 'Gone walk and walk and torment! Gone wish they find death but can't not find it, just walk and walk in all that sand.' She laughed again, and Sonya saw the wraithlike spirits, doomed to chase down mirage after waterless mirage.

'They'll be so thirsty!' she protested.

Telecea only nodded, tranquil, abstracted. When she spoke next, it was in the voice of an old woman. 'They will just have to make do. Aint on this earth to just take take take. Bad girl, seed of the devil, gots to be chasten, deliver you soul. He to punish. You to accept. Drought wif the plenty, storm wif the calm. Mirage wif the desert.'

On this last, Telecea's voice regained its original tone, and now she moved around the room again, calmly assembling materials. Sonya was amazed at her instinctive grasp of the collage form and its possibilities. She knew exactly what she needed and how to use it.

'A long piece of cardboard,' she murmured. 'That's right. Now some of that yellow sticky paper. Now I think I grind me some of that powder paint. Maybe some salt. Don't need no water, just stick that sand on. Piece of red velvet for the cactus flower. Wire for when it stick you wif them thorn.'

When she had assembled all the materials on the table, she sat down, completely absorbed, and, still talking quietly to herself, began to work. Across from her, Sonya watched her smell the powdered paint, then let it sift through her hands before putting it in place. The creative flow which she herself longed for and only rarely attained seemed to be Telecea's natural way of working. Her dream and fantasy material were as available to her as waking reality, there was no sharp cut-off between the two. The flow of energy was catching, and Sonya took a roll of brown wrapping paper and began a series of sketches in black ink of Telecea working.

When she recognized Ruth's knock on the door, she felt annoyed, but called out for her to come in. Telecea's reaction was more extreme. She jumped up, shielding her work with her body as if Ruth had been a dangerous stranger instead of her trusted therapist of two years.

'What you want here?' she panted.

Sonya hastily walked Ruth, who had come to ask her out for lunch, to the door. She had already decided to try eating in the inmate cafeteria again, to recruit some more clients, but she was sure Ruth would disapprove, so she told her she planned to work through lunch, and they arranged to meet at four.

When Sonya came back to her, Telecea was hunched over her desert, which stretched half the length of the table in a shallow cardboard trough. Only the bright wine color of the crown-of-thorns relieved the crumbling yellow desolation.

'Gots to keep them people *out*,' Telecea whispered. 'Ruth Foster-Candy! Why they gots to come after me everywhere wif they mess?'

'Telecea, Ruth didn't come here to hurt you. She cares a lot about you, you know that.'

But Telecea had covered her ears with her hands and was rocking back and forth, murmuring, 'Ruth Foster-Candy. Candy-Ruth Foster.'

'Do you remember how I told you there would be other people here, too?' Sonya asked her. 'How I said there'd be some times, like this morning, just for you, and other times, like when we were all painting the room, when a lot of people might be in here?'

Telecea still rocked, a finger in each ear. 'Oh my head!' she moaned.

Sonya had been about to say more, but she stopped herself, breathed deeply, and paid attention. Then she got up and stood behind Telecea, putting her hands on her shoulders and neck. She felt that Telecea had been alone in the dry desert for hours now. She needed a safe path back.

'Your desert will be right here,' she told her, making her words soft, warm sounds. 'It'll be right here waiting for you, when you come back from lunch. Right here.' She kept her hands on Telecea's shoulders, rubbing in a circular motion, and after a few moments she felt the tense muscles relax.

'You gonna lock it all up, now?' Telecea asked. 'Won't let nobody get to it?'

Sonya nodded solemnly. 'There will probably be other people with us in the room this afternoon,' she repeated. 'But nobody will touch your work.'

'OK.' Telecea sighed in relief, took off her smock, hung it on its hook, and disappeared. Sonya slowly took off and hung up her own smock, then locked the door and went down the stairs

She hadn't been back to the cafeteria since that first disastrous day, and now, abruptly afraid, she wondered what she was trying to prove by coming back. The impassive middle-aged Puerto Rican woman assigned to the cafeteria shoveled a round pale ball of mashed potatoes and three fatty pork sausages onto her plate.

'Hog dicks!' Sonya heard someone say. She stood alone with her tray, looking for a place to sit. Just like last time, she was the new girl at school, the fat wallflower at the dance. She recognized no one in the sea of faces, blank and mirage-like, which swam in front of her eyes. She couldn't tell if it had been seconds or minutes that she'd been standing there.

Then, 'Come on over here, baby.' It was Donny, gesturing to her to follow, and to the three others at her table to make room. Sonya went over, sat down, and smiled at Linda and at the familiar-looking woman on her right. She didn't know the two others at the table, but now that she was sitting, other faces in the room began to come into focus. She saw Billy, sitting with a scrawny looking white woman who was not Candy, and Alice, waving a newly bandaged arm at her from across the room. Her neck and shoulders were still tense, and now she realized that she'd been conscious of Telecea's need for transition but forgotten her own. Desert images still flashed across her mind.

Donny leaned forward and dabbed at Sonya's face with her napkin. 'This is the art teacher I was telling you about. Least it aint in her hair this time. They was painting the art room white, see, and all of a sudden all these girls starts walking round with white hair. This here's Jody.' Sonya now recognized the woman who had been

149

mowing the lawn right before the softball game. 'And that's Fran and that's Jocelyn,' Donny finished. Sonya smiled at them. She wanted to reach out and squeeze Donny's hand to thank her for doing, so gently and tactfully, what she'd done for Telecea.

'Speaking of the art room,' she said, instead. 'Are you all going to make it up there one of these afternoons? It's ready for you.' Glances were exchanged. After a moment's hesitation, Donny spoke for the group.

'To tell you the truth, you got too many nuts up there. . . .'

'I aint going nowhere that Telecea Jones is!' the heavy Italian-looking woman who was leaning on Jody spoke up. 'She gives me the heeby-jeebies!'

'Least you aint in her cottage,' Donny said soberly. She turned to Sonya again. 'I got all of them in there, see, and I just got to get away from them sometime. That Alice, cutting on herself every time you turn your back, that old one talking to God about everyone's private business. Then there's Telecea. . . .'

'And plus you got too many coloreds up there,' said the first woman, loudly. 'You get too many of them in one place and it's the same as putting up a Keep Out sign to the rest of us.'

Sonya was uncomfortably aware that her presence, and these comments, had not gone unmarked in the cafeteria at large. Gladdy, who was making the rounds of the tables begging cigarettes, now proclaimed, 'Art teacher sitting at a white table.' Sonya heard murmurs from another table, too.

'Who she think she is, switchin' up that way. Sit with us one day, them honkies the next.'

'The art room is for everyone,' she said quite loudly. 'It's for everyone who wants to do art, black or white.'

'Don't pay no mind to Fran, Sonya.' Donny was playing peacemaker again. She turned to the woman. 'How much time you got this round, Fran'

'Ten days.'

Donny nodded wisely. 'That's what I figured. You won't hear no one doing no real time talking that ignorant race shit,' she explained to Sonya. 'We all got to live in here together.'

Nevertheless, the mocking whispers followed Sonya when she got up to stack her tray with the others.

'You know who you are, lady?' she heard. 'Girl, boy, or thing?'

In her haste to get out, she jammed her tray on the rack too hard, and dislodged two others, which fell loudly to the floor. She bent to pick them up, hearing the laughter behind her, wanting to run.

'Slow down,' she commanded herself silently. 'This isn't high school. You don't live here. You can leave at the end of the day. This isn't your real life, it's just a mirage. They're just prisoners. It's not about you.'

TELECEA

Did not come, did not, no one else did not come. Up here to my room. Just me and Sonya, that's all. No one else. Put on our smocks get ready to start. Make me a desert, got no water. Just that trick water. They so thirsty they ready to die and oh that nice fresh blue water, drag theyself to it on they hand and knees all bended down to it try and drink. Gets sand in they mouth. Hot sand wif salt in it make them thirstier, bite them in the mouth. That what they gets.

Hurt they feets to walk on it, every step like a nail going in. They screaming, they so dry up and burnt and torment. Make me a good desert! Sand and that crown-a-thorns. Red velvet, look all soft, nice and soft red, they gone bend down put they face on it. Get pierced! In the heart, in the liver and soul. Right in the dick.

Not her. Not my teacher. Not Sonya. She aint got none, not at night, neither. They better watch it in my art room. When they gets all pierced and almost dead from thirst them birds gone come and eat they flesh off, then they be sorry. That Ruth Foster-Candy Cane better watch out! Better not try and mess wif my teacher.

She be making one of me. Telecea Jones in my orange artist smock. So I be safe. And can't no one come up here no more. Not no Candy. Not no Ruth Foster.

She put her hand on my neck all warm just like my dream I had. This head gonna stop hurting. Desert be all safe waiting for you. Come back this afternoon, make a mirage. That what you call, it a mirage. She told me.

WEDNESDAY, OCTOBER 7

RUTH

Ruth woke up full of a sense of anticipation and joy. She had dreamed about being a child in her mother's bed, squeezed like a young animal next to warm breasts and belly. She felt Victor stir next to her and pulled out of bed quickly, her feet touching the cold floor. Suddenly she was cold all over and breathless, like when Candy had said that to her in the office, about Sonya. The joy was gone and she was empty as if she'd been punctured.

In the kitchen in her robe, she felt herself fill again, but with something hard and heavy, like a rock in her chest. She thought it had to do with the dream, with the sudden chill of waking up from it too fast, so she went to run a hot bath. But once in the tub, the rock would not dissolve. Instead, it got bigger and more insistent as if she had to do something about it right away, as if it would explode inside her if she kept ignoring it. She felt an urgency, a need to act quickly although she didn't know what to do, and she jumped out of the hot water too fast and had to sit back down on the orange mat because of the dizziness. She closed her eyes, leaning her head on the tub edge and feeling her heart beat faster and faster like a drum, telling her there was something important, something she'd forgotten, something she'd better remember before it was too late. . . .

She thought she heard Victor, and tried frantically to pull herself together. At the same time a hard sarcastic voice came from somewhere inside her, 'You should have left long ago, you stupid fool. And you know it, too.'

She kept her eyes shut and images came flooding in. She saw the big self-portrait in Sonya's loft, but now it was repulsive, huge and fleshy and obscene. Then she saw Telecea's shaven, scarred head, like the head of a bruised cock. More and more nauseated, she opened her eyes and saw the orange fuzz of the mat and two long smooth white legs topped by sparse straw-colored pubic hair, not even enough to cover up a cunt which was too open, un ugly turkey-wattle, pink and unprotected. The different parts — legs, cunt, toes — seemed like separate fragments, floating pornographically free of each other.

'It's just me, my body,' she whispered aloud, fighting for control.

Then she heard Candy's voice, hard and mean, 'Stroking you up with one hand and the other up your ass.'

She couldn't bear to vomit, and after breathing deeply for a minute, knew she wouldn't. Her nausea was a little better now, but the panic was still there, and she knew she had to get out of the house. This was a goal she could concentrate on, and she held it in front of her, repeating to herself that she'd be alright, as soon as she got out the door she'd be OK. She willed Victor to stay asleep as she dressed blindly, combed her hair, grabbed her briefcase with sweating hands, and made it out into the hall.

She didn't wait for the car to warm up, but jerked it cruelly out into the street. Thank God, she was so early that there were few other cars on the road, and in minutes she was speeding down the freeway, the radio blaring. She inhaled deeply on her cigarette and felt her breathing go slowly back to normal, the rock lodged inside her begin to dissolve. She tried to tell herself she was getting sick, but she knew an anxiety attack when she saw one. And it had happened before. If a friend came to her with symptoms like these, she'd tell them to see a shrink. And if it were a client, she'd try to get to the bottom of it. 'What are you trying so hard not to think about?'

Her mouth felt gummy and she realized that she'd forgotten to brush her teeth. And, oh shit, she'd forgotten to pick up Sonya. She looked around, then pulled over to the side and backed madly up the exit she'd just passed, to reverse her direction.

TELECEA

Did not get no sleep all night. In my own room. My own desert. Turnt on me, stuck me in there. Make me die of thirst. Said, Trickt you this time, you bad girl, thought you was making that desert of yours for them others, now you the one.

Stript me of my artist smock throwed me in here all neked and no water. Said, Beholt, you a dreamer, child, you know too much, gots to slay you now, throw you in a pit in the dark in the black dark desert got no water in it so you throat burn up. Gots to sell you ass cause you found out what you aint spose to.

Dropt down on the sand and seen them bare white walls and this witch lady come up to me and say, It's OK, Telecea, it's just a dream, and I scream out, You aint tricking me no more I know you a mirage. Scream so loud I woked myself up.

In my room all thirsty. And hear them start in through the wall.

Oh Billy, come inside of me. Come inside of me wif her dick, she mean. All night long. Sometime Candy voice and sometime Ruth Foster. Can't tell which the dream and which for real. Torment me all night and if she think I'm going in her office Friday she crazy.

FRIDAY, OCTOBER 9

RUTH

'So, Ruth, I've managed to catch you alone at last.' Dave stretched out in the chair. 'I've come to talk about your favorite client and mine.'

Ruth wished he would say whatever he had to say and leave. His fencing around made her nervous. She raised her eyebrows politely, waiting.

'I mean the young lady whom we used to refer to, if you remember, as "TJ the man-eater." Also "The Terrible T." ' Ruth shrugged. These were his names, not hers.

'Fine, fine, you don't want to talk. But answer me this one.' Suddenly confrontative, he pointed his finger at her chest. 'Can you honestly tell me you've noticed no change in the young lady in question?' Ruth knew that part of the reason she wanted so badly to smash him in the face was that he was touching on her own unease.

'Well?' He sat back.

'Why don't you just tell me what's on your mind, Dave,' she said. 'I'm not sure what the purpose of the indirect questioning is.' Now he was staring at her with sympathy, as though she were very far gone.

'Why so defensive, Ruthy?' he asked gently. 'Do you know, I've never seen you like this before? I feel sure you do know what I'm trying to get at, but I'd be glad to verbalize it for you, if it's so difficult for you to do it. . . .'

'So verbalize already!' This was better, she knew, much more her old style, but he wasn't buying it.

'Fine, fine!' he reassured her in her sickness. Number one, as you might put it on one of your lists, a lot of reports have been coming in from different sources. Cottage and work officers, Telecea's social worker, everyone but her therapist in fact, has reported that Telecea's been doing a whole lot of acting out lately.' He stopped, trying to gauge the effect of this last thrust. Ruth tried to keep her face blank and polite.

'Now this is Telecea Jones we're talking about, Ruthy. She's psychotic, right? Everyone knows it. A little more or less of the bizarre stuff, no one's gonna remark on it. When these people do

156

start noticing things, there's something there.' She stopped herself from nodding, feeling her anxiety rise. Now he was counting things off on his fingers, like a prosecutor in court. 'Talks to herself all the time. Walks around in a fog, bumps into things. When she addresses someone it's to threaten them. More of the dick talk. Sits by herself rocking. Bizarre movements all around, checks out the food before she eats. The whole shtick.' He delivered his closing lines in a calm flat voice. 'People are getting scared, Ruthy. And with good reason.'

Ruth was unable to control the shrill defensiveness in her voice. 'I assume you have a theory? Or is all this just for the effect?'

Dave raised his arm in a forgiving, priestly gesture. 'Never mind. It's clearly a very touchy issue with you, so I'll just say it as simply as I can. Your friend. 'Sonny,' as I heard one of the girls call her the other day.'

'What the hell is that supposed to mean?' Amazed to hear herself shouting, Ruth forced herself to stop, take a few deep breaths, and try again. 'As I've been trying, apparently unsuccessfully, to convey to you, Dave, you're making me angry and nervous. Maybe it's a valid therapeutic technique, I certainly don't choose to use it myself, but I wish you'd stop treating me like a regressed patient and get to the point.'

'Well well well, we're all human, aren't we. Even SQ. Looks like you're due for another nickname, hmm?' At least he'd abandoned his professional act. But not for long. 'Sorry. What I mean is just this. Frankly, I don't think your friend is strictly professional. Take that nickname. It's no coincidence it's a man's nickname they chose for her. And, I'm sorry if this offends your tender sensibilities, but damn it, the lady does a whole lot of touching. You know damn well that if I'd had my hands all over those girls the way she does you'd have called me on it long ago.' He held up his hand to stop her before she could interrupt. 'I know, I know, you're going to say it's different because I'm a man. But this is an eighty-percent lesbian population.'

She began to protest, but he cut her off. 'I'm not saying the lady's out to seduce anyone. And I don't know what her particular sexual orientation is, and couldn't care less. What I am saying is, she's seductive as hell. Which just might be fine somewhere else. With very young kids. Or extremely withdrawn or passive patients. Nothing like a little seductiveness for a dyed-in-the-wool catatonic. But not here.'

Ruth was having trouble focussing. He was saying Sonya was a lesbian. Of course she was. How on earth had she avoided putting it together for herself? Something hammered deafeningly in her head as she argued mechanically with Dave.

'You seem to be unaware of it, but Sonya is working with all our sickest women. Gladdy, Alice Adams. Have you noticed the changes in *them*?'

'Of course I have.' Dave was snapping at her now, having apparently come to the end of his patience. 'And as I said, her style may be just fine with that kind of sickness. I'm sure she's a very talented lady in her own way. But she needs some supervision, and she needs it fast. I can do it myself, since you're obviously far too personally involved. Or Mrs Hanson can take over, I don't know if you're aware of it, but she's pretty dissatisfied with all this. I imagine she's up talking with Sonya right now. For all I know, she's no longer employed here.'

'How the hell should I be aware of it?' Ruth let herself shout now, feeling a tremendous rush in it. 'I wasn't consulted when she was hired and I'm sure I won't be when she's fired. One thing about this place is that you never hear anything first hand. I've been in my office all week. If Mrs Hanson was having problems with someone under my supervision, all she had to do was come to me. Or to Sonya herself. And if you,' she stood up and moved closer to him, 'have anything to say to me about my personal life or the friends I choose, you can tell me right now.'

'Calm down, Ruthy. Listen, don't get me wrong, of course your personal life is your own business. . . .'

The rush was waning, leaving a sour taste in her mouth, and a vague awful sense of shame, of having ruined everything. 'I'm sorry,' she began. There was a frantic knocking on the door and Lynda entered, her face important with urgency. 'Ruth, they want you over at the hospital right away. Something's wrong with Telecea!'

CANDY

Candy had decided not to go back to work after lunch. She was hiding out in the pool room instead, watching Billy shoot some pool with Donny Gitano. Delaney was out anyways, and Lee, who was on, didn't usually notice if you was there or not. All of a sudden, there was a noise from Hanson's office across the hall. Donny and Billy froze, and Candy went to the door to listen. Doreen, Hanson's secretary, was talking fast in her little mouse voice.

'No, no, Telecea, she's not here right now. Why don't you come back later. No, no, don't go in there. Stop that, stop that right now, or I'll have to call the deputy!' Then there was a big crash. Doreen's voice ended in a squeak, and she came running past them and down toward the deputy's office.

'What she don't know,' Billy told the two of them, 'is aint nobody home. They got that big union meeting over the academy. They're all up there but Hanson, and she's up in the art room giving Sonya a little talking-to. Jody went up there for something and heard them.' Sure enough, a minute later, here came Doreen again, right in the pool room, acting like she had forgot who they was.

'Would you three please go in there?' she pleaded. 'Telecea Jones just broke a window, and I'm afraid she's going to hurt herself.'

'Go on, Donny, your shot,' said Billy. Donny squinted up her eyes and took aim.

'Oh, dear!' squeaked Doreen. She looked to Candy next, but Candy made her face go blank, and after a few seconds the bitch ran out again.

Donny and Billy kept on playing, like they didn't give a shit so it was just Candy at the door watching, but they was all three listening. They heard Telecea's voice mumbling some shit about 'punish, venger' and 'break her power.' Then she started in with this spooky chant about 'mark her door with blood, fire her office up.' When she heard that, Candy took a step back.

'That's right, you better get out from that door, baby,' Billy told her. 'Aint nothing of *yours* gonna burn up in there.' She reached out with the silver tipped cue-stick that Candy had got for her and shot so all three balls went flying.

'Burn the hog up,' Candy heard. 'Set her on fire.' Then she smelled something burning, and right away that old picture flashed through her head. And then this other one of this Buddha man that burnt hisself right on TV. Without even thinking, she was out the door.

'Billy, come help me, that girl gonna burn herself up,' she called over her shoulder.

'And what you got to do with it, fool? Thought you was scared of fire,' she heard Billy call back. Everything speeded up now, and she heard footsteps behind her after all and grabbed out for Billy's hand, but it was just Donny.

They busted in the room and thank God it wasn't so bad – the only burning so far was in a wastebasket. Telecea had gone right off, and was all crouched up small, right under the window she had broke, making noises like an animal that would bite the first hand that touched it. She had cut herself from the glass and was holding onto her bloody arm with her eyes closed, probly thinking she had burnt down the whole place by now.

Donny stamped out the fire and went to dump the wastebasket somewheres, which would maybe save the poor nut from a arson case, not that it mattered much since she had life anyway, and Candy was left alone with Telecea. She could already hear the scary, echoey voices of men on those walky-talkies they carried around, and she knew what was coming down as good as if she'd already seen it.

Moody would round up three or four more men screws, and then they'd bunch up and come charging in like it was some big badass riot, or like a army charge from when he used to be in Vietnam, and probly got his kicks from charging into some village and killing off the little kids and mothers that wasn't doing nothing but standing by their houses being scared. When they saw it was just Telecea they'd be all let down and take off her clothes and beat her up good, since they wasn't allowed to kill nobody here. If Candy was fool enough to stay, she'd get it too, but it was hard to leave Telecea like that, all down on the floor. They was like sharks that loved the taste of blood and would hurt a wounded person more, and Candy knew if she just got the girl to her feet they wouldn't beat her so bad. But Telecea wasn't listening to anything she said.

Finally Candy got down on the floor next to her. 'Hey, girl,' she told her. 'Hey Telecea, now, come on, git it together. Aint nothing burnt. You're alright. Nothing bad happened. Come on, git up off that floor, girl. You know them. They like to hit you when you down.'

For the first time, Telecea opened up them big eyes, and looked right at her. 'Git off me Jezebel, don't you try and drag me down there! she screamed out. 'I know you, devil ho', git off!'

SONYA

While Telecea worked busily on her mirage, which was becoming more strange and beautiful every day, Sonya leaned peacefully out the window, absorbed in watching a woman who stood in the cold underneath, shouting up to a friend in Max. Sonya opened the window a little in order to hear better, pulling her smock and turtleneck out of her pants and tucking them around the old gray radiator to keep warm. As far as she could tell from being able to hear only the woman on the ground, the one in Max had tried to escape, but had been caught.

'Why didn't you take me along? You know if you had, we still be out there now . . . eating good . . . dressed in fur.' There was a pause for the response. 'Well, you should of thought of that before, girl. Uh-uh. No. Don't tell me.' Now she pulled out the empty lining of her jeans pocket in an elegant gesture. 'How I'm gone send you cigarettes? You think I got some my own self?' Then, with a dance of shivering, 'It's cold out here you know. What you mean have I messed with someone? You think I be standing out here in the cold with no cigarettes if I messed with someone?'

Sonya jerked around when she heard her name called, remembering too late that she was attached to the radiator. By the time she had untangled herself, taken off the ripped smock, and tucked her shirt back into her pants, Telecea had taken over for her.

'This room for artists only,' she was informing Mrs Hanson. 'You ain't got no business in here, get out.'

Sonya ruefully remembered the hour she'd spent with Telecea, working on the issue of other people having access to the art room. Ruth had gone on about the importance of her word choice with Telecea and so Sonya had told her, very carefully, over and over, that the room was open to all those who wanted to do art, and closed to those who did not. Now her words were being used against her.

Mrs Hanson fixed her with small beady eyes, apparently waiting for her to reprimand Telecea.

'Telecea, I'm sure Mrs Hanson is here because she needs to talk with me,' she said quite severely, hoping by this compromise to satisfy them both. As was her usual experience in such cases, neither one was satisfied.

'You *said*,' complained Telecea, who was being irritatingly logical today. 'You said you own self only ones can be up here is if they gots art to do.'

'Telecea! Mrs Hanson is the director of treatment. I wasn't talking about her, and you know it.'

Scowling, Telecea withdrew to her table, where she turned a rigid back on both of them. Sonya half expected Mrs Hanson to congratulate her on her firmness, or at least to comment on the appearance of the art room, which she hadn't seen yet. Instead, her color rising, she advanced furiously on Telecea and tapped her on the shoulder. 'Dear,' she spoke in her most poisonous sweet voice. 'Did you hear Miss Lehrman tell you that I wanted to speak with her?'

At the touch, Telecea jumped up like an uncoiled spring. Now she stood rigid in her blue sneakers and smock, her eyes rivetted on Sonya's face, clearly waiting to see whether she would allow this humiliation to continue.

'Mrs Hanson,' Sonya said urgently. 'Why don't we go ahead and talk. We can go right out in the hall if you'd like to see me alone, and Telecea can continue on the project she's working on. Or I'd be free to meet with you anytime this afternoon.'

'*Miss* Lehrman.' Each syllable was precise. 'Since you seem intent on misunderstanding me, I had better make myself crystal clear. I wish to speak to you, here in this room, alone. I'm afraid Telecea will have to finish her project at some other, more convenient time.'

Sonya felt tears of impotent rage rise in her eyes. If only she had explained Mrs Hanson's power to Telecea before, told her none of the rules applied to her. 'Why don't I just lock up the room,' she made one final effort. 'Then we could all three leave, and you and I could talk in the privacy of your office.'

'That will not be necessary,' Hanson spat out. Sonya was just deciding that she would not ask Telecea to leave the room, regardless of repercussions, when Telecea took action on her own. She tore off her smock, threw it at Sonya's feet, and made for the door.

As she often did in crisis situations, Sonya felt herself slip into automatic. She headed out the door behind Telecea, flinging 'I'll be right with you' back at Hanson.

Once in the hall, she took Telecea by the shoulders. 'Listen,' she told her in an urgent whisper. 'I had to do that. She has a lot of power over me. She can make me leave. Please try to understand, Telecea. I know you can if you try. I didn't want to kick you out, but if I don't do what she says, she can fire me.' Slowly, the blank stare seemed to leave Telecea's eyes.

'Alright.' She nodded slowly. 'I'll go now. Right now.' Her body was still rigid and her voice strange, but at least she was meeting Sonya's eyes. 'Fire her,' Sonya heard her murmur to herself, as she headed down the stairs.

Relieved that Telecea had understood this much, Sonya walked slowly back into the room. 'I'm good at people,' she reminded herself. 'I can handle this.' Taking a deep breath, she smiled at Hanson, sat down, and took the offensive, speaking cheerfully.

'This room's pretty different from last time you saw it, isn't it? I was sorry you couldn't make it to the opening.'

The purple hue of Hanson's face deepened perceptibly. 'I came here this morning out of a sense of urgency,' she intoned, 'and now I see that I was not mistaken. And I must say that I find your avoidance of the issue,' she paused and rolled the next words off her tongue with some enjoyment, 'rude and regrettable!'

Sonya forced her own voice to remain flat and unconcerned. 'I'm not avoiding,' she said. 'I just thought that perhaps we both might do better if we had a few minutes to cool down. But I'm certainly more than happy to discuss whatever it is you have in mind.'

'My dear girl!' Hanson's color was going down a little. 'I have been in this business for more than fifteen years. An incident of this kind is not likely to heat me up. No, my dear, unfortunately I'm all too used to it. Our girls have suffered from far too many well-meaning do-gooders who have lacked both judgement and any real understanding of their problems. We try to guard against these things, but one can't always tell from an interview. You for instance, had struck me, although inexperienced and idealistic of course, as a young woman with at least a modicum of professional insight.' She stopped to breathe, and Sonya grabbed her chance.

'I really don't know what you mean!'

Hanson shook her head. 'When I entered the room just now you were half undressed. This is of course, inexcusable around any inmate, but to think that you had Telecea Jones, one of our very sickest girls, with her sexual fantasies, alone in the room with you . . . it's unthinkable! To proceed, I then made it clear that I wished her to leave so that I could speak to you alone, and she responded by becoming quite violent and assaultive. Not only did you refuse to ask her to leave, but you supported her delusional system. My dear, have you any idea how dangerous this sort of thing can be?'

Sonya did not respond, and Hanson began to pant as her anger rose. 'Luckily, I was able to use my authority to prevent what could have been a most unfortunate occurrence. You then followed her out, and shut the door in my face! This is a paranoid girl, my dear! A very sick, a deeply schizoid personality. And every action I saw you take was supportive, yes, supportive, of that illness.'

Sonya felt herself sliding further and further down into her chair as the woman harangued her. The mountain of words was burying her like an avalanche. She must have looked repentant, because Hanson softened.

'Now, Miss Lehrman, I did notice, though you were so convinced that I had not, that you've done a very nice job with this room. Some of the wall images are perhaps overly stimulating . . . but we'll leave that for now. As I said, I'd like to give you another chance. I do believe in you, my dear. You can't convince me that you're incapable of learning!' She gave a merry laugh and shook her finger at Sonya. 'As a rule I leave supervision to Miss Foster, and I must admit that I'm quite surprised she hasn't spoken to you herself. So I think I'll take you on as my own special charge. We'll just lay down some ground rules right now, and from now on, you and I will work together, dear.'

From the depth of her seat, Sonya nodded despondently. 'First of all,' Hanson began, 'no, and I repeat, absolutely *no* physical contact with the girls. This was the complaint I came to you originally with, received, if I may say so, from numerous sources, including some of the girls themselves. You may think they like this sort of thing, my dear, and I know what a temptation it is to be popular.' She shook her finger humorously at Sonya again. 'But I think you'll find that our girls themselves will criticize you more than anyone else when you act inappropriately. They are the very first ones to remark on any irregularity of dress or language among the staff, and you, by the way dear, are dressed most inappropriately today. Your clothes must at the very least be in good repair! And the same rule goes for your actions. You must be a model for them, just as I myself must at all times be aware of serving as a model for both the girls and my own staff.' She patted at her hair complacently.

'So, I'm sure I won't have to mention it again. No more touching! Second,' she was smiling quite warmly by now, 'I'm calling an end as of right now to your hobnobbing in the cafeteria.' She leaned over the table at Sonya confidentially. 'You see, our girls consider the cafeteria their own territory. Their hunting-ground, so to speak. Territoriality, you know, all animals have it! So I'd like you to eat with the rest of us, in the staff dining room, when you don't go out. I'm sure that you'll find that we're not poison. I'm pleased to see that you and Miss Foster have become friendly. Miss Foster is one of our most deeply respected young staff. In point of fact, I'm quite disappointed with her at the moment, but that's not your concern. One thing at a time!' She giggled merrily. 'Anyway, there are other, very pleasant, and perhaps just a trifle more experienced people on the staff besides Miss Foster. Experience is the truest teacher, you know. You may be surprised at just how much you can learn from some of our old-timers. There has been talk, my dear. As you see, I believe in openness. They have commented on the fact that you don't socialize or eat with them, that, except for Miss Foster, you seem to prefer inmate company. Your private life is your own of course, dear, just as long as you do keep it private.'

'And finally, I'm going to ask you not to have Telecea Jones in here alone any more. Surely you have some other students by now, my dear, it shouldn't be that hard to arrange. Perhaps, just for the present, it would be better to try to have at least two girls in here at all times. That way you won't feed into their fantasies. Nothing to do with you, dear, just for security reasons. Your own security, let's not forget that, as well as our liability as an institution. You are our responsibility when you are on state property, you know that. All clear then? No questions? Good, good. I'm so glad we had our little talk and got things cleared up.' And Mrs Hanson left the room without waiting for a response.

Sonya didn't move from her chair. She felt as if she'd been run over by a steam roller.

She wondered if Telecea was alright. She'd seemed a little confused when she left, but somehow she didn't have the energy to go down and check. Instead, she put her head down on the table and waited for Ruth to come and get her.

TELECEA

That old hogface devil bitch it stink from her snout mouth when she breath at you from where she all rotted up inside. Just like that she come in my art room rip off Sonya smock wif them claw hands. Wif the skin on her all tough like they got. Little bird claw hands and them little hog eyes and poke her snout at me, talking bout get out my own art room.

Someone need to hurt that hogface, but Sonya she tell me do it with my sculpture don't be hurting no one with my hands not less I wants to go up to Max and can't make no sculpture up there. So I don't touch the bitch, not even when she put her claw hands on me. I would of kill her then, but Sonya she take me out and tell me what to do. Tell me that old hogface got power. Tell me fire her, and I know she mean that old office of her. Fire it up.

Time I gets down there all them talking at me. Mark her door wif blood. Break the pride of her power. Ruth Foster voice say, Wait till you see me, don't do nothing. But Ruth Foster turnt into that ho' Candy now so I know that voice a trick and I just listen to Sonya. Say be her Venger, do His will.

Fire and blood. Glass break and smoke and blood on the floor. Then I think what if Sonya aint mean that? What if I heard wrong and she won't let me back, never in my art room no more.

Now you done it, bad girl. Born bad, rotted up inside from your seed of the Dulter mother, devil father. Born marked, just like Cain that murder his own granny and curst from the earth.

Bad girl aint no artist, don't get no wall of her own. Stupid retard can't even read, how she gone deserve her a wall? Oh no, that wall gots to be took away, that wall a mistake. Gots to be painted over, all white blank like that other wall. Bad girl don't deserve nothing.

Then Ruth Foster-Candy voice. Up close to me wif her unclean self. Screaming at me, and her eyes got fire flames in. Got girls burning up. Tell me, Get up and come with me Telecea. Try and drag me down wif her. Down to the burning lake. Tell me, Now they gone come git you, git you when you down.

But I done resist temptation. Tell her Git off me, devil. Give her a good push, and she gone.

Then them others come. Well look-a-here. That bad little nigger gots to be punish. Gots to smash up that desert she made, smash up her mirage. Wif our boots. Take off her clothes. That'll show her. Beat it out.

SATURDAY, OCTOBER 10

RUTH

Ruth, Victor, Lisa and Bill sat around the dinner table, smoking a second fat joint. They had finished Ruth's excellent *coq au vin* and Victor's very successful apple pie and had already gone through two bottles of wine. The evening, which had started off boring and stilted, was picking up, and Ruth felt like getting high.

'Watch out,' Lisa warned, sucking deeply on the joint. 'It'll rob us of our disguises. Pare us down to our true naked essence.' She took off her sweater, as if to begin the paring down process, and Ruth thought she did look naked, with her round breasts perfectly visible under the pale blue leotard. Ruth wondered what it would be like to have big breasts like that, or like Sonya's. She realized that she'd been staring, and looked quickly away.

Bill smiled his wide innocuous smile. 'That's what I call a dinner,' he said. 'Where three hours later you're still sitting there, pleasantly high, talking ... reminds me of the dinners we used to have on weekends when I was a kid. I remember sitting around and feeling that the grownups had it all in control, that all was right with the world.'

Lisa grimaced, pulling on her cigarette now. 'You always manage to produce such good memories, sweetie,' she said. 'What I remember is watching the food jealously the whole time. To see if they were giving my brother the biggest piece as usual. After Daddy, that is. Boys were supposed to be hungrier.' Lisa reached into the pie plate and began to eat the crumbs. There was something appealing to Ruth about Lisa's frank greediness, and she especially liked it that Lisa smoked much more than she did, and with a kind of hunger that made her own habit seem mild.

Like Victor, Bill hated cigarettes, but put up with Lisa's smoking with saintly forbearance. It occurred to Ruth that she and Lisa had something in common – they were both ordinary mean people who were matched with saints. No wonder she was silent and Lisa was sarcastic.

'Why don't we go into the living room?' Victor suggested.

'See!' Bill was pretty high. 'That was like childhood too. Finally somebody would get up and say,' here he rose and spoke in an

169

uncharacteristically deep voice, "Shall we adjourn to the living room?" And we all would.'

The living room, unlike the other rooms in the apartment, which were Ruth's creations, was Victor's province. The bookcase sloped with paperbacks and records arranged at random and there were large Disarmament and Radical Therapy posters in clashing colors on the walls. A velvet sofa and two easy chairs from Vic's very first apartment stood against the walls, their cushions lumpy and worn bare in places. Ruth was able to like the room, as long as she felt quite clear that it had nothing to do with her. She sat with her legs curled under her, Victor's head on her lap.

'So,' Lisa asked her from deep in one of the chairs, 'don't you have any childhood dinner time memories?'

'Well, I remember tuning out a lot when I was eleven or twelve or so,' Ruth started. Lisa nodded in encouragement and she went on. 'My mother and my sister, Elaine, would be having one of their heavy conflicts, and my father would be getting angrier and angrier, building up to the point where he could fling his fork down and announce that he couldn't take it, he was leaving the table. And I'd be eating as fast and as silently as I could, just getting it over with, so I could go play. I'd say one or two phrases over and over to myself, something like, These people have nothing to do with me, this isn't my real life. And then, especially in the summer, when there'd still be a few hours of light left, I'd slip off and leave them there talking and arguing. There was a river about a half mile away, by a secret path I'd made through the woods, and I wasn't supposed to go there alone, especially in the evening, but that was when it was most exciting. When I was there was the only time I used to really feel like myself. . . .'

Ruth stopped. She felt as if she'd been talking for hours, and said much more than she'd meant to say. Now all three of them were beaming at her, as if she were a backward child who had for once performed well in front of company. 'Well, don't all talk at once.' She was suddenly angry and self-conscious.

'You are an unusually private person, Ruth,' said Bill. He had an annoying habit, probably picked up in his training, of always saying the person's name he was addressing. 'So it means more when you do share.'

Lisa got up, giving Bill an impatient look, and put on an old Joan Baez album. Ruth hadn't known it before, but it was exactly what she felt like listening to.

'Black is the color of my true love's hair,' sang Joan. 'Her face is something wondrous rare.' Ruth wondered why Joan hadn't changed 'her' to 'his.' She'd read in *Newsweek* that Joan Baez was bisexual, and she wondered if it were true. The song sounded better with 'her' in it, anyway. Sonya's hair was black . . . she wondered if Sonya used to listen to this song.

When Ruth had walked into the art room on Friday afternoon, after leaving Telecea badly bruised and heavily medicated in the hospital, she'd found Sonya sitting alone at the long white table, with her head in her arms.

'Hanson's been here, lecturing me,' she raised her head to say, 'but I got through it OK. Telecea was here at first, and Hanson started in on her but I think I managed to calm her down. That was hours ago, and everything's fine, really, I don't know why I can't seem to move. . . .'

She started to cry then, and Ruth decided to save the news about Telecea for later. She awkwardly put an arm around Sonya, from above, so the coarse black mane of hair touched her cheek, and she inhaled Sonya's special smell, of paint and turpentine and whatever that shampoo was. . . .

'I love the ground whereon she goes,' sang Joan, and Ruth remembered Dave's mouth moving like a robot, saying, 'Damn it, the lady does a whole lot of touching.' She suddenly felt that there were too many people in the room, and got up, a little shakily, to go to the bathroom.

'Come back soon, love,' Victor whispered, pulling at her. Grass always made him sexy.

In the bathroom, Ruth looked at herself in the mirror. Her face looked back, paler than usual, and somehow softer and less defined. When she came out, Lisa was in the kitchen, making coffee as if she lived there. Ruth leaned on the counter, watching her move around. They could hear the voices of the men in the living room, talking in a fast blur.

Lisa dried her hands on her jeans. Her breasts moved under the pale blue. 'I like you so much tonight, Ruth,' she said. 'I could picture you there, by the river. Thanks for telling about that.'

'It felt good to me, too.' Ruth smiled, liking her back.

'You look different tonight,' Lisa went on. 'You always look good, but usually you look . . . very well put together, you know? But tonight you look free. Like you must have looked by the river, those evenings.' She took two small steps toward Ruth, leaned forward awkwardly, and put her arms around her. Ruth felt Lisa's breath on her cheek, felt her warm soft body. Then Lisa's face came closer and she gave Ruth a long soft kiss. Ruth was amazed. She let Lisa kiss her and, for a long minute, she enjoyed it. Then it was over, and she stood there, holding on to the counter edge for steadiness.

'I just felt like doing that,' Lisa said in a small voice. 'Is it OK?' Ruth nodded, dumbly. She could still feel Lisa's breasts pressing warmly against her, could still taste her mouth. Then she went blank and cold, and felt nothing at all.

'We're just stoned, that's all,' she whispered, and turned mechanically back to the living room, where Victor shifted to make room for her on the couch.

CANDY

Candy was surprised at how alright it felt to her that Billy was gone out on furlough. Even though she knew, and had knew even before everyone had been jumping all over each other to be the first to tell her, that Billy wasn't gonna spend the weekend alone, it was different from when Billy was messing around in here and she had to have her face in it all the time and know that everyone was watching her to see how was she taking it. The truth was the only thing she was worried about was would Billy have her act together and not come back with no empty hands. Or empty cunt, in this case. She'd decided to go in on Lou and Frankie's plan to rip off the mental health wing but that wasn't till next week, and she could use some reefer now.

The thing that really made her feel alright was that her old girlfriend that she hadn't seen for three years, Loraine Bradley, had just came in. When Candy first knew her, Loraine had been a tall, pretty brownskin girl that came from some dumb little town in Wisconsin or Iowa or somewhere way the hell out in the Midwest, and talked like she was white. She'd been just getting started on the streets then. Earl had been tight with Loraine's man, Ritchie, so it had been Candy's job to break her in, and they used to work together sometimes. Loraine had been cool, too. She didn't try to pretend she knew all about the life, like most bitches that was just being turnt out, and she learned real fast. Not that you could really trust anyone out there, but Loraine was different. They used to split the cash right down the middle, regardless of who ended up doing what.

'Remember them two college boys that time?' Candy asked Loraine. They was sitting out in the sun on a bench with their coats on, but Loraine, who was coming off her habit, was shivering.

'Yeah, I think I remember,' Loraine said. 'What did we leave them with, their pants? They weren't the ones you had to cut, were they?'

'No, that was another scene,' Candy told her.

'What I remember was when Earl and Ritchie took us out after. To the Hub, you remember that?'

'Nah, not too good.' All the nights she'd spent fucked up and partying kind of floated together in Candy's mind like one big fucked up party. 'What I remember bout that,' she said, 'is feeling down, just fine you know, and then all of a sudden that jive peanut-prick bastard sees some straight motherfuckin' dude across the room looking at me and, hey, it's work time again. I hope his ass rots up at Lincoln!' Candy hadn't really knew she'd felt quite that way about Earl till she'd said it.

Loraine was surprised too. 'You never used to talk about him that way.'

'Yeah, and I used to be one stupid bitch, too.' Then Candy felt bad. 'I didn't mean to be putting you down or nothing,' she said. 'You still with Ritchie, huh?'

Loraine sighed and hugged herself. 'Candy, you know Ritchie's different from Earl and them. He really tried hard to keep me out of here. He put up the bail money right away when I was busted, without me even asking. Was up at Awaiting Trial the day after with the cash and this big bunch of American Beauty roses. You remember, that's our flower.'

Then, moving real fast, like it was a fix she had to get to quick, Loraine reached in her jeans pocket and took out a envelope. 'He told me not to show no one,' she said. 'But I know you don't talk.'

It was a tired looking card inside, that showed a black bride and groom with the bride's white dress and the groom's black old-fashioned hat made of that furry material and little green and silver glitters all around the edges. On the inside someone had scratched out the part that used to say 'Congratulations on being married,' or some shit like that, and wrote, in messy ballpoint,

'Baby you now what i mean by this. for when you out of there i now it may seem like a long time but you now i am for real so you keep cool and baby just remembur we gone be together sooner or later. Dont show noone this. YOU'R MAN, RICHARD.'

Candy put the card back in the envelope and handed it to Loraine. They was so many things she wanted to say. 'He used to always talk that marrying shit. Are you married yet?' And, 'Why *shouldn't* you show no one?' She remembered Ritchie, a cheap little bastard that was only five feet tall or so and liked to run his mouth bout how many fillies he had in his stable. He was always thinking somebody was laughing at him behind his back for being a little dude, and pulling his gun on people that hadn't done nothing to him. Earl was a motherfucker alright, but at least she'd made him bring her a diamond ring when she was first in, and not some cheap nasty little card with all the words spelt wrong. It was kind of hard to understand, because even though Loraine, who used to have a real pretty figure, had lost a whole lot of weight since Candy last saw her and when she smiled, which she hadn't hardly done yet, you could see a couple of teeth was missing, she was still a fine looking girl who was real smart and read a lot, who could of done good for herself instead of ruining her life for some jive midget pimp that couldn't even write. But Candy knew that as long as Loraine kept grasping onto that card like she was, it wasn't no point telling her nothing.

Loraine sighed. 'Fuck, it's cold out here,' she said. 'My lawyer says it looks like I can wrap it up in a year and a half. If I'm cool, and you know I'm gonna be cool. I'm too tired to be anything but. You just got a little time left, right?' Candy nodded, and Loraine sighed again.

'You know I'm glad for you, girl, but shit, Candy, I'm gonna miss you. I've already seen a few other girls that I know from outside, but nobody I'd cross the street to speak to. And anyway, these butches got me scared shitless. Girls been saying they fight you if you don't do what they want.'

Candy thought it was funny how every new girl that came in was worried about the same old shit. She almost knew the rap she was getting ready to lay on Loraine by heart.

'First time someone try to push you or make you do something you don't feel like doing, you be ready to fight. I'll get you a blade or if you got something else you feel more comfortable with, and you find a place for it. Hopefully, you won't never need it, but it don't hurt to have one. And then, if you say you're gonna fight, go ahead and do it. Don't matter if she's five times your size. Once will be enough, you know? And whatever you do, don't tell no screw nothing.'

'I know all that from the street,' Loraine said. 'And you *know* you didn't need to tell me that last.'

'Well, it aint really that different from the street in here,' Candy told her. 'Cept aint no one gonna force you to have sex if you don't want to.'

'What you mean if! I wouldn't go with no girl!' Then Loraine looked at her strange. 'You're going with someone in here for real, huh? They were saying you turned funny, but I didn't believe it.'

'Yeah, it's for real, alright,' Candy said. 'She's on furlough right now.' She could tell Loraine had plenty to say about that but she kept her mouth shut, just like Candy had about Ritchie. It was like they was both so glad to meet up they didn't want to spoil it by beefing.

'Listen, I got to lie down,' Loraine said. 'I got a terrible headache.'

'I'll come by for you suppertime,' Candy told her, and Loraine looked relieved they was still cool.

'Hey, I didn't mean nothing by what I said about, you know, going with girls,' she said. 'I mean, I don't dig it for myself, but that's just me. And I guess I got a lot to learn in here, just like when you first knew me, on the street. But you remember me, Candy, I learn fast.'

'I know you do, girl,' Candy said. She felt sorry for Loraine who looked like she was having a real hard time keeping her face together. 'When Billy comes back tomorrow, I'll introduce you two,' she said. 'And you're in on whatever she brings. I used to tell her about you, girl. Me and you's cool. And you're gonna be alright.'

Loraine nodded. 'I know it. Thanks, Candy. It's just, my head's hurting.' Then, like it was easier to say cause she'd already started to leave, she stopped trying to smile and said, 'It's just . . . I'm so sick of being a fast learner.' She had to stop herself from crying so she could get the words out.

'You know, Candy, it wasn't like I really wanted to get busted or anything, but at the same time I had this crazy picture in my head of what prison would be like. Maybe like this one time when I was in high school and my appendix bust, so I had to go in the hospital. I was real good at the time, you know what I mean, Candy? I was this real good colored girl that wasn't like those bad ones that took the secretarial course and then dropped out when they got pregnant in tenth grade. I was in straight academics, a cheerleader, all that shit. Only black girl on the fucking student council. Had a boy-friend that was captain of the football team who was good too. And then my appendix bust and I didn't have to do nothing for a week. Just lay there in the private room and no one was allowed to come in and see me and I didn't have to talk nice to no one or set no examples and everyone just left me the fuck alone!' She was crying now. 'It must be the medication they got me on. It's just, I guess I kept thinking prison would be like that, even though really I knew all the time it wouldn't. Seems like there aint no place they leave you alone unless you're dead.'

'Yeah, I know what you mean,' said Candy. 'But you'll get used to it, girl. Things'll look up in a day or two.' They squeezed hands and Loraine headed back to the cottage.

After she'd gone, Candy thought about her. 'Give her two weeks,' she said to Billy in her head. She was already getting looks from the butches, and she wasn't one to steady hold out. Plus she needed affection, and that Ritchie wouldn't be up here with no American Beauty roses in the near future, that was for damn sure.

She had knew that Loraine was educated, but not that she'd been all good like that. Candy'd always been a pretty bad girl herself, that people used to say was headed straight for jail, which was maybe why she assumed everyone else was the same way. When Loraine had been talking about her past, even when she'd been all upset and crying, she still seemed smart, like someone that understood why she was the way she was. It was like *that* Loraine was a whole different person from the dumb dizzy bitch that slept with that mangy card under her pillow. Maybe, like the songs said, love could make a fool out of the smartest girl. For a minute Candy worried about herself that way. It was true she put up with shit from Billy that she wouldn't think of putting up with from no one else. But at least Billy wasn't no pimp.

SONYA

Probably because she was a little high, the graffiti on the wall of the toilet in the bar seemed to Sonya to read like a tragic novel. 'World without men!' 'Jan even if you hate my guts I'll still love you forever until I die.' 'Barbara L. is to fine for her own good she'll be sorry.' 'Why don't you want me Mary? From you know who.' Someone banged loudly on the door, and Sonya got out, carefully avoiding the mirror.

Upstairs, the music was screaming, 'You're my own special woman!' The air was thick with smoke, and women kept bumping her with sharp elbows and spilling parts of their drinks on her.

'Dance?' It was a thin woman whose pallor contrasted sharply with her black leather jacket. Sonya shook her head. She knew that if she tried to dance, her feet would stick like magnets to the floor and the entire dance floor would stop and stare at her. Ruth was probably an incredible dancer. 'You're my horizon, you're all I can see,' blared the song, and Sonya replayed that last awful day at work, the ugly confrontation with Hanson and then her pitiful crying in front of Ruth, who must despise her now. She'd thought coming here and having a drink or two would get her mind off it, but it wasn't working.

She moved away from the dance floor and found a place by the wall where she could stand and watch the pool players. She loved the posed ritual quality of their movements, and had begun to mentally film them for a documentary to be called 'Woman Pool Players at the Side Door Bar,' when one of the players, a tall striking black woman in a white sweater, caught her attention. She looked like, no she *was*, Billy Morris. Escaped? On furlough? It was her, anyway, complete with her silver-tipped pool stick, and a small adoring blonde waiting on the sidelines. Sonya was about to move away discreetly when Billy, who had just shot, noticed her. She stared, then her mouth curled down in disgust and she turned and spat on the floor.

Sonya almost ran through the crowd to get to the door, propelled by the hatred of that gesture. The cold air was a relief, and she walked blindly through the narrow deserted streets, trying to shake the sense of being pursued. If only Billy would go staight back and tell the officers about having seen her in a gay bar. Then, on Monday, Hanson would fire her, and it would be simple gay oppression, and not her fault at all. She'd move out of this stupid city the very next week, and no one could possibly blame her or call her a quitter.

All of a sudden she smelled the ocean. She'd forgotten that this was a harbor city, but there, miraculously across the street, a pier stretched over the water. It was deserted and probably not safe at this time of night, but she walked out on it anyway, inhaling oil and fish and salt. She saw the gold lights of ships far out at sea, and yellow blinking ones from the airport across the bay. The cold wind felt good on her neck, and she shook her hair loose to feel it better. A plane took off, shooting up into the air from across the water, and now, suddenly, she loved this city as strongly as she'd hated it a few minutes ago. She felt the same way she had on her recent morning walk and, with a sudden clarity, understood that this joy and her misery in the bar were part of the same thing. There was a fine awareness which went along with being alone and uprooted, and it was this same awareness which made her skinless and vulnerable to random brutalities. Soon she'd have friends, would be a part of this city and would no longer be able to see so clearly. It was just as well to take advantage of this state while it lasted.

Sonya turned herself in what she felt was the direction of home and began to walk. She remembered walking home late at night in London, New York and Vermont, having left uncomfortable or undesired beds, parties or bars. She'd always found her way back, as she would tonight. And maybe she'd call Ruth in the morning. Now that Sonya thought about it realistically, Ruth hadn't acted disgusted at all.

TELECEA

They may think they got me fool, but I know they tricks. Send that ho' Candy in, try and drag me down in the black dark, but when I tell her bout herself she run alright.

Take and beat on me, kick me with they hard boots. Drags me over the hospital. Hospital, huh! Torture place is what it is and they takes and pierce me with they poison needles.

What they done, they find out bout my desert. Find out that where I'm sending them, so they torture me and send me up here instead. Up to Max wif no water and that thirst.

But He be watching out for me all the time. Done take that filthy ho' Proudy out. Say she got stomach ulcers, and I just laugh. Bitch gone think twice next time she try and starve someone the Lord love. Feel like a rat be chewing on her insides, thats what she got, stewin' in her own nasty juice.

Who they got up here instead, they got a old lady that really a inmate but they have told her she a police. Poor old lady all deaf and dumb, that why they pick her, so she won't bear no witness. And so when I cries out for water she won't hear nothing, make me die of thirst.

But He love me and need me for His Venger. So He help me, just like He done Joseph. And Daniel when they put him in with them lions. And that Samson. Only Samson a man so he need to have his hair long. I wears mines shave off cause it work the opposite for womans.

What they don't know is I been around my Granny when she start not hearing so I knows how to do wif deaf peoples. I just move my mouf and show her I need water. And she bring it right in to me, and juice too, not like that Proudy. This one aint scairt of me, and know He love me. She say it right out, He love you. And, Oh you poor child, what has they done to you? So I tell her all bout Joseph and how they done him. Just like my Granny told me.

How Joseph the youngest and smallest one in his whole family. Gots a daddy name Jacob that love that little boy the most. Have all these evil brothers that hate that poor child. Now his daddy he give Joseph a coat of many colors. Got all the colors of the rainbow in that coat. And the Lord love him and send him dream visions, just like He do me. But Joseph aint keep quiet bout his dreams like you spose to. So one day them brothers hides and wait till he come by wif all his sheeps. Jumpt him and say, Behold this dreamer come. Let's us take and slay him and leave him for the wild beasties to eat. And they would done it, too, but one of them greedy and he say, Let's us sell his ass instead. So they kill them sheeps and take and dip that pretty coat all in the blood. Spoilt it and show it to Daddy, say Joseph dead. And take and sell they own brother.

But the Lord He kept on sending Joseph them dream visions and now he know what you spose to do wif 'em. Make him a sculpture-picture and pretty soon he the one king and them brothers come to him all on they knees begging and pleading cause they starving to death.

He just laugh in they face, say, That what you get.

Old lady like that story, so I tell her bout Samson, too. Then she want to go on about that man, Jesus, that got trickt just like they done Joseph. How one time all them be sitting round the table and one of his brothers take and sell him for cash money. But what he done to them, he make them eat his flesh. Break it up and make them eat it right there at that table and drink his blood too. And then they nail his ass up, just hammer them nails right in his dick and he screamin' and cryin' and dyin'. And they give him that vinegar to drink, so he tormented wif thirst just like they done me. But he trickt them alright cause when they put him in the coffin he come alive and jump out and his ghost come after them devils. Jumpt right out the coffin in they face. Granny told me bout Jesus a few times but she say he too girlish. Let them do all that to him and don't lift a finger. Eye for a eye, that what you spose to do. Say that Jesus man don't know bout no vengeance. But I tell the old lady I like that story and she say, Jesus love you child, oh he do love you. She say they all told her I'm bad and violent and don't come near me but she known if she trust in Jesus he gone help her bring the Lord to me cause we all his children. Poor old thing don't even know she a inmate, and I already His Venger. But I aint want to hurt her so I aint said nothing.

MONDAY, OCTOBER 12

RUTH

'You look content,' Sonya said, as Murph buzzed her and Ruth through the front door on their way out.

'Yes,' Ruth nodded. 'I had a good day.' After last week's session she'd been afraid that she'd irrevocably ruined the therapy with Candy, but Candy had been especially open today, and they'd accomplished a lot.

Next she'd done an intake on Candy's friend, Loraine Bradley, whom she'd liked immediately and agreed to work with. Finally, and without Dave's help, she'd managed to convince Hanson to hold a special disciplinary board meeting for Telecea sometime within the next two weeks, with the goal of gradually reintroducing her to the compound. Hanson had even agreed to allow Telecea to continue her work with Sonya, as long as she also continued therapy with Ruth, a safeguard that Ruth felt comfortable with.

Now she and Sonya came out into the clear yellow light of the hour between afternoon and evening. In the field behind the parking lot, an old white horse ran in the long grass. Ruth whistled, long and low, and the horse pricked up its ears, hesitated, took a couple of mincing steps backwards, then trotted up to the low fence. Sonya, who'd been reaching out to him, jerked her hand back. 'Look at his big teeth!' she said.

Ruth rubbed the old white muzzle gently. 'See, he's alright, he's very gentle. Next time we'll bring him an apple,' she coaxed, but Sonya still hung back. She looked to Ruth like a horse herself, a shaggy-maned, large-boned Shetland pony, hanging back, unsure whether she wanted to be caught by the bridle and led home, or to take off and run wild. 'You know,' she said, 'you look like a pony, Sonya.'

Sonya laughed and backed off a few steps, imitating the horse. 'Are you going to whistle for me?' she asked.

Ruth tried to think of something witty to answer, but couldn't. 'Let's walk a little,' she said instead. They walked through the next field, the old horse following along the fence behind them. The grass, so tall it reached their waists, parted in two blond rivers behind them.

'I bet you loved horses when you were in junior high,' Sonya said, a little accusingly.

'Yes,' Ruth admitted, 'I did. I rode a lot, and wanted a horse desperately for a few years. How did you know?' As she asked this, she realized that she had the fantasy that Sonya knew everything about her, that she had always known, somehow.

Sonya shrugged her shoulders impatiently. 'WASP, upper middle class. The way you called to that horse, like a familiar,' she said. 'Not so hard to figure out.'

A little stunned, Ruth pulled her brown sweater closer around her.

'I'm sorry,' Sonya apologized. 'I didn't mean to categorize you. I know how I feel when people take one look and say 'New York Jewish,' as if that summed me up; as if there was nothing more to say. It's just that all the upper middle class WASP women I've known spent a few years of their lives as horses.'

Ruth felt typed, invisible, but now Sonya was drawing closer, walking more slowly through the grass, looking at her.

'What was it really like for you, growing up?' she asked. 'Never mind my stupid assumptions. Tell me about it.'

It was impossible to stay hurt. Ruth thought of Lisa who had also asked her about her childhood and then kissed her in the kitchen. 'When I was quite small, around this time of year, I used to play in a field like this, out behind our house,' she began with the first thing that came to mind. 'Elaine, my big sister, and I used to play hide and seek in the tall grass. I loved being the hider. Crouched way down you had a nest. You were invisible. It was a little scary, being the seeker. The only way you could find the other person was to stumble on her.'

Sonya did not kiss her, but she smiled in almost the same way Lisa had smiled when she'd told the story about the river. They had reached the end of the field now, and had begun walking into the beginning of a forest.

'Isn't it strange, all this, right in back of Redburn?' Sonya asked, but her voice lacked conviction, and Ruth thought that for both of them the prison had already become unreal, a place they had imagined. The trees were tall and far apart now, and the ground was soft with decayed leaves.

'What were *you* like?' Ruth asked, suddenly feeling that she had to know. 'When you were little, in New York?'

'Oh I don't know.' Sonya paused for a minute, and then said glumly, as if this fact alone explained everything, 'I was fat.'

Ruth imagined a chubby adorable little girl, with Sonya's dark mane and big eyes. 'Did you have brothers and sisters?' she asked. 'A best friend? What did you used to do?'

'I was an only child.' Sonya spoke in a flat monotone. 'My parents were old when they had me, I was their little miracle. Then when I went to school someone decided I had talent. They sent me to this special school for artistic kids from all over the city. It must have been the first time I'd been out of the neighborhood. When we got there, I remember the kids laughing at my mother, at how she looked and talked, I guess. Pretty soon I felt ashamed of them all the time, for using bad grammar and talking too loud and too much about money, for being old and dressing funny and being stupid. Neither of them is stupid really, just not educated, but who knew the difference then? I went on to Music and Art and all the other parents were so different, those middle class intellectuals, you know. I'd go over to someone's house after school, and there'd be classical music playing or else just silence and lots of books and furniture you didn't notice. My parents used to shout a lot. They weren't angry, it was just how they talked, and we always had this awful furniture from the store he worked in. . . . After a while I used to pretend that it was all a mistake, that I was really from some other family. . . .' Sonya shrugged her shoulders in her dark pea coat. 'They're good people, they really are. I was such a little snob. I don't know why I went on like that. It just depresses me. Let's talk about something else, OK?'

Obediently, Ruth changed the subject. 'The moon's already out.' It was a tiny sliver, barely visible. 'That would be a good Halloween moon,' she said. 'It'll be Halloween pretty soon.'

The idea didn't seem to cheer Sonya, who was hanging back, shuffling her feet in the leaves, but it excited Ruth. Halloween had always been her favorite holiday as a child. She remembered the ease, the lightness of her body, running through fields with her friend Liz, on Halloween night. Halloween hadn't been anything special for a few years now. Maybe this year would be different. Thinking of this, she put her arm easily around Sonya's drooping shoulders.

'Come on,' she said, 'don't be sad. We'll stop off at Nina's for a drink on the way home.'

CANDY

Candy stood by her tree. It was late afternoon, and Mabe's dope was alright. A long ways away she could hear cars going by, and they was a train too, that she usually only heard in the nighttime. They used to be a song on the radio, she remembered, bout a train going by a jail at night, tooting its whistle. It was the lonesomest sound of all, a train going somewheres and you stuck where you was.

A leaf drifted down from a tree that was over the fence, and Candy moved near it. You wasn't sposed to be more than six feet close to the fence. It was a D, and a major D if you was caught touching it, but it was such a puny little fence, easy enough to climb over if you wanted to. Girls did it all the time, even real pregnant ones. What if she climbed it right now? The only thing stopping her was Ginzer, standing right out there in the yard like a skinny old owl with her sharp little beak, and who ever heard of a bird stopping you from doing what you wanted? A yellow leaf landed on Ginzer's head, and she picked it off with a jerk, like in a speeded-up movie.

Candy felt more like a slow-motion movie herself, like on TV when they slow it down and the football players start up all over again, like they're swimming to each other to hug and kiss instead of fight. Or like when you're sposed to be in love in the movies and it goes foggy and different pastel colors and they start moving toward each other all slow. They was an ad too, about the closer she comes the better she looks. It was always guys and broads doing it in the movies of course or in that ad, moving closer and closer in.

What if she did start climbing the fence in slow motion, Candy wondered, and Ginzer did turn into an owl and fly to the top and peck at her. Only Ginzer probly couldn't move in slow motion if she tried – she was like on natural speed all the time. Some people was just that way, like Earl, who had always moved so smooth, like he was oiled, but fast, no matter if he was high or not. 'I'm a cat moves quiet,' he used to say, and she remembered him, a big black velvet cat, padding after her in fast slow-motion. And her the little mouse he was coming to grab.

'Hey Candy,' Mabe called. 'What the fuck you doing, girl?

Better get your ass away from that fence. Don't you see Ginzer out here?'

'Hey, Ginzer better not try no cat and mouse games with me,' Candy answered. The name sounded real funny when she said it aloud, just like a owl. 'Don't Ginzer sound funny, Battle?' she asked Mabe. 'Don't it sound just like the name a owl should have?'

Mabe's last name was Batelou, but she loved for people to call her Battle. Candy wouldn't do it as a rule, but today she thought what the hell, if it made her happy, why not? Plus she owed Mabe for the dope. 'Say it your own self, Battle,' she said. 'Say it one or two times out loud and see don't it sound strange.'

'Yeah, I guess it do,' said Mabe, looking around all paranoid to see had Ginzer heard them say her name. 'You better get your ass away from that fence, girl,' she said again. 'That stuff act on you funny!'

'But I am funny,' Candy said, for a joke. She was bored with Mabe, and pretended she was standing outside the fence looking in at the three little red brick cottages, playhouses for good little girls, arranged in a half-circle around the big mean one, with bars on its top windows.

That was a bore too, so she looked out. If you stepped right up to the fence, you could see through the holes just like you was out there, with no wire or nothing. There was a field that had wavy yellow grass, and a white horse running along. Beyond that, it looked like a forest. She put her nose through the hole, and it even smelled different. That must be the way fall in the country smelled, she decided. For a few years when she was growing up they'd lived sort of in the country or it would of been once you got out of that development, but she couldn't remember no particular smell.

'Girl, I'm a get Billy right now,' said Mabe's scared voice. 'Maybe she can talk some sense into you.' Candy wished the voice would go away. If she squinted up her eyes she could feel like she was really out there. She had never rode on a horse, just once when she was little on one of those ones they had tied together that went around in a ring. Not no real horse. This one kept moving in and out from where she could see it. She wondered where it was going to, and did it have some other horses to hang with.

She had never knew they had all that, right over the fence. When she had first got brung in she'd been too dope-sick to notice anything, and that time they'd escaped all she could see was the road with cars going by, that one just had to stop for them and the fence behind, waiting to close them in again.

She thought maybe on her way out she'd stop and pet that horse. Billy would probly laugh at her if she told her about it. She knew if she told Foster she wouldn't laugh, but it was Billy she wanted to tell.

In the city fall didn't smell no different than any other season. But even here inside the fence she thought she could smell a difference. 'What if every season in the country has its own smell,' she thought. She picked up a yellow leaf and held it in front of her nose, and smelled with her eyes closed. Then she looked through the hole in the fence again and pretended she was right out there, going straight up to the white horse. It licked her hand and she mounted up. It leaped away, real high, it could jump any old fence, and she was safe, galloping away into the forest.

'Candace Peters,' a loud ugly voice said in her ear. 'Just what do you think you are doing there?'

She pretended she didn't hear nothing.

'Are you asking me to give you a D report?' said the voice.

Candy turnt around. There was owl Ginzer and, a ways back, a whole group of girls standing there like little sheep, staring at her. She closed her eyes so they would go, but they was all still there when she opened them back up.

'All right Candace, that's it, I don't know what you're on, but we'll soon find out,' Ginzer said to her.

Candy sighed, and flipped on the switch in her head. She walked away from the fence, back to the others, with Ginzer following her.

'Mrs Ginzer,' she explained all soft and sorry. 'I didn't even realize what I was doing. I have a bad headache, and I was . . . uh . . . remembering the past.' She looked up at Ginzer-owl, making her eyes all big. Ginzer was looking at the other girls to see would they call her prejudice if she didn't say nothing. They was only Telecea Jones screaming out some shit so loud you could hear it all the way from Max. The others was quiet, or else saying shit like 'Hey, give her a break.'

Mabe spoke up. 'She's been very depressed all day, Mrs Ginzer, really, I think she got some bad news from her family or something.'

The old bitch said, 'Well, I'll let it go for this time. Just keep away from that fence, every one of you.'

Candy drifted off to the middle of the yard. 'Thanks, Battle,' she said. 'You alright.' She tried to look out from where she was, but everything she could see from there had wire in the way.

SONYA

Sonya was always attracted to Ruth when she was driving, and today, with her face still slightly flushed by the wind and her blond fine hair, for once not restrained by anything, falling around her face, she was almost irresistible. She'd put her arm around Sonya's shoulder in the woods with an easy authority. Now, excited by the idea of Halloween, she wanted to talk about her childhood, which she'd never done before.

'I wish you and I had known each other as children,' she said, and Sonya tried to imagine it. Ruth was three years older than her, which was about the same age difference as the series of girls she'd had passionate crushes on and had spent so much of her energy courting in high school. Her courting had generally been successful, except that the girls had always turned out to be surprisingly ordinary once she got to know them.

Ruth was still going on about her childhood Halloweens. Sonya remembered staying in the apartment on Halloween. The other kids would have asked her if she was supposed to be the fat lady no matter what costume she wore, and there were always bands of wild ones running around screaming and hitting and setting off fire crackers in your face. No one went trick-or-treating in her neighborhood. Someone would have been sure to poison the candy or put razor blades in it or something.

'Somehow, I think it must have been pure force of will, my friend Liz and I had both managed not to grow breasts that year,' Ruth was saying. 'I think we made some kind of pact not to, and it worked for a while. Everyone else we knew had already given in and gone off to boy-girl Halloween parties, which was probably why Liz and I were so wild that year – we knew it would be our last. Some of the boys hadn't gone to a party either, and they swooped down on us and tried to grab our candy, but we were tough. We got theirs, in the end. There was a chase. I remember running through fields like that one we were just in, right among the horses, climbing over the fences. After we'd lost them, we went into this graveyard, and sat on two stones and talked and ate the candy. We knew they'd be afraid to follow us in there.'

Sonya looked at Ruth in admiration. There were bits of straw in her hair, and for a moment she looked wild and fierce again, like the child who had run fearlessly shrieking through graveyards. Sonya reached out gently to take the straw out, and was surprised when Ruth's whole body shied away and the car swerved into the next lane.

TELECEA

Watch that white ho' walk right up to the fence. They's a rule you cannot go near that fence. Cannot do it. Ho' go right ahead and touch the fence, don't care bout no rule.

Think they got me hid. Think I can't see what they doing. Cannot witness. But I seen out the window and right over that fence too. Ho' looking at a white horse running out in the grass. Wish she could be like him. Free. Stupid bitch don't know He sent that horse. It name Death and it gone tramp her down wif it big old heavy feets. Stupid ho' look at that horse and don't even know he gone step on her head, crunch her up wif his big white teefs.

I touch that fence, how long you think it take before they carry me up here? But *she* don't feel right, oh the poor girl aint that too bad. Oh no of course we will not send her up to Max, oh no, not her, her hole made of candy. And gots her a black bomination to lick it right up. Take out her dick and do it. Oh no Max is not for them nice white girls like her gots to save it for them bad black girls. That Telecea Jones.

Soons I get back in my art room gone make a sculpture picture for them two. Make me a white horse wif one of them long sticky tongues like this animal I seen on TV, got one of them long snouts. It lick them ants up off the ground like a magnet, like it lectric or something, you should seen the way them ants come round and get lickt up! My horse gone have a snout like that dick Billy got. Gone put my sculpture picture right up in her bed. Cause I know she scairt. She don't want no one to find out but I watch and I lissen and I know. Gone put that beastie right in Billy bed and see how do she like her Candy Cane now.

THURSDAY, OCTOBER 15

RUTH

Ruth had promised Mrs Hanson to sit in on a class in the art room as part of her supervisory duty, but she felt highly uncomfortable with the role, and Gladdy Dwight's greeting when she opened the door didn't help.

'Here come Miss Foster. In our art room. What do she want in here, I wonder, Lord? Make her a self-painting? Come and make sure nobody have mess with her empty wall? Come to mess with my art teacher?' None of the other women around the table spoke to her or even raised their heads from their painting, and Ruth was about to give up and head back out the door when Sonya, who'd been mixing paint, appeared beside her, smiling and gesturing in welcome with two blue hands.

'Ruth, please, stay a while,' she said. Her red smock was spattered with paint and her hair was tied back with a red bandanna. At Sonya's signal, Alice Anderson, who was sitting alone at the end of the table, called out to Ruth in her whining voice.

'Hey, Miss Foster, how come you don't want to come look at my painting?'

Ruth still hesitated, but Donny Gitano looked up and told her not to be a stranger.

'If you're worried about that,' she gestured at Sonya's blue hands, 'it's not catching.' Ruth smiled and sat down next to Alice.

She remembered Donny, who had left therapy after two sessions, telling her that it was not her fault. 'It's just that I'm not ready to deal with this shit right now,' Donny had told her kindly. 'I think you do a real good job, and you're a nice lady with a cute appearance. So don't take it personal.'

Now Donny's chivalry had signaled to the others, who relaxed and continued painting and talking. Glancing around the table, Ruth realized that by 'self-painting,' Gladdy had meant self-portraits. Fascinated, she watched Alice work on hers. She had already ruled the white paper with an intricate grid pattern in pencil, and was now sketching a tiny figure which peered out from the lower corner of what looked like faint bars.

'That Alice got paints like everyone else,' Gladdy editorialized from her easel. 'All them fine pretty colors. But she want to use that old light pencil. Let her do what she wants,' she added, in a good facsimile of Sonya's voice. 'She doesn't interfere with *your* paintings.' Ruth found it easy to praise Alice's drawing. Although the tiny stereotyped female figure with its shelf-bust and bouncy hairdo was totally unlike Alice, with her scraggly oily hair and air of neutered sexuality, there was something in the entirety of the composition which made it a revealing self-portrait.

Donny's figure, done neatly, in bright blocks of primary colors, stood with a foot planted squarely at each bottom corner, and the head, with its block of rectangular black hair, exactly in the top center. Donny had painted herself as a weight-lifter, dressed in her usual sleeveless T-shirt and pair of red and black striped shorts, which looked here like an old fashioned prison uniform. In contrast to Donny herself, who was large-breasted, the figure formed a straight narrow line from top to bottom. The head was too small for the body, and the face was painted childishly, like a Halloween pumpkin, with dots for the eye and nose and a straight line of mouth. The muscled arms and shoulders, on the other hand, had received elaborate and loving treatment. Ruth praised this painting too, but she found it strangely disquieting.

Linda, in contrast to her lover, had painted herself as almost all face and no body. The head filled the page, with only vague lines extending downward suggesting the rest. The eyes were the main feature of Linda's painting. They were huge, ringed in different shades of blue, and had a sad quality which made Ruth turn from them to Linda's own sad eyes.

Neither Jody nor her friend had invited her to look, so Ruth sat down quietly next to Alice again, watching how Sonya passed from woman to woman, talking softly and pointing to parts of their paintings. Donny had set a tray of bright paints and a sheet of paper in front of Ruth, but she felt too uncomfortable to actually paint anything.

'Miss Foster don't want to make no self-painting,' Gladdy noted. 'Don't want nothing on her wall, nothing on her paper. Why she got to be so white, Lord?'

Ruth remembered the last time she'd taken art, in high school, when she'd felt ashamed of the clumsy images she'd produced, so unlike the images in her head, and hadn't enjoyed the mess that painting seemed to involve. What she did want was to be Sonya's student, to paint something which Sonya would bend over as she was bending over Donny's painting now, her arm lightly brushing Donny's shoulders, her voice low and intent.

Ruth noticed that Linda, who had finished her painting and cleaned her brushes, had allowed it to be pushed to the edge of the table. Now she edged it right off. The big sad face was under the table, being stepped on by Linda's pointed high heels. 'No!' Ruth wanted to protest. But Sonya had noticed what had happened too, and moving, quickly, she came to sit on Linda's other side.

'Your picture!' she said. 'Please don't ruin it!'

'It doesn't matter.' Linda spoke in a high-pitched little girl's voice. 'It was stupid anyway, I aint no artist. Don't want it.'

'Stop!' Sonya's voice was loud and angry now. 'Stop kicking your picture, I don't want you to destroy it. Pick it up!'

'It's mine, aint it?' Linda whispered, her voice almost tearful now. 'I can do what I want with it.' She was looking for support to Donny, who studiously looked away as if she wanted no part of the situation.

'That's your self-portrait,' Sonya repeated loudly, while Alice got up and crept, crab-wise, to the door, and Gladdy told them, 'Art teacher getting mad now, Lord. All upsetted. Time to end the program. Tune in next week tomorrow.' But ending was not what Sonya had in mind.

'What next!' Gladdy announced, with a kind of resigned disapproval. 'Art teacher gone under that table!'

There was a moment of suspense, then Sonya emerged, holding the paper. With more aggressiveness than Ruth had imagined her capable of, Linda grabbed at it. 'Gimme!' The paper, which was certainly no longer worth saving, ripped in two.

'Donny!' Linda appealed. 'Let's go!'

But Sonya was handing her half back, along with a piece of tape, smoothing it out. 'I don't mean to push you around,' she told Linda, very gently. 'But look at those eyes you painted.' Linda, openly tearful now, held one piece in each hand.

'Here, give me the tape.' It was Donny. 'You heard what the lady said, baby. She said it was good. You shouldn't rip your shit up. What she's trying to tell you is, don't put yourself down so much.'

'Yeah!' Jody, on the other side of the table, smoothed her platinum duck tail as she spoke. 'You make a picture of yourself, see, then you rip it up, it's like you tore up your own self!' The women smiled and nodded, pleased with their new insight and with themselves, and Linda shyly accepted the repaired picture from Donny. Alice, who had been hovering near the door, came back.

'Time for the music to start up,' Gladdy announced. 'Time for the lights.' They began to clean up now, putting their paintings, including the contested one, into individual large folders.

'It's all over, honey,' Ruth heard Sonya tell Alice. 'I'm not yelling anymore. But see, it was OK. Nothing bad happened.'

Donny lingered for a moment after the others had left. 'See you tomorrow,' she told Sonya. 'Long as you keep that little devil out of here.'

'I can't very well get her in here when she's up in Max,' Sonya told her, and Ruth felt a pang of guilt for not noticing Telecea's absence before.

Then Donny's eyes rested on Ruth. 'Take good care of my art teacher, OK? And you stay sweet.' She winked enormously, including both of them, and left.

Ruth sat frozen by the remark. So what Candy had said was true. The women were talking. Everyone had left too suddenly, and the silence was deafening. She was relieved when Sonya got up and unpeeled Gladdy's painting from her easel to show her. It was a bright, minutely detailed scene, without perspective, in which a small brown child and a large black woman walked together down a dusty road into the sunset.

'It's beautiful,' Ruth murmured. 'As good as Grandma Moses.' Her own words released her, and, unable to stop, she heard herself babble about the art room, the paintings, how wonderful Sonya had been, how much she had learned.

'Did you?' Sonya stopped her. 'Did you learn?'

Ruth nodded, speechless.

'I'm so glad!' Sonya looked at her with her direct, clear gaze. 'I respect your work so much, and after last week, I thought . . . I guess I needed for you to respect mine. I don't know whether you noticed,' she added, 'but I was really happy when you came in. . . .'

Joy welled up in Ruth. A few dirty brushes had been left on the table and she took them to the sink to wash. Sonya, who was sitting on the table, held up the paper which Ruth had left blank.

'What about this?' she asked. 'Want to take it home and paint?'

Ruth shook her head. 'I used to write a little,' she admitted, 'but I've never really been much good at art.'

'Well," said Sonya, 'if you felt like it, you could always look at the blank paper and see if you see anything there. The image you imagine, that's the first step, anyway.' Both of them looked at her blank wall, and Ruth had a momentary and frightening sensation that the monsters from Telecea's wall had invaded it, crawling over with their claws and deformed feet.

'So?' Sonya asked. 'Did you see anything?' Ruth smiled and shook her head as they left the room together.

CANDY

'It's all clear, Candy,' Lou reported. 'She's gone.'

'Where? Gone home?' Candy asked her.

'Nah.' Both Lou and Frankie, who'd come together to get her in the pool room, started laughing, and Lou did a quick handstand. 'She's gone up to get her baby. But she had her briefcase with her, so you know she aint coming back.'

'And if she did, she wouldn't notice nothing,' Frankie added. 'Blind.' The two of them exploded laughing again. It was getting on Candy's nerves, which was bad to start with. She hadn't taken no risks for so long it was almost like starting over.

'No, seriously,' Frankie went on. 'That is one nice looking bitch, especially now she got her nose opened up for her.'

'That's what I done for you, huh baby?' Lou pounced on her and they went down on the dirty pool room floor.

'Well, let's go ahead and do it if we're gonna, huh?' Candy wished she knew Foster had left the building, not just the mental health corridor, but it couldn't be helped. 'Frankie, you're gonna be out the window ready for what I hand you, right?'

'Yeah, I guess, in this rain,' Frankie grumbled.

'The rain's cool,' Candy told her. 'Hard to see through, and aint nobody with no sense out in it.'

Lou walked around them both on her hands. 'I'll be the lookout and grab the shit, both,' she said. 'Just hand it to my feets and I'll run off with my hands.'

'Hand it to your ass.' Candy wished they would stop acting so damn juvenile and get the thing done. 'I bet your key don't work anyway, Frankie.'

'What you want to bet?' Frankie took off for outside the window, and Candy and Lou headed down the hall, to the old iron door that separated the mental health corridor off from the rest of the floor. The key had been took so many times that the door was always left unlocked now, but it was noisy, and they opened it as quiet as they could, just wide enough for Candy to slip through. Lou stayed by the door, ready to kick it for a warning if anyone came, so Candy could hide in the bathroom till it was clear.

She walked down the corridor on tiptoe, even though it was so dark she knew they'd all left. They all left early, anyways, except Foster, and she was upstairs now, with Lehrman. Candy wondered what if Foster had forgot something and came back for it. Thinking about it spoiled her concentration, so she made her mind go blank, just paying attention to what she could see and hear, like when she was working the streets. She took the tissue out of her pocket and tried Frankie's key in the door of Lynda's office they all hung out in. It opened right up, and there was Frankie under the window. Candy looked all around, but there wasn't nothing to take except for Lynda's little clock radio that she knew for a fact wasn't worth more than twenty or so. She pushed up her window, slit a nice neat hole in the screen with her razor, and dropped the radio out into Frankie's hands. The typewriter would of been more like it, but it was so big they wasn't no way to get it out. They was some papers on the desk, and she gave the top one a quick read.

> Ms. Bradley, who was referred by another one of my clients, appears to be a tense but intelligent young woman, with considerable self-awareness, and potential ego strength. She appears to be a good candidate for long-term therapy.

That must be Foster, with all her talk about how she didn't repeat nothing to no one, talking bout Loraine for them all to read. At least she wasn't saying nothing bad, as far as Candy could tell. She looked at the paper underneath.

> Maria comes to us with a history of violent behavior and irrational thinking. She does not at this time appear to be a candidate for insight therapy. Her cottage officer has been instructed as to the necessity for regular administration of the medication prescribed.

That one had Thorne's name on it. Frankie was tapping on the window, and Candy snapped out of it. In Thorne's office, that she'd been expecting so much from, the cheap bastard didn't have nothing in there at all. Then in the desk drawer she did find a nice heavy fountain pen that had his name wrote on it in gold letters, egotistical bastard like he was, but that could be scraped off. And up on the rack was a good pair of men's furlined gloves. Candy was just starting to slice at the screen when she heard Lou bang, but real loud and crazy, like it was already too late, and then right away the iron door creaked and she knew there wasn't no time to make it across the hall to the bathroom. She closed Thorne's door, signaled for Frankie to get down, and flattened herself out behind the desk.

She could feel her heart beating double-time and her mind get speedy, the way it always used to do. What if it was Thorne, coming back for something he forgot, maybe his pen. She'd blow him right there. Or do any damn thing he wanted. 'God,' she prayed, 'just let me off this time and I'll be good from now on, I promise. . . .'

Thank God she heard girls' voices. And now the words in her head switched to 'Don't let it be Foster. Please don't let me get busted by Foster.' Whoever it was was probly going in the office where she'd already been, and she got ready for the scream when they saw the window. But it didn't come. There was some slamming and rustling noises and then they was coming down the hall again and it wasn't Foster at all but them other two.

'What gets me is the way she takes all the good cases and leaves us the pits and then she blames us,' one of them said.

'Yeah, but maybe she'll change her attitude to us now, if you know what I mean, Nan,' the other one went. 'Running up and down to that art room all the time. . . .' And then the iron door groaned shut, and Candy was home free.

She straightened up, all stiff, and heard a kind of thumping on the ceiling that was probly goddamn Telecea Jones banging her fool head on the floor. Now she wanted to get out of there so bad she felt like running without taking no precautions, but she was careful, and in a few minutes they was all three out in the rain, cussing out the shrinks for being such tightwads so they had to take all kind of risks for nothing, which was about what the radio amounted to, split three ways. Frankie hadn't seen her take the gloves and pen that was safe in her shirt, and Candy didn't see why she should open her mouth about them, seeing she was the one that took all the risks. She was glad she didn't say nothing a minute later, cause they both turned on her.

'How come you didn't get nothing out of Foster's office?' Frankie asked her. 'I know for a fact she keeps all kinds of shit in there.'

'Don't you know?' Lou came out of the side of her mouth all nasty. 'Candy-Cane just loves her shrinky-poo to pieces. She wouldn't touch a thing of hers.' Candy's fingers felt itchy on her razor and she was still speedy and hyper and ready to beef.

'I don't rip off people that's cool with me, unlike some bitches that would rob they own mother if they was something in it.' She waited, but Frankie just spat on the ground and grabbed Lou by the shoulder. 'She aint worth no D,' Candy heard her mutter, as they walked off. 'Least we know who not to do no business with no more.'

'You better give me my share if you know what's good for you, bitch,' she hissed after them, but she knew that was the last she'd hear about that radio. 'I got mine, anyway,' she thought, as she walked around the yard in the rain trying to slow herself down. She knew Billy'd be glad when she showed her the shit, which she wasn't expecting since Candy hadn't told her a thing about it. She didn't want Billy to take no risks, near as she was to her date.

SONYA

Sonya sat across from Ruth in one of the red leather upholstered booths at Nina's, taking footage for an erotic film. Ruth would photograph well, with her thin, taut lips, her perfect teeth which had almost certainly never been subjected to braces, her high cheekbones with the skin drawn tight over them, and her dark blue eyes. Sonya's mother had always maintained that blue-eyed people had no soul.

'Why you so white?' Gladdy had asked Ruth today in the art room. Sonya smiled, thinking of how impressed Ruth had been. There had been a positively passionate expression on her face during the episode with Linda. Crawling around on the floor was the kind of impulsive thing Ruth herself would never do, which was probably part of the appeal.

Lately she'd started taking down her hair as soon as she got in the car, having explained that she only wore it up at work to look professional and unseductive.

'So you're seductive with your hair down?' Sonya had teased her, and Ruth had blushed in that amazing way of hers, not going red all over, or blotchy, but just those two red spots high on her cheeks. Sonya wondered if there was anything she didn't do elegantly.

Ruth was still talking about the self-portraits, which had obviously made quite an impression, and Sonya noted again that although she was too uptight to pick up a brush herself, she had quite a remarkable eye. She noticed the waitress, a tall broad shouldered woman with short curly hair, watching the animated Ruth with obvious admiration. 'She thinks we're lovers,' Sonya thought. 'She envies me.'

'I keep thinking about all the prison imagery, the quaiity of being locked up in their work,' Ruth was saying. 'The stripes on Donny's shorts, the grid around Alice's painting. . . .' Sonya nodded.

'Gladdy's the only one who doesn't put some kind of cage around her pictures,' she said, 'and she doesn't paint in the present tense.' The waitress came to take their order, beaming at Ruth, who didn't seem to notice. Sonya wondered if she'd even noticed her, or the other women, mostly discreet lesbian couples, who patronized Nina's. Sonya imagined bending close to her and kissing her on the lips, then leading her straight out of this place to her loft. She imagined those thin lips opening as she slowly ran her tongue down Ruth's long white neck, then touched it to the tip of the small nipple. Would Ruth be shocked if she actually made a pass, or had she secretly been waiting for it for days?

'The woman's straight,' Sonya reminded herself. She'd probably act horrified. Or else leave Victor immediately and show up at Sonya's door the next day with wedding rings. 'Straight women are poison,' she told herself for the hundredth time. 'Keep your hands off.'

Ruth licked her finger, then reached over and touched a place on Sonya's cheek. 'Paint,' she explained, as Sonya's whole body reverberated from the touch.

'At a certain point,' she addressed the camera. 'Whatever's meant to happen will just happen.' After all, no one could expect her to resist this fervent snow queen forever.

TELECEA

Fools think they can put me up here, hide me so I can't bear no witness. Don't they know He see it all? Use me for His messenger, but He don't need me to see. His eyes got them cover with they filth and they lying, aint no place they can hide. They can put me up here, send me to the mental place, I been there before. Won't nothing save them now.

Took and grab that poor old lady out of here. Who know where they put her now. Got that devil Proudy back, ulcer stomach and all. Give them other girls up here whatever they wants. Recreation. Them card games for they ho'ing and gambling self. She say, Go on, take a shower honey. Don't pay no mind to that nut with her noise can't let her out can't no one go in there she just like an animal bite you in the throat. Job, they try him too, give him them worms and maggots right in his skin and all them boils, spit on him too, burn his skin and break his arm so the bone be digging right in him. Or like they done that Jesus, put nails in his dick to try and make him take it back.

Don't no one come in here. Aint seen no face. Just that rotten dickhead Moody when he put in the food smiling with them big yellow teef. That devil need to get smash right in them old stinking teef of his, that dick-face. Talking bout, Come on cutey pie they say you aint stopped your noise since you been up here well come on and try your tricks now, Daddy's here. Put his big old yellow dick fingers right in my food. And spit in it too and I seen his yellow cum in them mash potatoes. I will not touch nothing he give me.

That what they trying to do. Put me in a cage like an animal don't never let me out starve me to death. See can they make me do what they want. But I aint never said Sonya name. I know she be trying to come up here all the time. So I be waiting. Aint never said her name. Aint never give away our plan.

FRIDAY, OCTOBER 16

RUTH

Dave sat on the edge of the chair by Ruth's desk.

'It *is* strange the way they never touch your office,' he said speculatively, and she wondered whether he suspected her of breaking in to steal his gloves and fountain pen herself or merely organizing the plot.

'Nan's and Cindy's offices weren't broken into either this time,' she reminded him. 'Anyway, they'd better get the lock changed. How long did they take last time, a month?' There was a light knock on her door, and he got up.

'Let me know if you hear anything,' he said accusingly. 'That pen was a gift from when I graduated from med school.'

Ruth was surprised to see Candy waiting outside the door. 'Excuse me, you free now?' Her voice was hoarse and she flopped in the leather chair like a boneless rag doll in her faded jeans and white sweatshirt. She wore no make-up and her bleached hair hung limply around her pale face.

'I got the flu or something,' she sighed. 'I feel like shit, but I got this bunch of weirdos to take around. From some school for butches or something.' She handed over the tour slip. Ruth read 'Women's School Study Group on Institutional Oppression.'

'What I wanted to ask you,' Candy went on, 'was could you maybe just take them up the art room? The girls been coming around saying shit to them and I just can't take it today. I need to sit down.'

'Sure.' Ruth felt glad that Candy had asked her for something the way one might ask a friend. 'Why don't you just go back to the cottage and lie down, and I'll take care of them?'

'I can't. Shit's been missing out of girls' rooms, so all this week we're on restriction. You aint allowed back in there till five-thirty. Unless you're on bedrest, and you know I'd die before I'd let that quack mess with me. Listen, here they come.'

Ruth opened the door and was face to face with a group of six very young women and one slightly older one whom she thought must be their teacher. With their short hair and jeans they were obviously lesbians, but they looked nothing like the trim stylish dykes in their little leather vests who sometimes sat at the booths at Nina's giving each other soulful looks and holding hands under the table.

'This is a therapist that works here, Miss Foster,' Candy introduced her. 'She's gonna take you up to the art room.' The six young women stared suspiciously at Ruth, obviously disappointed at Candy's abdication. Only the teacher smiled and mumbled her name, Beth something.

Ruth led them up the stairs. She saw Mabe and Edie at the bottom, pointing and laughing, and understood why Candy had been so eager to hand the group over to her. Halfway up the stairs one of the women approached her.

'So you're a therapist here,' she said accusingly. 'Do you prescribe much medication?' Ruth looked away from the accusing adolescent face. 'I'm not an MD,' she said. 'I'm not authorized to prescribe medication at all.'

'But I'm sure you can make recommendations to the doctor.'

'I try to stay away from medication unless it's absolutely necessary,' Ruth told her. 'I stick to talking therapy myself.' The whole group had paused midway up the stairs, intent on her words.

'But is that what these women need?' asked another, sweet-faced one. 'Talking therapy?' She made it sound like a dirty word.

'Yes, I think they do need it, among a whole lot of other things,' Ruth answered. She was worn out already, and hoped that Sonya, whom she was sure they'd approve of more, would take them off her hands.

'But is it their problem anyway,' said the first one. 'Or society's?'

'It certainly starts with society,' Ruth said. 'But it becomes theirs too.' The teacher, who was attractive in a thin boyish kind of way, nodded encouragingly. Probably she and Sonya would fall in love at first sight.

Gladdy opened the door of the art room to them, a steady stream of talk already on her lips. Sonya's eyes met Ruth's from across the room, and she nodded slightly as if she'd taken in the whole situation at a glance.

'Now who we got here?' Gladdy broadcast genially, as they filed in. 'I would say cracker boys off a dirt farm down South. Way some of them crackers live, Lord! Wash theyself three times, when they gets born, when they gets married, and when they gets laid out! And they call colored people dirty!' All the women stared, transfixed, at Gladdy, who, pleased with the attention, went on. 'I would say cracker *boys*, but look here, Lord! Some of them boys got titties! But tell me, why any white girl want to come in here dressed up so nasty?' And, shaking her head, Gladdy turned back to her easel.

'Them nuts can make a lot of sense at times, can't they girls,' Fran commented loudly from the long table.

Sonya, who had been talking intently to the teacher, now turned back to the group of six or seven women, all busily making ashtrays out of clay.

'These women came in here because they want to learn what prisons are really about,' she said. 'They're afraid if they just ask the staff like most people do, they won't hear the truth. Would you be willing to talk to them a while? And you can ask them any questions you may have about them, too.'

Ruth knew she could go about her own business now. Donny had begun to organize chairs, and Sonya had that look she'd had at the opening, of a choreographer pulling strings for some larger effect. Telecea had been there too, that day. How easily they all forgot about Telecea when she wasn't there to remind them!

When she found Candy sitting on the bottom of the steps with her head on her knees, she was glad that she'd left the art room. The rush of feeling was scary. She wanted to take Candy home and put her to bed, to bring her soup and read to her. An anger rose in her that she was unable to do these simple things.

'Candy,' she said softly. Candy didn't raise her head and Ruth saw that the obvious way to make contact with this sick, sad child was by touch. A light touch on the shoulder? Sonya would have done it without thinking about it, but her own hand felt frozen. She wished they were in her office where it was so much safer.

'Candy, I left them up there, with Sonya. I . . . Are you OK?' she whispered absurdly. Candy, who was obviously not OK, said something into her hands.

Then she lifted her head. 'I told you, I think I got the flu,' she said hoarsely.

Making a tremendous effort, Ruth reached out and put her wet hand on Candy's forehead. It was very hot. 'Are you taking anything for this?' she asked, and immediately regretted it when Candy's eyes flashed at her suspiciously. She must think Ruth was accusing her of being high.

'They won't even give you no aspirin if you're not on bedrest,' she said. 'I don't want no medication anyways. All I want is for them to leave me alone and let me lay down.'

That a desire this simple should be refused was criminal. As Ruth began to speak she saw her words as objects, falling in some firm, unretractable pattern. 'Listen Candy, I have to go home now,' she said. 'But there's this cot just sitting in the closet in my office. I'll write you a note to give to anyone who comes, but no one should come. They don't have a key for the iron door so you shouldn't have any trouble getting out. You can just rest there until it's time to go back to the cottage.'

Candy looked amazed as they walked through the already empty corridors to Ruth's office. She hesitated at the door. 'Miss Foster, you got to watch yourself in here, you know that. I mean, hey, it's not such a big deal. I been sick on my feet before.'

Ruth shook her head. 'You don't need to stay in here if it makes you uncomfortable,' she said. 'But it's fine with me.' Candy nodded in bewildered acceptance.

'Why don't I stop off at the bathroom first.' She backed out the door. Ruth knew she was being given a final chance to reconsider, but she'd made her decision. She looked over her office. All her papers were filed away as usual. There was nothing to worry about there. She was the only one who was careful, although she guessed she could hardly call herself that any more. The others left everything out on their desks even though the wing was broken into every few weeks. For a moment she worried that she might be setting Candy up for trouble. If someone found her here, would they try to blame her for the break-ins? She'd write a note taking full responsibility herself and leave it with Candy. They could call her at home if there was any problem.

Ruth took the cot out of the closet and unfolded it. She laid the soft blue blanket on top of it, and plugged in the hot water. Next to the hot plate she arranged some cookies she kept in reserve, the tea bags and hot chocolate, and two aspirin, labeled and neatly folded into a napkin. Candy came in as she finished the note of explanation.

All of a sudden there was no space in the office. Ruth grabbed her briefcase and headed awkwardly for the door.

'Be sure to unplug the hot plate when you're finished,' she said. 'I fixed the door so it'll lock behind you. I said in the note to call me at home if someone finds you here and has any questions.' At the last minute she had to add, 'I know you won't let anyone else in here.' She wished she hadn't said it, but Candy was smiling gently.

'Don't you go home and worry now, Miss Foster,' she said. 'I won't get you in no trouble. I know how to be cool.'

'I hope you feel better soon.' Ruth heard her voice squeak, fervent and formal at once.

'Thanks, Miss Foster.' Candy's voice was a good solid sound behind her and Ruth tried hard to hold on to it, but as soon as she closed the iron door she felt a sense of foreboding. She could picture Dave coming for something he'd left behind, finding Candy, and shaking his head slowly and ominously at her note. 'I'm afraid I saw it coming,' he'd tell the others. 'Tried to intervene but it was already too late. Total disintegration of boundaries. . . .'

She decided to sit outside in front and wait for Sonya, who was the only one who might smile and tell her that it was alright, that nothing bad would happen. But when Sonya finally came out, she had the teacher of the women's group with her.

'I told Beth I was sure you wouldn't mind giving her a ride back,' Sonya explained. 'The others left, and we got to talking.'

'They were starting to get on my nerves, anyway.' Beth smiled at Ruth. 'They're sweet, but so young, you know? And I wanted to get to know the two of you if I could. Tell me about that women who showed us around first, Candy? She fascinated me.'

Ruth felt her initial anger at the intrusion dissipate. She knew it was more prudent not to tell anyone, even Sonya, what she'd done, and this decided it. It was fun driving back, with Beth talking an easy stream of impressions and observations of Redburn and Sonya squeezed between them in the middle. Ruth relaxed into silence, light-headed from the smell and feel of Sonya so close to her, and from the strangeness of what she'd done.

She got home before Victor, and sat at the kichen table with a block of yellow paper. 'I drove Sonya and a woman named Beth home today,' she wrote. 'They're both lesbians.' Then, underneath, she scribbled very fast,

> I wonder what it would be like to just leave things. To get sick of a job and go on to another one, to get sick of a city and move on, to get sick of a man and leave him one day. . . .

She read over what she'd written and wondered if she'd unconsciously been trying to get herself fired this afternoon. Where was Candy now, she wondered. Had she already gone safely back to the cottage? Or was she searching through Ruth's things? The phone rang and she jumped, crumpling the page guiltily.

CANDY

Candy was sick. Sitting in the ice-cold flag room, she shivered and sneezed, and her hands on the machine was freezing cold. Five minutes later, though, she was sweating, rolling up the sleeves of her sweatshirt to get some air. She knew she had a fever, but there was no way she was gonna let that bastard near her just to get on bedrest. Someone must of got on his case, cause he'd stopped prescribing hysterectomies right and left like he had the year he did her. Now all he did was breathe on girls with his nasty old-man bad breath, give their boobs a good twist saying he was checking for something, and get in a free feel with his spotty hands, then give you a cold pill or some aspirin. They could stuff their bed rest up their ass.

If the goddamn cottage wasn't shut up on restriction it would of been alright, cause even Delaney would of let her go early, the way she was sneezing on them flags, and then she could of gone to bed. And if Billy wasn't so fucked up around sickness she could of brung her toast and tea in bed and some magazines, 'True Confessions' and shit, that Candy liked to look at when she was sick and maybe watch her stories at the same time. But Billy always said sick people smelled bad and looked worse, so Candy had slept alone last night, and had to do for herself today. It was true she hadn't bothered to put on no make-up or do her hair this morning, but she knew she still looked a whole lot better than that Grace Powers bitch Billy was messing with again and had even brought in the flag room with her, that looked like nothing but street and smelled like cheap cunt and cum and dirty needles, no matter how much she tried to cover it up with that dime store perfume of hers.

Candy had to be excused to go to the toilet that she never used up here but now she was sick and couldn't help it. She wouldn't be surprised if she caught something off it. When she got back in the flag room, Delaney told her there was a tour for her up front. She thought of getting someone else to take it, but anything was better than sitting there freezing her ass and letting Billy make a fool of her, and anyways, maybe she could get something off of them. She hoped it was men in business suits, a bunch of johns walking in here to get petted up a little. Last time one of them slipped her a five after she'd talked real sweet to him and let him feel up her leg under the table in the library while he told her all about his wife that didn't like 'doing it.' She decided to look and see was it men, and if it was, run and fix herself up before taking them around.

But it wasn't no men, it was a group of them feminists. She guessed they was all butches except for one that looked more together and must of been the leader or something, but the butches she knew in the street or even in here tried to dress in a way that was pleasing to others, even it if was just them weird mans undershirts that Donny and them liked to wear, and these ones hadn't even tried.

They all had on either overhauls or jeans and the kind of nasty looking haircuts she remembered from when she was little and some kids would have their hair cut by their moms putting a bowl over their head and then you could tell by just looking that they couldn't afford no real haircut and was dirt poor and probly had cooties too. But these broads couldn't be that poor, or what were they doing in here touring some prison?

She took them up to the chapel and library first, cause there wasn't never anybody there, but they started right in fussing. One of them came right up in her face and started in with, 'Would it be possible for us to meet some of the women and really talk with them?' They was still up in the library, but Candy knew that sooner or later she'd have to take them back downstairs and past Four Corners on their way to the cottages, where everybody that had got out of work would be hanging.

'Don't worry, you gonna see plenty of women in a minute,' she mumbled, thinking they was probly going to hear some too. 'But you got any questions, you sposed to ask me, cause I'm your tour guide.' It hurt her voice to talk, and her head was hurting too.

'What reading materials are allowed in here?' It was the same broad, peering her eyes all over the library books on the shelves like she was some kind of spy or something. 'Are the women here allowed to receive gay and lesbian publications?'

'I don't know what they got in here, I don't use the library myself,' she said, acting good and retarded, but as soon as they got in the downstairs hall the same one started in again.

'Are many of the women in here LESBIANS?' she said, all loud and ignorant. Candy just shrugged like she never heard that word, but they was up to Four Corners now, and Edie was following them, with Mabe right behind her, both of them walking in that clumpy flat-footed white girl way all of them had. The leader had noticed them, and Candy felt mortified.

'Cut the shit, Edie,' she called out, meaning it to sound joking, but it came out nasty, probly cause she felt so damn sick. 'This my tour.'

Mabe and Edie started laughing. 'Oh, excuse me, Candy,' Edie said. 'I didn't know it was your tour. I figured it was your people, huh Battle?'

'Yeah,' agreed Mabe. 'We was just saying, Candy aint never had no visits before and now all her folks is up here to see her, well aint she got one big funny family, huh Edie?'

Candy knew if she stayed there any longer she was gonna have to beef, sick or not, cause bad as these creeps was, Mabe and Edie was going too far. She told the leader just a minute, ran down to Foster's office and without even thinking bout it, knocked on her door to ask her would she take them up to Lehrman's room. After a minute the door opened and 'the dick doctor,' like Telecea called him, walked out.

'Come on in, Candy,' Foster told her, obviously glad to get rid of him. She looked at Candy hard and told her she looked sick. Then she said she'd be glad to take the tour. Candy figured she was just as glad to have an excuse to go up the art room, but still, it was alright of her. After Foster'd took them up, Candy sat down on the steps. She knew she better get her ass in gear cause in a minute they was all gonna come trouping down again, but it was just too hard to move.

In one way she wished Foster hadn't said nothing about her being sick. No one else had even noticed it except for Billy if you could call that noticing, and she guessed she ought to be glad that someone cared, even if it was just her shrink that was paid to, but somehow it made her feel worse. It was like she'd been doing alright up to now, feeling like shit on the outside but not really noticing it too much inside, until Foster came along.

Foster came back down the stairs then, alone, and Candy put her head down on her knees until she could fix her face in one place. When she managed to get it together Foster was actually sitting down on the stairs next to her, with them red spots on her cheeks, probly cause she just came from Lehrman.

She wanted to know did Candy have a fever, and then she reached out real slow like it scared her to do it, and put a sweaty hand on her forehead. She asked was Candy taking anything for it, and at first Candy thought she meant was she high. Then all of a sudden she was speed-rapping about some cot in her office and how everyone else had left, she was just about to leave herself so why didn't Candy go lie down. Even though Foster was freaked and nervous and had probly started to regret it the minute she'd said it, Candy was still surprised. Here was tight-ass Foster that no one as far as she knew had even *tried* to get to bring nothing in, cause you could tell from one look at her that she'd rather die than break a fucking rule, doing something that only officers that really wanted something from you, probly some pussy, would do. And Candy knew in this case it wasn't bout that.

Foster was sure going through some changes. Before she wouldn't of been caught dead sitting down on no dirty steps in her little wool pantsuit, or touching no one like she had, or even talking to Candy the way she had lately, like they was both people or something. Candy didn't know how she felt about laying down in some therapy office, especially next door to where she'd been ripping shit off, but she said yeah cause she wanted to show Foster she heard where she was coming from. And anyways, it beat a blank.

She went and hung out in the bathroom a while so Foster would have time to hide anything she wanted to in her office, or change her mind, though Candy didn't really think she'd change it. She wasn't about that kind of back and forth shit, not like that Lehrman bitch, that would give you something and then five minutes later take it back.

When she walked back in the office, Foster had laid out the cot and made it up like a real bed, with this soft blanket on it and the hot plate plugged in with cookies in a little napkin next to it. She was all uptight, halfway out the door already with her coat and briefcase, probly worried that Candy would think she wanted to freak off with her.

'Hey, relax,' Candy wished she could say. 'I aint stone blind, I know you got the hots for Sonya, and on top of that we're both as fem as we could be.'

But Foster hadn't changed so much you could lay something like that on her. She fussed around, showing how the door locked itself and how to set the alarm clock and the hotplate and told Candy not to let anyone else in, and then she was gone. At first after she'd left Candy wished she hadn't said that last, like she figured the minute she left out, Candy would call Billy in for a quick fuck or something. But then she decided she didn't mind, cause saying that showed that she was still tight-ass Foster after all – she hadn't gone and traded in her whole personality for a new one.

Candy made sure the door was locked and the little curtain pulled so that if anybody walked by they wouldn't see her. She took the blue cup and made herself some nice sweet coffee in it. It was funny to be drinking out the cup she usually just looked at, and at first she felt good and cozy, like she was on the outside or something. Next to the cookies Foster had wrapped up these two aspirins in a napkin she had wrote 'aspirin' on, just so Candy wouldn't mistake them for some dangerous drug, maybe heroin or something. Candy laughed, thinking of her writing the little label. She was probly driving home right now wondering did she do the wrong thing and would Candy forget to unplug the hotplate and burn down the whole building. Candy's head was hurting bad, so she took the two aspirins with some more coffee, and set the clock.

At first she wondered would someone come back like they had that other time she got the gloves and pen, but it was real quiet, and after a while she lay down under the blue blanket, using her coat for a pillow. The blanket was pretty soft, but it itched her nose a little. It smelled like Foster, or maybe the kind of perfume she wore. Course her and Foster wouldn't never get down because of both being fem. They looked alike, everyone said so. And Foster was police.

It was a asshole thing even to think about. It was probly the fever that was making her do it. She played with her titties until they was hard, and thought about if Foster could see what she was doing under this blanket that smelled like her. Then she thought of Billy's mouth on her, which is what she always pictured when she did it to herself, with one finger on the inside pushing up and one tickling hard and steady on the outside and it was nice and long and slow just like when she was high, and right before she came she thought 'Better get used to it, girl, cause Billy's gonna be gone soon,' which wasn't what she wanted to come on, the tears wet on her face with the wet on her hand. That, along with the aspirin and fever, must of worked like a sleeping pill, cause she started drifting off.

Someone was screaming in her ear.

'Mom, I'm sick, don't send me to school today,' she cried out loud, but it was a alarm clock and she didn't know where the fuck she was and couldn't find where to put her finger to stop it for a long time.

She felt dizzy. There was a banging on her head and she knew she was in Foster's office, and she was leaving in two weeks, and a blanket was itching her face, and she couldn't stop crying. It was getting dark outside. Her heart was beating all fast and crazy. What was she doing? She hated Foster for leaving her in here. What the fuck was Foster trying to prove? She had to get out.

She neated up the office as fast as she could, folding the blanket and putting it and the cot back in the closet. They wasn't no way to wash the blue cup without taking it to the bathroom so she stuffed it down her shirt.

The hotplate was unplugged and everything was cool, and Candy shut the door, locking it behind her. Then she left out in a hurry, still feeling dizzy. The cup was a hard lump in her chest, and she wished she'd left it in the office.

SONYA

Sonya placed ashtray after identical ashtray on the shelf, glad that it was Friday. She'd proposed clay as a way to break out of the boring routine this group seemed to be settling into, but Linda had immediately discovered the coil method of ashtray making, and the others had joined in happily, ignoring Sonya's suggestions that they try faces or animals. She supposed that she ought to be deriving some satisfaction from the fact that the group was functioning so well together, even including Alice in their production line, but she was bored to death, and glad of the distraction when Ruth brought in the group of young dykes.

It was easy for her to get the two groups talking, and she enjoyed the obvious admiration of the teacher, Beth, who was quite striking with her hard, runner's body, her severe haircut and her bony Jewish face. Donny, Jody, and Fran had been describing the various injustices of the system to their visitors, who'd been listening respectfully. Now there was a lull which Gladdy seized on. She sauntered over to the table from the easel, and slowly pulled a large piece of clay out from under her dress.

'Bet none of these raggedy-ass crackers knew old Gladdy was pregnant,' she announced. 'Praise the Lord, it's another boy.' One of the women gave a small involuntary scream, and Beth, who had obviously been trying hard to take Redburn in stride, shuddered. Sonya decided it was time for clean-up.

'God don't like ugly,' she heard Gladdy tell the last of the visitors as she escorted them out of the door.

'Oh dear!' Beth shook her head. 'And I thought the less formally we dressed the better.' She'd been delighted with the offer to stay a while and ride home with Ruth, and while Sonya was pretty sure that Ruth wouldn't mind, she hoped she'd be a little jealous.

As it turned out, Ruth didn't seem to notice one way or another. She was in that remote, preoccupied mood that Sonya found especially appealing. She drove fast and silently, and seemed to barely listen to Beth's stream of talk. Sonya sat wedged between the two warm bodies, enjoying the ride and aware of how much she'd missed being touched in the last months.

TELECEA

What they doing now, they pretending I aint here. Try and disappear me. Girl, you so black you might as well be gone. Can't see you in the dark no-way. Not the light neither no more. Ruth Foster, Sonya spose to come. Somebody spose to come. But don't nobody come.

They be putting medicine, poison in my food, make me all mix up, make me sleep. In my water. Day and night come all together. How you spose to tell is you awake or asleep?

One time I seen that ho' Candy ride that white horse. Ride it up and over the fence and be gone. But then I seen her still in here. How you spose to know?

Been like this ever since when I throwed his piss-come food back in Moody dickface. You allow to beat peoples but aint spose to mark no one up. Aint spose to bang no one head on the floor. After that no one have came. And I seen and hear what I don't want to seen. See Sonya take out her dick and put it in Ruth Foster. Little childrens all burn up and scream. And when my Granny come and beat me, scream in my ear.

They be sneaking that poison food in at night. Put me to sleep so I can't see them come in. Wake up and it be there. Got so much maggots and shit that filthy food be moving, waving around by its ownself. But I try and eat something every day cause I know them.

Oh, why have she starve to death? We been putting in that nice good food each and every day. Mmmmm! Why aint she ate it? Poor thing must of went mental, it's not our fault.

Try and eat, but after one bite I gets sick. And my own bones be sticking me.

Now I don't care if they takes me to the mental place or what. Just so someone come in here. So I know they aint all forgot. So I know they aint disappeared me yet.

SATURDAY, OCTOBER 17

RUTH

Ruth sat in the kitchen, drinking tea for her sore throat and trying to read, but the horrible thing she'd done at work ticked inside her like a time bomb, and she couldn't concentrate.

Maybe it was already decided. Maybe she'd go in on Monday and they wouldn't let her through the door. If only she could be sure Candy was alright. 'Please,' she bargained with the gods. 'You can fire me, I don't care. Just leave her alone.'

Outside the window the young man from next door walked briskly down the street, holding his small blond daughter by the hand. He had discarded his suit for a bulky white fisherman's sweater. Ruth had run into his wife, who was about her own age, in the supermarket the other day. She was hugely pregnant, and told Ruth that her mother would be coming to stay when the baby was born.

Ruth imagined what her own mother would say when she told her she'd lost her job. 'Wouldn't it be a good time for the two of you to go ahead and get married and have a baby.' Or maybe, 'But Ruth, I thought at least your *work* was secure.' Then she'd ask Ruth not to say anything to her father, because of his heart. It would be better to make up some lie for them of course. She could always just say she'd decided to switch jobs.

Now Mary and Sandy came out together, both in jeans and sweatshirts, with their big dog straining on its leash. Ruth noticed the way they walked quite close together without actually touching and tried to imagine what it would be like to take the dog for a walk with the person you lived with and have to be careful not to touch hands. Of course, they could go to a gay bar at night. There had been one a few chapters back in *Sita*. She found the place and reread the description.

> The wonderful, near sinister rhythm of butch and disco and hard bartenders, the great, tall black beauties of women, tough and gay and at the edge.

It was almost impossible to imagine Mary and Sandy there, but she could see herself, drunk and with her hair cut short and messy, like the women on that tour. It would probably start happening to her now — Friday had been the first step. She'd be sitting there, sunk in despair, and Candy would come in.

'You spoiled my whole life,' she'd say. 'I just hope you know that.' Ruth tried to start it again, differently. This time it was Sonya coming toward her at the bar. 'Ruth — you — here? I've been looking everywhere for you, I was so worried. It'll be OK now. . . .' Sonya opened her arms, as the front door slammed, and Victor came in with the neatly folded laundry. 'I feel pretty lousy,' she told him. 'If I go back to bed will you come and bring me some orange juice?'

He brought the juice and his guitar, and sat next to her, nervously strumming cords. She could tell that he was trying to force himself to talk to her about something, and her own body tightened in rare sympathy.

'You know, I was just thinking,' he began. 'We ought to have Sonya to dinner one of these days. If you'd like to, I mean.' Ruth was startled. She'd been careful not to mention Sonya to him after the beginning, preferring to keep things separate.

'I know it's important to you to have a close woman friend,' he went on, 'and that you've missed it. I mean, I just wanted to let you know I'd noticed. . . .' He trailed off, waiting for her to respond somehow, to approve. She felt an exasperated tenderness, and reached out to him around the guitar. If only he weren't always so understanding and decent, so unfailingly nice. 'I know there are things I can't give you just because I *am* a man,' he went on doggedly, 'but I want you to have those things. And if you'd rather have her over when I'm out, that's fine, there are friends I'd like to spend more time with too, it's fine . . .' he went on agonizingly.

'Let me think about it when I'm feeling well.' She blew her nose. 'Right now I think I'd rather just be sick.' He shut up right away, apologetically. She hated the way she could push him around. She almost wished he would yell and break things or hit her, so that she'd have reason to leave him. She wished she wanted to tell him about leaving Candy in her office but she didn't.

He began to sing and play for her now, all of their old favorites, 'Catch the Wind,' 'Ramblin' Boy,' and 'Close the Door Lightly When You Go.' She had forgotten how sad they were. Then he started on a Mississippi John Hurt song.

'Don't want me, baby, got to have me anyhow,' he sang, in the black, country accent, the low, growly voice he'd learned so carefully. 'So lonesome here, can't see my baby's face.' She could see *him* clearly now, dark and curly, with his craggy, serious face, his eyebrows like a shelf all the way across, and his eyes that made people trust him at once, and rightly so. There were so few people one could trust! He sat there in her rocking chair that his bigness made seem flimsy, cradling the light wood guitar like a baby. She'd always known he would be a good, loving father to her children. When she'd first known him he'd been living happily in a room that was nothing but books, books and dirty socks, a few political posters crooked on the wall, his gray sheets on the bed. A drummer lived over him then, and the room was full of pounding which he never heard. She'd taken him from that. How could she throw him back now, five years later?

'Used to have a girl, but she went away. Some say Memphis, some say Leland,' Victor mumbled in the Mississippi John voice. She saw him, a senior in high school with a new guitar and a background in classical music, carefully playing the record over and over again, trying to get the inflection just right. By now it had become automatic. It was possible that he had even forgotten this long-ago scene himself, that she was the only one who still remembered. Knowing this, knowing so much, how could she leave him?

'I can't handle these songs today.' He stopped, and looking at him, Ruth thought that he knew what was going to happen as well as she did. She'd changed him terribly and unalterably, had cleaned his socks, sorted his books, made love to him on this smooth bed in this most female of rooms, and now she would leave him. He gestured, with his whole long body, to the bed, and she made room for him silently. He climbed in beside her, lying next to her slightly feverish warmth, and then they clung together, two creatures seeking comfort. She thought that neither of them would ever know anyone else as well as they knew each other.

CANDY

Candy's fever was down by Friday night, and Billy came back round like always. It wasn't like Candy wasn't glad to have her back, but something didn't feel quite the same.

'It's what always happens when somebody gets ready to leave,' she told Loraine. It was a sunny afternoon, and they was sitting out at a little card table by the cottage door, playing cards. 'People start backing off.'

'It aint only that she's leaving that's cooling you out, though,' Loraine said. She had already put on a little weight from when she first came in, and looked pretty with her hair in a full afro and the sun on her purple sweater. 'It's all the built-up bullshit between you two. Like yesterday when you were sick, and she was all over that little bitch, you said it didn't bother you none. Now, either you were just saying that, or else you had to have let go of something to get to that point, you know?'

It made Candy mad the way Loraine, who'd been in all of two weeks, was talking, like she had all the answers, or like she thought she'd turned into Foster all of a sudden.

'If you mean I had to realize she was human, I done that a long time ago, girl,' she said. 'In here, you got to face reality, even if you rather hold on to them illusions. You'd find out what Ritchie's really about too, if you was locked up with him.'

Loraine flushed, but she just said maybe so.

'No maybe about it,' Candy told her. 'You stick around a while and then tell me bout it.'

'OK, OK,' Loraine said. 'Let's just drop it if they got to you so bad. Sometimes I wish they didn't let those visitors come all in our place.'

Both of them looked at the spot where Mrs Morris, Billy, and Timmy had been sitting until just a few minutes ago. Tawanda was still staying with them, but Mrs Morris had never brought her out again and ever since that time Billy hadn't tried to get Candy and her mother together no more either.

Loraine was really getting on Candy's nerves. 'You'd be glad they let visitors in if you heard Ritchie was on his way up,' she told her. 'You wouldn't want no one messing with your grazin' in the grass then. Or do you already got your eye on some broad in here?'

Loraine pulled back. 'Well, scared-a-you, Candy Peters!' she said. 'Listen, if you're too pissy to be talking to anyone, you can just tell me, you know. You don't need to start no beef over nothing.'

'And you don't need to talk like no damn therapist, neither,' Candy mumbled, but she knew Loraine was right. 'Sorry,' she said, after a minute. 'I *am* in a pissy mood. Just, I don't like no one lecturing me. I already got me a therapist, you know.'

'Yeah, I know,' Loraine said. 'Seeing as I see her too.'

Candy wondered what Foster would do if she just brought the goddamn cup back with her on Monday. She'd probly think she'd ripped it off, then changed her mind. It would be better to get that motherfucking key back from Frankie so she could put the cup back before Foster came in, which was one goddamn hassle more she didn't need. It would be just her luck to get busted returning something. She wished Foster had never stuck her in that damn office, like it was really gonna make a motherfucking difference. The only one it made a difference to was Foster herself, who could go home and tell her boyfriend and Lehrman about the neat thing she'd done for poor Candy, that didn't have no place to lay her head.

'Thanks for sending me to Miss Foster,' Loraine said, sort of timid in case Candy still had a attitude. 'I really like her, don't you?'

'I guess she's alright,' Candy shrugged, 'for a screw.' *She* wished she'd never sent Loraine to Foster, cause she'd been acting like she was better than folks ever since. She'd turned down some real nice dope that Candy had talked Billy into letting her in on, which had made Candy look a fool, and for all she knew, Loraine had probly gone and run it all to Foster how Candy was trying to influence her to get back on drugs and shit.

'Later,' she told Loraine, cause the girl was really getting to her. She had just started back to the cottage to see could she find Frankie to get the key when Norma stopped her, all excited cause she was finally leaving after having her date put off two times cause she didn't have no place to stay.

'Mrs Schofield got it arranged so I got me a room in the Y paid a whole month ahead and that'll give me some time to find my feet again, so to speak,' she said, repeating the social worker's stupid words like they was magic. 'Candy, can you come in and help me pack for a minute?'

In Norma's room, Candy sat with her feet up on the stripped down mattress and watched Norma scrub the floor. She'd already folded her one or two outfits in a plastic shopping bag with her Bible and family pictures on top, so there wasn't no more packing to do as far as Candy could see.

'Now don't tell me I'm a fool cause they already been in here telling me that but I aint never left no place I lived in dirty and I aint starting now. You got time to come down the beauty parlor and do my hair nice for me once before I leave?'

'Sure,' Candy agreed. 'All my pressing engagements I got this afternoon can wait.'

'You think this here'll be alright for leaving out in?' Norma pointed to the same old-lady shiny blue dress that she'd wore to the art room that time.

'Alright for what, riding the state car from here to the Y?' Candy wanted to ask. Instead she nodded again.

'I been in here so long I don't know what they wearing out there no more,' Norma rattled on. 'But tomorrow is Sunday and just yesterday I received this letter from the preacher at my old church telling me come round the first Sunday I can, and everybody be glad to see me.' She took the letter out from between her boobs. 'You want to read it for me one more time? Just so I know I got the wording right?'

Candy read it to her. 'See there!' Norma cried. 'I would not have received it if I had left out of here last week the way I was sposed to. So He worked it for the best, after all.'

'The fuck He did!' Candy thought. She got up to leave cause she just wasn't in the mood today, but Norma gestured her down and then set herself heavily down on the bed beside her.

'You stay put a minute girl,' she said. 'I asked you to come in here cause I wanted to talk to you.'

Candy sighed. It seemed like everybody had a lecture for her today.

'Now don't you be getting no attitude before I even start,' Norma said. 'You know I aint got nothing against girls goin' with girls, so long as they good to each other. But that Billy Morris aint no good for you, honey. She don't treat you no different from how some no-good man would do, and you don't need that no more.'

Candy tried to get up, but Norma pushed her back down on the bed with her strong old arms.

'Don't be walking on my wet floor, now,' she said. 'Aint no reason for you to be tied to that girl. I known her mother on the streets years before you girls was even born, and Billy take after her mother. I aint talkin' bout her mannish ways now, I'm talking bout what goes deeper, how they treats people. Now Billy due to leave here before you, and you got a good chance to get your life together without her. Get in that program you told me that lady that be helping Telecea have in mind for you. The one about helping girls get off the streets. You'd be real good at that, Candy.'

Candy tried to picture Norma and Billy's mother hanging on the street together before she was born but Norma was on a whole new tack now. 'Donny told me how you tried to help Telecea last time she went off. I know you spose to be so bad and all, but I seen how you watch out for folks that can't help theyself.' She took a envelope off the dresser.

'This here is a little goodbye card I wrote my name in for Telecea. I'm gonna shout up to her before I leave out, but she aint been answering me lately and I'm worried bout her. I wouldn't trust most of them others to give it to her, Candy. But I know you will.'

Candy took the envelope even though she didn't want to. 'Telecea can't read,' she said.

'That don't matter,' Norma answered. 'You know I aint so much on the reading myself, but I manages. You can let her know it's from me on the side like, without humiliating her. I don't need to tell you how, Candy.'

The floor was dry now. 'I'll see she gets it,' Candy promised, taking the envelope. 'You meet me at the beauty parlor in half an hour and I'll do your hair.'

In her room, she put the envelope down next to Foster's goddamn cup on her dresser. She wished people that couldn't deal with their own lives would stop laying all this shit on her, and just leave her the fuck alone. If she was so fucking good and trustworthy, why was she here in the first place?

SONYA

When Sonya tightened the piece of wire that held the two figures together, the board they sat on tipped to one side, and the smaller figure bounced off, dragging the other one along with it. She wanted them across from each other, each one straining backwards, with the four hands locked together, balancing the seesaw and keeping the piece in permanent stasis, but achieving this was turning out to be harder than she'd expected. She was having fun working the problem out, though.

She put Laura Nyro on the turntable and decided to work on the two figures and the seesaw separately for now, and balance them later. She'd already made skeletons out of heavy, hard-to-manipulate wire, and now she wound soft fine wire around and around the smaller figure, giving it large breasts, broad shoulders, and big feet and hands. The other one was taller, but much thinner, so they ought to balance fairly well. She didn't want a frozen balance anyway, but instead a slight swinging up and down. It was when the balance got permanently weighted down on one side that things got boring, and it was worst of all if you were the one left sitting on the ground, holding all the power on your side. If you were the one left hanging in the air at least it was exciting, you never knew when you might get banged down with a jolt. Ruth had been intriguingly distant on the ride home yesterday, but mostly being with her hadn't been too exciting lately. She was so eager to give herself up that there was no fun to it. With Mira, at least it had been back and forth for the first three or four months.

'Uptown, going down, the old lifeline,' sang Laura. Sonya decided to cover the seesaw in velvet. The figures themselves could stay pretty bare, mostly wire, but the seesaw would be deceptively soft, almost like a pillow, with foam lining it under the black velvet cover. She'd applique the velvet with words in pink and red silk. 'Let me go.' 'Hold me.' 'I love you.' 'I can't breathe!' She jotted them down as fast as they came, glad that it was only Saturday so that she could finish the piece tomorrow. Then she could finish that subway sculpture she'd started a while ago, which would complement this one. Both involved two female figures, balancing each other as they jockeyed for position. It was too bad not to be able to work during the week, but at least the prison was inspiring her.

'Looking for my baby in time,' she sang along jubilantly, as she brushed her hair into an electric cloud and put on her leather jacket to go out.

TELECEA

What I don't know is if it a trick or the real Norma. Sometime He send the one He love a angel. But could send a devil too. They have got me so mix-up and confuse how I'm spose to tell? Like this one time a devil come and tell this man take his boy up the mountain and kill and cook him, eat him up. Little boy get suspicious, ask his daddy, Where the meat we spose to cook up here? Daddy say, You the meat, son, ha ha ha. Just like that, bout to eat up his own child, but the Lord send down an angel quick, tell him stop.

So how you spose to know? Like in here where they got the inmates drest like police. Or when I first seen Sonya she was drest like a witch. He say don't suffer no witches. But I seen through that costume and I knowed.

What I seen, I seen someone that look like Norma down there, tell me, You aint alone up there Telecea, cause I always be thinking of you. Tell me They sending me home now, send me to a free room in the Y for a whole month and your time come too, child. Tell me, Just you try and hold on cause He aint gone let it go on like this for you and that nice lady be trying to get you out right now and I have gave Candy Peters a message for you. Then when I blink my eyes she be gone.

Now how I'm spose to know is it a trick or Norma? Cause if it Norma, why she got to say that ho' name? How I'm spose to tell?

MONDAY, OCTOBER 19

RUTH

Ruth's first feeling when she got in Monday morning was one of tremendous relief. Candy had locked the door, turned off the hot plate, and replaced the cot and blanket neatly in the closet. Only the blue cup was missing from its place, and compared to the enormity of what she'd imagined, this seemed a small price to pay. 'Let a thief stay in your office, then don't be surprised when you get ripped off,' she could hear Candy say. As ten o'clock approached, she tried to believe that Candy had only borrowed the cup and would bring it back when she came in for her appointment. As the hour came and went, she thought that Candy might still be sick and unable to get a message to her. By eleven, when Mabe came in, she was still turning it around in her mind, trying to make sense of something that already made perfect sense.

Mabe had first come to Ruth a year and a half ago, saying that she was depressed because she missed her children, who were with her mother. Now she was due to be released in a week. 'So,' Ruth asked her. 'How are you feeling about leaving?' Mabe smiled widely.

'He was here,' she said, as if that told it all. 'He come up on Friday and stayed at least three hours.'

'Was it a good visit?' Ruth asked her. There was no need to ask who 'he' was.

'Yeah.' Mabe nodded dreamily. 'He brung me some clothes and make-up and stuff I been needin' for a long time. That wig I told you bout I thought he gave away. But he been savin' it for me all the time. And told me he got his eye on a nice little place for me, right near where he stay. . . .'

'How do you feel about that?' Ruth asked her, hopelessly enough, as it was quite clear how Mabe felt. 'How about your plans for getting back the children?' Mabe ignored this last.

'How you think I feel?' she demanded. 'Some girls, they leave out of here, and aint got no place to go. You know that old lady, Norma? They made her wait two whole weeks past her date cause she didn't have no one to take her. But I got nothing to worry bout. He gone be there to get me. Aint many mens would wait that long. And he know I been waitin' too. Aint never messed with no bitch the whole time I been in here, and he know it. He can't stand that shit, it make him sick,' she added proudly, staring at Ruth.

Ruth wondered what she could say that would make any difference. That Clay was a well-known pimp? Over the years she'd actually had three different clients who claimed to be his main lady. That he'd only begun to visit her in the last two weeks, after she'd got her date, that she'd be stepping right back into the same mess that had brought her to Redburn in the first place and to Ruth's office in the second, that she'd undoubtedly be back within a matter of months? Or years, if she was very lucky.

Mabe shifted a little, comfortably, in her seat. She was wearing the new wig, which looked hard and brittle and was a strange reddish color, foundation make-up which didn't match her skin tone, and bright purple lipstick which covered about half her lips. Her blue nylon blouse was too tight and strained at the breast. She looked to Ruth like a picture-book whore, one created in the mind of some male novelist.

'Mabe,' she made an effort. 'Are you remembering your kids when Clay talks to you? Are you really telling yourself the truth about this?'

Mabe snapped to attention, offended and defensive. 'What you mean, the truth? He come up, aint he? What's he gonna drive all this way for if he don't love me?'

'I don't mean whether or not he loves you,' Ruth said, as gently as she could. 'I mean about the kind of life he's involved in. You've been talking to me for a long time now about how you didn't want to go back to that life, how you planned to stay with your mother for a while so you could get your children back.'

Mabe's face was hard and angry. 'I know you can't understand about this,' she said. 'He say seeing girls together make him sick,' she went on, staring openly at Ruth's body, and then, under the desk, at her crossed legs. Ruth squeezed them protectively together. She had the sudden and eerie sensation that she was talking not to slow, plodding Mabe, who was nasty enough but incapable of insinuation, and who got into most of her trouble in the institution by following her friend Edie, but instead to some slick, slippery-minded man.

'What are you saying, Mabe?' she asked. 'You feel I can't understand your feelings for Clay?'

Mabe shrugged and seemed to change her mind.

'Hey, I know you're trying to help me, Miss Foster. But you

know, so far when I been talkin' to you it's like I ain't had nothin' real to deal with, see, cause I been in this place, and the shit that come down in this place aint bout nothin', you just be passing the time waitin' to get out. But now, hey, I got my life to think about. It's like all this was just practice time, you know, and now I'm gettin' ready to step out.'

All this was said at top speed, and looking at Mabe, Ruth could see, like a subliminal image, the quickly shifting expressions and movements of the person she assumed was Clay.

'What you just said, Mabe,' she said impulsively. 'It didn't sound like you. It sounded like somebody else talking.' A flush rose under the make-up on Mabe's face.

'I aint stupid!' she said. 'I know how to talk my own self.' And then, rolling the long words out proudly, 'So what if me and Clay has been discussioning this incarceration and the result on a person that been inside too long. How they could get a tency to get institution-alize. How the man be fuckin' with your head.'

Ruth wished she could tell Mabe goodbye and good luck now, as she was clearly through with therapy. As Mabe herself had put it, she had her life to think about now. Too much truth telling would only get in the way. But Mabe, who had always explained her attendance at therapy to herself and others in terms of the good time reports that would get her out sooner, was not about to quit before the bitter end, and Ruth was reluctant to terminate what had actually been quite a positive experience with a rejection on her part. Instead, they would agree together to mark time through one more session this week, and then Mabe could start all over, with someone else, on her next trip back.

After Mabe left, Ruth tried not to let herself get discouraged. It was still possible that Mabe would come in at the end of the week ready to work, and then the hopelessness on her part would be destructive. Still, she couldn't help looking back on their year and a half's worth of therapy with a sinking feeling. She remembered reading that women who, in the throes of childbirth, screamed 'never again,' would forget the experience of pain immediately afterwards. This, the book had said, was nature's way of assuring that babies would continue to be born. The effect of Redburn seemed to be to assure society that there would always be enough whores to fill the need. The place had acted on Mabe like a wet sponge on a slate. It had wiped her clean of memories and would send her back to the mean streets healthy and rested, a little older, fifteen pounds heavier, and ready for more.

Ruth heard the banging over her head again. Unlike Mabe, Telecea would not get any street breaks. She imagined her thirty years from now, old and wrinkled, still banging her head on the floor of Max. She got up to find Mrs Hanson and try to arrange for the disciplinary board meeting.

CANDY

Because she hadn't put back the goddamn mug, Candy skipped therapy on Monday. She was wrote down for it, though, so Delaney let her out the flag room, and she sat, not under her tree cause it was too cold and windy out, but at a bench at Four Corners. The more she thought about it, the gladder she was she decided not to go, cause she could see she'd got sucked into this therapy shit like she really believed it was gonna do something for her, like she'd forgot the only way these motherfuckers could help her was to let her out the door.

'This white twenty-six year old woman still has too many issues to work through so I advise retaining her in protective custody for a few more years.' That was the kind of bullshit Foster would write down on her. True, Foster'd forgot herself a few times lately and acted like a person, but that didn't change nothing. She'd probly go overboard the other way to make up for it now.

Mabe walked by to meet her visit at the front door, twitching her fat ass stuffed into jeans that was at least two sizes too small, and wearing some kind of nasty wig. 'Better make sure the state buy you some nice half-size slacks before you leave out,' Candy yelled out.

But Mabe just called back, 'Later for you, bitch,' in too much of a hurry to stop and beef.

Next Lou wandered by, all sad and whiney like she'd been since her and Frankie had broke up, a few days back.

'I keep thinking Norma's still here,' she complained. 'You know how it is, Candy, I keep thinking of things I want to say to her, and then I remember she gone.'

'I aint noticed you having all that much to say to her before she left,' Candy told her. 'You dropped old Mama quick enough soon's you found someone to fuck with.'

Lou gave her one surprised hurt look with her big eyes, then she got all hard and jumped off the bench.

'Everyone knows you just evil cause Billy fittin' to leave and got someone else waiting on her out there,' she snarled out, and then her face scrunched all up like a kid's face before it starts to cry. 'I'm glad she do, too, cause I hate you!'

And she ran down the hall where Candy could hear her tell some new scared little white girl to hand over them cigarettes or else. Candy wished she hadn't talked like that to Lou. The kid hadn't done nothing to her.

No one came by for a little while, and then Billy did, in her grey sweatshirt with the cute little hood up over her head. 'What's this I been hearing' she said. 'Something bout some fresh little broad with a attitude sitting out here looking for trouble? Come on back the cottage, baby. I got some Columbian reefer that can't wait. Plus you and me's got to talk.'

Back in Candy's room after they smoked, they sat on the bed and Billy took Candy's face in her two hands. 'Don't look away, baby,' she told her. 'You think I got it made now I'm getting ready to leave, don't you? You think it's gonna be easy for me, leaving you?'

Candy shrugged. 'I don't know.'

'You already forget I told you I love you?' Billy asked. 'Listen, you think I waited all my whole life to tell someone that just to have it forgot?'

Candy couldn't answer cause tears was blocking up her throat. 'Yes, you do want me to forget,' she thought. 'You want me to forget all about Grace, and your mother's plans for you, and that one they all say you got waiting on the outside. And the times I'm sick and needing you and you aint there. . . .'

'I aint forgot,' she said out loud. Then Billy pulled her near, all gentle and soft, and snuggled her head down on her shoulder.

'What you is forgetting is with me you can't just look on the outside,' she said. 'You got to look at what's underneath. And underneath I'm scared, Candy.'

Candy tried to stay hard but she felt herself melting with Billy needing her again. 'Tell me what you scared of, baby,' she whispered.

Billy lit another joint. 'Everything, I guess,' she said. 'It's been a long time since I been out there, for real, I mean, not on no furlough. What if I can't make it? They got this college thing hooked up for me, but how you think I'm gonna look in some whitey college? And you know the way people slide their eyes at you when they see you come crawling back here, like you some kind of slime or something. I guess I'm scared of that.'

Candy smoothed Billy's face with her fingertips, soft but steady the way she liked it. 'You aint gonna be alone in that classroom, baby,' she said. 'I'm gonna be right here thinking about you and loving you and just waiting till I can get out there with you.'

'Yeah, I know,' Billy said. 'Only I wish you was coming right out with me, so we could start together.' They sat quietly for a while and then Billy gave her a suspicious look. 'You already got your eye on one of these butches for when I'm gone?'

'You know I aint,' Candy started, but Billy was up, pacing up and down the little bit of a room.

'What's that up there?' she asked, pointing to the blue cup Candy had stuck on the bureau on top of the card Norma had gave her for Telecea.

Candy hesitated. Billy hadn't been around when she came out of Foster's office Friday night, and she hadn't told her nothing about it.

'The card is from Norma to Telecea,' she told Billy slowly. 'She made me promise to give it to her when she came out of Max. And you really want to know what the cup is?' Billy nodded yes, and Candy got up off the bed, sort of floating. She picked the cup up off the bureau and saw the ocean swimming in it.

'It aint right,' she thought. 'How come Billy and me aint never been to the ocean together?'

'I'll show you what it is,' she said, and threw it down, as hard as she could. The cup lay on the floor, broke, in little pieces of speckled blue and white. Billy laughed.

'You better clean that mess up, girl,' she said. 'Or somebody gonna get her feet cut up. And I got my shoes on. Tell you what,' she went on. 'I won't ask you nothing else about it. And I'm gonna believe what you said bout that letter, too. Won't even look at it. But I don't want no damn roots letter round my baby, neither. Anything meant for that crazy bitch got to have some roots or something in it.' Billy picked up the envelope and took out her little silver lighter, keeping her eyes on Candy's face the whole time to see was it really what she said it was, and would she try to stop her. It burnt slow, just the envelope first, then the shiny card, going all bright and smelling bad. Candy remembered how Norma said all she wrote on it was her name. When it got to her fingers, Billy dropped it on the floor. It was gonna catch the throw-rug, and Candy ran to stamp it out.

'Shit!' she screamed. She had cut her bare foot on something.

SONYA

Donny stayed late in the art room on Monday. She'd told Sonya that the more she'd thought about her self-portrait, the more it bothered her. When the others had left, she and Donny took out the painting and looked at the muscles, the small blank face, the T-shirt, the neat blocks of color.

'You think it really looks like me?' Donny asked.

'No,' Sonya told her. 'Or only one part of you, anyway.'

'That's what I thought myself,' Donny agreed. 'I thought maybe I could do another one, but I don't know how.'

'Why don't you paint the parts of you that didn't get into the first one?' Sonya suggested, and was pleased to see Donny select large brushes and begin painting at once, without her usual outline in pencil. It was past four, and Sonya had missed her ride with Ruth, who had left early today, but she didn't mind taking the bus back for once. She was in a good mood, and found Donny's presence easy. Her eyes rested on Gladdy's latest painting, left on the easel to dry. It was of the inside of a one-room house, and the details of pallet and four-poster bed, wood-burning stove and range, and even a checkered quilt hung over a tiny rocking chair, were done with incredible delicacy. She wondered about arranging a show for Gladdy somewhere. 'Gladdy Dwight – paintings from Behind the Walls by a sixty-five year old black woman.' The feminist community would love it and love her too, as Gladdy's discoverer.

'Afraid?' she asked, as the camera panned in closer. 'No, I guess I never thought of being afraid. I find it very nurturing to work with these women. My own art has expanded tremendously since I started here –'

'Well?' Donny looked softer than usual, even pretty, as she held up her painting for inspection. This time she had painted a face only, a long oval face outlined in blue. It was simply done, with dots for nostrils, and large eyes, one with a teardrop falling from it. One half of the mouth aimed up, smiling, and the other half drooped down.

'It's very fine, Donny,' Sonya told her. 'Very honest.'

Donny considered. 'I don't know,' she said. 'I aint got it yet. Who knows, I may need to make a whole bunch, huh?'

The two smiled at each other as they cleaned up and got ready to go.

TELECEA

I know what they been trying to do. Don't let no one near me. Sonya she try and see me but they aint let her. Think if they can get me all weak and mixded up they get what they want. Make me say Sonya name, tell them our plan.

But He be protecting me. Send this girl I used to know Dina Porter up here only now her name Dina War cause she make war on all them. On the system, that what she say.

She say, What they doing to you, girl. Look at you you aint spose to treat no dog like that let alone no human being if they keeps it up they gone have a law suit on they hands. Tranden gone hear bout this if it the last thing I do. She tell me go on and eat the food cause or else you be giving them just what they wants. She here for escape but they don't keep her in no cage. She walk all round, come and see me by my door.

I close my eyes so I don't have to see that nasty shit and try and eat something. So I can get my strength back for when they come and try and trick me, make me talk.

TUESDAY, OCTOBER 20

RUTH

Mary Proudy gave Ruth a rare smile, complimented her on her new red sweater, and asked her whether she had come up to Max to see Dina.

'No,' Ruth shook her head. Dina Porter, already a seasoned con at the time, had been Ruth's very first case at Redburn. 'I'd like to say hi to her if there's time, but actually I'm here to see Telecea Jones today.'

Proudy's face quickly resumed its usual belligerent expression. 'You got to talk to that one from outside her cell,' she said. 'And if she get loud, down you go. I don't want no trouble on my shift. I told Tranden hisself when he begged me to take my job back cause he couldn't find no one else that was capable of handling it. I don't care if you offer me twice what I'm getting now, I told him. I got ulcers that act up when I gets nervous. The only way I go back up there is if you give it to me in writing that I don't have to have nothing to do with that girl. They say she knows roots and I don't mess with that stuff. Seen too many funny things happen if you know what I mean. And anyway she gives me the creeps. Her mouth was half of what made me sick in the first place. Go on down the hall. Last door on your left.'

Ruth had already begun to move when Proudy thought of something else. 'You thinking of getting her moved out of here, Miss Foster? Maybe they could take her over State or something where they *sposed* to be crazy? It aint doing none of us no good to leave her up here all the time. Not her, not the other girls, not me neither.'

The long narrow corridor which was Max had always reminded Ruth of a prison in some late-night old movie. It was lined on either side with tiny cells which contained neither toilet nor sink and were barely large enough for the cot which was the only furniture. These cells, cited in yearly futile complaints by various prisoner's-rights groups, were always sweltering in summer and freezing in winter. Each one had a small barred window which looked out on the compound's yard, and could be reached only by standing on the cot. The cell wall which looked out on the corridor was covered with two

236

layers of heavy wire grill, which the women stuck their fingers through as Ruth passed, exactly like caged animals.

'Hey Miss Foster, you know me, I gotta talk to you!'

'Lady, mail this letter for me? Please?'

'Got a cigarette, Miss?'

'Hey, tell Proudy she better bring my medication!'

Knowing that to stop and talk even once would mean she'd never get to Telecea, Ruth tried to walk straight by, giving quick nods and smiles, but feeling her belly wrenching alarmingly. The last cell was separated from the others by several empty ones. It was dark there at the end of the corridor, and at first Ruth couldn't see Telecea behind the blur of grill. When her vision did adjust to the darkness she was shocked at what she saw. Telecea sat crouched on the cot, her dark eyes sunk alarmingly into her head, and her pajamas hanging loosely on her wasted body. She looked as though she'd been up here fasting for two months instead of two weeks, and Ruth wasn't surprised when she didn't answer her greeting. 'You're so thin!' Ruth finally got out. 'Haven't you been eating? Are you sick?'

Telecea just stared at her.

'I'm so sorry I couldn't come before,' Ruth went on blindly. 'What would you think about leaving Max for a few hours every day?'

'Don't matter what I think or don't think.' Telecea had finally spoken and Ruth couldn't argue with her. She wanted to run away from the corridor of caged women and never come back.

'Listen, Telecea,' she tried to pull herself together. 'I know you feel helpless up here, like nothing makes any difference. But sometimes it helps to know what's going to happen before it happens.'

She began to describe the schedule she'd gotten OK'd, the therapy hours twice a week with her and three times a week with Sonya, the lunches in the cafeteria with the others. Although Telecea's expression changed when Ruth mentioned Sonya's name, she gave no other signs of having heard. Lamely, Ruth passed a typed copy of the schedule she'd been so proud of obtaining through the bottom of the grill.

'You could ask someone to read it to you,' she suggested helplessly. 'Maybe Dina?' Ashamed, she'd turned to leave when a barrage of words stopped her.

'Don't you walk off like you all safe now! I know you! Give me

237

some old paper. Alright, you can come out, Telecea, we gonna treat you nice now if you don't tell. But it too late for that. He know what you done, you Ruth Foster-Candy ho', you. First be one then be the other, think you can trick someone like that but He give me my vision and you aint trickt me, ho'! He gone break the pride of your power. Gone fall on one another eat each other up. So only you hands and you feets be left, ho' Jezebel. Too late to trick someone wif some old paper! He seen and I witness. I been chose. Gone be his Venger. Think you can turn back to plain old Ruth Foster? Too late for that, ho'!'

Shaken, Ruth made her way down the corridor.

'Miss Foster!'

Dina Porter's voice stopped her.

'Don't you let her get to you, now. She's just a little upsetted from remaining up here too long, got a little mental disturbance preying on her mind, that's all. I'll go over that schedule with her. Don't cause yourself no anxiety, she'll be alright.'

CANDY

For no good reason, Candy was feeling the weight of what she'd did get heavier and heavier. She had left one or two dudes bleeding where they fell, and never did find out if they made it or not, and had ripped more people off all their shit than she could even count, but she had never felt as bad as she did now, about a motherfucking blue cup and a fifteen cent card.

'You know, they gone and rehabilitated me,' she told Loraine. 'Against my will. You think I should sue?'

Loraine laughed. They was playing cards in the TV room. 'I wouldn't worry,' she said. 'I haven't noticed you getting a whole lot less larceny-hearted.'

Candy wished she could tell Loraine about the cup and card but she didn't cause of the way Loraine had been lately. 'I'm gonna see if Dina wants anything,' she said instead.

Ever since Dina had came back from her last escape, they had almost always been someone standing under her window in Max, shouting up. Candy had known Dina a long time, and she didn't fall for her jive raps the way the new girls did, but she still liked her, maybe cause the broad could always make her laugh.

'Hey Dina, what's happenin?' she called out from below Max, shivering cause it was cold out.

'That you, Sugar Candy?' Dina's voice came back nice and clear. 'What you think's happening up here in this hell hole? Everyone's quiet except this poor child Telecea Jones they have took and drove mental. They better remove her out of here soon, though, cause we all gonna go off if she don't shut up her yelling.'

Candy could hear some kind of commotion up there and Dina turned back to shout at someone inside.

'That Telecea you talking to?' Candy called.

'Who else you think be hollering out the Bible in broad daylight?' Dina asked. 'How come you so interested in Telecea, all of a sudden?'

'I got this message a lady that went home left for her,' Candy told her. 'Would you give it to her for me?'

'Uh-uh, no. You know me, I don't never carry no messages for no one. Her window's right round in back.'

'But it aint even from me,' Candy pleaded. 'And anyway, she don't listen to me, she call me all kind of devil.'

Dina ignored this. 'What's the matter, honey,' she asked instead. 'You sound all tensed-up. Aint Billy treating you good? You both leaving out of here some time soon, aint you? You tell her from me she better shape up and take care of her woman or she gonna have some competition on her hands when I come out this hell hole.'

Candy tried to laugh but it didn't come out. 'I don't carry no messages,' she said. 'You need some cigarettes or something, Dina?'

'No, honey. You just go ahead round and tell her what you got to say. Girl can't do nothing to you from up here no way, and anyways she aint mean, long as you psychologize her the right way, listen to what she say and answer her back like it made some sense, you know? Reassurance her a little, you know?'

Candy went round to where she knew Telecea's window was, cause of all the noise that come from it. She might as well get it over with.

'Hey Telecea, I got a message for you from Norma,' she yelled. She didn't hear nothing at first, then a dark shape appeared up at the window.

'You aint got me fooled, Ruth Foster-Candy ho',' it screamed. 'I know your unclean devil switch-up tricks with two different faces and them messages and papers. Think you can come up here and talk like Ruth Foster through my door and then come up under my window dresst up the other way!'

Candy thought she'd just go ahead and say what she had to say and, if Telecea wouldn't listen, she couldn't help it. She would of done what she told Norma she would do, or anyways as much as she could without no card.

'Norma wanted to talk to you, cause she didn't know did you hear her when she said goodbye her ownself. She said she was gonna miss you and she hope you doing OK and taking care of yourself and don't let no one mess with your head. And she wanted to tell you she got a nice room in the Y for free and her old church to go to, and she gonna be praying for you every day and God bless.'

A funny thing happened to Candy when she was talking. It was like she was Norma, like she was talking with the old lady's voice.

Telecea must of heard it too, cause she went quiet. Then, 'Who are you?' she asked in a quieter voice.

'I'm Candy Peters,' she called back up. 'You always thought I meant to hurt you, but I never did. And that's why Norma asked me to be sure and give you her message. What I just told you. That's what she said.'

Telecea must of been thinking it over. 'I aint saying I believe you,' she said finally. 'And I aint saying I don't. But I heard what you said.'

'That's good.' Candy went back to the cottage feeling like half her load had lifted.

In her room, she sat down on the bed, got out her notepaper, and wrote a letter. It came out real fast, like she'd been practicing it in her head.

> Dear Miss Foster, The reason I didn't come on Monday you might
> of guesed, because I broke your cup when I was in there and I felt so
> bad I didn't want to come back. And then I started thinking maybe I
> better start learning to make it on my own without you because you
> know pretty soon I'll be out. But I know you have always tried hard to
> help me and I do apreciate it and I am sorry about the cup and if you write
> and tell me how much its worth I will make out a store card for you,
> because I have got some money saved, and it means a lot that you cared
> when I wasn't feeling well. So you take care of you now, and please don't
> think I just don't care.'

Before she signed her name to it, Candy read the letter over. It sounded too emotional to her, especially the end part. She thought of Miss Foster reading it. She would wrinkle her forehead and get that sad look and think, 'Why didn't Candy just come and tell me what happened, why did she have to write me a letter?'

Candy shivered. It was something weird going on with her today, the way she kept hearing all those other people's voices in her head.

She signed her name to the note and decided she'd bring it to Miss Foster in person the next day. She'd just say, 'I don't really want to talk no more, Miss Foster, but here's this note, and thank you.' It would be harder that way, but maybe then she'd have some peace.

SONYA

Sonya had known that Ruth was compulsive, but she'd never seen her the way she was on the drive back this afternoon, speedy as hell, chain-smoking, and talking obsessively about her visit to Telecea up in Max.

How she'd fucked everything up by getting so guilty that she'd arranged for Telecea to leave Max part time, when she was in no state to be on the compound at all, how it might possibly be alright if she had a one-to-one guard with her at all times but Hanson would never approve that and would just decide to keep her up there, where she'd get worse and worse and finally kill someone when she did get out, if she hadn't died of malnutrition by that time, how she didn't mind being alone in an office with her herself but she was damned if she was going to expose Sonya to that risk. . . .

'Slow down there,' Sonya stopped her. 'Aren't you talking a little double-standard, there?'

'Are you even listening to me?' Ruth almost screamed. 'I keep trying to explain to you but you never really take it in, do you? This isn't some kind of power trip on my part, Sonya. Two people associated with Telecea have already died. OK, we don't know what really happened but it's nothing to play with. I'm scared for you, and I want you to be scared, too. It's as if, without meaning to, we've been playing her like a goddamn bull in the ring or something. We lock her up in isolation for two weeks, did I tell you that it looks like no one but that horrible Moody even laid eyes on her for most of that time? And then, when she's all ready to explode, we let her out. I mean, what the hell are we asking for?'

Ruth honked at a truck that was moving too slowly. Then she passed it, narrowly squeezing between two speeding cars.

'Do I understand that you don't want Telecea in the art room because you think that she might kill me?' Sonya tried to say this seriously, but a laugh kept threatening. 'Why aren't you afraid for yourself, then, if she's so dangerous?'

Ruth's answer was a little calmer. 'We've gone over this before. For one thing, you work with her at a much different level than I do.' Ruth paused. 'Also, you've got to realize I've been here four years now. I couldn't stand it if you got hurt as a result of my stupidity.'

She reached for another cigarette as she drove, but couldn't light it because her hand was shaking so badly. When Sonya did it for her she felt a kind of electric energy coming from Ruth's body. Even the fuzz on her mohair sweater seemed to stand up on end. Sonya remembered the cold angry Ruth she'd met that first day, when she'd barged into her office.

'Why don't you come up for a while,' she suggested, as Ruth pulled the car up by her house.

Ruth stared at her with surprise as if this was the first time she'd noticed she was in the car.

'Oh, I can't, not today,' she said, still speeding. 'I have to spend some time by myself and figure this one out on my own. For one thing, I've got to understand how I let things get to this point. It's not like me to let things go like this. If anything, I've always thought of myself as being too responsible, but I guess this isn't a job where you can afford to stop concentrating, even for a few weeks.'

Then she opened the door for Sonya to get out, as if she couldn't wait to get rid of her.

Sonya slammed it behind her, resolving that she'd never ask again. Ruth could be the one to do the asking, and then maybe, just maybe, if she was in the mood, she'd consider it. At the end of her little speech Ruth had sounded as if she blamed Sonya for her own preoccupation with her! She'd probably go home and fuck with Victor to get rid of her tension.

'Shit!' Sonya stomped around the loft, talking in her new Redburn voice. 'Who wants you anyways, tight-ass Foster? Not me!'

TELECEA

Think they can fool me with they tricks. Come like a thief in the night in all them different faces and other people voice. First she come up to me in her Ruth Foster self in her red sweater wif all them little standing-up worm heads. Say, Telecea you can come out now, go to the art room twice a week just like before and come in my office once a week your chair still there and drink that chocolate like you done and everything be back where it belong.

I seen it on TV one time, they catched this big old lion in a trap. Out there in Africa. Talk to him all nice and sweet, hold a piece of meat right in front of his mouf and you know they had to of starve him before, cause you can see that old lion mouf start in to water and first he think better of it. But then he give in and follow that meat. They saying, Come on, kitty, come on, and lead him up into that truck. Then bang go that truck door and they throwed that meat away. Aint even gave him it, just got him in there be whipping him with them metal whips every time he roar. And if he die, well, never mind, they get them another one from the same trap they got him out of.

If everything gone be so nicey-nice, tell me this, how come I aint seen Sonya up here yet? What they done with her?

Must think I aint got no sense cause next thing they do, they try it from down there. This time she take the Candy-ho' part like she don't know He see everywhere and aint no hiding. And then have the nerve to take Norma voice, when I knows good and well Norma done left out of here two weeks ago cause she came herself as a angel and told me so.

But the voice do sound like Norma so just in case I say, Yeah, I hear you.

Only if Sonya come here her own self then I will come out. That the only way they move me out of here on my two feets, if Sonya come and tell me do it.

THURSDAY, OCTOBER 22

RUTH

By Thursday afternoon, Ruth felt a little more comfortable about Telecea. She'd somehow managed to convince Hanson of the necessity, at least for an initial period, of a one-to-one officer to be assigned to Telecea during the time she spent out of Max. She was pretty sure that Sonya had finally taken in her warning, and would keep it in mind in her contact with Telecea. Sonya was scheduled to see Telecea in Max today, and Ruth thought that if she was reachable at all at this point, Sonya would be the one to do it.

As Ruth walked back to her office, she saw Candy standing at her door. She had ached with that loss and guilt all week too, and now she almost ran to get to her before she disappeared again. But Candy would take only two small steps into the office, and stood there looking at the floor holding out an envelope. She wore a beaded, bleached-out pinkish sweater stretched over her small breasts, and her newly streaked hair was pulled back into an especially tight pony tail, giving the skin around her hairline a tight, sore look. Her face was almost masked with heavy make-up. Ruth wanted to go to Candy and take her in her arms, to tell her that she had missed her, and to undo the cruel rubber band. Instead, she stood helplessly while Candy shifted from foot to foot.

'I got to be somewhere.' she held out the envelope like a shield. 'I just wanted to give you this myself.' Ruth could feel Candy's conflicting pulling away and toward her in her own body.

'Why don't you sit down for a minute while I read it,' she said firmly, trying to eliminate choice. Candy shrugged. She wouldn't sit down, but stepped a little closer and half-closed the door while Ruth sat at her desk with the letter. Down the hall, Ruth could hear Dave repeating something over and over, in a loud voice. She pretended that the letter was taking her much longer to read than it actually took. 'So you take care of you, now,' she read over and over again, 'and please don't think I don't care.'

'I don't want to pressure you to stay in therapy if you really think it's better for you not to, Candy,' she said finally. 'But I think it might feel better to both of us to sit and talk about it now, instead of just breaking off like this.'

Candy hesitated, fingering her pack of cigarettes.

'If she takes one out now,' Ruth decided, uncomfortable with how much it mattered to her, 'she'll stay.'

Candy lit a cigarette, her fingers shaking in a way that reminded Ruth of herself lately. Then she came and sat on the very edge of the chair, tapping her feet rhythmically, like a scrawny, streaky city bird, poised for flight. Ruth needed to make Candy's presence more definite, and got up to close the door.

'I'm glad you're here,' she said, when she got back to her chair. 'I've been concerned that by leaving you in the office, I put you in an uncomfortable position, set you up somehow.' She found that she knew the words, which rattled primly in the air, by heart.

When Candy answered, her words had the same prim, rehearsed quality to them. 'Hey, don't worry about it,' she said. 'That's why I wrote you that letter, cause I thought you'd think, you know, that you done something wrong, but it aint about that. I wasn't worried about staying in the office or nothing, it's just like what I said, I got to start dealing with things on my own. And like I said, I do want to pay for the cup. I mean, I know it meant a lot to you, and all. What you said about your friend made it and all.'

Ruth wanted to scream. She felt Candy slipping away, both of them caught somehow in this play with mediocre lines and a stupid, unnecessary ending. But the last time she'd acted impulsively, she'd made everything worse, messier. She wished she were Sonya. Sonya wouldn't have to agonize. She'd just act, and it would be the right thing.

'Shit!' She didn't know whose voice she was using, breaking the sound barrier of polite softness. 'Never mind the damn cup! What I care about is what's going on with you!'

Candy stared at her for a moment. The she answered, and her voice, too, sounded different, shakier. 'How bout what's going on with *you*? I aint the only one in this room, you know!'

Ruth would have spoken, but Candy wasn't through. 'You just don't want me to quit cause then you might have to worry about your own self. You couldn't walk out the door telling yourself what a good job you done then. What a good therapist you are and how much you care. That's what you get off on isn't it? But the minute I say something about you, like that time I said the shit about Sonya, then you turn right back into Miss Tight-Ass Social Worker. Like this expression comes on your face. . . .' Candy's face copied it, cruelly. 'Who the hell are you?' she mimicked in a prissy, unpleasant voice. 'Please get your ass right back where it belongs.' Candy reached up impatiently and tore out the rubber band herself. She shook her head and her hair fanned out like a streaked mane.

'I asked her to be real, I started it,' Ruth reminded herself, but she felt her own feet tapping on the floor now, her shaking hands reaching for a cigarette.

'I'm not so sure you really want me to stop being that "Miss Tight-Ass Social Worker," ' she said. 'Look what happened when I stepped out of that role – you skipped your appointment and just came back to tell me you're quitting.'

'Oh yeah!' Candy seemed to be enjoying herself now. 'That was really steppin' out of it, alright! That time you let your feelings get the better of your job, didn't you? I was sick and sorry so you helped me out. But I don't need it, you hear me? I make out fine. I don't need no favors from no one, especially not from no screw.'

At this name, Ruth felt tears start to her eyes. Candy was crying too when she spoke again.

'I'm a adult just like you, Miss Foster. I aint your fucking child!' Neither of them said anything for a minute. Ruth remembered the dream in which she'd rescued Candy, the two of them running to freedom through the rain on their bare feet.

'I don't think you're a child,' she said finally. 'I respect you a lot, Candy. Maybe I've never told you how much I learn from you. I'm your therapist and you're right, I don't think I should talk to you about my personal life. But if you want to know how I feel right now, or how I felt about leaving you in the office, I could talk about that.'

Candy gave her a half-smile, and nodded.

'I felt like a fool,' Ruth said. 'I felt like I set you up, Candy, I closed my eyes to the reality of this place. Because the truth is, it isn't a place where if you're sick you get to lie down. And I wanted it to be, I didn't want to see that it wasn't, so I acted like it was. And the worst part was that then I went home and left you with the way it really is. So when I saw that the cup was gone, I thought that's what you were trying to tell me, that I couldn't have it both ways.'

'Maybe,' Candy agreed. 'I didn't say it like that to myself, though. I fell asleep and then I woke up and it was dark and I was so mad. And scared. And I don't know why, I just grabbed that cup and run. And then I felt so bad. Cause it didn't make no sense. I really like you so much, you know. . . .'

Ruth paused to let that sink in for a moment. 'After I did it I kept thinking that I shouldn't even be a therapist, that there's got to be something wrong when every time you go by your feelings, it means you're making a mistake.'

'Hey, that don't have to be true,' Candy comforted her. 'It's just this place. When you do something good in here, it gets turnt around. It's the opposite of how it should be. If I was you, I'd leave. I really would. I mean, it's not like they're keeping you in here. You aint done nothing wrong.'

They both laughed, feebly.

'No, seriously,' Candy continued. 'Aint they got therapist jobs someplace else you could do?'

Ruth smiled. 'But I like working here in lots of ways,' she said. 'I like my clients here. I like you a lot, Candy.'

Candy smiled, and shook her head again. 'Listen,' she said. 'Remember what I talked to you about a while ago? About feelings? Like take my case now. Billy's been treating me like shit. And she's sposed to leave next week. Now what good is it gonna do me to come and see you and talk about how that feels, and get all stirred up? I got to live here. I can't just go off, like Telecea Jones or them, you know. Or take that time when I was sick. No one hadn't even noticed it but Billy, and she just noticed it enough to stay away. And I was hurting, but I turnt it off, you know. I was making it, I was doing real good. And then you came down them stairs, and put your hand on me, and told me to lie down, and the blanket and office and shit. . . .' Candy shook her head. 'See what I'm trying to tell you is it aint the feelings that's wrong. It's just you can't have them in here. So why not go work someplace normal, where you can?'

'I understand what you're saying,' Ruth told her. 'Thank you. But I think I'll hang on here a little while.'

Candy nodded. 'Well, seeing that you're so stubborn, and if you aint put anyone in at my place, how bout Monday at ten next week?'

Ruth nodded. 'Monday at ten,' she agreed.

CANDY

When Candy came out of Foster's office, that bitch Lehrman was standing right outside. The thought that she might of heard their conversation made Candy want to punch her in the jibs. This broad was always showing up someplace she had no business being and she was gonna get her ass kicked for her one of these days. Candy wished she could tell her that the only reason her pretty little art room hadn't been cleaned out but good yet was cause a lot of people that had respect for Miss Foster knew they was tight. Sonya-baby probly thought it was cause she was so cool, just one of the girls.

Candy took a good look at Lehrman to see could she see what Foster saw in her. She was dressed fairly butch today, with black corduroys, a plaid blazer jacket and these kind of bad black boots, and with her crazy witch hair all down and bushed out. Like the first time she saw her, Candy had to admit there was something there, some style or energy or something, even though it wasn't nothing she could go for herself, not in a million years. She looked a little better when she was dressed butch, or maybe it was just easier to picture her with Foster that way. She hoped at least she wouldn't treat Foster too bad. You could tell she was the kind that was gonna turn nasty one way or the other, but maybe these educated type butches didn't beat on their ladies. Cause what would Foster do if someone hit her? It was hard to picture. Candy was pretty sure Foster hadn't never let no man do her like that. She probly had never even run into the problem.

'Hi Candy, how are you?' Lehrman had the nerve to ask, like they was old buddies or something.

Candy just halfway nodded her head, but the bitch went right on.

'You know, Candy, I was on my way up to Max for the first time, and I chickened out. Had to come talk to Ruth about it.'

'Scared you just thinking bout Max, huh?' Candy asked, wishing she could smack the dizzy bitch. 'Well, it scared me too. When I did three months up there after my last escape. So maybe you'll get over it.'

Lehrman stared at her, like she'd hit her or something. 'Did I say

249

something wrong?' she asked. 'Or are you still angry at me from the tour?'

Candy thought of her and Foster hanging out together after work. They'd sit in a restaurant somewheres and hold hands and Foster would tell her all about her 'personal life' that was such a big fucking secret. Probly Foster would tell the bitch how she'd persuaded her poor disturbed patient, Candy, to stay in therapy. 'I aint angry,' she told Lehrman, all flat and hateful. 'I don't have no feelings concerning you. Got better things to do with my time.'

SONYA

'Yes,' Ruth had told her, 'it's important, you have to go.' Now Sonya stood downstairs in the hall, waiting for Moody to escort her to Max and thinking about her plan for a prison dollhouse. It would be the kind of dollhouse where you can take the roof and sometimes the side wall off, and reach your hand in, like the way it looked when they were tearing down an apartment building, and for a day or so you could look in and see intact rooms with pink wallpaper and the table set for breakfast. Only her prison dollhouse would have an area called Max which would be at the center, but covered up or veiled somehow, the dark mysterious energy source of the whole place.

When Moody finally arrived Sonya decided she'd put him in too, as a large, human-faced dog, its mouth hanging open, panting and waiting for permission to attack.

She followed him silently up the stairs and to the left, where he paused and worked with his huge bunch of keys on a black iron door. Behind that door was another one, and when that opened onto a tiny square office, she was surprised to see a small copper-colored woman in a yellow terry cloth bathrobe sitting on the desk smoking a cigarette.

Moody headed back down the stairs, locking the doors behind him, and the woman motioned to Sonya. 'Why don't you sit down and relax yourself? Proudy'll be back subsequently, she went down there to check up on a new girl. Nine and one half months pregnant, and would you believe this is where they brung that poor child when they picked her up on escape! Don't even speak no English, aint it a shame?'

'Yes,' Sonya agreed, pondering the nine and one half months. 'Why didn't they put her in the hospital?'

'Oh you know how these people in here's minds work,' the woman answered. 'By the way, I'm Dina War. I know you must be Sonya, that poor child Telecea speaks of you constantly. They tell me you're an artistic therapist, and as it happens, the field interests me. I feel you can derive a lot of interior type insight from a person's art work they produce.'

Sonya nodded in bewildered agreement.

'I myself tried my hand at it, so to speak, at one time,' Dina continued. 'During an unfortunate incarceration at the unfamous Ramsey State Hospital, I'm sure you've heard of it. Come to find out, three weeks later when I was home again, I receive a letter in the mail informing me that my paintings had been selected for a nation wide tour, that is international, if you get my meaning. . . .'

A harried looking black woman who must be Proudy appeared from down the hall where a radio blasted, and Dina jumped off the desk and disappeared.

'Miss Foster said you'd be coming up here one of these days.' Proudy looked at Sonya hard. 'Go right down the end. But just like I told her, if she gets noisy, out you go. I aint putting up with it.'

As Ruth had warned her, the long corridor was a shock. Women yelled and sobbed requests at her from their bare cells. A sour smell of urine came from one of them, where a plastic pail had spilled on the floor. There was no cot here, only a mound on a bare ripped mattress. One slim bare arm and a delicate breast were left uncovered by the army blanket. Sonya's palms began to sweat and she wished she could leave.

'Suicide risk,' she heard Dina's voice from the cell across the narrow hall. 'That's the little Riquan I was telling you about. You're sposed to take all their clothes and the sheets, so they can't hang themself. And you gotta check on them every hour. It's the law.'

As Sonya got further down the hall, the radio got louder. It hung from one of the exposed pipes just outside the last cell, where Telecea was standing, pressed tightly against the harsh grating. She looked much thinner, and her shaved hair had grown out in uneven little peaks. Her eyes, always enormous, now seemed to take up her whole face. 'You my delight alright tonight,' the music screamed, hurting Sonya's ear.

Telecea's fingers reached through the holes in the wire. 'Come here,' she said in a piercing whisper.

Sonya came as close as she could.

'They got one of them things in the radio,' Telecea whispered. 'To listen to me, find out what I'm thinking. Try and protect theyself gainst the Venger. Fools don't know it don't make Him no difference. He hear it all anyway. The noise spose to drive me crazy. Mess wif my ears.'

Sonya nodded. 'I can see how it would do that.' She reached up to turn it down, waiting for some repercussion.

Telecea smiled at her. 'I know you come,' she said. 'Dina tell me, don't you count on it you know how they be, but I knowed you would. Don't worry, I aint say your name to no one else,' she added quickly. 'Even that time they make me drink cum.'

'Why not?' Sonya was afraid that Telecea had built up some fantasy in which they were lovers, but instead she whispered frantically, 'You know! The sculpture pictures. Be His Venger!'

Confused, Sonya decided to ground them both by talking about the art room. She described Telecea's desert sculpture, safe in storage, and the other one she'd just begun, still waiting for her. Telecea listened hungrily, pressed so close to the wire that Sonya thought her face would wear its print all day.

'We goin' on with it huh?' she demanded. 'When I come out of here next week in the morning, Monday Wednesday Friday ten o'clock.'

Ruth had instructed Sonya to repeat this schedule several times to Telecea, emphasizing that she'd be pretty fuzzy. Such a repetition appeared to be unnecessary. Instead, she decided to talk to Telecea as she usually did, as a fellow artist. She described her plans for the prison-house sculpture, and Telecea leaned closer to listen, motioning from time to time for her to speak more softly. When she came to the part about Moody as Dog, Telecea's eyes lit up.

'See how he gon like that, his unclean doggish self,' she gloated.

'I doubt he'll ever see it,' Sonya reminded her.

But Telecea continued to laugh to herself. 'A big stupid dog that get his ass whip. And kick.'

Proudy's voice hollered from the office. 'Time to go, Miss.'

Sonya gripped Telecea's fingers through the grating in goodbye. The first horror of the place had worn off, and she saw herself walking fearlessly and compassionately through Max, the only one Telecea trusted.

The mound under the blanket in the still smelly cage had shifted position now. A young girl's head looked out, her eyes dazed and confused.

'Mami, Mami,' she cried, looking directly at Sonya.

'Never mind that one, she don't speak no English,' Proudy told her. 'And what you turn down the radio for? Why don't *you* try and listen to that nut seven hours a day sometime with no break? I leave it up like that for the girls,' she explained, softening a little. 'If they hear her carrying on, it sets them all off. Then I got a whole floor full of nuts instead of just one.'

As Sonya waited for Moody to open the doors again, the radio blared out defiantly. 'When your friends start acting cold to your face, when you start feeling so out of place . . .' The song followed her down the stairs. 'When your troubles come down like the falling rain.'

TELECEA

Sonya been up here. Just like I knowed, all this time she been trying to come and they aint let her. She gots to be careful so don't no one find out. She tell me, Telecea, your wall is waiting for you. And no one have touched your desert sculpture. She making a prison house sculpture her own self. All bout this place. Put anyone she want in there and even Max too and that Jezebel Proudy her ho'ish self and Moody that done me like that. She make him a dog, one of them big old stupid dogs that the spit come out his mouth when he breathe and when you see it you kick it good. Kind of dog got no fur on it fat old ass, everyone be kicking it so much. The way she gone make it, the front be open up, and you could just put your hand in. Like He do. Like that time He got sorry he made the world cause everyone so evil and ho'ish with they dicks in each other mouth and they unclean filthy ways. So He just move his little finger and let that water in. Forty days and forty nights flood, and every time He see something live crawling round moving or breathing, let that water come in on it. Peoples be searching round for some dry land screaming and hollering and just grinching they fingers up, try and hold onto something. Call out, Help, help, I'm sorry I done you that way, I promise I be good now. He tell them, Ha ha ha, honey, well aint that just too bad cause it too late now.

Lock me up in a cage, make me drink cum out that nasty old dick. Now they gone see how it feels. All that water come up over they head and they belly all swole up and torment and take a long long time to drown!

Make her a prison house sculpture and we just reach right in and do it to the one she pick. Just her and me be the only ones left when it all over.

SATURDAY, OCTOBER 24

RUTH

'Phone!'

Victor came in to yell at Ruth, who was vacuuming the living room and hadn't heard it. He'd been reluctant to answer it all week because he was sure it would be Sonya for her, even though it never had been Sonya, and was usually for him. Now he withdrew ostentatiously into the bedroom, closing the door behind him. As she picked up the phone she could hear the faint sound of his guitar.

'Hi, Sweetheart.' It was her father, who always talked too loud on the phone so that she had to hold it at arm's length. Her mother, who was on the other extension, almost whispered, which made it hard to talk to them both comfortably. She'd given up asking them to call separately a long time ago.

'Enjoying your weekend?' her father asked.

'Yeah,' she said. 'We're just hanging around being lazy.'

'That's good.' It was her mother now. 'You work so hard all week. How's the weather up there? You know it was warm enough to use the pool one day last week?'

When the weather was exhausted, they asked how Ruth's work was going.

'Fine,' she told them. 'Just fine.'

Her father made the usual joke about how he told people he had a daughter in prison, and her mother reminded her to be careful in that place. Ruth told them that Victor was fine, and so was the apartment, and that she was thinking of taking up jogging. She was beginning to get a headache, and carried the phone into the kitchen, where the lentil soup simmered on the stove and she'd arranged a bunch of red and orange leaves against the old brick. She tasted and spiced the soup as she talked to them.

'How's everyone down there?' she asked. 'Have you heard from Elaine?'

There was a short silence, then her mother cleared her throat.

'Elaine and Tim are having their problems,' she said. 'We're hoping for the best, of course. Those poor children.'

'Yeah, well I told her she's got to handle it on her own this time. No more running to Daddy to fix things up.' Her father sounded like he'd had a drink or two. 'I always tell Mom it could be worse. We could have two like her.' He laughed loudly. 'What I want to know is when are you and that young man of yours going to take the plunge and give me the chance to give away some of this money I've been saving for you? You wait much longer, that sister of yours will spend it up right under your nose. Seems to me the two of you ought to know each other plenty well by now. Gotta take a few risks in life, Ruthy.'

'You leave Ruth alone,' her mother cut in. 'She knows what's best for her, she always has. She and Victor will get married when they're ready to, not to please us, Dad. And they'll stay married, too, right Ruthy?'

Ruth made a noncommittal noise. Now her stomach hurt too.

'Well, you tell that young man of yours hello from me,' her father yelled. 'Can't say I approve of this living-together business, but he's a good boy. . . .'

As she hung up the phone, Victor appeared in the doorway.

'In case you wanted to make plans for tonight with Sonya it's fine with me. Actually, Bill sort of asked me to drop over if I could. He could use some support right now.'

Bill was always in need of support lately, because, according to Victor, Lisa was spending all her time with her new lesbian friends and had refused to sleep with Bill any more.

'Go, then,' part of her wanted to shout. 'Since you've got it all figured out anyway.' But she felt empty and shaky after the phone call and didn't want to be alone.

'That was just my parents,' she told him flatly. 'My father says hello.'

'You're entitled to your own life, you don't need to tell me who it was,' he began, but she pulled him close and buried her head into his familiar solidness.

'Lisa's her and I'm me,' she mumbled into his sweater. 'It's not an epidemic. Why don't you bring your guitar and play to me while I finish the soup?'

CANDY

It was a rainy Saturday afternoon, and Candy was in the cottage, cooking dinner for her friends. She'd made cornbread, beans, fried up some chicken, and she'd baked some brownies. They was even some of that homemade hooch they made with them pop cans of grapefruit juice you could get at the store, that wasn't too bad if you drunk it a little at a time. Ginzer was off, and the little dyke screw Bobby Brown, who was on duty, didn't care what you did as long as you let her in on it and there wasn't no beefing involved. Candy had already gave Bobby a plate and cleared her out, and all the other girls in the cottage was in their rooms sleeping or watching TV or something, so now it felt almost like it was her own kitchen, with her friends so underfoot she couldn't hardly take care of the food. Finally she told them scram till it was done. Lou and Loraine and Donny moved, but Billy, who was high, stayed where she was, in one of them folding chairs set right in the middle of the kitchen floor.

Dina stayed too, jumping after Candy from the counter to the stove to the icebox and talking a mile a minute. The food was sposed to be to celebrate that Dina had came out of Max that day, and Dina was celebrating all right, catching up on all the gossip both in here and on the street with her speedy self, and keeping her eyes on Loraine's curvy little ass, where they had landed the minute she walked down them Max steps.

'You say Fran Minelli's gone? That's good, but the bitch'll be back in a month, see if she aint. Edie Sampson's still here, though, right? You watch, the minute it starts in smelling odiperous that one will make her appearances.'

And sure enough, a few minutes later here came Edie, hanging her big tits on the counter and telling Dina, 'Well, my Lord what a surprise, how you doing, Sister,' as if she hadn't know Dina was up in Max all the time and was just too lazy to take her fat ass under the window.

'I'm doing excellent, thanks to some friends that came to see about me all the time I was incarcerated in that rat hole, and no thanks to them that had more proficient things to do,' Dina told her.

Then Edie turnt to Billy, who was her next best chance of getting over cause of knowing her mother.

'I just now thought about some nice fresh greens I got that I could add in to what you-all got going,' she tried.

But Billy just sat there nodding, so Dina had to speak for her and say, 'Oh now, aint that a shame, but greens just don't fit in appropriate with the menu,' which of course they did.

Edie stuck out her lip and high-tailed it on out, and Candy laughed loudest of all.

Then the food was ready, and Candy gave everyone a plate to carry back to Billy's room, that she had fixed up before with this purple shade on the light she made out of a old slip. She turned the radio on to her jazz station, and the DJ cooperated by playing her favorite, Ramsey Lewis's 'Love Notes,' just as everyone squeezed in the room, all talking about how fine and mellow it was with the rain starting to fall outside.

Feeding people had always been special for Candy. She wouldn't feed just anybody but you knew when she cooked for you that you was alright with her. Food was a funny thing, she thought, meaning real food that someone had prepared, and not the shit they served you in the cafeteria. It seemed like it had a way of reminding people of past memories.

Loraine, who was sitting on the floor kind of leaning up against Dina's legs but acting like she didn't know she was doing it, started talking first. She told them about when she was a kid on Sunday afternoons in summer, and they used to go to this lake.

'We used to come out of that water,' she said, all soft, almost like she was singing it to the music, 'and they'd be that hot warm barbecue smell, you know, and the mothers would grab us with those big towels, not necessarily their own kid, just the nearest kid, and rub on us. And they'd tell us 'You *know* you-all don't get nothing to eat till you change out them wet suits. Catch your death.' And by the time we had changed, and started in eating, the sun would be just coming down, and a radio would be playing, and the teenagers would of started snuggling up together and sometimes the grownups too, and us kids could watch them and giggle, and then after all the food was gone, we'd go off on our own and tell ghost stories and scare each other to death . . .' Loraine trailed off, remembering.

Candy wished she was there, and they all must of felt the same way, cause just then Lou said, 'I wish it was summer right now and I was by that lake, just the way you told it.'

'Yeah,' Loraine said. 'But I would keep the food and the company we got right here. Just change the location.'

Candy couldn't quite believe that about the company, but even if it wasn't true, it was a sweet thing to say. She would of felt real good herself, if only Billy wasn't nodding off, away in her own world like that, hardly eating or drinking. Someone was passing round reefer, and Candy dragged hard and tried to listen to Dina tell this real long story about some family reunion she'd gone to, going into every single person that was there, and how they each made it big this or that way, and got wrote up or had a TV special on them, and just what they was each doing now.

'God*damn*, Dina,' Donny finally said. 'You gonna tell us what color underwear they all had on?'

Dina looked mad at first, but her and Donny was butch-buddies from way back, so she just laughed.

'How bout you, Candy?' Donny asked her. 'Who taught you to cook so good, your Mom?'

Candy shook her head. 'My Mom didn't teach me shit. I must of found out by myself. Or else I was born knowing.'

'Maybe you were a cook in a, you know, premature carnation,' said Dina.

Nobody knew what that was, so she started in explaining bout how you could be carnated in all these different people's bodies before you was born, but Candy didn't listen.

She was thinking bout cooking and eating memories too, the summer right before she left home. She was skinny now, but before that one summer she'd been even skinnier, starved-looking, people used to say, and the reason was, she always hated mealtimes so much. Her mother hated cooking. She usually fed them shit out of cans, that she had cooked too long, or else out of packages that used to be just a little bit still-froze inside, or the milk would be off. There was always something bad about almost every meal, probly cause she'd been drinking the whole time she was cooking. Then, right before dinner she used to get scared, and try to pull it together, acting like one of them mothers on TV, and calling out, 'Catherine, come in here and set the table, dear.'

There was these glittery silvery plastic tablemats that Candy remembered real good for some reason, with a hard gritty feel to them she used to hate. And cloth napkins that was dirty a lot, cause her mother said nice people didn't use no paper napkins, but she used to forget to wash them. And a bunch of fake flowers in the middle. When they was still living home, Sally and Stan usually tried to be somewheres else at supper time, and Candy wished she was old enough to skip out too. But every so often they was all there and that was the worst of all. Candy remembered pushing her food all around her plate. She could never really eat with her Dad there, but leaving food was enough to set him off. They was so many things that could do that, though. The phone would ring and it would be some boy asking for her or Sal, and that would do it. Or maybe something would come up about her not going to school. Or else he would suddenly notice how fast Stan was eating, and push his face right down in his plate, so food'd fly all over. Then he'd yell some shit about 'Here I work hard all week to put food in your worthless stomachs and this is what I come home to, a pack of stupid worthless kids that don't have no respect, and a worthless lying trickster drunk for a wife, that don't even deserve to have a good home like she got.' No matter how pissy mad he was he wouldn't never swear cause he didn't believe in it. He said it was against God's laws. And then Mom would either cry or start in on her hysterical drunk laughing and run out the room. Which is when Candy would book out fast, cause it was her turn next. And just cause her mother always put herself in the way of his fist and took whatever shit he dished out to her didn't mean Candy had to.

That summer she'd decided she wasn't going to, ever again. She was just thirteen at the time, and small, but she knew how to talk real grownup and she put socks in her bra and a shitload of make-up and they believed she was sixteen, or said they did, and hired her for a waitress at the rootbeer stand out on the beltway. Dad was always talking about how he'd been working on his dad's farm from when he was seven years old or something, and how lazy his kids was, so he couldn't say nothing to her about it, and she didn't have to come home for supper all summer.

It was hard work, but she liked earning money and wearing that skimpy uniform that showed off the figure she was faking and just beginning to get, and she almost felt sweet sixteen for real. She'd ride her bike in to work in the morning, and when she had a date for after work, they'd just put the bike in his car, and the guy would let her out a block from home with it. But sometime she wouldn't have no date, and then what she'd do was pack up some food, a cheeseburger and fries or onion rings and a rootbeer float or something, in her bike basket, and stop to eat it at this place she'd found that was a big old river with a bridge over it. It didn't look like nothing when you drove over it in a car, but underneath there was benches and rocks that was worn smooth from people sitting on them, and they'd always be a few old black people that had came fishing around sunset. She thought they must of been coming there forever. She'd sit on a rock and mind her business and eat her picnic, and every so often she'd hear a snatch of conversation that sounded soft and gentle, not about any certain thing or in a hurry, and just the opposite of the way her Mom and Dad talked to each other, or the other grownups she knew. Sometimes the old people would smile at her, but nobody ever bothered her or spoke, and she'd eat in peace, then throw the bag in the water and watch the slow old river take it away. It was the first time she could remember food tasting good. She'd just sit there a while thinking till it got dark, and by the time she got home, whatever shit had gone down that night would be over and her Dad would be snoring in front of the TV.

'What's the matter, Candy, lost in your thoughts?' Donny asked her gently. Candy nodded. The room was quiet now, with Loraine and Dina gone off together, and Billy nodding into her food up on the bed. Candy took Billy's full plate from her, and her and Donny carried everything back in the kitchen.

'Shit, I hate to see her hit the street like that,' Donny said. 'Way she's going, she'll be back in about the time you're ready to leave out.'

'I know,' Candy nodded, 'but aint nothing I can do. She won't listen to me.'

'She aint much good to you like that, is she?' Donny asked. Linda was out on furlough, and Donny moved her arm round Candy's waist, trying it out. Candy smiled and moved out the way. Billy had been known to come out of a nod fast before, and there wasn't no way Donny turned her on anyway, with her slicked back greazed-up hair and her pasty white skin.

SONYA

It was noon, and Sonya was eating hot oatmeal with raisins and raspberry jam and cream. She tasted and chewed each mouthful very slowly, the way they'd said to do in a compulsive eating group she'd once been in briefly. She tried to concentrate on her eating, instead of on the terrible dream she'd had. Ruth had warned her that everyone had Max dreams after their first visit, and she was no exception. Someone had been reaching at her with bony starved hands, trying to drag her in with them. The worst part had been when she'd smashed and smashed the hands with a brick so they'd let go of her.

She got more oatmeal. There were gray clouds outside. A storm was brewing. It was the perfect kind of weekend morning to get up and have a slow, luxurious breakfast with your lover and then go back to bed for a few hours. She thought of calling Ruth, who'd decided to take up jogging and had asked her if she wanted to go running together over the weekend, but Sonya didn't feel like making a fool of herself running, or like a whole lot of small talk and preliminaries.

'Will you come over and come to bed.' That's what she'd really like to say to Ruth. Then, if she appeared, they wouldn't have to talk at all. Sonya would just lead her, firmly and silently, to the still-warm bed. There was something sexy about a morning bed before it was made, with its warm sheets and body smells. They'd get up much later, maybe five or six or so, and she'd send Ruth home and start working. She was beginning to think she couldn't work well if she didn't get some sex, or at least some physical contact. There was a kind of flow that came from being touched that she didn't seem to have any more.

TELECEA

Stay awake all night. Thinking and planning. Planning and thinking.
Bout when I get out of here. Back to the art room. When it start to get
light, I climb up on the bed and look out that little window. Cloud
coming, got a animal zipped up in it. Then it unzip itself out that grey
cloud its furry self. Half black and half white. Them red eyes. Smoke
out its mouth. A long dick-tail wif stingers at the end. Big old feathers
on it head.

It talk to me. Tell me, I the Venger and He send me down to you,
Telecea Jones. Then that beast climb back in that cloud and zip itself
up nice and warm. And the rain come down.

Saturday now. Only two more days till Monday. When I get out
of here.

MONDAY, OCTOBER 26

RUTH

'It was my same burning dream,' Candy said. 'Only it was that little
kid that came in with Billy's mother that time, Tawanda, that was
getting burnt, and I couldn't do nothing but just sit back and watch.
And then I had this other dream, that I was pregnant. . . .'

In a new costume of a loose sweatshirt and jeans, and without
make-up, Candy looked casual and almost boyish this morning,
except for the streaked platinum hair and the lines around her eyes
and mouth. Her glance kept going to the mug which Sonya had
helped Ruth to pick out to replace the broken one, a heavy, squat
mug, with a blue-grey speckled glaze a little like the other. Ruth
forced herself to stop thinking about going to buy the mug with
Sonya, and to concentrate on what Candy was saying to her.

'I was getting all the signs. Morning sickness, and breasts and
belly swole up, everything. But even in the dream I knew it wasn't
possible, right, so I went to this lady doctor. Come to think of it, she
looked like you. Or anyway, how you used to look, with your hair all
pulled back in a bun, sort of stern, you know, but kind. And I told
you, I mean her, that I had a hysterectomy, so wasn't no way I could
be pregnant.'

'But she said while I was in jail they'd figured out how to do it,
how to grow your womb back. She said that's what I did, without
realizing it. And first I believed her, but then I had the thought she
was trying to trick me. That what really happened was this tumor
started to grow in me from when they fucked with me for the
hysterectomy, and she was just telling me this other shit so I would
die without making no noise about it.'

Ruth thought how much she liked Candy. Even her dreams were
sharp with intelligence, pain, and rage. 'Remember what we were
saying about how sometimes dreams are a way of talking to
yourself?' she asked. 'Telling yourself what maybe you know but you
can't say out loud yet?'

Candy nodded. 'Yeah, I've been thinking about it like that,' she
said. 'First, what I thought was, that womb shit came up cause Billy's
sort of been taking up that part of me, the part that wants a kid, you
know? But now she's gone, I mean she's going, right, and that part

feels empty again. But I aint been letting myself really think about it out loud you know, because what good is it gonna do, I can't have no baby. So in the dream it's like I solved it the only way possible, by a miracle. Which is what everyone in here wants if you see what I mean.'

Ruth shook her head. 'What do you mean?'

'Well, you know how Frankie goes to them Jesus ladies? Them born-agains? At first I thought she was just trying to get shit from them, cigarettes and stuff, but now I think it's this miracle thing. A whole lot of girls go to them fools. Plus a lot of them go to that Catholic priest that comes here on Sundays but you sposed to pick one, you aint sposed to go to both of them, but a lot of them does. That way they got a back-up, see. In case the miracle don't come through one way, it still might another.'

Ruth nodded, impressed. 'Do you think everyone in here has a miracle in reserve?' she asked.

'That's what I been trying to figure out,' Candy said. 'And I think so. Take Billy, she goes to dope, and so do a lot of them. Plus, she got me for a back-up. Lots of them got their man on the outside, no matter what a asshole he is, like Mabe for instance. And Telecea and Gladdy and them, they go to the crazy place, cause when you go off you can believe you're anywhere you want to be, or anyone, like you know how Telecea thinks she's God's messenger or something?'

Ruth nodded again.

'Loraine used to go to Ritchie, but now I think she goes to you, the way she's always talking about 'Everything's gonna be alright, now Miss Foster's helping me to understand.' Now you know and I know it aint that simple.'

'Maybe that's it,' Ruth suggested. 'The knowing that it isn't that simple that makes you different. If you know you can't depend on some miracle, then you have to look to a lot of different things. And to yourself.'

'Yeah, sometimes I look at it that way,' Candy said. 'And then other times I think I aint no different. I go to Billy first, and then you, if that don't work. Plus, I always got good old dope back there if I need it.'

'And me,' Ruth thought, 'I'm no different either. I go to Sonya. And then to my work.'

She thought about how Sonya looked when she first came down to the car that morning, with her hair tangled and sleep still in her eyes. She'd gotten in without greeting Ruth or even smiling at her, like a sulky, sleepy child. Ruth had wanted to reach over and stroke her good morning, to comb out her lovely tangled pony hair and smooth out her clothes. But even in the short time they'd been driving to work together, she'd learned when to hold back. She'd driven on smoothly as if immersed in her own thoughts, and after a while Sonya had slowly shaken herself awake, had combed her hair, and then had reached out to Ruth, squeezing her hand on the wheel for good morning.

'It's like a Bingo game,' Candy was saying. 'If you don't get your miracle in one card you still got another.'

Luckily, Ruth hadn't quite lost the train of thought. 'But in a Bingo game, somebody has to win,' she said, to show that she was listening.

'That's right.' Candy's voice was grim. 'But in here, aint none of us gonna get no miracles.'

'Listen, Candy, there are other ways besides miracles. Just hearing you talking, I keep thinking what a good counselor you'd be, how much understanding of people you have. And there's that peer counseling program for street women I told you about that my friend Ann runs. You go to school part-time and work part-time. I'm sure they'd take you if you're interested. You could do that without a miracle.'

'Yeah, I guess,' Candy nodded. 'But first I'd have to stop believing in miracles for real. Like I got to stop wanting shit from Billy. And I just aint ready to. Take this morning, some of us was talking bout Telecea Jones, cause she's sposed to be coming out of Max. I told you how Billy is when it comes to Telecea, right? Well, I said we all ought to watch out for her a little bit, now Norma's gone. And Billy came out of her nod just long enough to tell me, 'You aint speaking to her.' I started arguing, cause really someone got to speak to that girl or she'll go right off again, but then I saw Billy wasn't paying no attention. She was off in her nod again. Now I don't dig being told what to do, but at least she used to stay around long enough to back up what she said. I mean if she fuckin' hit me it would beat a blank, you know?'

Ruth nodded. 'Still, it sounds to me like you're not relying too much on those miracles,' she said. 'Even though you just told me that part of you isn't ready to give up the Billy-miracle, you're still going ahead and doing what you believe in instead of what she wants you to do. Look at the stand you're taking about Telecea. . . .'

Candy shrugged. 'She aint come out yet,' she said. 'Who knows, maybe I'll turn on her first of anyone. Seems like everything's in opposites. Either I help her or I turn on her. Either I get all cured, like I aint even had no hysterectomy, or it's a big trick, and I'm about to die of cancer. And like in one way I feel like I'm just waiting for Billy to go so I can clean up my act, and in another way I want her to get busted and me right along with her, so can't neither of us get out. How do I know which is real?'

'Probably both are real,' Ruth suggested. 'Part of you really wants to make it this time, and then there's the part that doesn't want to.'

'Yeah, that sounds right. But don't you think Billy's got a part that wants to make it? I never thought she'd mess up like this.'

'I'm sure she has one,' Ruth said. 'But maybe it's just not as strong as yours, right now anyway.'

Candy nodded. 'Yeah, I mean, my life hasn't been easy, but it's been a piece of cake compared to hers. There's a lot from before that's still fucking with her. But, like I thought I could change it. Make it go away or something.'

Ruth noded in recognition.

'I used to lie there.' Candy's voice was dazed. 'Next to her. She'd be asleep, and I'd be awake, and I'd be feeling so much I thought I'd explode. And I just knew it had to be going somewheres. I guess I thought it was kind of floating into her, you know? Healing up them hurt places. But now that seems like just one more bullshit miracle, you know?'

'I don't think so,' Ruth said. 'I think it was working. Maybe not as fast as you needed it to, or as she did, and not all at once like a miracle, or even enough to make her get it together on the outside yet. But that doesn't mean your love didn't help her. Maybe you can't even know how yet. But I'm sure it did.'

Candy smiled grimly. 'Thanks, but no thanks. If she goes out now, with a habit, she's gonna need to sell. And she aint gonna be careful bout it, cause she's gonna be sick. Which means she gets busted soon. She comes back in here. So how the fuck my love gonna help her? Or help me?'

She got up. 'I don't know how you stay in this business,' she said. 'Trying to put people back together that's too far gone to be helped. If Billy's too bad hurt, how you gonna help someone like Telecea Jones? I'd give up and go on home. They aint no miracles.

Like if you had a hysterectomy, how the fuck you gonna turn back around and have a kid?'

She paused at the door.

'See you next week,' she said gently. 'Don't get me wrong, I aint disgusted with you this time, Miss Foster. Just plain disgusted.'

CANDY

In the cafeteria at noon, Dina was joining in with Billy in putting down therapy while they was all eating rubbery spaghetti.

'You know that quote Karl Marx said?' she asked them. 'Religion is the opium of the people?'

None of them did, though Candy had heard of Karl Marx, and they had all heard of opium.

'Well, opium is a kind of dope, right?' Dina explained, getting so enthused that she gestured with her fork and spilled tomato sauce on Loraine's shirt. 'So this dude, Marx, that started off Communism, was saying that people get so they depend on religion the same way as dope, for their fix. And this going to therapy shit is the exact same thing.'

'That's just what I been telling her.' Billy spoke to Dina over Candy's head, ignoring her. 'This girl here needs her therapy fix every Monday morning. If she don't get it, she act up. You know how these mental people is.'

'I wish you'd both stop,' Candy said. Something in Dina's rap reminded her of what she'd been saying to Foster a few hours ago, but she was afraid all this talk about mental people might remind Billy of Telecea, who was out of Max, sitting right on the other side of the dining room, with her own private officer, this little black dude, Edwin, otherwise known as Tom White. So far, Billy didn't seem to of noticed Telecea.

'Watch that fork, baby,' Loraine told Dina, who she was calling Her Woman out loud now. 'Anyway I don't agree with what you just said. There's a difference between junk you get addicted to, and something that helps you put your head back together.'

'Girl,' Billy gave Loraine a mean look. 'Sometimes when you talk I wonder where you coming from on the for-real side.'

'From the suburbs, that's where,' Candy thought. 'From the only colored cheer-leader,' but she didn't say nothing.

She could hear some noise from Telecea's table, something about 'sinning and laughing and stuffing they face like a pig,' and she talked real fast so Billy wouldn't hear, imitating one of them white ladies from the suburbs that Loraine had reminded her of for a minute.

'I hope all of you are planning to participate in the nice Halloween party they have planned for us, girls,' she said. 'I'm sure you're all going to put on your nice costumes and dunk for apples and carve some nice jack-o-lanterns.'

'I'm gonna carve me a jack-o-lantern, alright,' said Billy, as loud and hateful as she could be. She was staring right over at Telecea now, and Candy realized she'd seen her all the time. 'One of them bald-headed ones.'

'Cool it, now, girl.' Dina skipped over to Billy like a little pixie and said something in her ear.

Billy smiled and Candy knew it had to of been something about dope. 'Hey, maybe I will par-ticipate after all,' Billy said.

SONYA

Monday morning, Sonya let herself into the art room, appreciating all over again the way the sun fell on the painted walls, the clean spaciousness of it. The full-length mirror which she'd put up as an aid to self-portraiture made wavering circular patterns of reflection on Ruth's white wall, creating an art form of its own. Sonya looked at herself in the silver mirror, trying to see what Ruth saw when she gazed at her with those adoring eyes.

'Soft and rounded,' she whispered in Ruth's voice. 'Sensual, voluptuous.' Did Ruth think about her breasts, she wondered, maybe imagine burying her head in them. Or did she think like that at all?

Telecea was due in an hour, and she moved quietly around the room, locating Telecea's work and her orange smock, which she'd sewed up. Then she sat down on the bench beneath the white wall and opened her idea book to the prison-house plan. It was too logical, she decided. It needed more of the nightmare quality of a fun-house.

At exactly ten o'clock Telecea appeared at the door accompanied by the promised male officer. He was small and dark, with a balding head a little like Telecea's freshly shaven one and a general look of being some distant relative produced to wait on the wronged queen.

'You can go now,' Telecea commanded.

He immediately scuttled out, stationing himself outside the door, and Sonya wondered how he could possibly constitute protection to anyone.

Telecea hadn't yet looked at her. Instead she closed her eyes and took a step forward, extending her arms. Sonya realized, after a worried instant, what was required. She slipped the orange smock onto the painfully thin arms, and Telecea sighed with satisfaction and opened her huge eyes. The pathetic, childish look she'd had in Max, where her hair had begun to grow in, was now gone. Sonya looked down at the blue sneakers in order not to be overawed.

Telecea shook her head rapidly, breaking the trance. 'We only gots one hour today. Gots to work fast.'

She began pacing around the room, checking for changes, or possibly spying devices.

'Hm-m, still empty,' she noted, when she came to Ruth's wall.

When she reached the mirror she shook her head in disapproval, then turned its face to the wall. Finally she returned to her own place, and the almost finished mirage sculpture.

'No time for this today,' she decided. 'Yours done yet?'

'My what?'

'You know, your prison sculpture you told me about. It aint done?'

Sonya had forgotten Telecea's occasional perfect recall.

'I was working on the plan for it,' she explained, gesturing toward her idea book. 'Right before you came in.'

'Tell me who you got in it.' There was a definite note of impatience in Telecea's voice, and Sonya was beginning to feel uneasy.

'I told you, I haven't finished it yet.' She tried to make her voice firm and calm.

'Well, I needs to know,' insisted Telecea. 'Cause if you already got Moody, I aint putting him in mines.'

'Moody?' Sonya remembered saying something about seeing him as a dog. 'Why couldn't he be in both our sculptures?' she asked.

'Because! That be a waste of time. Once you dead you dead.'

Sonya shivered. It was not that Telecea was exactly unfriendly to her today, but rather as if they were two scientists, working so intently on the same desperately important project that their intimacy would have to be temporarily forfeited under the necessities of the work. Sonya still wasn't sure what the exact nature of this work was supposed to be, but she didn't much like the idea she was getting.

'Listen, Telecea.' She tried to invest her words with both authority and affection. 'You know that putting someone into a sculpture doesn't change anything in real life, right? Making Moody a dog in a sculpture doesn't mean he'll really turn into a dog?'

Telecea shook her head back and forth rapidly in an effort not to hear.

'You never used to waste no time,' she complained. 'I guess I will just take Moody myself, it do that evil dog good to get killed twice anyway.'

Immediately absorbed, she began to make light pencil marks on a large piece of cardboard.

Watching her, Sonya could hear Ruth scolding her, telling her she didn't understand Telecea's potential for violence. But even if Sonya had understood it correctly, what harm could this belief do anyone? In a way, it might have the opposite effect. If Telecea was busy killing her enemies symbolically with paint and cardboard, she wouldn't need to do it in reality. Was it that different from what any artist did, anyway? How about those peaceful, nonviolent writers whose characters butchered one another, or those gentle painters whose canvases oozed blood? It was all sublimation, really. Telecea's was just more overt. Even so, Sonya felt uneasy. Because Moody wouldn't actually turn into a dog, and the people Telecea was busily putting into her newest sculpture would presumably not all die off within the next month. And then would Telecea feel some obligation to help them along their way? She tried to think how to ground Telecea in reality without denying the power of her art.

'There are artists who don't work with hatred or punishment,' she tried, a little feebly. 'There are other kinds of power, Telecea, do you understand? Loving, forgiving power.' Telecea turned to her, smiling a little.

'No,' she said. 'Gone too far for that. There is a time. For every thing. Seed of the harlot, child of the devil. Gots to beat it out. Rape what you earn. White horse done come and Venger be on his back.'

Sonya shivered. For some reason she didn't understand she went over to the mirror and turned it back around. She saw her face in it, tight with anxiety, invaded with Telecea's craziness. Why had she been accepting Telecea's terms at all, treating them as if they existed in some kind of rational system?

Still standing, she turned and pointed to Telecea's cardboard. 'It's a sculpture you were beginning, on a piece of cardboard. It has no magic powers to hurt anyone.'

Telecea stared at her blankly, like a stone.

'I know!' Sonya continued loudly, as if to a slow child. 'We still have a little time left, let's paint pictures of each other. You looked very nice today in your orange smock. I'd like to paint you.'

As she said this, she moved purposefully to the closet and began to take out paints. She'd better start working with Telecea in the way she had with the most disturbed of the patients in the hospital in Vermont, where she'd stuck to still-lifes and portraits – anything that would tie them to reality instead of allowing or encouraging further disorientation.

Telecea seemed agreeable enough. She followed Sonya to the closet and began rummaging through its contents.

'Yeah, that right! You can paint me. Them feathers in there. Make us some horns. Then I be the sculpture picture. My own self!' She paused, and then added, in a flash of inspiration, 'For Halloween!'

'No!' protested Sonya, feeling herself slipping again. 'What I meant was to paint you the way you are now. No feathers or paint, just a picture of you, on paper. Not scary. Pretty.'

It was the wrong word to use in relation to Telecea, and Sonya wasn't surprised to hear that spooky laugh.

'Venger got no time for pretty. No time for forgiving neither. You aint gots to pretend.'

It was too late for Sonya's portrait idea, and she'd lost the urge anyway. They cleaned up until the little guard knocked and then came timidly into the room. Telecea hung up her smock obediently, nodding rhythmically to herself.

'Yeah. Uh-huh. I be the sculpture alright. My own self. Saturday. For Halloween. Uh-huh.'

TELECEA

Mr Edwin White the police I got. They know they better not put no Moody in with me if they wants to keep his old fat ass alive. This little man like that old lady they put up in Max that time tell me bout Jesus. They got him so he don't know what he is.

Just like that cartoon, Little Red Goldilocks. Bout that old lady she had this wolf skin on her and the wolf gots the old lady skin. They calls it a sheep in wolf clothes but if you look good you can see them sheep eyes looking out. That how you know.

They better watch theyself with all they switching up in here. Wrong one could get hurt, like when that chopper he come in to get the wolf that have ate up the little girl. How he spose to know? All he can see is the skin so he chop that Granny all up, just leave the feets and the palms of her hands. Poor old lady. Aint her fault, she try her best to do God's word. Brung up a child that born bad and need to be punish every day, *she* can't help that.

I tell you, you gots to watch out cause when it come for Venging you gots to know who who. Like what if He tell me go chop me up some Candy Cane Peters but she be inside the Ruth Foster skin? Bitch try and fool me with Norma voice, well now I am out here, even if I do gots to go back to Max at night and I can lissen and I can watch and find out for myself who really here and who be stealing someone else voice.

That little sheepwolf police dude, I ask him, How come you lets them dress you up like that?

Aint no one can say I don't be giving people they warnings. But Little Sheep Dick want to play ignorant. Tell me, Hey Telecea, you know I aint got no costume on, this is me man, the real me.

Better get that little pointy dick cover up with some fur, I tell him. Don't you know wolfs and sheeps both got fur on they dick?

We in the cafeteria and he almost choke on his spaghetti, looking to see do his dick got fur on it.

Them evil girls just the same since I been up there. With they nasty talk, just spraying that bloody sauce all round. Billy Morris talking some shit bout how she gone carve on me, Halloween. Something happening Halloween, she got that part right. Don't no

276

one but Sonya and me know what, but it aint Telecea Jones gone be cut.

     That butch bomination can talk all she want, but she scairt. Or else why she go the other way soon she see me? Why she start in shaking? Come in a room and look to see do I be in it before she sit down. Oh yeah, that one know alright. Got the mark on her forehead just as sure as she got that dick curlt up inside her, and she know it, too.

WEDNESDAY, OCTOBER 28

RUTH

Loraine Bradley started off her therapy session with Ruth late Wednesday afternoon by asking her if she was on something.

Ruth was so startled that she laughed out loud. 'You mean whether I'm on some drug?' she asked.

'Oh, I don't mean a street drug, Miss Foster.' Loraine's golden-brown skin flushed. 'I know you wouldn't be into nothing like that! But sometimes a person might be taking some medication, you know, to lose weight or something . . .' She shook her head in confusion. 'Not that you need to lose weight, there wouldn't be too much left of you if you did. Well, maybe for a cold, you know, they put all kinds of things in cold medication these days.'

'Do you think I'm acting speedy?' Ruth asked her.

'Oh, not exactly speedy,' Loraine assured her. 'I don't mean you're doing nothing bad. I mean anything bad. You just seem kind of different. Even how you look. . . .'

Ruth looked closely at Loraine, who seemed disproportionately upset by this conversation, almost to the point of tears. She had lately begun to wear her long hair pulled back into a knot at the back of her head, in the style Ruth had recently abandoned herself. She wore neat tailored tan slacks, and a yellow Fair Isle sweater with a multi-colored border, which had struck Ruth as somehow familiar. Now she realized that it was almost identical to a light blue Fair Isle sweater of her own, which was one of her regulars for work. Even the stiff way Loraine was sitting at the edge of the brown chair with her legs pressed neatly together reminded Ruth somehow of her own posture, although today she'd been leaning back in her chair as she listened, her hands stuck into the floppy sleeves of her new red shirt. She began to understand.

'Do you mean I look different? You've been sort of trying to look like me, and now all of a sudden I'm changing the way I look?'

'I told you,' Loraine nodded emphatically. 'That very first time I came in here. That I wanted to change. To have a, you know, a normal type life. And you're the only straight person I know that I like.'

Ruth laughed a little. 'And I've already stopped looking so straight! Almost right away!'

Loraine nodded. 'That's all I know how to do,' she explained, 'is pay attention. And then imitate. Like in high school I knew I wasn't gonna be nobody's raggedy little nigger. So I watched till I knew which kids to pay attention to. And once I started dressing like them, that was when my English teacher told me to stay after school, had I ever considered college and that. I mean, my schoolwork was good before and nobody ever talked about no college!'

'So it was worth it?' Ruth asked. 'All that paying attention?'

'I don't know,' Loraine shrugged. 'Guess I always thought they'd see through me. That was probably why I did what I did. They accepted me at this hot shit college in the East, you know, and they were flying me up for orientation. The pressure was really on. They'd invited all these down-South relatives to my graduation to hear me get my scholarship and everything. I was sposed to be an example to my race and all that. The first one in the family to make it to college. What happened instead is I got on that plane and there was this one-night stopover in the city, I was sposed to spend the night in a hotel and go on to school the next day. And I went out that night and met someone and I never did make it to that school. I guess I thought by going bad all the way I could at least relax for a while. What I didn't know was there was a whole new set of dressing and talking and acting rules that went with the life. To pay attention to.'

The fifty minutes was over, but Loraine was Ruth's last client, and she decided to let her go on.

'So what am I going to do now?' she wept ten minutes later. 'You said the answer isn't copying you, but how do I know what to do, then? How am I supposed to be real when I don't have anything inside? Or a hairstyle? Or a voice that's mine?'

Ruth tried to tell her that during the last hour she hadn't sounded like a woman without a voice. She described the pain and struggle she'd heard, the deep need to discover herself.

'Do you think you understand me so much cause you're changing a lot too?' Loraine asked. 'You look so different with your hair down!'

'Maybe,' Ruth agreed. 'I guess I have to think about it.'

It was true, she thought after Loraine had left, that the quality of her work had changed radically lately with almost all of her clients. It was as if she'd been able to experience them much more deeply, almost from inside. Her session with Telecea yesterday had been especially powerful.

She'd understood that in Telecea's mind, she and Candy had become somehow confused. They'd spent the hour defining and clarifying the basic boundaries between people, and she felt sure that Telecea would be able to continue the process on her own. She wondered how Sonya's session with Telecea had gone today. Sonya had seemed a little disturbed about Telecea on Monday, although she hadn't actually said much to Ruth about it. It would be important to keep checking in over the next few weeks, she thought. Telecea was still pretty delusional, and Sonya, for all her brilliance, was still new.

Sonya hadn't come downstairs yet, and Ruth decided to stop in at Lynda's office for a few minutes. It was a long time since she'd stopped in just to chat, and she was in the mood. She was more energetic in general, these days. She'd just bought new running shoes, and she itched to try them out. Maybe Sonya would run with her, on Halloween day, before the party.

CANDY

Early yesterday morning when she couldn't sleep, Candy had got up and seen Bobby Brown who was still on, making out with a new little girl. Bobby had seen Candy too. Which was why, when Billy came out the shower and sat down on the bed all naked and sweet smelling, Candy knew wasn't no one gonna hassle them.

She pretended like she was blind, closed her eyes and went exploring with her tongue and the tips of her fingers both, down the long sweet ridge of Billy's back, and then in front, all over her face, licking all round her eyes and soft cheeks and stopping for a long moment to drink in her sweet lips and taste her mouth. Then she started down Billy's long proud neck and rested for a minute on her little nipple, all hard and tight in her mouth. She had just got it in mind to slip right down her long flat belly to her cunt when all of a sudden Billy jerked away.

'Don't touch me like that!'

'What the fuck?' Candy gasped.

Billy jumped off of the bed, pushing her away like she was an irritating fly or mosquito or something, and kept right on shrugging her neck and shoulders, like when you already kilt the bug but could still feel it bothering you.

Candy just laid there. Even though Billy had been all the way naked, and *she* still had on her bra and panties, she felt much too bare all of a sudden and crawled under the covers. Billy must of felt the same way, cause she was getting dressed super fast, like it was a race or something. When Billy was all put together and standing a little way from the bed, she looked down at Candy and started shaking her head.

'You know what time it is, for Christ's sake?' she said.

Candy felt cold under the blanket. She didn't know what the fuck time had to do with anything.

'How come you don't want me touching you?' she asked in a small voice.

'I said, you know what time it is?' Billy repeated.

Like a scared, obedient kid, Candy turnt and looked at the clock up on the dresser.

'Three-thirty,' she said. 'So what, I told you we was cool.'

'It's broad daylight, for Christ's sake,' Billy said again. 'Here I am, just coming out the shower not thinking bout nothing, right, and here you come, all over me like some damn nympho, in the broad daylight!'

Candy tried to get mad, but she was hurting too bad.

'You used to like for me to touch you, Billy,' she whispered. 'You didn't use to care what time it was or if it was light or what.'

'Yeah, well.'

Billy was walking up and down in front of the mirror, patting her hair and making sure her shirt collar was laying right from where it came out her sweater. Her hair looked extra fine cause Candy had just cut it for her, short but not too short. It had a nice shape to it, and was so soft it made you want to put your hand in it, like a lamb or something.

'Who's gonna do your hair?' Candy asked.

'I don't know, I been wondering,' Billy mumbled.

Candy could just see the thoughts pass through her head, how she could probly find her another bitch who could do most things, get her dope and cash and cook and do for her, and even maybe pick out nice clothes like Candy had always done, but where was she gonna find one who could cut her hair the way she liked it?

'What's the name of the store you said you got this at?' Billy asked, pinching on the sweater, and Candy knew the way she'd been reading her mind was right.

She was gonna say something bout it, but the way Billy was standing up with her down low on the bed was a good way to get hit, so she just whispered, 'I don't remember the name no more.'

Billy sat down on the edge of the bed then.

'Baby, I didn't mean to hurt you or nothing,' she said. 'Like, hey, you just picked the wrong moment to freak off in is all. These things got to be timed just right, aint I taught you that, baby? Like, you got to be paying attention to where *I* am at the moment, and not just concentrating on where the hell you is, you know?'

'I'm sorry, Billy,' she said, even though she didn't know exactly what she was sorry for, but she did feel it though.

'Come on out that blanket, now,' Billy told her. She started rubbing Candy's head a little bit. 'Before someone come in and bust us.'

Candy pulled the blanket up a little higher. 'You know I

282

wouldn't start nothing unless I knew good and well it was cool. What you think, I want to get you busted so you can't leave?'

She meant it as a joke, but Billy was staring at her all suspicious, like that was exactly what she did think. Candy reached for her clothes. Her whole body hurt, like she'd got a beating, even though Billy hadn't touched her. She had got her shirt on and was pulling on her pants when Billy stopped her again.

'You're high-tailing it back to your own room, am I right?' she said. 'So you can shut the door and feel good and sorry for yourself.'

Candy had to nod because it was true.

'Hold on a minute girl,' Billy said. 'Why you always moving so fast? Don't know what you want from one minute to the next, do you? Now how you gonna come in here, get me all turnt on, and then just leave out?'

Candy was beginning to wonder if she'd smoked too much reefer or something cause she was feeling all crazy and mixed up back and forth, like she couldn't do nothing right, or at the right time.

'Take them clothes back off,' Billy said, 'seeing that you on the bed in the first place.'

Candy took off her clothes, only it was so damn cold.

'Don't be going back in the covers, now,' Billy said, right before she was about to. 'Lay down and relax. How come you so stiff, white girl?'

It used to be a joke between them that meant she really wasn't like a white girl at all. But this time it didn't feel like no joke. Billy's face was hard and mad, and the room, that could sometimes feel like it didn't have no walls at all, seemed tiny and tight, like one of them cages up in Max.

When Candy laid back down, Billy bent her head over, and started sucking hard on her cold nipples. First Billy's mouth was on one nipple and her fingers was around the other, and then her mouth and fingers changed places. Even though Candy knew what was coming next, it still felt too sudden when Billy slid her head down and started eating her. 'What's the matter, baby?' she said in that same pissed-off voice, after a minute. 'I'm doing it the way you like.'

Candy had completely forgot to breathe hard or make noise or something. She'd been thinking of how Billy danced. She was a good dancer, but she always danced the same way. And she would only dance to certain old records that she'd heard a whole lot before.

What Candy liked best was music she hadn't never heard, that she could just turn her body loose into. But when she danced like that, Billy would get embarrassed and tell her don't shake your titties in front of everyone, even if everyone was just the other girls in the gym at one of them juvenile dances like the one they was having Saturday for Halloween.

Billy's mouth was sucking at her harder now, and her tongue was sliding up inside. Candy could see her hair with the nice shape and her shoulders moving in that white sweater. She could tell Billy was real into it from her breathing, so even though she wasn't hot at all she moaned a little and acted like she was.

'Yeah, girl, yeah,' Billy was saying, in between. 'Oh yeah I'm doing it to you alright.'

After what seemed like enough time Candy made a noise like when she came, and changed her breathing.

Billy sat right up, smiling. 'That was more like it, baby,' she said, all relieved. 'That other stuff, shit girl, you had me feeling like a bitch for a minute there. You gots to watch that shit, baby.'

She butted Candy with her head and tried to put her arm around her, ready to be sweet, but Candy had started putting her clothes back on again. What little high she did have was gone, and she felt cold and tired and disgusted with herself.

'All I know is,' she said, not even caring if it made Billy mad, 'you used to like it. Just a few weeks ago you didn't even be worrying about what you was sposed to be feeling. You was just feeling it.'

'Shit!' Billy was all up in her face. Then she grabbed her by the two wrists.

'Don't you know nothing?' she said. 'That was then, baby, that was then. Seem like you keep forgetting I'm leaving out of this motherfucker in about one week now. Or else you remember and be trying your best to fuck with my head. How you think I'm gonna make it on the streets if I come back all messed up, used to some little white fem treating me like her bitch?'

'It aint me that's messing you up!' Candy shouted, trying to get her wrists loose. Billy's nails was cutting into her skin. 'It aint me that's fucking with your head. You're motherfucking right, you gonna be messed up when you get out there. But it aint me that's doing it.'

Billy dropped her wrists then, and slapped her hard across the

284

face. Candy didn't even feel it, but just like that her own hand came up and slapped Billy back good and hard.

'You don't do me like that, bitch,' Billy breathed. 'I could kill you for that.'

For a moment it seemed like they would fight, but then Billy pointed to the door.

'You aint keeping me in this place like I know you want to,' she snarled. 'Git.'

With tears all in her face, Candy backed out the room, just like Billy was some stranger out to get her instead of the only person in the whole world she had ever really loved.

SONYA

Wednesday afternoon Sonya came down from the art room a little early to find Ruth and talk to her about Telecea. She'd been putting it off for a while because of the way Ruth always overreacted about Telecea, but the requests for feathers and paint were getting increasingly urgent and she was getting nervous. Also, she was in a good mood because her friend Barb had called that morning from New York, inviting herself for the weekend and promising to go along with her to the stupid staff Halloween party on Saturday they were all so into.

She was surprised to find Ruth in Lynda's office, giggling with the others about the costumes they'd all worn to last year's party.

'Your Victor's was the best,' Lynda sighed as Sonya came in. 'I just couldn't get over him, with those cute bunny ears and that little tail, and the carrot cake he baked himself. It takes a man that's really secure in his manhood to wear a costume like that, that's what I told my Steve at the time. Steve went as a cowboy, remember? He finally told me he didn't want to hear the name Victor once more in his house!'

'Have you met Vic yet?' Shaking her newly polished nails in the air to dry, Cindy turned to Sonya.

Ruth gave her brittle laugh. 'As a matter of fact he's not going to be the hit of this year's party, Cindy. His own office party's the same night, and he can't get out of it.' She turned to Nan, who immediately blushed deeply. 'What are you wearing this year?'

'I don't know.' Nan ducked, as if she wished she could make all five feet nine of her disappear. During Sonya's first couple of weeks at Redburn Nan had gone out of her way to talk to her, confiding that she still lived with her parents in some suburb about an hour away. Sonya had found the obviously pre-planned and possibly rehearsed overtures so painful that she'd cut them short, and now Nan usually stuck close to Cindy, who seemed to watch out for her in her own nasty way. Sonya couldn't imagine what had brought either of them to Redburn in the first place.

'Ruth!' Cindy's effort at archness did nothing to conceal her hostility. 'Don't change the subject on us. I bet there's a new man in your life. I was just telling Nan and Lynda you've been looking awfully sparkly these days. Any objections to my giving poor old Vic a consolation call?'

'Be my guest.' Without looking around, Ruth picked up her briefcase and walked out. In the ensuing chill Sonya felt all their eyes on her.

'Sonya, tell her nobody meant to . . .' Lynda's sentence faltered and stopped.

'Gotta catch my ride,' Sonya mumbled, making her escape awkwardly. By the time she caught her, Ruth was already halfway down the hall and Sonya felt ridiculous, scurrying after her like some clownish attendant to the queen.

'I don't know what's wrong with me,' Ruth muttered in the car. 'You'd think I'd know enough not to get personal with them by now! It happens every damn time.'

'It was really just Cindy, wasn't it?' Sonya asked timidly. 'And she's obviously jealous of you.'

'Oh please, do we have to waste our time talking about them?' Without meeting Sonya's eyes, Ruth lit a cigarette and turned on the radio. Sonya felt as though she'd been slapped. Maybe Ruth did have a new man in her life. Why had she gotten so furious at the suggestion otherwise? Maybe the heat Sonya had been picking up all this time had been totally out of context. Sonya decided to keep her mouth shut for the rest of the ride. It was definitely not the time to bring up Telecea.

TELECEA

Little Sheep Dick spose to take me right up there after lunch but this day he gone off somewheres fast in a hurry. Probly run to the toilet, check his dick. Man got to have something wrong wif that little fur dick he got, way he keep taking it out to check do it still be there.

I glad he gone, cause I gots something I been meaning to check up on too. Go on down the hall to watch and see do she really stay the same Ruth Foster like she say, or do she change up. Spose to see her tomorrow, and I got to find out first.

First thing when I get down there, I hear her voice from that office where they stay, make they evil plans. What I do, I duck in that dirty filthy bathroom they gots across from it and leave the door open so I can hear and see. Lord, do it smell! Them white people so nasty wif they pussy dead white hairs all in the sink and crawling wif them little white maggots. I would not touch nothing in there not if you pay me a million dollars.

When I first hear Ruth Foster voice I know something aint cool. She aint never use to go in there. Plus when I see her in there, she all drest up like a ho' in them tight black pants and red shirt. The old Ruth Foster aint never wore nothing like that or have her hair all out and snakey to drag someone down wif her! Then I hear her say something bout costume and I know what she doing. That ho' drest up alright and when I seen Sonya go in there I know who she doing it for. Looking at my art teacher all hot like she can't wait to get them unclean hands on her, come all close, whisper take out that dick so can't no one else hear. Then she leave out and Sonya follow right after like some little old ghost, like she don't want to but she can't help herself.

That devil ho' Foster got hold of my teacher alright and now I knows I gots to work fast. Only three more days now. Gots to make sure Sonya bring me them things I need. For my Venger costume, Halloween.

FRIDAY, OCTOBER 30

RUTH

Ruth was in a shitty mood all day Friday. She didn't know what was wrong with Sonya, but thought she'd been put off by the 'ladies' stupid cracks about Victor and 'her new man' on Wednesday afternoon. Sonya had been cold and unfriendly since then, only speaking to her in the car that morning to tell her that she wouldn't need a ride home because she was leaving early to meet a friend who was coming in from New York for the weekend. She hadn't said who the friend was, but Ruth thought it was probably that woman from Vermont, Mira, whom Sonya sometimes talked about. She'd move right in and that would be the last Ruth would see of Sonya outside of work. Now the run with Sonya tomorrow was off. Worst of all, Sonya would bring her friend to the party. Halloween would be spoiled.

Her mood didn't improve when two clients in a row didn't show, or when Telecea did, and proceeded to sit in silence during the entire hour, fixing her with a malevolent stare. It was the first time she'd behaved in quite that way and Ruth thought she should probably do something about it, but she had no idea what, short of sending her back to Max full-time. She was in no mood to deal with it anyway. It would have to wait until Monday.

Just as she was walking out the door her phone rang. It was Lisa, sounding nervous and hassled.

'I know this is horribly spur of the moment, but do you want to meet me for a drink? I'm still at work. We had an emergency with one of my clients today, she found Jesus and he told her to stay a man like she was made. Unfortunately, she's already had several operations. Anyway, there's a little place called Nina's I go to sometimes, I can tell you how to get there.'

'OK,' Ruth agreed eagerly. 'I know where it is.' She'd been wondering whether Sonya would take her friend by Nina's, and now she'd find out.

Half an hour later, she pushed open the door to cool darkness and Nina Simone singing, 'I Need a Little Sugar in My Bowl.' It was the song Sonya always put on the jukebox, and there she was, in one of the booths in the middle, sitting with a stylish-looking woman with very short hair and a green quilted vest who must be Mira. Ruth walked toward the back. She'd be just as surprised as Sonya, and explain that she was here to meet Lisa, which was true. But just before Ruth reached her, Sonya moved and turned into a stranger, an unknown woman with a horse face and only her long black hair remotely like Sonya's.

'Ruth, right here!' Ruth jumped, but it was just Lisa, calling her from the next booth over. She tried to swallow the disappointment which rose in her throat.

'Hi Ruth, you're looking beautiful as usual,' Lisa told her sarcastically.

Ruth noticed Lisa's thinness, and the dark shadows under her eyes. She hoped she hadn't been invited here to provide a little free therapy, because she wasn't in the mood.

'So you come here sometimes?' Lisa asked.

'Yeah, my friend from work, Sonya Lehrman, and I come here a lot,' Ruth said. Saying these words out loud had been the most pleasurable thing she'd done all day, but Lisa hadn't heard them. She had already launched into the story of the changes in her life in the past month, talking compulsively and stopping only long enough to order a glass of wine. Ruth had heard the plot already, from Vic via Bill. She felt bored and absurdly miserable, as if she might burst into tears at any moment without warning.

'There are so many feelings inside me,' Lisa was saying. 'Rising and rising.' Ruth pictured her as a damp puddle of unbaked bread, set to rise in an oven.

'So in one way I may seem like an entirely different person to you now, but really I'm not. The feelings were there all the time, it's just that the top blew off. The rocket exploded.'

'The bread,' Ruth corrected. The mixed metaphors annoyed her, and she felt something rising herself, an anger at Lisa for having dragged her here, where Sonya was not, to talk at her without seeing her. 'As I recall,' she said, horrified at her own tone even as she spoke, 'the last time I saw you some of those feelings were already surfacing, no?' Lisa's face went stiff, and Ruth could tell she was remembering that scene in the kitchen, both of them stoned, the two men waiting in the living room.

'Of course I remember,' Lisa said finally. Then she leaned across the table and spoke in a stilted, vaguely British voice, which Ruth understood was supposed to be her own. 'Lisa kissed me after dinner. How *immature* of her! How amusing. I must tell Vic!' Now she spoke in her own voice again. 'It's all a big game to you, isn't it? You can just sit there looking lovely and remote and throwing out a sarcastic comment from time to time and it's enough. You get by.'

Ruth drew back from the force of Lisa's anger, and from her voice, which was getting louder. She could see heads turning at the bar.

'I guess it's because of how you look,' Lisa went on in a slightly lower tone. 'Women like you never had to learn the shit the rest of us did. All you had to do was sit back and wait till people came to you. While the rest of us were busting ass trying to learn all the tricks, how to be charming and mothering and intelligent but not too, how to listen just right. But why bother, if you don't need to, right, Ruth? And why listen to another woman's pain? I don't know why I even called you!'

'I don't either!' Ruth tried to speak over the lump that was forming in her throat. She groped for her coat and purse. 'I don't know whom all this belongs to,' she said, 'but it sure isn't mine, and I don't have to stay and listen to it.'

'Of *course* not! You don't have to do anything you don't want to do. *What* women's movement?' Lisa asked hatefully in her Ruth voice. 'I'm not a group person, actually. I never did like cliques. No, I prefer to stay out of the prison politics. I'm there to do therapy. Feelings? What are those? No, I'm afraid they're too much trouble.' Ruth wanted to leave but somehow she couldn't. She thought of reaching over and taking Lisa's shoulders and shaking her as hard as she could, until all her bones were loose, to stop her stream of talk. 'It's you who'll miss out in the end, though,' Lisa was concluding, triumphantly. 'Because *I* may be in pain now, I *know* I look like shit, I didn't need to see it on your face. Well, it's hard. I'm coming out, I'm fucking leaving a six-year relationship, if you think that's easy . . .' Tears threatened. 'But at least I'm in touch with myself, which is more than *you'll* ever be.'

Ruth opened her mouth but nothing came out. It was hard to keep from crying, and she wished for her rage of earlier in the day. 'What was all that?' she finally got out. 'A prepared speech? Ready for the first person to come along? Excuse me, for the first pretty woman.' Now that she'd started, it felt good to be saying all the hateful things that came to her. She could taste her whole day's anger, and some from earlier too. 'What did you do, go through your phone book until you got someone who would agree to come down here? Because it didn't matter who it was, did it?' She gave Lisa a chance to yell back, but she said nothing. 'I'll tell you one thing,' she went on. 'You are so totally self-involved at this point that you have no idea *who* you're sitting with. You're talking to someone you made up in your head and named Ruth Foster. If you'd bothered to check out the reality of who I am, if you'd ever bothered to really address me, you might have found out some things about me that would have surprised you. We might even have had a real conversation.' Ruth took a deep breath and realized that she felt better than she had all week. She put on her coat and walked to the door, then realized that she hadn't paid for her beer. She stopped, groped in her pocket, then began to walk back. There were two men at the bar, staring approvingly at her. One of them formed his thumb and forefinger into a circle of success.

'You tell her, Blondy,' he said.

The other one waved some money in the air. 'It's on me, babe. Anyone ever tell you you're cute when you're mad?'

Ruth's anger returned in full force. 'Why don't you stuff it?' she told them in a fierce whisper. 'Why don't you stuff it up your ass.' Then she went back to the booth, hoping she wouldn't get hit from behind, and threw a dollar and two quarters down on the table. Lisa was still sitting there, struggling with tears as she put her jacket on. Ruth hadn't meant to throw money at her. She didn't want to leave her here, with these assholes. 'Please, let's start over,' she said to Lisa. 'Let's get out of here.'

On the sidewalk, feeling strangely buoyant, she took Lisa's hand and Lisa didn't take it away. 'I've never done that in my life,' Ruth told her. 'I've never made a scene in public. And I don't think I ever told anyone to stuff it before. Let's get out of here before they come to kill us.'

'You were great,' Lisa said. 'Their mouths are probably still open.'

They were laughing as they walked, and then they were hugging each other, right there on the street. For a second Ruth closed her eyes and pretended she was hugging Sonya. But it was much too thin. It was Lisa. She opened her eyes quickly. 'Could we go and talk for real?' she asked. 'Where are you living now?'

CANDY

Candy could just picture Foster saying that the D she got Wednesday night was her own fault cause of the pissy mood she was in after her beef with Billy, but what was she sposed to do when she walked in the shower room and seen three of them on one? Edie was leaning on the poor bastard to make sure she wasn't going nowhere, and her two buddies was holding her head down in the toilet.

It was that new girl, Liz somebody, that Bobby Brown had been freaking off with in her office that day that Candy seen them, and now she was finding out what happened when you messed with a screw. True, the dizzy bitch had brought it on herself, but she was only seventeen on her first time in, plus Candy didn't even like to see no kittens drown. She told them get the fuck off, but Edie just said mind your own business, bitch, and didn't move. By this time Candy was getting scared the girl would drown for real.

'Hey Edie, your Moma's a ten cent ho' and she taught you real good,' she screamed, which was getting right down to their level but what could you do, so she kept it up until Edie finally got so aggravated she let go of the girl, who was choking and blue by this time, told the others stay back, and came at Candy.

Which was why she was sitting on the dirty filthy floor outside the D-Board office now, with her face all scratched up. They was a lot of them up this week: Edie and her buddies, plus two others that had came in on Candy's side when they heard the commotion, plus eight other broads from Daisy and the two other cottages, Violet and McCune. At least Candy didn't have no scratches that wouldn't be gone in a week or so, while Edie had one eye half closed and a whole clump of hair gone, which wasn't too bad when you compared their two sizes. The people that knew who did it to her kept looking at Edie and laughing.

'You'd think these fuckers could put some chairs out here.' That was Anita Knight, a tall fine looking broad from McCune that was sitting next to Candy.

'Hey, what you think this shit's all about anyway?' Candy asked her.

'Bout humiliation,' answered Anita, who wasn't nobody's fool.

293

'Damn right,' agreed Candy. 'So what they need chairs for?'

'I hear you, white girl,' yelled Edie from down the row. There was something about D-Board that could make you feel on the same side as your worst enemy. Candy even felt a little sorry for that pitiful Grace Powers that Billy messed with, that had been busted bringing dope in, and was gonna get a new case for it. They had already called Grace in one time to hear her side of it as they put it. Now Riley came out the room and said for her to please step back in.

'I really don't know why you bother with all this in and out shit,' Candy said to Riley's face. 'Why don't you just send us a slip of paper with what you got to say wrote on it. You know damn well you got your minds made up from the jump.'

Riley gave her a surprised look, cause she wasn't used to no mouth from her. 'Are you trying to earn another D?' she asked. 'Isn't one enough for you, in one week?'

'You can't give me no D,' Candy told her. 'I aint threatened you and I aint used no bad language. I know the rules!' Riley pushed Grace in and slammed the door. Candy felt like making more of a commotion. One of them big Redburn silverfishes was crawling on the floor next to her, and she jumped up like a snake bit her. 'A roach went up my leg!' she shouted. Just like that all the girls started yelling and screaming and jumping around too.

'Bugs, cockroaches crawling on us!' they went. One new girl from Violet even started crying.

'Someone gonna hear about this!' growled Edie. 'This aint right, no sir them motherfuckin' bastards.' Candy watched her hike up her half-size pants to see did a roach climb in, and tried not to laugh. She hoped she started a riot.

'Which of you girls is out here asking for trouble?' It was Moody they sent out this time of course, with his fat redneck self.

'Cockroaches crawling all over us!' screamed Edie. 'Gonna get my lawyer on you bastards.'

'Well give him a hug and a kiss from me, big Mama,' Moody told her. 'And that roach too. You ought to be old friends, seeing where you come from.' Then he started in with his crazy laugh and went back in, slamming the door.

'You-all ought to protest,' Dina said after he was gone. She had stayed in her room during the beef and didn't have no D, but had come out now to keep them company, dancing back and forth in her little black turtleneck. 'If I was in you-all's place I would refuse to set my feet inside that room until they gets some chairs and a 'sterminator in here. Don't you know they trespassing all over your human rights?'

Grace came out of the office. She was sobbing hard, and where the tears had washed off her makeup you could see old acne scars. Dina was right there, putting her skinny arm around her and curious as hell. 'What they do you for, sister?'

'Sister, huh,' somebody snorted, but Grace sobbed out that the welfare was gonna take her kids for permanent now, like they told her they would if she got any more cases.

'The fucking cunts,' they all said, cause it wasn't right to mess with no one's kids even if it was a dumb whiney bitch like Grace.

It was a whole two hours later they called Candy. When she went in they was all sitting there waiting for her: Moody and Riley and Delaney and Hanson. It was a shitty board alright. They was letting Hanson do all the talking cause she was boss.

'Have a seat, Candace,' she said in her fake sugary voice, pointing a claw at the pink plastic chair next to her. She had on her purple leather outfit today and Candy thought she should of been in a freak show, with her bald head and animal skins.

'You aint offered me no chair out there,' Candy told them. 'I been sitting on that floor for two hours now, and aint no one offered me no chair.' They all looked embarrassed, like she had farted or something.

'You may stand if you prefer, Candace,' Hanson said, sending the others a see how good I can handle this one look. 'I must say that I am both surprised and disappointed to hear you speak to us this way, just as I was both surprised and disappointed when I was handed your name on a D report. This is the first one you've had for over a year, isn't it? Since you and your – er – "friend" returned from escape. I think we'd all like to hear what happened in your own words.'

'You got the report right there, don't you?' Candy said. She knew she was sounding more like Billy than herself, but she just couldn't be bothered to kiss no ass today. It didn't take much to make the old bitch blow her cool.

'You are not here to play games with us, Candace!' she shrieked out, and Moody must of figured this was his signal to start messing with her. He held up the report and pretended he was reading it.

'Says here the officer caught this one trying to hold another girl's head under water. Sounds like she wants a little vacation in Max to me!' Candy almost had to laugh at their asshole tricks. Wiggins had wrote the report and she knew damn well it didn't say nothing like that. She was sposed to get mad when she heard it and tell them what really did happen, naming a whole lot of names while she was at it. Instead, she kept quiet and thought about if Moody came to her on the street as a trick. She would cut his fucking balls off him, and his cock too, slow as she could, and send them to his wife in a little package, like that artist on TV did with his ear.

'Mr Moody may sound a little harsh to you dear,' the old freak had got her cool back again, 'but he is making a good point. If you don't give us your version of what happened then we have no choice but to go by the report, which may not be accurate. Now I know the schoolgirl code as well as you do, dear, but aren't we getting a little grown up for that now? Miss Foster tells me she is thinking of recommending you for a peer counselor program. Tell me, Candace, can you really picture the bad little girl standing here as a counselor for others?'

Candy shrugged. 'If you got officers that lie on their reports that aint my fault,' she said. 'Can I go now?' She started to book, but Hanson reached out and grabbed hold of her by the wrist.

'When you're feeling hurt, it's easy to strike out at the whole world, isn't it, Candy?' she said, like she thought she was someone in a TV story. 'I've known you for a long time now, and I know that this angry little girl isn't the *real* Candace Peters. So I'm going to act like that little girl isn't even in the room with us.' Just then Moody let out a belly laugh, which Candy figured was the one and only favor he would ever do her. 'Now Candace —' the old bitch tried to go on, but Riley and Delaney had caught it too, and was giggling and trying to cover it up by coughs. 'Perhaps the duty of sitting on this board is too much for some of you?' Hanson said, all nasty out the side of her mouth. Then she turned back to Candy, sweet as poisoned sugar again.

'Now Candace, we both know that your turn to walk out of these doors a free woman will come soon, just as your "friend's" turn has almost come. That is, of course, if the behavior you're here to see us about today is, as I trust it is, an isolated incident. And when that date comes I think part of you is going to be very very glad that your precious Billy left when she did. The dates we give our girls are not purely accidental, you know that, dear. We try to plan ahead a little, to do what's best for our girls, and sometimes, maybe just because we've been around a little bit longer than them, what we feel is best may be just a little different than what they think they might prefer at the moment. Because Candace, especially when you smile – and I hope to see that pretty smile before you leave this room, don't you officers? – especially when you smile, you are a very attractive young lady! And there are some young men out there, not pimps and addicts dear, but nice young men who are working or attending school just as we hope you will be doing. Well, let me just say that I wouldn't be at all surprised if, maybe a year from now, I may open my mail one fine day and find a wedding invitation with a little note in it saying how glad you are for our arranging things the way we did.'

'Would you let go of me? You make me want to throw up.' Candy tore loose of Hanson's claws and made it out the door.

'What happened?' everyone out there wanted to know, but she just shrugged and went on back to the cottage. So she could of been out with Billy if that motherfucking cunt hadn't decided she ought to be making it with a dude! She wondered what the bitch would do to her now. They weren't sposed to put you in Max for one minor D, and a cottage lock up didn't bother her none. She'd almost decided not to go to the asshole Halloween dance tomorrow night anyway, and she didn't get no visits for them to take away. Most likely they'd mess with her date, but no matter what, they had to let her out by Christmas. And even if they did take another few weeks of her life, it would of been almost worth it, to of told them off for once.

SONYA

When she got home from work, an hour early, Sonya arranged her new sculptures around the loft, including the one which she'd just finished in time for Barb's visit. Barb would be the first person to spend the night here, and it felt right that it would be her, not a lover, but an old friend and fellow artist. Just as she finished cleaning up, the phone rang.

'Listen Sonya, I'm really sorry, but I'm still home, I can't come down this weekend after all. Wait till you hear, I think I have a show! You know the new women's gallery-school I told you about, the one Leah was involved in? Well, one of the directors, Janet Smith, called me up yesterday, she saw my work at that group show last year and she wants me to come in and talk to her Monday about being one of the three artists to open up the place.'

'Great,' Sonya got out. 'But why can't you come? I've been counting on it.'

Barb sounded like she'd just taken a hit of speed. 'I'm working on this big painting, a dream landscape, which I want to include in the show. I just may be able to finish it if I work on it all night, of course it may not be dry in time to show her . . . Listen, I'm sending you a notice about a competition this same place, Womenarts, is sponsoring. It sounds like it was made for you. Sculpture with social content, that's what they're looking for, and the winner gets to be part of the faculty next year. They're going to exhibit lots of the entries, it's really a big deal. One of those International Endowment of the Arts grants, you know? This Janet Smith is a dyke, she's worked in prisons herself, it's made for you. And I've already mentioned your name to her. Things are changing, Sonny, it's our turn now! Look around, the only vital art any more's coming from blacks and women. The white men have dwindled into dried up abstractions, they're bloodless. If you won you'd have to move back here, but that wouldn't kill you would it? You don't sound exactly overwhelmed with the scene there. Have you made it with the social worker yet, by the way?'

'No,' Sonya told her glumly. 'I think I've dwindled a little myself.'

After she'd hung up Sonya felt lonelier than she had since she'd moved. She hadn't particularly missed Barb before, but the way she'd been looking forward to her visit and now the crushing force of disappointment made her realize how isolated she really was here.

On her way to the icebox to find something to eat she saw her few pieces, arranged childishly around the work area. They were amateurish, that was clear now. You could tell at a glance the artist didn't live in New York, hadn't studied with the right people, was, in fact, a pretentious fool.

She sat on the edge of her bed eating a sandwich with the phone in her lap, trailing its long umbilical cord.

She could call Ruth, but it would be too humiliating to admit that Barb had changed her mind, especially after the way she'd mentioned the visit, leaving plenty of room for Ruth to assume Barb was her lover. She would probably bring her new man to the damn party, which would leave Sonya with no one. Maybe she just wouldn't go. The phone seemed to be growing. Insistent and intrusive, it was taking on a life of its own. She could use a real phone with a long cord and snake it all around the tiny realistic figure of a woman, as if the phone were eating her up like a boa constrictor. It would be easy to do, unlike that prison house idea. She wondered if it would be political enough for that competition. She wondered if she would ever have anyone to talk to again, to share feelings with, or dreams, or ideas for sculptures. She decided to call Mira.

The phone rang and rang. Then, 'Hello?' Mira sounded warm and sleepy and Sonya heard her own voice tremble, already near tears. She could imagine Mira sitting cross-legged on the bed, her eyes wide-open in surprise, nervously ruffling her short feathery hair.

'Is everything alright?' There was a strange formal note in Mira's voice now. Probably she was warning herself not to be vulnerable.

'You sound like a robot.' Sonya let her own voice break a little. 'I'm really lonely. I've been thinking about you all the time.' She was just about to offer to fly down for the weekend or pay for Mira to come, when Mira said, 'Listen, Sonny, this isn't the best time for me to talk.' She sounded embarrassed now, and something clicked. How could she have forgotten? This was how Mira used to sound when she'd get up to answer the phone when they were in bed, making love.

'Better watch it! She might get impatient and leave. I didn't know there were any dykes out there, by the way. Or did you import someone? Or convert a straight woman? Oh. Excuse my assumptions, maybe it's a man?' Sonya heard her voice cutting and slapping at Mira in the old way. It was Mira's own fault though. She had deliberately made a fool of her.

'Man, woman, or fucking robot!' Mira screamed. 'It's none of your business now!' She hung up but Sonya had heard her start to cry. At least she still had that much of an effect.

TELECEA

When I come downstairs wif my feathers and paint all safe in a bag she give me, I seen them sitting in line like for judgment day. Like some D board gone take the sins off they heads! Too late for that now.

I seen how it be starting already. All of them falling on each other, destroying each other they ownself, don't hardly need no Venger. That Candy ho' been in the shower room wif them other bominations got one girl head under the water and drownded her. Then Candy and them start in scratching and biting, got each other blood under they nails, flesh in they teeth. Just like Norma used to call them, a pack of dogs. Oh yeah, it be starting alright, but that ho' don't know enough to be scare.

Her bomination, Billy, she scairt alright. The sound of a shaked leaf making her ass shake now. Like the other day, I hear the two of them in there starting in on they ho'ing and moaning. Billy gots her dick all out and then all of a sudden she pull it back. Say, You know what time it is? She mean Venging time, but that ho' don't understand and want to keep right on wif it. Billy tell her, get away from me bitch and nympher and all that. Call her a white ho'. That Jezebel will not leave her alone so Billy hit her one good.

'I could kill you, ho', now git.' Filthy bomination think she can change up now, hide that dick. But it too late. She already markt. She know it, too.

But them others don't know. Gone be took by surprise. All line up on that floor screaming cause them cockroaches and maggots eating on they flesh right now. And they aint even died yet. Good as dead, though. Venging time getting near, Lord. Good and near.

SATURDAY, OCTOBER 31

RUTH

Ruth woke up early as usual on Halloween, before the full light. 'The party,' she thought, and then remembered that it would be spoiled, Sonya's friend was coming with her. She was wide awake anyway, and decided to run around Silver Pond. Since Sonya wouldn't go with her, she'd go alone. As she got her sweatpants, T-shirt and new running shoes from the closet, Victor stirred, mumbled something that sounded like 'exaggerating' and went back to sleep.

In the kitchen, lacing her new shoes which were ridged on the bottom, with white racing stripes over a bright green body, she thought fleetingly of Telecea's tennis shoes. As she went out the door into the morning, though, she forgot about Redburn. She felt much younger than that, more like the hopeful young college girl who used to sneak back to the dorm early in the morning after some all-night adventure.

The pond was only half a mile off, so she started running right away, taking long strides along the dim grey sidewalk. Was it possible that she hadn't run for years, except maybe to catch a bus? In high school she'd liked running, and had wished there was a girls' track team for her to join.

The air was cool and the wind blew against her face. The almost round moon was setting as she reached the pond. It would be full tonight, for Halloween.

Ruth began to run along the cement track, the stiff frozen grass which grew between the cracks snapping under her feet. Everything was still colorless, with only the outlines clear, and a faint white mist rose from the pond. The one or two people whom she passed, going in the opposite direction, were gray silhouettes who ran by silently without speaking. The long unused muscles in her legs and thighs were aching a little now, and she had a pain in her side. If she was really going to do this seriously, she'd have to stop smoking. It was two miles around and she was determined to make it. She concentrated on an image of herself, running every morning, growing stronger and stronger until she could circle the pond three or four times without even feeling it.

She wondered if Sonya would ever run with her. Sonya seemed

to worry a lot about her body, didn't seem to know how beautiful she really was. Maybe that mysterious Mira had nagged her to lose weight, had loved her in spite of and not because of her body. Why else would she move in that ashamed way sometimes, her shoulders hunched in as if she wished she had no body at all? *She* would love Sonya exactly the way she was, and then Sonya would begin to move differently, would love to dance instead of being afraid to. Ruth decided not to let herself imagine dancing with Sonya at the party tonight because that was all spoiled. She could hardly breathe again.

She'd concentrate only on what she could see. The grass was thawed, softened now. Everything was taking on color. Her lungs were on fire. Thinking about people seemed to work better. She tried to picture different women she knew, running. Beth, that teacher who'd ridden home with them the other day, would be a natural. It was harder to picture Lisa. Finally she succeeded in seeing her running alongside another woman, talking and panting as she ran. Candy probably wouldn't run, even if she could. Billy would run, gloriously and without effort. Alice and Mabe wouldn't run. Lorraine might enjoy it, especially if she knew Ruth was running. She had the body for it, the long legs. Could Telecea run off some of that rage? Possibly. It would sure be a lot better than banging her head on the floor.

Ruth felt a much sharper pain in her side, like a knife. She'd probably been going much too fast. Everyone said to start slow, to do no more than a mile the first time. She should have paid attention. She hurt a lot, but she had to keep running because if she let herself stop now it meant that nothing would ever happen. Sonya would never hold her in her arms. They would never kiss. She'd go on the same way, living with Victor, working at Redburn, for ever and ever and nothing would ever change. Like that old Otis Redding song on the jukebox at Nina's, 'Seem like nothing gonna change. Everything still remains the same.' She noticed that she was breathing in quick shallow breaths and tried to slow down. Yes, that was better. Maybe she was getting her second wind. Now she heard footsteps, neither passing her nor falling behind, but paced at her own speed. She turned to look.

It was a tall skinny man with shiny blue trunks and fancy rainbow striped shoes. Ugly veins stuck out in his legs. He sped up, running parallel to her. He was chinless, his hair slicked down to his sweaty head.

'Do a lot of running?' She ignored him, but he kept right with her, assuming whatever speed she switched to. He wasn't panting, didn't seem tired at all. 'Never seen you before. After a while you get familiar with them. Most girls, they tend to run a little later, after it's light. They're scared. I like an early start, myself.' He fell behind her, so she had to turn back to keep track of him. Her mouth was very dry and her heart was beating, but the running was easy now. She knew he'd be on her if she stopped. When she looked back she could see his erection, sticking out in the shiny blue shorts.

'Leave me alone,' she panted. If only some other runner would come along.

'Not very friendly, are you?' He sounded excited, as if he was working himself up to grab her. She got ready to scream, but her voice felt frozen, like in a dream. She couldn't feel her body any more. He teased her, running a little closer, falling back.

Thank God, she heard footsteps behind them. She turned and saw three more men and a dog in the distance.

'Look,' she told him, 'people are coming. I'll scream.'

'Cunt.' But he disappeared immediately, sprinting far ahead. 'He's had practice at this,' she realized hysterically. 'He must do it a lot.' The others were approaching now, trim middle-aged men, professorial types, running in formation. One of them called the dog, a golden retriever, to heel.

'Morning,' he nodded to her, flashing a smile. She wanted to stop them, to call out, but the man was gone now, what could she say? The words stuck in her throat and now the moment was over, they had passed. There were other runners on the path now, anyway. He wouldn't, couldn't wait for her up ahead and jump out at her. She tasted hot leftover fear in her mouth. If only she had a small sharp knife with her. She stopped picturing anything now, just concentrated on making her feet go on, not stopping.

Finally she saw the open place she'd started at, and knew she was safe, that she'd made the full circle. 'I made it,' she thought, proud of herself. As she'd been instructed, she walked slowly home, stretching her legs so that they wouldn't stiffen and cramp afterwards. She had almost stopped trembling. The sun was bright and the sweat running down her sides and between her breasts felt good. There were a lot of women out running now. She wondered if she should warn them, but none of them seemed to be alone, and he was probably gone. Even if she started later next time, she could still make it to work on time. The leaves were brilliant in the sun – bright reds and oranges, and some which were the color of dried blood. Ruth felt a long shiver go through her. Victor would probably still be asleep when she got home. She would pretend it hadn't happened.

CANDY

Candy was dragging a mop and a bucket of dirty water around the cottage. She was sposed to do all the floors for her lock-up punishment, but somebody had already done them for their regular job and they was perfectly clean. It made about as much sense as most work they gave you in here. In the TV room the girls was sitting in front of the box like a bunch of retards, watching some damn kiddy show, and Candy slopped some water under their feet to wake them up a little.

'Baby-Go-Too'. On the TV, a blond woman with a oily voice held up a oversized baby doll. 'She talks she pees and when she wants your attention she knows how to get it!' The doll's hand moved like it was haunted or something and clutched onto the blonde's skirt. 'Only nineteen ninety-nine, plus tax.'

'Aint that cute, I'm gonna order me one for Michelle.' Jocelyn Brown shoved at Candy with her foot. 'What are you trying to do, flood the place? Git out a here.'

In the kitchen, Ginzer was drinking coffee and rapping a mile a minute with old Moore, a screw that had been around ever since the place got started or something.

'That's what I told her, just like I'm telling you.' The old bitch clacked her lousy pair of false teeth in and out. 'I said, Go right ahead and let that little faggot take that nut out in that dark gym, that's what make you happy. You the professional, not me, we both knows that, I told her. But I got my personal day coming.'

Ginzer nodded so hard her coffee jumped out the cup. 'That's exactly what I told 'em too. Let her slaughter the whole lot of them. But not on my shift, you don't.'

'Shit, Rae.' Moore sucked her teeth all the way in. 'I wouldn't let that one out to go to the john, no sir. Keep her up in Max where she belongs, that's what I'd do. Talk bout extra security so we don't have no escapes during the party. That kind don't need to run. Don't know if she's in or out or up in heaven anyways. Do her damage perfectly good right here. Then, next time she slam some girl's head up against the wall, they got someone to blame. "It was Miz Moore's shift," that's just what they tell em downtown.'

'Aint that the truth!' Ginzer got so excited she started to throw her hands around. 'Therapy this and art room that. Party-in-the-gym! You know them college girls aint gonna be in that gym tonight, Betty. Not that old rhino hide neither. You know who takes the weight soon as the sun goes down.'

Moore nodded. 'You know I do, Rae. Got my personal day coming tonight, that's what I told her right to her face.'

'Scuse me.' Candy was getting sick of pretending to mop the floors so she sloshed some water down between their feet. Ginzer turned on her just like she knew she would.

'What on earth are you doing with that dirty water, girl? Don't you know Jenny cleaned this floor half an hour ago?'

'Miz Hanson told me to,' Candy whined. 'For my D.'

'See what I'm telling you.' Ginzer and Moore was both nodding their heads up and down like a Howdy Doody puppet show. 'How on earth you supposed to do your job with them interfering every time you get something straight? Empty that nasty water out this minute, Candy Peters, I don't care if the President of the United States told you to do it his own self! I'd quit tomorrow if I didn't need the money so bad!'

Moore stretched her creaky legs. 'Got my retirement coming in six months,' she said. 'Be glad to leave this place behind!'

'You and me both,' Candy muttered as she threw out the water. 'You and me both!'

Fran Minelli came up to her on her way back to her room.

'Hey Candy, got some git-high for the party tonight? I can pay.' Candy shook her head no. 'Oh come on, girl. Billy's out there high as a kite. I know you-all got some shit. Or at least valium or reefer or something. I'd even take some of that homemade booze you-all make if you aint got nothing else.'

'I said no, you got a hearing problem?' Candy went in her room and slammed the door shut, but she could still hear Fran out there, threatening one of the nuts for her crazy pills. She lay on the bed and wondered what would Billy say if she ran tonight. So they was gonna have extra guards. Big fucking deal. She could make it out of this place blindfolded with both hands tied behind her back and the whole National Guard sitting on the fence. It would be a hell of a lot less boring than the stupid-ass Halloween party they was all so hot for, that was for damn sure.

SONYA

Sonya had decided to practice running around Silver Pond on her own before trying it with Ruth. It had been hard, getting right out of bed and stuffing herself into the uncomfortable bra, the hot sweat pants, and the new shoes which didn't feel right. She'd ended up drinking too much coffee to get herself going, and now she felt it sloshing inside her, an added heaviness.

She was dragging too much with her, anyway. Her breasts swung around and dripped sweat into the tight binding bra, even her long hair, tied with a string, seemed to weigh a ton. Most of the other women running were slim, with flat chests and sleek short hair. Their legs looked thin and taut, as they passed her with the inevitable dog trotting along behind them, stopping for a quick sniff or possibly a bite of her. Sonya wondered what the fuck she was doing here anyway. She hated dogs and strenuous exercise. Running had sounded romantic when Ruth had mentioned it, but now she saw that it was lonely and unpleasant in its very nature. For one thing, there was no way to make real contact with anyone else, no way to distinguish the artists from the women execs, the gays from the straights. All you could see about a person running was the condition of his or her body.

There were little markers on the cement which told you how far you'd run. The one below her said 1/6. Only one sixth of a mile and already she felt like this? She forced herself to keep running, but she was dizzy. What if she fainted? And there was an image from her dream that kept coming back. She'd been in bed with Ruth, about to start making love. Then she realized that her flesh was swelling, rising like bread dough. It reminded her of some horrible twist on Alice in Wonderland, or of the soup story, from a book she'd had as a child. A hungry woman had wished for some soup, and the soup came, but wouldn't stop once it had started. In the picture it was a reddish brown color, maybe cream of tomato soup, and it filled the entire two-story house and overflowed into the street. Animals were swimming in it and drinking it and people had stopped collecting it in pans and were standing at the top of their houses, screaming for help. It seemed like an extreme punishment, just for having wished for some soup.

There were so many stories about women who got punished for wishing for things. She tried to think of them to take her mind off the running. There was that fisherman's wife, who'd had the audacity to wish for too much, and had ended up destitute. And then there was that really horrible story about a mother whose son had been killed by machinery and wished him back to life and he came, but all mangled. The story ended with his monster footsteps, dragging in the hall. She didn't think the mother had been allowed to change her wish. You only got one, which always backfired, and that was that.

Sonya wished she hadn't brought in the damn feathers for Telecea, or that she'd at least mentioned it to Ruth. Not that a few feathers for a Halloween costume could do any damage but the whole thing was spooky somehow. She'd be glad when the Redburn party was over.

This running was just too hard. She ached all over, and sweat ran down between her loaf breasts like melted butter. She'd decided to do at least one mile, but the little marker only said 1/4. Maybe she'd get a heart attack right here. Then she wouldn't have to finish the mile, or go to that damn party tonight. In a minute she was going to start walking, mile or no mile. Walking was exercise too. In case she ran into Ruth she could always say it was her second time around.

Once she started to walk she could really look around her. The sun was out and the water on the pond rippled gently. Some ducks circled, preparing for a landing, then swooshing down in perfect formation. Sonya stepped off the path, into a patch of weeds and high grass. The milkweeds, in different stages of delicate opening, reminded her of cunts. She touched the softness of their feathers against her cheek, tried the texture against her tongue. She wondered if she could use some in a sculpture, and gathered up as many as she could hold, then walked along the path, admiring the brilliant fall leaves. She stuck a bright red leaf, a duck feather, and a milkweed pod into her hair. Now all the runners smiled at her, and she smiled back. So this was the kind of harmless recognition Telecea had been looking for, with her feathers. Sonya laughed at her own folly in taking on Ruth's obsession. She decided to go to the Halloween party as a forest gypsy. Maybe she'd have a good time, after all.

TELECEA

Today I stay in my room and He talk to me. Send me a dream vision, tell me what to do, cause today the day. Show me how it spose to look. Say, Telecea child, stay with me now. I show you the way. Aint no one gonna stop you no more. He right too, cause first they tell me I can't go to that evil bomination of a party they got, and today they come and say come on. Just like I knowed they would. Little Sheep Dick he spose to come wif me. That what he think.

This the first time I make me a sculpture without Sonya. She gone now. Done gone wif the ho' and grow her a dick. No one left but me now. I don't need Sonya no more. She brung me the feathers and things and I took me some paint. Don't need no one no more.

Half of it gots to be black and half of it white cause some of them bominations white and some black. Got ears like the devil, stick right up in the air and hear what be in peoples mind. One of them long tails like a whip wif sparks burning off the end of it. Curl it up and whip it out, just like one of them dicks. Feathers all up and down that tail and on the head too cause when it need to, it can fly. Just up and leave when it done what it spose to. Can't no one catch it, it just fly on out of here. Cause it name the Venger and it belong to the Lord.

No one come in my room all day. Got the Venger ready now. To do what it have to do. No more ho'ing then, Lord, no more changing up. All of them busy wif they costumes, think they can turn theyself into someone else and escape, well aint no one escaping tonight. Not this night, Lord. Halloween night. When it get dark, that when I spose to do it. Gots to wait until dark. Then it out of my hands.

SATURDAY, OCTOBER 31

RUTH

Victor had gone out, thank goodness. When Ruth had first told him that she wanted to go to the party alone, he'd withdrawn into wounded silence, then made some secret plan of his own which he had now embarked upon. The neighborhood children, dressed as ghosts and cowboys and witches, had come and gone, hours ago.

Standing naked in front of the mirror, Ruth chopped at her hair with the kitchen shears. When she'd decided to cut it she'd vaguely pictured the short stylish cut she'd seen on some of the women at Nina's, but there was no time for stylishness now. It was alright though, because Candy had often offered to cut her hair at the beauty parlor at Redburn, and Ruth decided that it would be an appropriate thing to do together towards the end of therapy. This way, Ruth could have her hair wild for the party, Candy could trim it into respectability for her on Monday morning, and it would all contribute to the termination process.

The yellow hair fell on the floor, where she'd forgotten to put down newspaper, and Ruth felt lighter and lighter as she cut. There was something sexual about the process, like stepping back into one of the wild, untamed Halloweens of her childhood, and she was glad Victor was gone. 'I'm not like myself,' she said aloud to the tall, naked, half short-haired/half long-haired woman in the mirror, who was looking less and less like her. 'Trick or treat.' Her thoughts were racing too fast to follow. Maybe Victor had dropped some speed into her coffee before leaving, in a jealous rage at being excluded? She giggled wildly at the highly unlikely image of him slipping in the little pill. 'Manic,' she diagnosed herself in the mirror, and went into another fit of laughter.

She forced herself to stop cutting, because her hair was already very short, and Candy would have to take a little more off when she trimmed it. She threw the scissors on the bed, and turned to the odd pile of clothes she'd assembled there. She'd never sat down and figured out her costume, or made any kind of list of the things she needed for it, but she'd been thinking about it off and on all week. The only thing she'd decided on for sure were the silver pants Elaine had sent her from L.A. She held them up to the light, noticing the many tiny holes, and then pulled them over her hips, remembering the note that had come with them. 'I couldn't even get one leg into these, but thought my skinny little sister might be ready for a change of pace. E.' Elaine had been the sensitive one of the family, entitled to angry tantrums and fits of hysteria followed by long intimate sessions with their mother, neither of which sensible Ruth had even contemplated. Thinking of how she'd timidly worshipped Elaine, who'd alternately ignored and bullied her all through their child-hood, Ruth was surprised to find herself shaking with anger. Usually she never thought about Elaine, and would throw out the occasional silly packages she sent (most often second hand clothes) as soon as she opened them, but something had prompted her to make an exception for these pants. They were certainly very old. The material, which had probably once been harsh and metallic, was now soft as a second skin, and the silver color was worn transparent in some places. She wondered who had worn them before, and what had made the many tiny holes. Probably cigarette ash. She tried to remember how Elaine used to dress up on Halloween night but couldn't. Maybe she'd been too old to dress up.

Over the silver pants, she put on a long vest she'd picked up at Goodwill the other day on her way home. It was a soft worn blue and gray pinstriped material that might once have been the inside of a small man's tuxedo. Worn without a shirt and buttoned all the way up, it was decent but sexy. She took out the package of silver bangles she'd bought at Woolworths, and pasted one in the center of her forehead like an Indian woman, and one, in the shape of a leaf, under her eybrow. Then she smudged lots of green mascara on her eyelids and stepped back to look.

The pretty, ordinary young woman was completely gone. Instead there was a strange, long-necked figure, half androgynous bag-lady, half sexy French vamp. It felt exactly right. It felt like her. She put on her old black balletslippers so she could dance. The pants were too long, with little puddles of silver trailing on the floor, but she didn't have time to hem them now. She could always roll them up. Sonya wouldn't want to dance, though. She'd said she didn't like to, and anyway, she'd be with her friend. Ruth kept forgetting that.

She didn't want to wear her tidy suede jacket, so she grabbed Vic's old painting sweater with its leather patches at the elbows and deep pockets for her cigarettes and money and keys. She didn't feel like carrying a purse. In the bedroom, she took a last look in the mirror. There was the hair, lying on the floor like evidence of a crime. Fuck it, she'd sweep it up when she got home. She could leave a mess one time in her life!

It was fun driving to a party at night without Victor. On side streets masked and costumed figures grouped in doorways. On the river-way, the full moon shone on the water and the colored lights danced up at her. She turned the radio onto AM rock as loud as it would go and squealed around corners, pretending she was the cab driver Sonya admired. 'You're my reason for living,' blared the radio. 'My day and my night.'

The party was at Cindy's house, in an ugly modern building across the river. There was a musty elevator to ride up in, and Ruth felt sexy and anonymous, any woman at all going to a costume party anywhere, Paris or New York or London. She was suddenly hit with nervousness in the elevator, and almost wanted to go back down again. The music was loud from down the hall. If only she knew whether Sonya had arrived yet. She hoped so, but in a way it would be better if she hadn't. Then she'd have time to get settled, and when Sonya came in she could show her where to put her coat and get her a drink. She'd forgotten about the goddamn friend again! Well, she could show them both around. She wondered what Sonya would be dressed as.

Lynda let her in, and took her to the bedroom to drop off her sweater. As soon as Ruth saw her, looking the same as she always did except for a silver cardboard crown on her head, held on by an elastic around her chin, she knew that this was not an anonymous Parisian party at all. 'Ruth, you look so different I almost didn't recognize you!' she gushed. 'And you don't even have a mask on! I hardly recognize anyone, but they mostly have masks on.' Ruth didn't like the sound of this. She stood hesitantly outside the living room, watching the crowd which was squeezed in there. As far as she could tell, there were only a few staff members and a lot of strangers. Although of course some of the seeming strangers were probably staff in disguise. She thought of the man at Silver Pond, and forced him out of her mind. He couldn't be here. It occurred to her that Sonya might be here, but unrecognizable, and this made her even more nervous. An enormously fat chicken came towards her and grabbed her arm with a large wing covered with real white feathers.

It was squawking something about joining the party, but because it was only a chicken, Ruth felt no obligation to be polite. She pulled away, into the crowd. She felt eyes on her, and heard a few gasps.

Then she heard Dave's voice. 'Well, what do you know!' He was a pirate, with a red bandanna, a big floppy mustache, and an eyepatch. His mask was pushed up on his head and there was a real looking pistol at his waist. He grabbed her elbow, just as the chicken had done, and pulled at her, yelling above the music. 'Happy Halloween! I swear I didn't know you at first, SQ! Guess we can't call you that tonight, can we! Well, well, well, and alone too. Who would of thunk it.' He was harder to ignore than the chicken had been, since he knew her and since he, like Lynda, looked just like himself, only more so. On the other hand, Ruth had practice ignoring him from work. The Rolling Stones were screaming about brown sugar. She decided that Sonya was definitely not in the room. Now that Ruth thought about it, it wouldn't be like her to come in chicken form or anything like that. But what if she didn't come at all! It was the first time this possibility had occurred to Ruth. 'And I cut my hair off and everything!' she thought, illogically.

Dave had led her to a punch table at the back of the room, and was insistently pressing a fat joint into her hand. She'd left her cigarettes in the bedroom, in the pocket of Vic's sweater, and was itching to smoke something, so she accepted it gladly and lit up. She also accepted the paper glass of punch he was holding out, then said, 'Excuse me!' as if she suddenly had to run to the bathroom, turned her back and escaped, pushing through people like a lawnmower. When she stopped moving, she was in the kitchen, another room where Sonya wasn't, facing another man who looked just like Dave, only this one was a clown instead of a pirate. The grass was beginning to hurt her throat, so she stopped smoking and swallowed down the punch in her glass. The resemblance was so strong that it occurred to her that maybe the clown really was Dave, who had hurried to change costumes in order to confuse her, but she knew that there hadn't been enough time. And this one was a little taller, anyway. Maybe his twin brother? She offered him the end of her joint, to stave him off, but he shook his head and leaned at her, breathing alcohol and repeating his name. He produced another cup of punch and handed it to her.

'Aren't you the something-something-something-something,' he kept shouting at her, but the music was just as loud in here and she couldn't understand a word, not that she was really trying. It was the Supremes now, 'Take back your love!'

The joint was burning her fingers, and she dropped it on the floor. The clown got very upset. 'I-something-something-I-something-me!' he bellowed, stamping it out. She thought she would pretend to be a severely disturbed person who had ended up by mistake at this party.

'Clowns are supposed to be funny. So do tricks. Make jokes!' she said, in the sort of loud flat voice she thought such a person might use. She drifted to a spot next to the refrigerator where she could see both the living room and the hall outside, and was surprised when he followed her. There was Lynda again, slapping at a small man who kept snapping the elastic holding her crown up.

'Quit it, Steve,' she said.

A tall pretty black woman in white face, who Ruth thought might be one of the cottage officers, was leaning up against the stove, looking bored. She was wearing a black shirt and white pants and Ruth noticed that she had painted the inside of her hands black and the outside of them white. She reminded Ruth of the cookies they used to call half and halves, because they had half black and half white frosting. She was beginning to feel a little dizzy, and was just thinking of going to lean on the stove too, when she saw Sonya come into the living room.

Sonya had on funny patched knickers, a low-cut white peasant blouse, and big gold gypsy hoops in her ears. She was hung all over with autumn leaves and milkweed pods, and had tangled them into her black hair, which stood out, electric. Like Lynda and Dave, she looked even more like herself than usual, but in her case this made Ruth happy. She wanted to run right over, but when she began to move she got dizzy again, and now the chicken had caught Sonya. Then Sonya was coming slowly toward her, stopping to talk briefly to people, moving closer and closer, but not yet meeting Ruth's eyes. Ruth understood that it was a kind of game, a Halloween game. Trying to play her part correctly, she turned her back and began sipping her punch and talking to the clown, who was still there. She found that even without seeing her, she could feel Sonya coming closer and closer. She got a whiff of her scent, wood and paint and turpentine and soap, and tonight some kind of perfume. Lily of the valley? Hyacinth? She'd have to ask. The new short hairs on her neck stood up with excitement. Then the Sonya-feeling was abruptly cut off, and she turned around. Sonya had stopped at the stove, and was talking intently to the half and half woman. Now she had put her hand on her arm, and suddenly they were walking off together, into the other room. Their two backs vanished. Ruth knew that Sonya had seen her, a while ago, but she hadn't even greeted her. Her throat felt parched. Trick or treat, and she'd gotten the trick. The clown was asking her, again, to dance. 'I'll be all ready to dance,' she agreed, digging her voice-for-men up from memory, 'with just one more refill.' He went to get it, and while he was gone Ruth tried to keep perfectly still. Somehow it felt as though if she didn't move the last few minutes could replay themselves, and Sonya would come in again. But Sonya was gone, into the other room.

Aretha was screaming that all she wanted was a little respect, R-E-S-P-E-C-T. Ruth danced hard with the clown out in the middle of the floor. Sonya and half-and-half were gone, they must be in the bedroom. The clown danced by wiggling his shoulders a very little bit and looking embarrassed. 'You're too much for me,' he mumbled, very soon, and slunk off. For a little while Ruth danced with herself, but she began tripping on her pant bottoms, and stopped. She was ready to get her coat and leave, but she didn't want to go in the bedroom if Sonya and that woman were in there. There was another creature blocking her path now, a man wearing a horse's head. It was made of wire, and reminded Ruth of a small cage, maybe one for rabbits. She thought of Redburn. This cage was much smaller than the one that Telecea was locked in, up in Max, but Telecea couldn't carry hers along with her. Ruth wondered whether they were having their Halloween party right now too, and what Billy and Candy were dressed as.

The horse head was speaking to her, saying the word Equus, and something else she couldn't understand. 'I can't hear you,' she told it. It came closer, to speak in her ear, and the wire bruised her face. She jumped back. 'Go away! You're hurting me with that thing!' It reached up and seemed to be trying to remove the wire head, but it was stuck on very firmly. 'No wonder, hooves aren't very dextrous, you know,' she said, glad she could still be witty, and tried to do her lawnmower act. It followed her, though, pushing people aside with the wire head. It was accusing her of something. Its adam's apple jumped and she remembered the man at the pond again. This one was the same size. She heard the word bitch. He couldn't get her here, there were too many people. 'You shouldn't go around with a cage on your head, then,' she said. 'Go away, I have to find my friend now.' She went into the kitchen again. There were people there, some of whom looked familiar, but not Sonya. She noticed that the icebox was very shiny white, and had notices stuck on it with magnetic Smile buttons. One of the notices was a cartoon about shrinks. It showed a naked woman with large pointy breasts lying on a couch in a shrink's office. 'Vat seems to be the problem?' the shrink was saying.

'Have you seen my friend?' she asked the nearest person, who turned out to be the clown again. 'A woman all silver and gold with leaves in her hair?'

'Now Ruthy, don't you think you ought to . . .' he began, trying to sound like her father, for some reason.

'How do you know my name?' she screamed at him. Then she remembered that of course Dave had told him, since they were a team. The clown held a kind of fencing foil with a sheath around it that she hadn't noticed before. 'At least you could have been a little more creative in your choice of phallus,' she told him. Now Horsehead had joined them. And Dave was approaching from the other room. It seemed the collusion was more widespread than she'd realized. It had started that morning, on her run. Now she was sure he was here, one of them. But she had to act like she hadn't figured it out. She had a better chance of escaping if they didn't know she was scared. 'A cage but no phallus,' she said in a foreign accent, like the shrink in the cartoon. 'Ve-ry in-ter-esting.'

'Calm down, baby.' They used a kind of ventriloquism, so that she couldn't tell whose mouth the words were coming from. 'If you're looking for your girlfriend, she's making out with the black chick, on top of the coats. High school all over again.'

'What high school did *you* go to?' said one of the others, like a comedy team. 'Don't remember any dykes at *my* high school parties.'

'Well, you can't always tell,' said another, pointing. 'Now those two over there are obvious, but somehow, even in her get-up, I wouldn't have picked this little honey out of a crowd.' Ruth followed the point of his finger, hoping to find Sonya, but instead there was Nan, standing by the sink with a tall red-headed woman. Neither of them was dressed up as anything, and they both looked uncomfortable. The music had stopped for a moment, so Ruth knew that she could get their attention.

She cupped her hands like a megaphone. 'Never mind all these

317

pricks, Nan,' she shouted. 'You two go on and hold hands if you want to.' Nan turned and stared at her like a rabbit, with shocked, wide open eyes, then she and the other woman almost ran out of the room. The pointing finger had led to Ruth. The horse's head loomed very close, as if he meant to hurt her with the wire again, only worse.

'And you, Ms. Fem?' he said, in a scary voice.

She felt suddenly violently sick, and managed to break away from them and run down the hall to the bathroom. Shit! There was somebody in there. The walls of the narrow hall swayed back and forth, threatening to crush her between them. She pounded at the door. 'I am not a person who is sick on the floor,' she told herself. Nan and the other woman came scurrying out of the bathroom. Ruth made it inside, closed the door, locked it, walked very slowly over to the toilet to prove to herself that she could, and was horribly sick. While she was throwing up, the floor began to rise, so she sat down on it. After it was over she got up and tried to stick her face under cold water, but she bumped her head on the faucet. This was a lethal place. Everything was trying to hurt her. She had to get out fast. Above the sink was a cartoon of the same naked woman as on the icebox. She was sitting on a toilet this time, reading a book. 'Take time for yourself and relax,' read the caption. Ruth couldn't understand the joke. Another caption came into her head. 'I wouldn't have picked *this* little honey out of a crowd.' He'd meant her. Did this prove she was a dyke, once and for all? Scenes from her life started flashing by at lightning speed, like a movie gone wild. She wanted badly to stop them, to go home where she could show herself the movie slowly and figure everything out. But there was something else she had to remember, something bad. 'She's making out with the black chick, on top of the coats.' That was it. As she remembered, another wave of nausea rolled through her and she vomited into the toilet again. It felt like her insides were coming out, but she felt a little better afterwards. The floor had stopped moving up and down, at least. There was a timid knock at the door.

'Ruth, are you alright? Can I help?' It was Nan's voice.

'What do you mean, I'm fine,' she answered angrily. Then another wave hit her, and she was sick again. There was nothing solid at least, just more and more of that awful pink punch, and now she remembered that she hadn't eaten all day, she'd been too excited. No wonder she'd gotten drunk so fast. Because that's what she'd done alright, gotten disgustingly drunk, for the first time in her life.

She was setting all kinds of records for herself tonight! She washed out her mouth, brushed her teeth several times with a lot of toothpaste and someone's toothbrush, and splashed more cold water on her face, which was perfectly white, with strange red and blue spots. Someone was pounding on the door.

'One sec,' she called out, and looked at herself in the mirror. The bag-lady had taken over, except that now she also looked like a whore who'd just gotten beaten up by her pimp, who had cut off her hair with a meat cleaver. A down-and-out whore who had needed a fix four hours ago.

She had just one aim now – to make it to her car and leave. She was still shaky but much less dizzy, and she found the bedroom easily. At first she thought she saw them, lying together, but it was just the pile of coats. She kept looking and looking through the pile, but she couldn't find her bag or her suede jacket. She wouldn't have cared, except that without her keys she couldn't get home, and without money she couldn't call a taxi. Panic filled her as she sorted again and again through the heavy pile. It was another trick.

'Ruth.' Sonya stood next to her, handing her a man's sweater. The sweater smelled like Vic. How had Sonya know it was hers! She felt in the pockets for her money and keys.

'Ruth.' She was saying it again, speaking so slowly that her name made a whole sentence. 'Let's go, honey. I'll drive you. It's OK now.' Sonya's hand was touching hers, and Ruth froze, sure that as soon as she moved Sonya would disappear again.

'I can drive,' she managed to get out. 'I'm not drunk anymore. I was just leaving.'

'Never mind all that.' Sonya had her whole arm around her now, and the warmth of it, so different from the other hard hands which had handled her tonight, made tears come to her eyes. She could feel them, wet on her face. 'It's OK,' Sonya said again. 'Never mind this fucking party now,' and they moved out into the hall, and out the door, and into the elevator, which Ruth remembered riding, a long time ago. Then they were standing together, in the cool, sweet smelling night. Ruth looked into the sky and saw the full round golden moon.

'I went running,' she remembered. 'This morning.'

'Me too.' Sonya laughed. Her arm was still around her, and now her other hand was on her face, gently touching the place the horse head had hurt her and pushing back the funny jagged hair. 'Do you

319

think you can show me where your car is?' she asked. 'What happened to your face?'

'A horse bumped me,' Ruth said. 'Of course I know where the car is.'

'I'm sorry I left you alone like that,' Sonya told her when they stood in front of it. 'I'm sorry I didn't come over.'

'It's OK.' Ruth had given Sonya up to the coat room, and now here she was, taking the keys from her and unlocking the passenger side for her to get in. It felt like a miracle.

'Sorry if I'm jerky at first,' Sonya apologized. 'I haven't driven a shift for a while.' But she pulled out smoothly and started to drive. Ruth opened the window for some air, and leaned her head out.

'I don't know what the fuck is wrong with me,' Sonya was saying. 'That kid was all of nineteen! I was just trying to prove some damn thing to you. You looked too beautiful or something, too unattainable. And surrounded by all those men. I got scared. Are you still there?'

'Yes,' Ruth said, from the window. There were still a few ghosts and masked, weird figures on the street. She thought Sonya was driving her to her loft and now she felt as happy as she'd felt awful before.

'Maybe what I was trying to do tonight was warn you off,' Sonya went on, 'with actions because words don't ever work. See, that's how I behave when I care for someone. So you don't want to get too close after all, honey, you really don't.'

Ruth heard that Sonya had said, in a roundabout way, that she cared about her. She had called her honey. She heard, too, that Sonya was sad, even more than the time in the woods when she'd talked about her childhood. This time was different, though. This time she'd be able to do something about Sonya's sadness. 'I do want to know you,' she said, speaking very clearly so that Sonya would know she wasn't drunk anymore. She was glad she'd brushed her teeth so well after being sick. 'You're wrong,' she said. 'I do want to know you.'

They were stopped for a red light. Ruth moved closer and they kissed, very gently. She tasted Sonya's mouth for the first time, and thought she might crack in two pieces from joy.

'We're going to your house, right?' she whispered, and Sonya looked at her, shrugged her shoulders, and nodded.

CANDY

The way it all got started was Candy and Billy was in the shower room Saturday night. Candy was just getting ready to bang Billy's fucking hard head on the floor and Billy probly had the same thing in her mind, when all of a sudden they stopped. Maybe it was the girls and screws right outside the door, waiting for the two of them to hurt each other. Or maybe it was just the dope wearing off. Whatever it was, their eyes met, and Billy said, real slow, 'They got us just where they want us, don't they?'

'Yeah,' Candy agreed. 'Made us a trap and we almost fell right in.'

'Hey,' said Billy, and she was laughing a little now. 'Even if I did hate you, which as it happens I do not, I wouldn't give them the satisfaction.'

'I know I don't hate you,' Candy said, and then they walked out the room together. Candy looked at the crowd outside like she was surprised to see them there. 'Something real exciting must be about to jump off,' she said, 'cause I know you-all broads aint standing out here like a bunch of stupid sheep for no reason at all.' Then the two of them went in her room and shut the door.

'You know,' Billy said, 'everyone got some kind of stake in us not making it, when you think about it.' Candy thought about it for a while, and she saw that no matter if it was because they was inmates, or both girls, or one black and one white, it was true.

'We got to show them we aint got nothing to do with them or who they think we are,' Billy said. 'That whatever ideas they went and made up about us don't affect us at all.' That was when Candy had her idea.

'Listen,' she said, 'this gonna open their noses for them but good. Aint no one gonna be able to take this one in.' Which is how it happened that her and Billy was dressed up as each other for the Halloween party. Billy got out her pinstriped suit that she'd had altered to fit her, and that Candy had always admired, and Candy gave Billy her pink state dress from reform school that was the only girls' clothes Billy could relate to at all cause the last time she wore a skirt it was back at the state school. Billy went back in her own room to change, and Candy put on the white silk shirt, then the pants and the vest, and last the jacket and the wide blue tie. She was amazed it wasn't too big on her. She'd knew that her and Billy was both built about the same, but she'd never really thought of them being the same size, like two girl friends that could share clothes and make-up or something. When Candy looked in the mirror and saw what a good butch she made she felt funny, like maybe the idea wasn't too cool after all. The only thing wrong was her hair, and when she put it up under the hat, she looked like the real thing.

Billy stayed out a long time, and when she came back Candy didn't only think the idea wasn't so cool, she knew it wasn't. Billy had plaited her hair into two pigtails. The pink dress came down to about the middle of her knees and she'd put on sneakers and white socks. She looked as cute as shit and about fourteen.

'Like this is real interesting and all,' Candy told her. 'But not for wearing to no party in the gym, you know?' Billy didn't say nothing, just stared at her like she didn't know who it was. Just then Edie and her new sidekick, a sorry looking broad named Avis Parker, banged on the door and barged in.

'Well!' Edie's eyes went from one to the other of them. 'Avis told me she seen someone that looked like Billy's teenage daughter come in here and I knew Billy didn't have no daughter so I had to see what all this was about!'

'Well you seen.' Candy was pissed as hell and more than ready to put her own clothes back on. 'So now you can leave. Aint no one invited you in here in the first place.'

'Well!' Edie jumped back playing the fool. 'Bad old butch, aint you, Candy-Cane. Better watch out for her, Billy, cute little thing like you is.' Billy, who must of renewed her high when she was changing, cause her reactions was all slow, had just picked up on what was coming down.

'You don't dig our Halloween costumes, huh?' she said, slow but mean. 'Maybe you think this dress makes me less of a man?' That sounded kind of funny the way Billy looked, but Edie backed off, with Avis right behind her.

'We was just playing, Billy,' she said, but Candy could hear them laughing outside the door, and telling the others to come look. Billy heard them too.

'We're going just the way we are,' she said. 'They got some laughing to do they can do it to my face.' Candy shrugged and pinned her hair up good inside the hat. She was sposed to be on lock-up but didn't look like nobody was gonna stop her.

'You gonna let me in on what you got in your room before we go?' she asked, all aggressive and shit, seeing that she had the look.

In the main building, it was Halloween party, alright. Every last one of them had got hold of something, and dry as the compound was, you could be sure all the nuts would be missing those crazy pills they'd been hoarding. The screws must of reasoned that the best way to bring down the tension that had been building was to let the girls freak off with each other as much as they wanted to, cause lights was off where they should of been on all over the building. In the gym they was turned down low, with orange and black streamers hung across the ceiling, like for some half-assed high school dance.

Candy knew lots of girls must be on shit they had never tried before, or that hadn't got tested out yet, just like when it was real dry in the street and people started to get their asses poisoned. Cause instead of freaking off in the corners like they was sposed to, they was falling asleep or getting all paranoid and seeing shit. Even Candy, who had always had a real good toleration, was feeling weird from the shit Billy had gave her. What it felt like was she wasn't in the gym at all, but way the fuck up in some damn plane, looking down on this place, that was just a bunch of little people jerking around inside a closed box, like this ant farm she'd seen once. Then the plane came down closer and it looked like a high school dance again, and then down a little closer, and she could see that what had looked like a broad and a dude dancing together was really one broad dancing with another broad dressed up as a dude, and two broads dancing together had went out way back in junior high. Billy had went over to the other side of the gym to pull off some dope deal with Grace, which Candy couldn't very well object to, seeing she had just now took advantage of Grace's dope. She didn't really care, anyway, because of being up in the plane, and she danced a few numbers with Lou, who she usually enjoyed moving with, only tonight Lou was treating her all weird like a dude or something, and the music didn't sound right either, screaming some shit about burn baby burn that she never noticed the words to before. And then the plane was too low and she had to stop, cause she couldn't see no more whole people, but just these close-ups of faces with real big open pores and pimples and shit, and she hoped to hell wasn't no high school around where the kids had so many track marks, on their arms and legs where you'd expect them, but also places like faces and necks and hands. And then there was the getting cut and shot scars, and more than two or three girls had lines that went right *around* their neck like someone must of tried to cut their heads the fuck off. And she'd never noticed before how many of the girls had tried to slice their wrists sometime or another. Candy was more than ready to split and she was just trying to locate Billy and tell her stay if she wanted to, but she was leaving the fuck out, when something touched her from behind that wasn't Billy and she spinned around and saw this dead-white face with staring eyes and sticking out black lips and two horns coming out its head and some kind of feather tail in back. She froze still and her hand grabbed onto her razor in the pocket of Billy's suit, and she smelled the smell coming off the thing, that was the smell of killing and death.

'I know you, white cunt Jezebel,' Telecea said (cause of course it was her), speed-talking in this scratchy whisper. 'I know it all now, how you change with Ruth Foster. How you stole Norma voice your unclean self, come under my window with your bominations in His eyes. Think you can trick me putting on Billy's clothes, well hiding time over, Ho', and Venging time here. Aint no hiding place left now, the Venger ready for you.' Telecea went right on with her shit, all about beasties and dogs and white horses, and how the palms of Candy's hands was gonna be all that was left of her, and Candy just let her talk. Even though the gym was full of people it was like this wall had came down around them, as if Telecea was invisible, and no one but Candy could see her.

'Cool out,' Candy kept telling herself all the time Telecea was talking. 'Cool out now, girl, let go that blade, you don't need it.' Cause she was almost sure Telecea didn't have no weapon on her, the way she thought she was one of the monsters out of her own head and even looked like one of them she'd painted on the wall of the art room. 'She probly thinks a Venger or whatever can kill just by wanting to,' she told herself. 'It's the bad dope scaring you more than anything else, let that blade go.' But she couldn't make her fingers in the suit pocket let it loose and she just prayed that Telecea wouldn't jump her right now, and give her a case. Cause she'd kill the bitch. She knew at least her fear didn't show, cause that was another thing she got from hooking, how even when you was high as a kite and ready to piss your pants from fear of some maniac, wasn't no way you let him sense it, not even from your breathing or your smell, cause plenty of them was like dogs that bite you if they know you scared, or sharks, when they're around blood – just like the police. So that when she did speak, she was cool in her voice and body both, cutting through the garbage talk.

'Lehrman help you with your costume, Telecea? She brung in them feathers and shit for you, huh.' Telecea took a step back and her tight painted-up face went soft all of a sudden, just like a balloon when you start to let the air out. 'It's a real nice costume, Telecea,' Candy went on, talking all bright and smiley like some social worker or kindergarten teacher or something, and keeping her eyes right on the bitch, cause even if everyone else was too high or scared or something to act like Telecea existed, someone better bring her out of it, cause as long as she thought she was some kind of monster or devil or something, the girl was dangerous.

'You almost had me scared for a minute. That's some bad Halloween costume, alright.' She could tell it was working, so she let herself look around for Billy for a minute, and that was her mistake. The high she'd got rid of out of necessity came right back and she felt like she was up in the damn plane again. She couldn't see Billy nowhere but Loraine and Dina was standing together just a few yards away with their backs to her. They was close enough to hear her over the music if she shouted, but for some reason she knew she couldn't. It would feel like shouting at store mannequins or people made out of cardboard or something.

Just then two little claw hands grabbed her by the collar, choking on her. Telecea had gone right back into her devil self, and was whispering the same thing over and over in that high screechy voice.

'Something bad done happen to Billy, something bad done happen to Billy.'

Candy jerked away, but Telecea held on and let herself get drug right across the floor like a skinny mangy rat when it gets its teeth into you good. Candy held her off her neck with both hands so she could breathe.

'Shut your lying mouth and let go of me, girl,' she yelled, but Telecea had went off for real now, rattling off at the mouth like a jammed-up machine gun.

'Something bad done happen to Billy,' she started up again. 'You drug her down wif you, ho' Jezebel, made her put her big old

dick in your pussy, now you both gone burn burn burn in that fire.'
When Candy heard that burning shit she shivered, and for some
reason Telecea let go. Candy moved across the floor to Loraine and
Dina but Telecea's voice followed her.

'I know you, bitch, I know you. You the one lets mens stick they
guns up your cunt.' And even high as she was, those words hit Candy
like a stone in the belly. And then she was sweating and shaking at
the same time but at least the crazy bitch had let go of her and she was
next to Loraine and Dina and panting out, 'Where's Billy?' But oh
God, it was just like she thought it would be – they turned real slow
and just stared at her, and part of her said, 'They're high, that's all,'
but the other part knew they had turned into fucking cardboard
statues. She took one arm of each and pinched but neither of them
moved much and on the side that was sposed to be Dina all she could
feel was cardboard and on the side that was Loraine it was like
pinching fucking air.

And then she realized she had let Telecea out of her sight. It was
the one thing she could of done to watch out for Billy and she'd
panicked and blew it. Everything was going too fast, she was having
trouble getting her breath and seeing them dots in the air so she sat
down on the gym floor and closed her eyes and put her head down
between her legs. Cause wasn't no way she could afford to pass out
now.

When she opened them again she wasn't up in no plane no more
but down lower than everyone and there was Dina, talking and
gesturing with this black magic marker that she had just used to write
'Kiss Me I'm Funny' on her T-shirt for her Halloween costume. She
was talking to Candy, saying all these words like 'Don't you worry
we'll find Billy I'll take care of business I'm here now you know you
can depend on me' but to Candy it sounded just like a TV
commercial run too fast or like a Western with the sound all run
together, which she didn't know why she thought of, maybe because
the sets was made of cardboard in Westerns, you could tell if you
looked close. And she knew she *couldn't* depend on Dina, not for
nothing. And then she looked over at Loraine, who was dressed in a
plain white T-shirt with nothing wrote on it and baggy jeans, her hair
pulled back, no make-up, and she thought, 'Loraine's dressed up as
Nothing tonight, that's her costume, fucking nothing,' and then
Loraine opened her mouth and leaned down and said, 'Candy . . .'
and her voice was flat and way far off but it wasn't quite nothing.

There was this little part there that was different from all Dina's cardboard shit, but the trouble was this part was flickering off and on like a fucking candle that couldn't make up its mind was it gonna light up for real or not, and she thought 'If it goes all the way out forget Loraine too,' but she needed her bad cause it was hard to hold out against this bad dope alone and so, hoping she wasn't wasting as much time as it felt like, but time always *did* get weird with dope, she said to Dina 'Give me that magic marker,' and she took and wrote on Loraine's white T-shirt, as big and black as she could: 'LORAINE BRADLEY.' Then she turned Loraine around and wrote her name on the back, and then stretched the shirt off Loraine's belly so she could read it, and told her, 'See that, Loraine, that means you aint disappearing on me now, cause I need you.' Thank God, Loraine answered her, and her voice was alright.

'You afraid Telecea's gonna do something to Billy?' she asked. 'You want me to go get the police?'

Candy thought for a second. 'No way,' she said. 'We got to find Billy ourself, fast. Or Telecea.'

Dina had just started a rap about how she was gonna organize a institutional-wide search, and how this just illustrated how the system did something or other, but Candy didn't stay around to listen. 'Let's check out the cottage,' she told Loraine. Dina had went off somewheres so the two of them moved out the gym to the dark hall, sort of holding on to each other.

'This shit aint no good; it's poison, aint it, Candy?' Loraine asked her.

'Yeah,' Candy said. Both of them was having trouble with their walking, but it helped to know it was hitting them the same way and wasn't nothing personal.

Wiggins was in the cottage, and when Candy asked her had she seen Billy or Telecea, she didn't answer, but just started in babbling about how Telecea ought to be in Max where she belonged and not at no party. They finally had to just barge through, but wasn't no one in the rooms but three girls, asleep or passed out, and the shower room was empty. Then they went back out in the yard, where the assholes had dimmed the lights too, and Loraine asked her, 'Do you think they could be out here somewhere?' Candy closed her eyes, cause usually she could feel it with her body if Billy was anywhere near, and she thought she could feel if Telecea was near, too, by that smell. But there was only the cold air and she breathed it in deep and wished she could just leave her eyes closed and sink down in the grass. Billy was probly OK anyways, freaking off with Grace somewheres and not in no trouble.

'You're the one.' She made herself repeat it in her head, what Telecea had said about that thing that happened to her the time her and Billy was on escape, that she hadn't told no one in the world about, not Billy and not Foster. 'You're the one lets mens stick they guns up your cunt.' That thing that happened to her that she hadn't hardly told her ownself about, cause all she wanted to do was forget it as fast as she could, and here was this crazy bitch knowing all about it.

And here *she* was, ready to pass out on the grass and leave Billy to her. She opened up her eyes and slapped her face hard two times to wake herself up. 'It's somewhere inside,' she told Loraine. 'Somewheres in the main building, I know it,' and they went on in. Past the gym down the hall, and then they seen it, a little strange moving light in the hall bathroom, and Candy started running.

SONYA

Sonya walked to the party through the night, dressed as a forest gypsy. She'd worked productively all day. Now she allowed herself to know that Ruth wanted her, had wanted her ever since they'd met, might very probably want her tonight, at the party. In a way this being desired was more important to her than its aftermath. She thought she could do without security or sex or even love, all of which most women seemed to need, but not without some steady affirmation of her own desirability. She pictured a series of Pandora-like boxes, called 'What I Need Most.' The hinges would fly open when the right button was pressed, to reveal a mirror, a wedding veil, a reaching hand, a mouth . . . Each to her own.

She'd been tense about the party before, dreading the men and the dancing but she was light and detached now, a friendly observer. She could stay and watch, or she could leave in ten minutes if she felt like it. These people had nothing to do with her. It was already past nine, but there were still small groups of kids roaming the streets in masks and made-up faces. A long-legged girl with wild black hair giggled and screamed in Spanish, dodging a shorter dark boy who moved after her, pushing the swings so they swung crazily in the night as if mounted by ghostly children.

Sonya walked across the still, moonlit river and reached Cindy's building, still full of the evening's easy rhythm. She rode the elevator up and was met at the door by Cindy, a distracted and frilly witch, who took her into the dark bedroom where coats were piled on the double bed, then walked away without speaking, jarring Sonya out of her peaceful mood.

Then she stood at the entrance to the living room. There they all were, in their unimaginative ugly costumes, gathered into a tight knot and moving jerkily together and apart in time to the loud music. She took a step into the room and felt its currents pulling at her containment. Ruth didn't seem to be there. She did see several unrecognizable creatures, but they all walked like men.

'Hi, Sonya, don't you look pretty.' Lynda, a small stout princess, touched her on the shoulder, then shouted in her ear. 'Listen, have you seen Ruth yet?' Lynda looked worried and

329

Sonya followed her back out into the hall to find out what was going on.

'I think she might be upset because Victor couldn't make it or something. She's not acting like herself at all, and she looks funny. I think maybe she had sort of a lot to drink . . . I'm so glad you're here, Sonya, I didn't know what to do. I admire her so much, but you're the only one of us she's really friendly with, you know?'

Lynda sounded genuinely concerned. The situation was like one of Sonya's fantasies come true, and she was intrigued. Maybe it was just as well that Barb hadn't come.

'She's probably in the kitchen.' Lynda pointed through to the open door between the living room and kitchen, where Dave, absurd in swords and mustaches, was in close conversation with a man with a wire horse's head. 'I think Dave's looking for her too. But you know, he's not always that sensitive, I'm afraid he'll just upset her more.'

Sonya wondered whether all the men in the party were competing for the prize of taking care of Ruth. She didn't feel much like entering the competition. There were too many men here anyway. She pushed her way through the throng of dancing people to a place near the kitchen door, and saw Ruth, who seemed to have cut off her hair, standing as if pressed into a corner by a man in a clown suit who was talking to her intently. She wore tight silvery pants and looked beautiful and somehow dazed. Ruth's eyes found Sonya at once, but she stayed where she was, waiting passively to be approached, and Sonya felt her anger rising. She was damned if she'd play it their way. Let Ruth come to her if she needed her so badly.

'Dance?' It was a fat white chicken with a male voice, so well-stuffed and bulging that it didn't look capable of dancing. Sonya refused, but started a conversation with it. When she finally disentangled herself, Ruth's back was to her and she was still talking to the clown. Her slightly bent back, her bare slim arms, and her neck with the new jagged hairline were touchingly waiflike. Her hair wasn't even cut properly, it was chopped off roughly and unevenly, as if by some blunt instrument. Sonya imagined Ruth doing it herself in a strange little ceremony before coming here. She looked prepared to offer herself up for sacrifice, and Sonya, remembering Telecea and the feathers, wondered uncomfortably what her role in it was supposed to be. No wonder Ruth overreacted to Telecea. There was some sort of affinity between them. She wished people would stop casting her in their melodramas without her permission.

'Hey, Gypsy Mama!' It was a tall, vaguely familiar black woman, now in white face, whom Sonya thought she remembered seeing sitting outside at Redburn, although it was hard to tell if it was the same person. 'Excuse me, but you know the lady standing over there, rapping to the clown, right? How bout an introduction?' Sonya stared at her, speechless, and the woman winked drunkenly. 'She's your old lady? Better go take care of her then.' Sonya tried to get away, but the woman grabbed her by the hand.

'Don't try and play straight with me,' she said. 'I know who you are. The word gets around. Listen, excuse me, I'm not too sober I know, I've been trying to leave for the last half hour. Just couldn't take my eyes off her. Couldn't even get up the balls to talk to her or nothing. Very weird vibes, you know? Like she's about to break or something. Not that I'd object to her doing it at my place, I'd be glad to pick up the pieces.'

'Go talk to her then, I'm not stopping you.' Sonya tried to jerk away, but she kept hold.

'Hey, don't go away mad,' she said. 'Anyone ever tell you you have pretty eyes? I like broads that aint all skin and bones myself. You want to come help me find my coat?'

Sonya followed her back to the bedroom and kissed her among the coats. She closed her eyes and tried not to notice the taste of beer, the grease paint that was getting on her face, the raccoon fur scratching her, or the openings and shuttings of the door. After a moment the woman sat up, belched a little, and shook herself free. 'Hey, Gypsy Mama,' she said. 'You're sweet. But I gotta go now.'

By the time Sonya had made it back to the kitchen, Ruth had disappeared. Sonya stood in the hall, wiping half-heartedly at her greasy face, picturing Ruth, with her terrible vulnerability tonight, probably halfway home with some asshole who could hardly wait to get his prick in her. She stood there watching the loud ugly people jerking back and forth to the loud ugly music, and knew that she'd blown it once again. She'd been offered something precious, something rare and tender and she'd turned her back on it.

'Oh Sonya, there you are! I'm so glad, I thought you already left.' It was Nan, urgent and sweating, at her elbow. 'Did you know Ruth's been looking for you all over? She was drinking and she got sick, and now she's in the bedroom getting her coat, she says she's going to drive home, but she's in no shape to drive!'

'Thanks, Nan, I'll go find her.' Quick to snatch her reprieve, Sonya went to the bedroom, conscious at the same time of a curious feeling of having been tricked.

TELECEA

Halloween time now. Venging time now. Aint about no more Telecea Jones. White horse have came and flyed her on out of here. Told her, you done what you can, now it out of your hands. Gots to do His will now. Send His Venger in the gym. Make it dark in there. All of them too scairt to see the Venger. Make a space round it like when He part that sea round Moses, pull them waters up.

What that Venger gone do? Could be cut, and could be burn. How I'm spose to know? It out my hands now. Gots to do His will. Could be burn or could be poison.

Pretty soon they all start in moaning and holding they stomachs so I seen He pick poison. Poison first.

Talkin' bout sick this and bad dope that and every time they look over at the Venger start in puking. Puke they nasty guts out all rotted up inside. Try and get away but it too dark. Too late now.

That Candy come right up to me all drest in man clothes like her butch wear. Dirty ho' think she can hide from Him in some old costume. Try and act like I am still Telecea. Don't she know the Venger can see through any old costume. See right in her belly where it all rotted up wif them maggots. Right down in her cunt. Seen a gun in there just waiting to go off blow her insides out. Ho' try and act all cool but when I tell her bout that gun she start to shake. Sweat pour down and she run off.

He tell me take the Venger in the hall bathroom. Lights all off in there. All dark and nasty but it out of my hands. Tell me make the Venger scrunch up against the wall, get that lighter out. Wait and lissen.

After a while she come alright. Not that Candy ho' but her Billy come. I known it be one or the other so I aint surprise. Just keep still and watch what happen.

That Billy aint no big bad butch tonight. Oh no! What done happen to her, He must have snatch her up. Tell her, You think you so much of a man, well I turn you back. Back to a little girl. Born bad. Seed of the Dulter. Child of the devil. Bomination in His eyes got to save her soul. Just a little girl in pigtails and a pink dress. Holdin' on to her belly, all sick and scairt. Call out her ho' name.

Candy, Candy!

What she think her ho' gone do for her now?

Candy, where are you, this shit poison!

She right, it poison alright, and now she start to feel it. I been all
still and scruncht up but I know she feel it. Feel she aint alone in here,
ha ha ha. Feel that Venger in here wif her. In the black dark. Want to
get away now but the poison too strong and that little girl too sick to
go nowhere. Sick out both ends. Nasty and unclean and so scairt she
aint close the stall door.

So I seen what drop off. That dick! He take it off her, flush it
right down. I seen! Bitch aint got no more dick now, just a little
nappy black hole.

Then He tell me it time so when she start to step out that stall the
Venger step out too. In the dark, wif my lighter right up under that
devil face. All black and white and feathers and horns. Let the Venger
tell her.

Well Louisa Ann child, look who we gots in here wif us tonight!
Nice little girl in your pink dress, too bad you been evil and gots to be
punish.

When she first seen, her mouf go wide open like a fish mouf.
Open and shut, open and shut and don't nothing come out. Tears
start in rolling down her face and she be shaking. That one know a
devil when she see one. Tell her, Don't you move, Louisa Ann, child.
Too late to get away now, little girl. You been knowing this was
coming. Then I move my fire all close, get ready to burn her up.

Who that! Aint no one else spose to be in here! Watch out now,
Venger get you too if you come too close!

Who you talkin to? Aint no Telecea in here! This is the Venger in
here, ho', bitch, better get the fuck off me now! Git off, I tell you.

Let go my feathers now, ho'! Let go my tail! He gone kill you
now, watch out, he gone. . . .

Better git away from me wif that magic writing on that shirt,
ho'! Better not try and put no spell on me! Who you think this is, this
the Venger, ho'! Better get the fuck off!

Oh, you gone die now. All of you gone die.

See, I told you you was gone burn.

SUNDAY, NOVEMBER 1

RUTH

Ruth finished her second cup of the amber tea, and now she didn't feel high anymore, but empty and new as if she'd just been born, her body tender and raw and alive. From where she sat on the rocking chair she could see Sonya's sculptures: a mobile in silver wire which moved gently at the window and reminded her, she wasn't sure why, of Telecea, a floppy life-sized stuffed woman, sitting at the table in a resigned attitude, and another one which looked like two wire women, balancing on a see-saw. It was growing faintly light outside, and she wanted to stop time, to slow it all down, because it was already morning, and it was going by too fast.

Now Sonya came back to her, and Ruth saw her face clearly, her dark eyes and the softness around her chin. 'Are you alright?' Sonya asked her. 'Ruth you know we don't *have* to do anything. . . .'

Sonya stood above her, and Ruth, reaching up to her, heard a sadness and a wanting, and then Sonya put her hands in Ruth's new short hair, stroking her head and her naked neck, then slowly kissing her forehead. Then Sonya raised her from the chair, holding her close. 'Let's go to bed, hmm?' she said. 'I'm just going to the bathroom, I'll be right there.'

Ruth took off her clothes and got into Sonya's bed, in her loft. She could hear Sonya in the bathroom, and then she came in, and Ruth got a quick look at her wonderful nakedness in the light.

'Wait, I want to look at you,' she said, but Sonya got right into the bed and lay still next to her, not touching. Ruth thought Sonya looked scared and young, hiding under the covers. Feeling braver, she reached over to her and touched her shoulder which felt different than with clothes on. It was warm and soft, and Ruth got up on one elbow and leaned over her, kissing her neck and the deep hollow of her collar bone and every part of her face again and again. They'd been kissing before but it was different with Sonya naked, next to her. It was almost too much, too overwhelming, because she had never even touched her face against Sonya's neck before, or smelled her, or rubbed her lips against the soft curls around her face, but she had wanted and wanted to, and now Sonya was here, all of her, and she could.

'I can't believe I'm really here,' she whispered to Sonya. 'I've been wanting you so much all this time,' and as she said it she knew it was true even though she hadn't really known it, not out loud, not like this, with her whole body flooded with wanting.

'You have?' Sonya whispered. 'You really have?'

'Yes, always, in the car, everywhere. . . .' And Ruth pulled the light blue sheet over both of their heads so they were like children in a tent and now she could see all of Sonya: her great sloping hips and her soft creamy breasts, so luxurious she was almost afraid to touch them. She did, softly, with her fingers and then her tongue but she couldn't tell if Sonya liked it and for a moment she felt frozen and scared but then Sonya began to kiss her back, began to touch her all over and it was terribly exciting but too fast and flickery.

'Lovely, you're so lovely,' Sonya whispered, and she pulled Ruth over on top of her, so that Ruth felt all of her at once, and then she felt Sonya breathing, in and out very slowly and they were breathing together and her body was part of Sonya's.

'I want to stay here, I want to stay right here like this forever,' she whispered, and when Sonya laughed a little Ruth could feel that too, in every part of her body, how Sonya's stomach moved up and down, and then they were pressing together, their wet cunts pushing and sucking on each other, and Sonya slid her hand in between them and Ruth felt Sonya's fingers exploring, touching her wetness and right away too soon she was coming exploding into Sonya drinking her in, sucking on her neck.

They lay like that for a while and Ruth was filled with a tremendous joy. She wanted to sing and shout. 'I love you!' she whispered to Sonya, and then, because that didn't say it all, 'Sonya, I want to know you.'

They lay side by side, Sonya half covered with the sheet, and Ruth leaned over again, her love so powerful inside her she thought there was nothing she couldn't do. 'Don't hide please,' she whispered. 'Don't hide, you're so beautiful.' And then she began to kiss Sonya with her lips and tongue and fingertips, taking her time, slowly exploring her hips and belly down to where the little ridge of curly hair began. She stopped there and felt afraid again, with Sonya so quiet above her. She'd never touched another woman's sex, only her own, and she was afraid it would be too different, and she wouldn't know what to do. She lay her cheek softly on the coarse black hair, then put her hand there, parted the two lips, and looked.

The soft flower-like shape of Sonya's cunt filled her with wave after wave of tenderness, so soft and open, and moist, waiting. She kissed Sonya there, softly at first with her lips, and then more surely, with her tongue, and Sonya's legs opened wider and she was deep and wet and Ruth put her fingers deep inside her and she felt Sonya moan and she moved with her, feeling the building inside Sonya, more and more until she felt Sonya contract and expand, felt her cunt tighten and let go around Ruth's fingers, and Ruth lay for a moment with her cheek gently on Sonya's cunt, and then Sonya pulled her up so they lay close together again, Sonya's arms around her.

'I can't believe it,' Sonya whispered to her. 'I can't believe you've never been with a woman.' They lay still for a little while and then Sonya's hand was exploring Ruth again, softly, teasingly.

The phone rang. Sonya's hand stopped dead and Ruth's whole body clenched. The giant red phone by the bed kept ringing and ringing. loud and hateful, until Sonya pulled her hand and her body away. 'No one calls me this early,' she said in a hard flat voice. 'Does Victor know you're here?'

'No, unless he guessed,' Ruth faltered.

Sonya picked up the phone. 'Hello,' she said. Then angrily, 'hold on.' It was seven now by the bedside clock. Sonya moved to the furthest edge of the bed and lay with her back to Ruth, her head under the quilt. Ruth wanted to refuse the phone, to throw it across the room, screaming that it wasn't fair.

'Hello,' she said, instead, and at the sound in Victor's voice, immediately stiffened with dread.

'I'm sorry to have to call you there,' he was saying. 'I just couldn't think where else you'd be,' and she knew in a flash that someone was dead and saw Candy lying murdered. When he went on draggingly, 'Don't worry, it's no one in your family,' she screamed out, 'Is it Candy' and at this, beginning to understand, Sonya took her head out of the blankets and came closer, letting their bodies touch again. Ruth felt a fleeting triumph and then Victor said, 'I don't know who it is. Dave just said there's been an emergency, to call him at the prison right away.'

'Did he say anything about Candy?' she begged, but he repeated stonily that Dave had told him nothing, that he was there if she needed him, and hung up. Ruth dialed rapidly, wishing suddenly that she was home where she belonged and not in this strange angry woman's bed.

337

'I'm sorry I pulled away, I didn't know anything was wrong,' Sonya said from far away. The switchboard transferred her to Dave uncharacteristically fast.

'Listen Ruth, sorry to call you like this,' he began.

'Just tell me,' she interrupted. 'Is it Candy?'

'No, she'll be alright,' Ruth was so flooded with relief she didn't hear what else he said, and he shouted at her. 'Listen to me, Ruth, goddamnit. I'm trying to tell you, Loraine Bradley's dead. I've been here for an hour and I still can't figure out what the fuck happened. As far as I can make out, Telecea staged a psycho at the party they had in the gym last night, God knows why they let her go, but she burned Loraine with a lighter. They took Loraine to City, and apparently she had some kind of bizarre reaction to the medication or something, went into shock, who the hell knows. She wasn't burned that badly, anyway. Candy and what's her name, her girl-friend, were involved too somehow, and Candy got burnt too, but not badly. We've got her in the hospital here, totally freaked, I've given her enough valium to knock out a horse and she's still scream-ing. The staff's totally useless, they're just falling all over each other to disclaim responsibility, and meanwhile I'm supposed to be on the phone to Loraine's goddamn family in Wisconsin, and I just got a call from Proudy up in Max saying she's going home if someone doesn't get up there and do something about Telecea before she pulls the whole damn building down on our heads. I don't know what the fuck they were all on last night but we got a whole lot of sick girls here today, and the news about Loraine's already out. Tranden's out in California, but they've called him, he's supposed to be on the next plane and be here by this afternoon. Listen, how fast can you get here?'

He wasn't asking her where she was calling from, or referring to last night, she noticed. He needed her too much.

'I'll be right there,' she said. 'I'm leaving now.' But when she put down the phone and reached for her clothes, she found only the vest and awful silver pants.

'Here.' Sonya handed her a pair of pants and a gray sweater. 'The pants shrunk in the dryer, I can't even get into them. They shouldn't be too bad. Just keep the coat on and you'll be OK.' Ruth put on the baggy pants and funny smelling sweater. Sonya looked at her and shook her head. 'It doesn't work. Let's go by your place and get you some clothes. And you need a scarf or something over that hair.'

Ruth didn't understand why she was going on about the way she looked while everyone had burned up. Sonya was too big and bouncy beside her and Ruth didn't want her along, but it was too hard to tell her not to come, and they went down to the car together.

CANDY

Candy was having her burning dream. She knew she had to wake up or she would get burnt she had to keep her eyes open but someone had drugged her she couldn't shake it off she was in a nod. If only she could just get her eyes open it would be alright but they was stuck shut and she kept trying and trying to wake up and scream out but every time she'd go under again and now she dreamed her arm was burning up like a hot dog on the fire shriveling all black and she was screaming and screaming and nothing would come out her mouth.

And then it started all over again trying and trying to keep her eyes open and then she did get them open and it wasn't the cottage it was some white room and they was a girl's voice coming from somewheres screaming, 'Mami, mami,' and she didn't know was that part of the dream or was she awake but her arm was burnt for real she couldn't even move it, it hurted so much and then she went under again.

And she was running and running down a long tunnel trying to find Billy and warn her and then she run up smack into a hard steel door and she could see another tunnel and she started to run down that and it stopped too and then she saw it was a maze like they ran rats through to get their reactions, and someone was watching her from the watchtower it was back at Watsonville and she thought why bother to have them men with guns cause can't no one find their way out of here anyway, they built it like that and set your arm on fire too, and now they was behind her, getting closer and closer. . . .

Then she jerked awake again in a white room smelling of medicine and she thought, 'A hospital, oh my God they took out my insides, they burnt out my womb, not my arm after all, and now I can't never have no kids,' and then she remembered they had already done that to her so that couldn't be it. But it had to be some kind of hospital she knew, cause of the smell. 'Billy,' she screamed they must of killed Billy somehow and drugged her so she wouldn't tell. 'Billy, Billy!' And then Miss Putnam came and kept saying Billy was alright but she knew it was a lie and she kept on screaming and screaming. She could hear someone else screaming too, 'Mami, Mami,' and then over and over 'donner ester me nino, donner ester me nino' and

Candy kept trying to understand it in case it was something about Billy but she couldn't make it out and then she went back under again.

And then she woke up for real and started screaming again and finally after a long time Billy walked in the room so she stopped. She tried to get up and go to her, but her arm was all on fire and she had to be sick. She started to cry then, and said, 'Billy where the fuck is this, I gotta be sick.' And Billy sort of took her by the other arm like she thought it was gonna break off, and took her out the room and it wasn't no real hospital after all, just the fucking Redburn hospital with its filthy dirty bathroom that she made it to just in time.

So at least she knew where she was now, though she didn't remember how the fuck she had got here, but she knew she had to of been unconscious though, cause that was the only way they could of got her in here. There was a big white bandage on her arm, that was still on fire, so she knew *that* part of the dream was real. When she got out in the hall Billy was still there with this funny expression on her face.

'Come on,' she said. 'You got to lie down again. Girl, you was screaming for me so loud they heard you all the way the other side of the compound! They called the cottage and said get over here as fast as I could.' Just then this pregnant little girl in a raggy blue housecoat came wandering by talking to herself in Spanish and crying for her mama which kind of depressing shit was just one of the many reasons Candy always kept way the hell out of this place plus the dirt and the way they drugged you up so you didn't know was you coming or going and then sent you off to get experimented on.

They was back in the room they started in, and she lay down on the bed cause the pain in her arm was making her dizzy.

'They better give me something for this,' she said to Billy, 'and then I'm getting the fuck out of this place, but first someone better tell me what went down. I didn't hurt no one, did I?'

'Fuck, no.' Billy had her hands in her pockets and was pacing up and down in the little room like she couldn't wait to book. 'You really don't remember, huh?' she asked. At first Candy was hurting so much she didn't pay a whole lot of attention to Billy's expression, but now she took a good look and knew it had to be something bad and anyways something must of really jumped off for them to of let Billy in here to see her cause wasn't no inmates that wasn't on sick list ever allowed in the hospital. But it couldn't be nothing too bad, cause Billy was alright and not in Max or nothing and neither was she.

'Come on, baby, you got to remember, it was just last night.' Billy sounded pissed off. 'It was the Halloween party, right, and we was all high on that bad shit?' Then Candy did remember some of it. She had got dressed up as a butch and Billy as a little girl in that pink dress, that was it, and then things had got all fucked up, running down tunnels in the dark, like in the dream. It was so confusing, but she knew if she could just shake them nightmares out of her head it would all come clear. Billy sat down at the foot of the bed and then got right up again.

'You remember the way Telecea went off and had me trapped in that bathroom?' she said, real soft. Candy didn't, quite, but she nodded her head anyway.

'Fuck it.' Billy pointed to the bandage on Candy's arm. 'Telecea had a lighter, right?'

'Oh,' Candy said. 'She burned me?' That was a relief cause it was the thing she'd been most scared of always, and here it had happened and she was OK.

'You remember who was with you when you came in after Telecea?' Billy asked. Candy tried to remember. She thought of writing something with a black magic marker on a white T-shirt.

'Loraine,' she said, feeling like she might be sick again. 'Loraine was with me.'

'Yeah, baby, you got it. Listen, I got to go now. They told me five minutes, just long enough for you to see me and calm down. They gonna be coming after me any minute now.' And Billy booked as fast as she had came, so that when it finally did come back to Candy, she was alone.

How they'd all been tripping out and Loraine had seemed shrunk down to nothing so Candy had wrote her name on her T-shirt and made her come with her to look for Billy. And the two of them in the cottage and being so sick together out in the grass. And then the dark toilet and Telecea all painted up and feathered coming at the little girl that was Billy with something. It was confused then but she remembered a flame and Loraine's white shirt lighting up with the black letters running together and someone screaming and screaming. Her rolling Loraine down on the ground and hitting at the flame and someone shouting at her stop, it was already out, and pulling her off, and her arm hurting and after a while the siren of a ambulance and now she knew what it was that Billy wouldn't tell her. That Loraine had got burnt to death. That she had pulled Loraine with her to get burnt to death.

Candy heard a noise coming from somewhere that she stopped when she realized it was her. And then it was like she couldn't get her breath and whatever they had gave her kept pushing her back on the bed fogging up her head and she was trying to scream for them to come and give her something else, to put her all the way out, because it was like that nightmare again and she kept trying to wake up and it kept on stabbing at her, telling her, 'You killed her, you killed her, you burnt her up.'

And then after a long time Miss Foster was there but not the real one – it was a ghost Miss Foster, with her hair cut off and her face all bruised up like she had got in a accident or something too.

'Miss Foster, I killed Loraine,' Candy said out loud, to the ghost Miss Foster.

'No, Candy, you didn't,' Miss Foster said in her regular voice, so Candy thought maybe it was her after all. Foster said that Loraine was dead, but she hadn't burned up, it was something they did in the hospital. 'It wasn't your fault, Candy, it had nothing to do with you,' she said about ten times, and then she came closer and held Candy in her arms and said it again and the stabbing went away for a little while and then Miss Putnam was there saying 'Miss Foster, please, Dr Thorne's been waiting for you up in Max,' and Foster was gone too.

SONYA

Sonya walked down the road, kicking stones and cursing herself for having come along on this fool's errand in the first place. Buses came irregularly during the weekend and she'd had more than enough waiting around today, so she decided to walk as far as the main road, then hitch. Probably she'd get raped, it would be the perfect ending to this day. She'd been so caught up in Ruth's hysteria that she hadn't even taken the time to wash before leaving, and her legs rubbed together, sticky and uncomfortable. As she walked she reviewed the ridiculous morning, starting with getting interrupted by that phone call.

No one could accuse her of being unsupportive this time, that was for sure. She'd fallen over herself in her eagerness to accompany Ruth to Redburn, and then once she'd seen how Ruth looked in her clothes, with the pants half falling off, she'd tried her best to persuade her to take a few minutes to stop and pick up some of her own clothes or at least to cover her slashed hair with a scarf, but Ruth wasn't even listening. Apparently she preferred to go in looking like some ridiculous bag-lady, maybe as a kind of self-punishment. From the moment they got in the car she'd done nothing but blame herself. 'If only,' she kept saying. 'If only I could just take last week back and do it again. If only I'd paid attention to what was building up. If only I hadn't been so preoccupied.' She hadn't actually said if only she hadn't gone to bed with Sonya, but the drift was clear enough. Well, Sonya had a few if only's of her own, and that was certainly one of them. She hadn't intended to go to the stupid party in the first place and certainly hadn't meant to bring Ruth home with her, and now look what had happened. This would teach her to keep her distance from hysterical straight women from now on, anyway.

She'd done her best to swallow her anger and be nice to Ruth. It was a real emergency, after all, with someone dead. On the ride in, she'd told Ruth over and over that it wasn't her fault, that no one could possibly blame her, and that blaming herself was the least productive thing she could do. She'd suggested that they stop for coffee and that Ruth use the time to pull herself together. In response, Ruth had only driven faster, going into some long explanation of

344

some other burning death in Candy's distant past which made it absolutely imperative for Ruth to be with her immediately.

'Listen,' Sonya had reasoned with her. 'Candy's a big girl. She's survived on the streets for years without you to hold her hand. I'm sure this isn't the first death she's witnessed. She's probably in a whole lot better shape than you are right now. Plus she doesn't have a job to keep.'

But Ruth had just given her the same look she had right after she'd gotten that phone call, like 'What is this unpleasant stranger doing here?' Then, as soon as they'd pulled into the parking lot she'd dissolved into tears. 'It just hit me about Loraine,' she got out. 'She would have made it, she was one of the few who would have really made it.'

The tears hadn't done anything to improve Ruth's appearance, and Sonya had begun to wonder if the two of them would even be let through the door. But Ruth produced a pair of dark glasses at the last moment, along with her haughtiest manner, and the unfamiliar weekend guard stared, but buzzed them in. 'Telecea's up in Max . . . if you want to see her,' Ruth had told Sonya and then had vanished in the direction of the hospital.

But when Sonya had gotten up to Max, Proudy wouldn't let her in. 'I got plenty on my hands right now,' she'd shouted through the door. 'Aint no one coming in without no authorization.' Sonya had heard screams and thuds through the door. She'd finally managed to locate Riley, the weekend deputy, but it had been an exercise in futility. She'd asked her to call Ruth, Dave, even Mrs Hanson, to get her the necessary authorization, but the woman just shook her head at her like a bull getting ready to charge. 'I'm the deputy in charge here, young lady. Now you say you work here, and I'd advise you to come back when you're scheduled to. We've got enough foolishness on our hands without importing more.' Then she'd gone so far as to walk Sonya down the hall and watch her leave.

She kicked a stone in her path with all her might. Maybe they'd somehow already connected Telecea's feathers and paints to her. For all she knew, Telecea had told everyone she'd been acting on Sonya's orders. Well, she wasn't going to start accusing herself, that was for sure. She'd leave that game to Ruth. Let them go ahead and fire her if that's what they wanted to do. She had had it up to here with this place anyway.

TELECEA

Forgive me, Lord. I done what I can. She born too bad for saving. Granny standing there praying over me like every time after she beat me. I try to save her soul for you, Lord, but it dint do no good. Wif her devil father staring out at me from them eyes of her. You take her now, Lord. Send her where you want. Don't never let her go to no art room no more. Never see Sonya no more. I wash my hands of her now Lord. She all your. Stand there in her black church dress rubbing her hands together. Tell Him. You see me Lord. You know how I have try.

I start to slamming my head on the floor cause that make her go. Bitch Proudy out there spying. Stop that noise, girl. Don't you know, worse you fuss, worse that doctor gonna do you? On his way right now, with his needle. Gone put you to sleep, put you out of your misery. Done kilt that poor child never done you no harm. Burnt her up. Keep that noise up and I'm a tell him don't ever wake you up no more when he put you to sleep. Just like they do a mad dog.

MONDAY, NOVEMBER 2

RUTH

Dave had suggested that those of them who'd had to come in on Sunday should take Monday off, so when Ruth woke up automatically at seven, she turned over and closed her eyes again. She wanted desperately to be back asleep, but Victor was talking at her, his hand on her shoulder, shaking her awake.

'Please, Vic,' she said, 'leave me alone, I'm not going to work.' It felt like a tremendous effort to get the words out and she turned to the wall and curled up, sinking back. But he wouldn't leave her alone.

'Ruth, wake up, listen to me, please.' He was sitting on the bed, cross-legged, in blue pajama bottoms. She sighed and turned over because it seemed easier, in the long run. 'Are you sure it's a good idea not to go to work today?' he said. 'Wouldn't it be better to go in and deal with it, to get it over with instead of avoiding?' He was earnest and tough, a style that was possibly successful with his more depressed clients. She didn't need it, this morning.

'It's all been arranged,' she tried to forestall him. 'None of us who went in Sunday have to go in today.'

'I see. You could have told me.' He jumped off the bed and left the room, slamming the door, then came right back and sat down in the rocking chair.

'Listen, Ruth, I know you're upset about Loraine, but you have to take some responsibility for what you're doing!' He waited, but she had nothing to say. 'You vanished Saturday night and I literally haven't seen you since. I don't even know exactly what happened yet. How the hell am I supposed to help you?'

By letting me go back to sleep, she thought, but that wasn't the right answer. She knew her silence was infuriating him but talking was too hard.

'I feel like you're trying to punish me somehow, but I didn't have anything to do with Loraine's death, Ruth. I'd like to help, if you'd just give me a chance.'

'Vic, if you really want to help, please, could we talk about it later?' She got up to go to the bathroom and felt again how terribly tired she was.

When she got back to bed, Victor was still there, waiting. 'It won't help to walk away from me,' he said. 'Or from what you're feeling. You've already been sleeping for twelve hours, now.' She wondered what he wanted from her, what she could say that would make him be quiet and leave her alone. Probably it was something about Sonya. Victor went on, 'Listen, you told me that Loraine got killed by some medication they gave her at the hospital and that Candy and Telecea were somehow involved, and that's all the information I have. Why don't you at least tell me what happened, for God's sake! I'm still living here, you know.'

'Yes, I know,' she agreed. How could she not know? He was sitting closer to her now, almost on top of her, his hand pushing on her shoulder. She forced herself not to pull away, to just tell him the truth and hope it was good enough.

'Vic, I know I have a lot to explain, I know you must be furious and upset with me and you don't want to wait. But I feel terrible, and I really can't talk now. If you could just treat me as if I were sick for a little while . . . maybe you could bring me a cup of tea?' She was glad to have thought of something concrete she could ask him for. It was too late to go back to sleep now, and her throat was parched and scratchy. She could almost taste the hot, lemony tea.

'Shit!' He slammed something down on the bureau. 'I get it already! You don't need to make up excuses to get me to leave. I'm not stupid, Ruth, even if I am invisible to you!' He stomped out of the room and she heard crashing noises in the kitchen. Apparently he wasn't going to bring her the tea, but she didn't want to get it herself with him in there. Well, he'd have to go to work eventually. Now she could hear him on the phone, probably complaining to someone about her. She closed her eyes and stuffed the pillow over her head.

'You gone kill me now?' Telecea asked, when she and Dave came in to her cell in Max. 'Put me asleep?' There was blood on her head, where she'd been banging it.

'Did you say you're a friend of Loraine's, dear?' Mrs Bradley's voice was tight, brittle, begging her not to tell. 'A teacher too? Isn't that sweet of you to call! Hank, come here, there's a friend of Loraine's on the phone. Passing through town, I guess.'

Ruth took the pillow off her head and tried hard to concentrate on the present, on Vic's voice on the phone. She couldn't hear his words, though, and those others kept pressing on her, banging in her head. He was hanging up now, coming back into the bedroom.

'I have to go. But if you're planning to go back to work tomorrow, I'd advise you to do something about your hair.' Ruth put her hand to her hair. Sonya had kept on and on about it in the car, then Dave had mentioned it a few times, and now Vic. Why were they so concerned with her hair when between them all they'd killed Loraine?

'Thanks, I'll fix it,' she said, to make him go.

'Well, it won't get fixed by lying in bed.' His anger smashed right into her, and she had forgotten how to protect herself.

'Victor, don't, please,' she whispered, but he was relentless.

'Acting like your hair's just fine isn't going to make the party go away.' She didn't know if he meant the staff party or the Redburn party and didn't want to ask. He was on his way out again, but paused at the door.

'Well, maybe when I leave, as you so obviously can't wait for me to do, and Sonya comes over, she can help you pull it together. Since she was with you at the time and I wasn't.'

He stomped out and she heard the front door slam. Now was the time to get up and get the tea, but she was afraid to. The rush of remembering was bad enough when she lay still, and she was afraid it would come at her faster than she could handle if she moved.

The door opened and he was back again. Maybe he'd just keep doing it, she thought, coming and going, coming and going, all day long.

He stood with his back to her where she lay on the bed, and she could tell he was crying. She was supposed to jump out of bed and throw her arms around him. Then they would hold each other, both crying now, and he would say how much it had hurt him to talk to her like that, it was just that he was so hurt himself, so jealous that it was eating him up inside. She'd lead him gently to the bed, and, as the guilty party, initiate their lovemaking. He stood there for what seemed like an endless time, waiting. Finally he gave her a last look of betrayal and went out. Probably he'd be back a few more times.

Ruth lay as still as she could in bed, trying not to remember.

'Go on dear, now you can go on, Hank's on the other line, that's Loraine's dad.' She tried to make that one go away but what came instead was Telecea, arching her back in terror as Dave approached her with the needle.

'Help, Ruth Foster, don't let him kill me!' She saw herself ineffectually arguing with Dave, begging him to stop what he was

349

doing, to let her try to calm Telecea down. And Dave, armed with that needle, sweating and cursing.

'Fuck it, Ruth, will you hold her arm for Christ's sake!' Until finally he yelled for Moody who came in laughing and kneeled on Telecea, his weight on her skinny chest, her head still banging on the floor, while Dave fumbled, missed a few times, and finally got the needle in her arm. Just as Telecea started to go under, she looked right at Ruth and mumbled something about Sonya. Maybe she was saying goodbye to her, since she believed she was being killed.

By the time Ruth had finally been able to leave, about five in the evening, Sonya was long gone. Telecea was already gone too, by that time, shipped out to some maximum security, computer-run jail in Kansas. And they'd already shipped Loraine's body out to Wisconsin. For all Ruth knew Telecea and Loraine had gone on the same plane, in some special hidden compartment reserved for unconscious and dead bodies.

It was all so fast, as if they were trying to pretend nothing had happened. Was it possible that they'd try to cover it up? They'd certainly given Candy enough drugs to make most people forget anything. But how could they expect Ruth to forget what she'd seen? A few hours after she'd gotten to Redburn, Tranden had arrived. Dave had stuck to his side, so she was the one who had to go to the hospital morgue to identify Loraine's body.

Ruth had thought Loraine would be burnt, but there was almost nothing, just some little burns on her stomach, where the shirt had caught fire. It was just Loraine lying there looking the same but dead and it didn't make any sense. And no one would tell her anything at first. They just wanted her to sign a paper and leave but she refused to sign until they told her what had happened.

On the piece of paper it said that Loraine Bradley, black female, age 27, inmate of Redburn Prison and ward of the state, had been admitted at 11:45 Saturday night with second degree burns. That she had lost consciousness at approximately 2:00 A.M. and had been found with vital signs missing at 2:34 A.M. That attempts at resuscitation had been unsuccessful and the deputy of Redburn had been notified at 3:15 A.M. That Ruth Foster, director of mental health, had arrived to identify the body prior to its release to prison authorities. Then there was a space for her to sign. After about two hours, they finally produced the young intern who'd been on duty when Loraine was admitted. He was sleepy and testy and had obviously been told to keep his mouth shut, but he finally talked to her.

'We gave her a great deal of codeine,' he said. 'It's standard procedure with burns, one of the only things that'll touch the pain. Not an unusual amount, you understand, just the standard. And as far as I can tell she OD'd. She must have been pretty heavily medicated already. Which isn't the hospital's responsibility, see, it's the prison's.' And he'd showed her the admission papers, where 'none' had been checked under other medications. 'The guy that brought her in said she wasn't on anything. And we didn't bother with any kind of blood test or urine. She was hurting bad, you know. We just got that codeine into her. She quieted down right away, and the nurse left. When we checked her next she was cold.'

Ruth thought she'd done OK with the doctor. At first he'd stared at her but she'd explained that she'd been called out of a costume party in the middle of the night and had had to borrow someone's clothes. She'd acted calm, professional, upset about what had happened, but not personally involved. She hadn't even winced when, halfway through the explanation his face had started to change on her, turning into Dave's, then into the pirate's at the party, and finally into the man at the pond's. That had made it hard to concentrate, but she'd gotten through it.

Now she just needed stillness and quiet, a blank empty mind, with no pictures in it, but they wouldn't stop coming. Now the switching business had started all over again in her head, with Dave's face becoming the young doctor's then some other man at the party's. 'It's not our responsibility,' he said. 'She's making out with the black chick, on top of the coats. We're completely covered of course. Any suit would implicate the Redburn staff as I guess you know. Not very friendly, are you? Are you, Ms. Fem?'

It was all too much, and her mind wouldn't stop. The pillow was damp, and Ruth smelled her own body, sweaty and strange. She got up and had to sit down again with dizziness, probably from not having eaten for so long. Not since the day before the party, and that felt like about a year ago. In the kitchen, Victor had left a half-opened can of baked beans on the counter. Some sticky beans were trailing out from the can and had spilled on the floor. A carton of milk was out too, and had gone sour. Ruth poured it into the sink. At first it wouldn't come and then it all plopped out. Ruth's stomach turned over. She put some water on the stove and went back to the bedroom.

She wondered if Candy needed her, if she'd noticed that Ruth wasn't there. She pressed her head into the pillow and now she remembered pressing her face between Sonya's great, soft breasts, sinking in, and then it was Loraine's body that she was sinking into and all the time Loraine was dying. The water whistled from the stove and Ruth got up to make tea. It was hard to do it, hard to concentrate with all the voices hammering at her. She wondered if she was going crazy.

CANDY

When Candy woke up, the pain in her arm made her remember where she was. Then about Loraine. They must of gave her something heavy-duty after Foster went cause she felt like she'd been sleeping for a million years and she couldn't tell if it was morning or afternoon. Her mouth was all dried out, and she had to piss bad, but when she got up her legs was shaky. She went down to the nasty bathroom without running into no one. It was real quiet, like a ghost place and she had the scary feeling that maybe she was the only one left there. Her jeans and T-shirt and her jacket that Billy had brung was on the chair back in the room so she put them on, scraping the shirt on her sore arm. She was sick and dirty and she thought of going in the shower room and washing, but it was more important to get out. She walked down the corridors past the locked doors. Through the wire grills on top she could see girls sleeping on some of the beds, probly drugged. In the TV room the set was on, playing one of the soaps, which made it afternoon, but the clock on the wall was stuck at seven-thirty.

'Hey!' she yelled. 'Anyone home?' Finally, after about five minutes a young nurse that Candy hadn't seen before came out the office.

'You're sposed to let me out now,' Candy told her. 'I was in here doing my clean-up job, and now I'm sposed to go back to the cottage.'

The nurse stared at her in a confused kind of way. 'They didn't say anything about that,' she started in, staring at Candy's bandaged arm.

Candy cut her off. 'Well then, they must of forgot. You can call the deputy and check if you want. Go ahead. See, I come in here and get my arm took care of, then I clean up. Then you're sposed to let me out.'

She didn't know if it was the con in her getting over or that the girl was so new she would of done whatever anybody told her, but she unlocked the hospital door and Candy was out in the cold air. It was gray and raw and no one was in the yard either. She walked toward the cottage, feeling light and empty, as if a vampire had came and drained out all her blood in the night. If she could just see Billy it

353

would be different, she thought, it would start to seem real again.

When she got in the cottage she saw on the kitchen clock it was three in the afternoon which explained the quiet – everyone was at work. She passed Loraine's room quick without looking in and came to her own room that was all dark and locked up, like they thought she had died too. Then she heard noises coming from Billy's room, across the hall.

The door was open and she stood there, quiet and invisible, watching Billy and Dina mess with a suitcase they had up on the stripped-down bed. As she looked, the breath went out of Candy's body cause it wasn't even Billy's room any more, it was all packed up, with even the pictures gone off the wall and lighter patches where they used to be, that one of her and Billy standing together, the school one of Timmy, and the small one of Angela Davis, out the book. She stood there wondering would they ever look up and see her, or had she really got turnt into a ghost. She remembered feeling like this in the gym that night. Then it was her and Telecea, the invisible twins. They had probly already sent Telecea away somewhere. Loraine was dead. And now it looked like Billy was packing to go.

Dina saw her first. 'Hey girl!' she said, like everything was just routine. 'It's about time you made it over here. We three's got some very heavy rapping to do. I was just about to anticipate goin' lookin' for you.' Billy turnt around slow, then.

'Hey, baby,' she said. Candy stood there staring at her.

'You aint sposed to be leaving yet,' she finally got out.

'They are removing Billy *now* today!' Dina jumped up to shut the door, hyped up as usual, and not seeming too shook up that her girlfriend had just got killed. 'These motherfuckers don't want no witnesses! They came in here and informed her she was leaving early this AM!' Candy felt lost and dizzy. Her arm hurt her bad. She sat down on the edge of the bed and started eating from a box of crackers that was there. She hadn't ate for what seemed like days.

'You watch,' Dina told her. 'You're gonna get your papers real soon too, maybe this week. And I wouldn't be surprised if some of the strings that's been attaching *me* in here starts to cut loose too.' Candy wished Dina would get out so she could at least talk to Billy.

'How come you didn't come get me this morning?' she asked her like Dina wasn't even there. 'Soon's you heard you was leaving today?'

'Me and Dina have been figuring this shit out,' Billy told her real slow. She was high as a kite. 'There may be some big bucks in here.'

'That's right,' Dina broke in. 'They is scared shitless, man. They getting previsions of lawsuits, losing their little jobs and etcetera! And we got them right over a tub. Only thing I'm surprised at is they haven't separated us yet. Locked us up in three different places so we can't share the information. We were the only ones that was on the scene at the time, see'

'Why should they lock you up, Dina?' Candy asked her. Eating the crackers had made her feel a little stronger, and a burning anger at the fucking unfairness of it all was rising in her. 'From what I remember, *you* wasn't nowhere near the scene. You was too busy running your mouth about what-all you was going to do to help. Institution-wide searches and shit.' Billy and Dina both stared at her like she was nuts.

'Only reason I'm gonna let that shit slide right now, Candy,' Dina said, 'is cause you're still recuperatin' from the side effects of shock! And plus, too, I know you're upset. Probly blaming yourself for what happened. But listen, girl, that's my former woman you're talking about. And you know good and well I was damn near busting my ass trying to develop a plan of action that would of worked in a more subtler way, instead of just busting in there like you done, which you ought to of known would send a crazy person right off. Just like it did do. And what happened as a net result? You tell me. Now I aint blaming you cause you was panicked, you probly couldn't help yourself at the time, but don't let me hear you turning it round on me!'

Candy had to admit Dina was right. She hadn't done nothing herself but get Loraine croaked. 'I'm sorry,' she said, and sat as far away from them as she could. It was gonna be time for Billy to leave and they wouldn't of planned nothing about after. Wouldn't of even said goodbye. A dark pit was opening up in front of her, deep and black, and she couldn't stop herself from falling in.

'Now listen up, both of you,' Dina was saying. 'This may be the last time we're all together, so we got to get our story straight. From information sources I got, I hear they are trying to put it all on the hospital on the outside. Saying they the ones should of gave her the tests to see did she already have any drugs inhabiting her blood stream. Which they probly did not do, but that is not the point if you gather in my meaning. You know good and well Telecea Jones the one really did it. You see that girl up in Max today? No. They shipped her ass out of here quick, fast, and in a hurry so she wouldn't talk. Now what we got here is a case of criminal neglectitude. All of us know that girl was sposed to be locked in Max on account of attacking people. They had her as a maximum security risk, sposed to be under one to one guard all the time, am I right?'

'Right,' agreed Billy. Candy closed her eyes, but then she remembered it was her last time for a long time to see Billy, so she opened them back up. Billy had on creased blue flannel pants and the white sweater. She looked like she was in a dream and didn't want to wake up.

'They knew good and well that girl was dangerous,' Dina finished up. 'To the well-fare and well-being of herself and others. So why'd they allow her out like that, all by herself? We're gonna make them pay through their noses, for our sister's death. And make sure that little freak gets hers, too.'

'What the fuck does it matter?' Candy asked. 'Telecea's got life already. And you know if they shipped her out it wasn't to no country club. Loraine's already dead. And aint nobody gonna give *us* no money, even if they do end up losing some law suit.'

'Aint you never hear of no shut-mouth money?' Dina asked her. 'Pay-off bucks?' Dina kept running her mouth bout money and bucks and cash and plans and Candy tried to tune her out. Dina was as high as Billy, she thought, but in her case it wasn't even no drugs that had did it, it was thinking bout being rich. When really, there was about as much chance they would get rich offa this thing as that her and Billy would settle down on the outside and live happily ever after.

Finally, Billy woke up a little and asked Dina to leave 'So I can say goodbye to my woman.' Once they was alone, though, she wouldn't even look at Candy, just kept pacing up and down the room, talking bout big bucks.

Billy,' Candy stopped her. 'I can't concentrate on what you're saying. Please. Just lay down with me a minute. Before you go.'

Billy did lay down with her then, but carefully, so her clothes wouldn't get messed up. She kept looking at the bandage on Candy's arm in a scared kind of way, like she thought it was catching or something.

'Hold on to me for a minute, baby,' Candy said, but Billy acted like she didn't hear. She kept shifting round on the bed, running her mouth.

356

'Listen, girl, you probly saved my life in there! And I'm not gonna forget that when I'm out, either, I can promise you that. I'm through fucking around, you hear that, baby. We play our cards right with this shit and we'll have us a little nest-egg to start up on. Get us our own place. Aint nothing coming between us now, you dig? No dope, no other ladies, nothing.'

Her voice went on and on and Candy stopped listening and put her cheek on Billy's. She rubbed the top of Billy's soft head with her face. She could feel Billy in there somewhere, and smell her, and she guessed that was gonna have to be enough. Billy was getting more restless now.

'I aint even gonna say goodbye, baby, cause you'll be out there with me next week, you watch. Won't even have the time to notice I'm gone, that's how it's gonna be.' She got up, smoothing down her clothes. 'Mama should be here by now. They told me four o'clock, and you know I aint staying a minute later.'

Candy and Billy and Dina each took one suitcase, and they started walking across to the main building. Through the window at the front desk they could see Timmy and Mrs Morris, waving like mad. Billy kissed the bunch of girls that had came out at the last minute to say goodbye. She kissed Dina and then Candy. Then they buzzed her through and it was over. Billy was out there. Free.

Candy picked up one foot and put it in front the other. She was heading back to the cottage when she realized they was one thing she hadn't done yet and she went back past Four Corners to the deputy's office and knocked on the door.

'Could you give me Loraine's folks' address?' she asked Riley. 'I'd like to send a card.'

Riley stared at her all suspicious out her little eyes. 'You're gonna have to go to Mrs Hanson for that,' she said. 'I got nothing to do with this whole mess.' Candy walked back down the hall.

'Mrs Hanson's in a meeting, Candy,' Doreen squeaked at her. 'She said not to disturb her.'

'OK,' said Candy. 'I'll wait.' She sat herself down in the chair cause it didn't matter if she sat here all day or someplace else. Finally Hanson came out. She took Candy by her good arm and pulled her in her office so hard it hurt the bad one.

'Now you just sit down and make yourself comfortable, dear.' She pointed at one of the pink plastic chairs. 'Mrs Riley has told me about your sweet thought. And I want to tell you I think you're a very brave girl, worrying about poor Loraine's parents. It's good to see the old Candace Peters back, and I want you to know you did just right to come in here and share your feelings with me. I want you to realize how deeply concerned and sorrowful we are too, dear, at this tragic event. Loraine was a very sweet girl, and we of the staff have contributed to send her family a very large bouquet as our expression of sympathy.' Hanson was just like Billy and Dina in a way, talking on and on with her garbage like she was on speed.

'I just want to know her folks' address,' Candy interrupted, 'so I can send them a card.'

'You just deliver your card to me,' Hanson said. 'And I promise you it will be delivered with the others. I'll see to it personally, dear.' Candy realized Dina and Billy had been at least partly right. Not about all the big bucks they was down for, but about the other part. Hanson thought she wanted to start some trouble with Loraine's folks and wasn't no way she was gonna come through with no address.

'Never mind this bullshit,' she said, and moved her feet out the office. Now she had did everything she had to do, so she went back and lay down on her bed. Once she had laid down, though, she couldn't think of any reason to get up again. After a while she remembered like from a dream when Foster had came and talked to her in the hospital. Foster hadn't talked like the rest of them. She had talked like a real person, that knew Loraine was dead. She had held Candy in her arms. Her hair was all messed up and she looked weird. Candy thought she would maybe like to see Foster again. Not to say nothing to her, just to see her face. But probly she wouldn't come back no more either. She shut her eyes and lay as still as she could on the bed.

SONYA

Sonya woke up with a headache. At first she could remember only the color – an emerald blue green. As she sat up, the rest of it came back.

She had been walking up a mountain trail with some kind of large group when she saw a flash of blue-green among the stones. She bent to pick it up, and discovered it was not a stone after all, but a small turtle, almost completely frozen. She knelt, feeling the heat of her cupped hands warming it back to life, pleased with her power. The turtle began to rock back and forth convulsively in its shell, and then she realized with disgust that it was badly damaged, probably dying. The small snakey head emerged, the pointy worm tail, then the beginnings of little soft claw feet which tickled her hand. The whole thing had a too-soft, deformed feeling to it, but the head was the worst of all, small and slimy, with a gaping toothless mouth and horrible popping glazed blue eyes. She was about to fling it as far as she could when the others in the group surrounded her, bending to see and then exclaiming in sympathy. Now she knew she could never get rid of it. She'd have to carry it with her everywhere.

She got out of bed, feeling cramps tugging at her belly. There was blood dripping down the inside of her legs, and now she remembered the day before, in all its sickening detail. There were no tampax in the bathroom. She grabbed a towel and started to walk back to bed when she put her foot down in a plate of yesterday's yogurt and jam. It was too much. She threw the plate against the wall, but it hit the Telecea mobile instead, making it crack and dangle crazily. Sonya stood there looking at it, crying with frustration, the dripping blood making a little puddle on the floor.

TUESDAY, NOVEMBER 3

RUTH

'It's alright,' Ruth reassured herself. 'Other people take weeks off. I get two days.' She'd woken up with the alarm, prepared to go back to work, but the voices had started up in her head again, and she'd called in sick, then gone back to bed. Now she'd been awakened by noises in the kitchen. Victor should have been at work hours ago, but he was there, shaggy and bearish-looking because he hadn't shaved for a few days, banging dishes around in the sink. When he saw her he jumped guiltily and said he'd thought she was still asleep.

'I was.' She pulled her yellow robe around her, noticing that it needed washing. She hadn't washed or brushed her teeth yet, and she felt dirty and ugly, at a disadvantage. Victor sat down at the kitchen table, moving strangely, as if he were stiff all over. 'Are you alright?' she asked him uneasily.

He hesitated, then shook his head and began what sounded to her like a prepared speech. 'I took today off, too, Ruth,' he said slowly. 'I don't think you have any idea,' he raked his hand through his curls, 'that this has been a very hard time for me, too.'

'Yes, I know it has, Vic. I do know. But let me go wash and brush my teeth before we talk, OK?'

'You see, Ruth!' He was heavy, solemn in his accusation. 'You never really *see* me.' She sat back down, resigned. Maybe the catastrophe could still be averted.

'I haven't really been able to see anyone but myself in the past couple of weeks.' She spoke fast, 'I've been pretty much in a state of crisis, and I know I haven't communicated it very well to you. But that doesn't mean I don't love you. Because I do. . . .' She wondered as she said this whether it was true, or whether she'd simply decided that she was incapable of handling one more crisis at the moment. 'Let's go in the bedroom,' she said, leading the way. 'I need to lie down.' As they went in she planned quickly, feeling like some woman on a soap opera. 'We won't talk at all. We'll fuck, then he can't leave me today. A couple of more weeks, that's all I need.'

But he wouldn't get into bed with her, and sat down on the rocker instead with something of the pained, uneasy manner of a doctor delivering bad news at a bedside. She pulled the covers around her head. It was such a strange time – eleven o'clock on Tuesday. Everyone else on the street must be at work.

'Stop, Vic,' she whispered, but he wouldn't.

'Ruth, I know this isn't the best time to say this, but I'm human, too. I have feelings just like you do, although half the time you don't seem to know that.' She could tell that he was trying to work up an anger he didn't feel at the moment, to gear himself up for what he was going to say. 'I've tried to wait,' he went on, 'but I can't anymore, or I'll fall apart, too. And that wouldn't help you any. We're going to have to split up, Ruth, and as soon as possible. I can't take it anymore.'

Ruth got out of the bed and sat at the edge of it. This was all wrong. *She* was the one who was supposed to be saying this, not him! 'Is it because I stayed at Sonya's?' she asked. 'You don't even know what happened.' She was ready to lie, but he stopped her.

'No, and I don't want to know. It isn't just that, anyway. It's not like this is happening out of the blue or something. You know it's not like me to leave as soon as there's trouble, Ruth. You know it's been going on and on! Think of the camping trip this summer. We can't even go away for a weekend together!' Ruth sat in her dirty robe at the edge of the bed, silent because it was all true but he'd always refused to see it before. And now he had worked himself into a real anger.

'It may be fine for you, the way we've been living, it may be what *you* want out of a relationship, but it's not what I want. Or maybe it's easier for you, because I'm always nice to you, I never learned how not to be. But you don't know how it feels to me to be around you constantly, and to feel that half the time you hate me, and the other half my presence is some kind of irritation to you. You're wrong that it was spending the night with Sonya that did it, because I couldn't have taken it much longer anyway, but sure, that had some kind of effect. I was *worried* about you, Rooey. I thought you'd been in a goddamn car accident or something. I mean, I figured you'd at least call if you'd decided not to come home. I'm sure it was an important and meaningful night for you, and no, I don't want to hear anything about it. Well, it was an important night for me, too. I just sat in the kitchen and waited for you and thought and waited and thought. That was when I made this decision. It all came together for me. That being with you, I had stopped loving myself somewhere along the line. And that's not how I want to live.'

It was the end of the speech. Ruth knew that she'd lost anyway now, so it didn't matter anymore what she said or did. She stood above him in her dirty robe and screamed in his face.

'I assume you're already packed? Or maybe you intend for *me* to leave? Preferably this afternoon, so I don't finish you off totally?'

He got up and backed away from her, looking scared. 'Let's be rational about this,' he began, but she was screaming again.

'Fuck rational. Six years together and you couldn't wait maybe another week, maybe three more days, just enough time to see me back at work, halfway functional again. Six fucking years together, and you had to pick this one time, the *first* time since you've known me, isn't it, that I'm in really bad shape. The first time, and you grabbed it. Remember what you said to me on the phone, Vic? When you called me at Sonya's? Something about you were there if I needed you? Remember that bullshit?'

Ruth caught sight of herself in the mirror. She'd looked in the same mirror to cut her hair what seemed like a million years ago. She saw a raging madwoman in a stained yellow robe, with a splotchy face and jagged hair. No wonder Vic had picked this time to leave her. He had always loved her containment, her cool, clean, pretty surface. Despite what he'd been saying, he had wanted her when she was cool and unavailable. It had turned him on. Now she was messy and out of control and he wanted a refund. She wasn't the same package he'd picked out.

Vic was in the doorway of the bedroom by now. 'I didn't mean I'd go today, this afternoon,' he said in a slow calm voice, as if he were setting limits with one of his hysterical teenage clients. 'But at this point, I'm not so sure. If it's gotten this bad with us, maybe I *should* leave right away. The apartment's yours, of course, it always has been, hasn't it. I'll try to get someone to stay with you, Sonya or Lisa, whoever you want. I know you're in bad shape, but clearly my presence isn't doing you any good.'

She began to scream at him again, and her own voice frightened her. It was a voice she'd never used in her life before, although she'd heard it often enough. It was the voice of her sister, Elaine, in one of her moods, the voice of one of the women at Redburn, going off in the cafeteria. It was an enraged madwoman's voice, and for the first time Ruth recognized it as her own.

'Stop talking like that,' she shrieked. 'Where do you think you are, in one of your little encounter group sessions? What did you do, hold a group consultation to get advice on how to tell me you were through? Maybe you role-played it with your peer-supervision group, hmm?' His face looked strange, and she thought that he probably *had* done just that.

'I think what you'd like is for me to join in with you, to scream and shout and then it would be all over and we'd make love and go on. But it's too late for that, Ruth. I can't do it any more. It makes no difference whether I got support to do this from my friends or not. I still mean it.' She wanted to strike out, to hit him in the face, but she already knew what he'd do. He wouldn't hit her back at all, but just hold her arms down until she calmed down, 'containment' they called it at Freeport.

CANDY

Tuesday afternoon Candy surprised herself by getting up, not cause someone told her to, cause they was all leaving her strictly alone now, but cause she was sick of laying in bed feeling like death warmed over. She sure as hell wasn't taking herself up to no flag room, though, without no one making her, so she went to find Foster and explain to her about missing her appointment yesterday and see could she make one for today. It felt strange on the compound, sort of like in this story she'd seen about a man who goes to sleep one night and when he wakes up it's a hundred years later or something, and don't nobody even know him. It was only three days since the Halloween party, but it seemed like a hundred years. Billy and Loraine was gone, and it was empty cause everyone was at work, but it was more than that that reminded her of the story. It seemed like the few people she did run into, staff and girls both, looked right through her.

That was one reason she wanted to see Foster, cause this ghost thing had been with her ever since the party and she wasn't sure if it was all in her head, or for real. One thing she'd thought was maybe the bandage on her arm reminded them of the fire and Loraine getting killed, and didn't nobody want to have to think about that so they rather not think about her at all. But there was three new girls hanging around the social workers' office waiting to get assigned, and even they seemed like they turned away a little when they seen her, and they couldn't know who she was.

'Soon as they get rid of one of us, whichever way, they got space for another,' Candy thought. She wondered if someone had left a little note with the judge on the bench that said, 'Three beds free at Redburn.' So the next three girls that had came before him had got sent down regardless of what they was up for. Of course it was always regardless anyway. If you was up for pros or drugs or robbery or assault you could more or less know what they was gonna charge you with, but your sentence depended more on if the judge had got his rocks off the night before than anything else.

In the mental health corridor, at least, it seemed more normal. Lynda was typing something in her office with the radio on and them other two was sitting around gossiping as usual. Another new girl was hanging outside of Thorne's office.

'You got a cigarette?' she asked Candy. Candy gave her one, but the girls's hands was shaking too bad to light it. 'My nerves is just totally shot,' she said. 'That's why I'm waiting to see the psychiatrist, ya know?' She was one of them sort of washed-out almost pretty white trash girls, a little like Grace Powers. Billy would of probly dug her if she was still here. She was just dying to tell Candy all about her problem with her nerves, if Candy had gave her any encouragement at all, but Candy just wanted to rap with Foster.

But Foster's office way down the end was closed, with a note on it that said, 'Miss Foster is out sick due to illness.' Candy thought what it meant for real was she wasn't coming back ever, not that she gave a shit. She'd just wanted to see her cause she was bored anyways. On the way back she ran into the new girl again.

'So you got bad nerves?' she asked her.

'Sure do,' the girl said. 'They aint never been that good anyways, see, but he got to change my room, cause if he don't I'm gonna go off.'

'You sure you aint gone already?' Candy asked her. The girl just stared at her with her mouth hanging open showing the big holes where her teeth used to be, like she didn't even know she was being cracked on. Candy gave her another cigarette that she lit up for her to make her forget the crack.

'What's the matter with your room?' she asked.

'They was a dead girl in it! That girl that got burnt up right before I come in, that's her same bed they got me sleeping in. And, I'm psychic, see, and I seen her last night, she come to me!' The bitch started sniveling. Thorne would load her up with medication, Candy thought, and in three weeks she'd be fat and puffed up as a big white balloon.

'What this dead girl look like?' she asked.

'Oh, she was real big, maybe six feet, almost like a man,' the new girl said. 'One of them real dark niggers, you know, like one of them wild Africans they got on TV? And she had one green glass eye that shint in the dark. I know cause I seen it when she come to me. I knew it was her cause some girls that knew her told me that's what she looked like.'

'I knew her too.' Candy came real close and stared at the girl hard. 'Didn't they tell you there was someone else that almost got burnt up with her?' The girl nodded, backing off, her eyes stuck on the bandage on Candy's arm.

'Did you know the nigger that done it?' she whispered. 'That they say got evil powers?'

'Yup.' Candy moved her right up against the door. 'I'm gonna tell you this for your own sake,' she whispered. 'That one told me she had something against that room and anyone in it. That she was gonna come back in the night and git whoever tried to sleep in that same bed.' The girl went right off, screaming and screaming, and right then Thorne opened up this door so she almost fell in. Like the rest of them, he acted like he didn't even see Candy, shutting the door in her face.

'Never mind them assholes,' she whispered to herself in Billy's voice, but Billy was gone. She went in the nasty bathroom across from Lynda's office to look at herself in the mirror. So she had a bandage and was pale looking, that was no reason to treat someone like they didn't fuckin' exist! Maybe if she did her hair and put on some make-up people would see her again. But come to think of it, her eyes looked kind of strange, too. 'Ghost eyes,' she thought. 'That's why won't nobody look.' Loraine would know who she was, she thought. She'd come over and put an arm around her and tell her she was glad Candy was alright and not burnt up. But maybe they was burying Loraine right now, throwing dirt down on her coffin. She wanted Loraine back so bad it bent her in two. That was when she heard their voices from Lynda's office.

'If I were you I wouldn't even bother with that presentation, Nan,' Cindy was saying. 'Bet you anything we don't see her back this week.'

'I bet she'll be back, Cindy.' That was Nan, sounding embarrassed or sorry or something. 'You know she never misses work.'

'Yeah, well you know what Dave said. He was telling me what a risk it is for someone like her to drink or get high, you know. I mean, the more repressed the individual is, the more she's keeping in, right?' Cindy laughed in her shitty way. 'God, if it was me I'd never come back to work after acting like that at the party, I'd be too embarrassed. And you know what, Dave said her hair was still like that when she came in on Sunday. He said he felt really worried about her, the way she cracked under the pressure. Kneeled down in Telecea's cell in Max, started to cry and wouldn't let him give her her meds. I mean he was having a hard enough time as it was.'

'Listen, Cindy, of course Ruth was upset on Sunday.' That was Lynda, getting her two cents in. 'That girl that was killed was her client, and you know how much she cares. Plus I think she and Victor are having problems. I think we should all go out of our way to be nice to her when she comes back.'

'I don't know why everyone has such a soft spot for poor little Ruth!' That Cindy was really a bitch. 'She sure doesn't have one for us. You know we'd all be out on our asses tomorrow if it was up to her. And if you want to know about her little problems with Vic, why don't you ask Sonya. I just wonder if her hair will still be like that when she comes in next. Anyone want to put some money on it?'

Candy listened a while more but all she could hear was giggling and whispering. She decided that as soon as these bitches left for the day she'd steal that key from Frankie and clean out Cindy's office, but good, and leave her a little note.

'You know that girl that got kilt well your next.' That's exactly what she'd say, wrote out all crazy and spelt wrong so wouldn't nobody know it was her. She pictured herself walking right out of the wing with all she could carry including the goddamn typewriter and the police just staring at her and letting her go cause now she was invisible and didn't nobody want to mess with her.

Back in her room, she took Dina's black magic marker that someone had left in there, and wrote out the note for Cindy. Then, for the hell of it, she wrote another shitty one, that she signed 'The Ghost that used to live in your room' to put in that new girl's room, that used to be Loraine's. And then she took her pen and wrote a different kind of one for Foster, to slip under her door when she went in Cindy's office that evening. Lucky it was her left arm that got burnt. She'd be able to cut Foster's hair easy. After all the notes was done, Candy didn't know what to do. She didn't want to go back to bed, cause that just made it worse. These days the minute she stopped still and let herself think she started to feel like she wanted to die, like that black pit was just there sucking at her, trying to pull her down in.

SONYA

When she came in on Tuesday, Sonya was surprised to find that she'd been missed on Monday. Loraine's death had affected all the women, not only those most directly involved, and it pleased Sonya to reflect that it was she, the irresponsible one, who was now at hand to reassure and patch up, while Ruth stayed home in bed. Within minutes of her arrival, Donny, Linda, Jodie, and Alice showed up, and when Gladdy, taking up her position at the easel said, 'Our art teacher did come back. Did not get burnt up. Did not go away,' no one bothered to tell her that she was mental.

Sonya moved around the room in her dance of watching and listening, contributing to conversations and commenting on the many images of flames, gravestones, and death. It was late by the time she'd finished a final private conversation with Donny, and she was halfway down the stairs before she remembered that Ruth wasn't there, waiting to drive her home and hear about her day.

For the first time, Sonya let herself take in the fact that Ruth hadn't been in for two days. She considered calling or dropping by, but then she remembered the Ruth of that awful morning after, cold and hard, her jaw set, treating Sonya like some very distant acquaintance. If she called, Victor would probably answer the phone anyway. Maybe Ruth needed time alone. Better to let her call when she was ready. She'd probably come back to work tomorrow anyway.

368

WEDNESDAY, NOVEMBER 4

RUTH

With Telecea sent to the computerized prison in Kansas, Mabe gone home, and Loraine dead, Ruth had no morning appointments on Wednesday, but she went in early anyway. She had somehow counted on work to bring her back to herself, had looked forward to being buzzed in at the front, to the familiar smells of coffee and doughnuts and smoke in the mental health corridor, and most of all to the feel of her office. But nothing seemed to help lift the steel band of guilt and dread which had encircled her body for the past week, the repetitive voices which would not leave her alone. She watched herself woodenly going through the motions which would get her into her own office, walking, opening doors, smiling. They stared at her. Even Murph at the front desk, who had always liked her, stared at her as if she had turned into someone else.

She saw with relief that there was nobody in the mental health corridor yet. She locked herself into her own office, needing to know that Dave couldn't open the door suddenly and catch her off guard. Or Sonya, who had left Redburn that Sunday without even leaving her a note, and had not bothered to call since, even though she, more than anyone else, must know what Ruth was going through. Sonya would be at the compulsory staff meeting this afternoon, and Ruth felt a sickening mixture of need and dread at the thought of seeing her.

Maybe Sonya would reach out and try to touch her, and then she'd shatter all over the floor like Martha's cup must have done when Candy had broken it. That wasn't quite right, because the cup had been whole before, and she was already in a million pieces, held together very carefully without glue, like one of those huge jigsaw puzzles that you could destroy just by jiggling the card table it was on. She wished Martha's cup was still in the office. The new one wasn't the same. She looked up at the Gauguin painting, and wished there had been time to give it to Telecea before she left, although probably they weren't allowed paintings in that place.

Ruth shivered, and noticed two slips of paper which had been pushed under the door. Probably one was from Dave. It would say, 'And you, Ms. Fem?' The other was an official memo, which would read, 'Due to criminal negligence and mental imbalance Ruth Foster is hereby banned from this institution.' It seemed to take a long time to get up, unfold them, and sit down again to read the terrible news.

The first note was from Sonya, written in her large, bold artist's script, in red fountain pen. 'Dear R—,' it said. 'I am here. Would like to see you, when it's right for you.' The pen had leaked blood in an ornate pattern around the edges of the paper. Ruth imagined Sonya picking up some of the pieces of her, a few of the prettier ones, from where she'd shattered on the ground, and taking them home to use in a collage, like that one she'd done of Telecea. She balled up the note and threw it on the floor. Then she picked it up again and smoothed it in her hand, filled with an enormous longing. She smelled it to see if there was a trace of Sonya, but she couldn't find one. Then she put it in her pocket.

The other note was on institutional notepaper, in light blue ballpoint. She recognized Candy's neat rounded handwriting, with the little circles over the i's.

> Hi Miss Foster. Glad your back. I'm feeling better now and hope you are to. Sometimes theres no place to go but up (Smile!) If you didn't get your hair done yet come down to the beauty parlor anytime before noon and I'll do it for you like we said. Sinserley Yours. Candy.

Ruth put her hand up to the jagged hair on her neck. She had forgotten about it again. She held onto Candy's note, which with its tact and kindness gave her back to herself in some essential way. She was especially touched by that last phrase, 'like we said,' reminding her that the offer was a long-standing one which had nothing to do with recent violent events. Ruth thought it was Candy's way of affirming that the world had been going on long before the present trouble and would continue to do so.

It was easier to leave her office then, and even to walk past Dave and Cindy who were standing in the doorway of Cindy's office, which had just been broken into again. Apparently this time there had also been a threatening note. 'How upsetting,' said Ruth. 'Do you think it's the same person as last time? How are you two, anyway?' She thought she'd achieved the right note but they both stared at her in an embarrassed way.

'I'm just fine, Ruth,' Dave said in his doctor-to-patient voice. 'Glad to see you back.'

Down the hall, Ruth knocked on the door to the beauty parlor.

'It's open,' called Candy's voice, and Ruth walked into a clean pink room, full of a strong sweetish smell which she thought must be straightened hair. Pictures cut out of glossy magazines, demonstrating various black and white women's hairstyles were taped on the walls, and there were three pink sinks which folded back, just like in a real beauty parlor, and two hooded pink hair dryers.

'Hey, Miss Foster!' Candy turned from where she stood combing out the hair of a bulky black woman who sat in one of the pink plastic chairs with her back to Ruth. Lou Ann Williams, the very young southern girl whom she'd seen a month or two ago for intake, sat perched on the counter, her straightened hair rising in two stiff wings around her small face. The large woman turned and Ruth recognized her as Norma Lewis, who'd served a short term for killing her husband in self-defense, and who had befriended Telecea. Ruth remembered that Norma had been released a few weeks ago, and wondered what she was doing back.

'Pleased to meet you, honey.' Norma reached out her hand, and Ruth was shocked to see that she had a black eye. 'Candy here been telling me how much you done for her, and how hurt you was, the same way she was bout the sister's death. I didn't put it together till I seen you just now that she was talking bout the same lady that used to watch out for my friend Telecea.' Norma's hand felt hard and warm and real. Ruth held on to it for a few seconds, realizing that this was the first time she'd shaken any of the inmate's hands since she'd worked here.

'You see someone in here?' Norma prompted Lou Ann, who had not greeted Ruth and now dissolved into laughter.

'Aint they got no more beauty parlors on the outside?' she finally got out between giggles.

'I've been waiting for Candy to do my hair,' Ruth explained.

'Honey, don't pay this one no mind.' Norma gave Lou Ann a little slap. 'Seems like she forgot all her manners just as soon as I left out the door. This place!' There was something so reassuring and motherly about Norma that Ruth felt sorry when she and Lou, with her wings of hair meekly curled under, left the beauty parlor.

She was uneasy too, to be left alone with Candy, whom she'd last seen in the hospital, drugged and in pain. Almost always before, Ruth had been the comforter, the caretaker. But Candy seemed comfortable with the reversal. There was an ease and authority about her which Ruth had never seen before.

371

'C'mon over here,' she said, and Ruth came obediently to the pink chair by the sink, and let Candy, who moved only a little awkwardly to favor her left arm, tie a white towel around her neck, as she kept up a steady, comforting stream of talk which required no response.

'Oh, this'll be a pleasure to cut, Miss Foster. You've got such pretty hair. Real fine. Mine used to be like that too, only I put so many colors in it, it's all coarsened up. When I get out I'm gonna have it cut nice and short by someone real good, and let it grow natural. I've been, let's see, a blonde, a brunette, a redhead, one time I had silver streaks put in . . . let your head down now, and I'll wet it.' Ruth let her head fall back, and Candy turned on the hot water, her fingers still stroking, massaging. Ruth closed her eyes, relieved that she didn't have to talk.

'What I like to do, I shampoo it after,' Candy's voice went on. 'Cut it wet, shampoo it after and like that you won't have no stray hair floating around. You want it any special way or just let me do what I think? You can put your head up now.'

'Whatever you think,' Ruth whispered, and now Candy began, sliding her long fingers with their sharp nails through Ruth's hair as she cut it. Small tongues of yellow fell on the floor, joining with Lou's black hair and Norma's gray curls, and Ruth shivered, remembering how, the night before the party, her hair had fallen on the floor.

'You're sort of scary today, huh?' Candy said comfortably, and Ruth nodded, clearing her rusty throat. 'You don't need to say nothing, Miss Foster. I dig it. See, I was just like that too, let's see, till last night or maybe this morning. I think what pulled me out of it was Norma coming back. I mean shit, I hated to see her back here, but I needed to see a friend, I mean someone I at least halfway trust, you know? That's how come I'm glad you're back, too. They moved Dina out yesterday, did you know that?' Ruth shook her head.

'Is Norma back for long?' she asked.

'Naw, just a parole violation. Protective custody, really,' Candy explained. 'These dudes that like to call themselves her ex-old man's people tried to mess with her a little, is all. Can't give folks like that no room or they'll just stamp you out. Gotta be tough to get along out there, you know, Miss Foster?' Ruth nodded, meekly. Candy put one hand on either side of her face, looking at the results like a painting she'd just finished. 'This is gonna look nice, now. You got a face that can take a good short cut. I always told you you could do more with yourself than what you was. Look there.'

Ruth looked. To herself, she looked, as Candy had said, 'scary.' She liked the word used like that. It was halfway between being scared herself and being frightening, and it fit the reflection she saw – a thin intense face with sharp almost bird-like features, big lost looking blue eyes, and a little bit of pale hair plastered flat to her head.

'I look nice like a drowned rat,' she joked feebly.

Candy laughed. 'You'll see when it dries,' she said. 'It's gonna be nice-nice. I'm gonna shampoo you now, then we'll stick you under the dryer. Let go your head again.' Ruth did, and now there was hot flowing water all around her, and she closed her eyes again and felt Candy's gentle strong fingers touching her deeply. She knew that her face was wet with tears, but there was so much other water it didn't matter.

When she came out of the dryer, Candy shaved and powdered her neck, and combed out her hair. It was very short now and layered, like the feathers of some delicate bird. Ruth had worn her most conservative shirt and sweater outfit today, but dressed differently, she saw that she might be mistaken for one of those slim stylish lesbians she'd admired. She looked less ordinary, or pretty, than she'd ever looked in her life, with her cheekbones more prominent since she'd lost weight, and her eyes in evidence.

'It's lovely,' she said. 'It's just right. Thank you, Candy.' Candy stood behind her, reviewing her handiwork. 'Are you alright, what happened with Billy, do you know what you just did for me, do you know that I love you?' Ruth wanted to ask, but she knew that this was not the time. She looked into the mirror instead, and their eyes met for a moment there.

At the door, Ruth paused, remembering other business.

'I have a meeting at one that will probably last a while,' she said, 'but could you come by my office later this afternoon, maybe three? I want to get the papers in for that peer-counseling program for you right away. For all we know they may send you out of here tomorrow. Or me.'

Candy nodded, agreeing. 'I'll be there, Miss Foster.'

Ruth walked down the hall toward Hanson's office. She still felt the band of guilt and pain pressing in on her, but she no longer felt in danger, at least for the moment, of breaking into a million pieces on the floor.

CANDY

Candy had finished with Foster's hair and she'd gone off to her meeting. Now she was trying to do something with her own hair. 'You're scary today,' she'd said to Foster, but it was more than that, really, it was like this girl that she remembered from Watsonville when she'd been up in Admitting there, that they had brung in fresh from croaking her man. What they'd said she'd did was call the cops herself and then just sat and waited for them with the blood from it still all over her and it still would of been there when she came in the joint too, if someone hadn't made her wash. She was like that the whole time, she would do anything as long as you told her just exactly what. That girl reminded Candy of a fucking robot or computer or something, that wouldn't talk unless you asked it a question. Then she'd answer and it would be alright, at least the words would be alright, or on the right subject anyway, but there would usually be something wrong about it, like the volume would be way off, or else the feeling to it would be all wrong, like laughing when she talked about something sad. After a while no one hadn't talked to her at all, except Candy tried to sometimes cause she felt sorry for the poor bastard. No one messed with her either, and at first Candy thought it was cause they felt sorry for her too, but then she realized this girl had them all spooked. She was a nice, straight girl that had went to church and worked in a store and had never messed around or did nothing wrong in her whole life before, and it seemed to Candy like she was gonna just stay in shock for the whole rest of it.

Of course Foster hadn't killed nobody, but still she was acting sort of like that girl. When Candy did her hair she livened up, but she still didn't act like her old self. It was like instead of being numbed out, she started feeling everything twice as much. She reminded Candy of a sad little girl, all skinny with her hair plastered down and her crying eyes, like she was just waiting for some grownup to come along and take care of her. Which was just the opposite of her old tight-ass self, the way she never used to show no one her feelings. Not that she'd got exactly trusting now, it was more like she was hurting so bad she couldn't even worry bout keeping it hid.

Candy tried to make her hands be gentle and strong both and

374

give Foster the best haircut she knew how, cause it was all she could think of to pay back all the times Foster had took care of her, and that last time in the hospital where she was the only one who even acted like Candy was a person and not some old ghost. She thought of asking Foster what else was wrong, cause bad as she might feel about Loraine, Redburn wasn't where she went home to at night, but even though Foster was acting real different she still might not appreciate no personal questions, so Candy kept her mouth shut. She was sure it had to be something about that Lehrman, though. Candy could just picture that bitch telling Foster if she really wanted her she had to leave her man, and then when Foster had went and did it, the bitch wouldn't want her no more. That was just the kind of shit she would do.

It was a smoking haircut if Candy said to herself. Foster looked just a little butch, but that was cool, cause the way she was going around letting all her insides show, looking tough on the outside wouldn't do her no harm.

Now she was alone, Candy shampooed her own hair and tried to decide should she really get it cut when she got out. She'd had more than enough of looking butch herself after that awful night, but of course there was more to the look than just hair length. Billy liked her with long hair, but Billy was gonna have to be disappointed in her in more ways than that. Candy took Billy's letter she had got that morning out her pocket to read again. The beauty parlor was about the best place to think, and she knew nobody would come and bother her or tell her get to work, cause Delaney had walked right past her in the hall and hadn't said shit.

'To My Woman Candy' the letter, that had no return address and no phone number on it, begun.

I wouldn't be surprised if by the time you get this you may of already got your date cause like I told you they want all of us that was involved in you know what *out* and so I wouldn't be surprised if I will be seeing you out here any time now which I'm glad cause this is only my second day out here and allready I am missing you so bad it hurts. Well maybe sometime it takes a separation to let you know how much you really do need and miss a certain person. And its like theres people around but I can't really relate to none of them cause they don't know where I'm coming from plus they are all into the same old shit plus they aint you. Well you remember how big they talked about that so called 'college' program they was going to get me into, well now what I hear is I will have to wait for the next fall September semester to start school which is a whole year off plus it won't even be no real 'college' program, but some special bullshit they got rigged up for 'ex-offenders' which is just there bullshit per usual a lot of talk and aint nothing hapening. My mistake was to ever believed it in the first place. So you know I aint gonna work in no factory or no cleaner now but I am waiting on my lady Candy cause I know she can take care of business so we can get our lifes together and go to school and get our own place like we always planed and get ourself started. Now don't worry or get no attitude if these bitches that come out here on furlough start bringing you there he-said she-said shit cause you know how they are and it dont mean nothing and I am waiting for you.

Candy you will understand what I'm going through when you get out here yourself, it is fucking wierd being out here again it blows your mind you feel like your from another planet or something. But when you come out I will be here waiting to take care of you and make you feel OK like only I can do so don't worry.

Listen theres a dude Rich you will remember him from the old days well hes coming to see one of his lady's that just got in and I told him look you up he's got some cigarettes for you your brand. (Smile.) So I hope you are not upset like you were before and be cool and remember I love you.

The letter was signed 'Your Man Billy,' and it was getting it, along with Norma coming back which was the part she'd told Foster about, that had brought Candy back to life when she was feeling so scary and ghosty and invisible. At first she'd mostly just noticed how long it was and the part about how much Billy missed her and remember I love you. But now, as she started to clean up the beauty parlor what kept sticking in her mind was, 'I am waiting on my lady Candy cause I know she can take care of business.' The more Candy thought about that the colder and madder she got cause Billy wasn't talking bout no peer-counseling program, that was for sure. She wrote a letter back to Billy in her head as she finished sweeping up.

"Well, they sent Dina home and its my turn now so it looks like what you two was saying was true but I don't see no big money do you? I got your letter where you say you love me but if you love me so much how come your asking me to be a hore? If I loved someone I wouldn't ask them that cause its a dogs life and you know it too. So where you coming from on the for real side? And tell that fucker Rich stay the fuck away from me cause I aint coming out there no junky and anyway don't you remember his last lady in here he didn't come to see? If you forgot already you got a short memory.'

Candy was shaking she was so mad as she tied up the plastic garbage bag full of blond and straightened and nappy black hair. The garbage bag made her think of something dead, of Loraine burnt up and down in the ground. Her arm started hurting bad and for a minute she thought she was gonna puke. She took a deep breath, started gathering up all the towels, and put them in the laundry bag. She couldn't really write Billy no letter like that, and anyway she wouldn't know where to send it, but she thought she'd go back to the cottage and write it down not to send but to show to Foster when she went to see her that afternoon about the program. Shit, Candy hoped Foster would of pulled it together by then. And that she was for real about this program and not just jiving like they done to Billy. Because she had got another letter too, early this morning. It was so short she didn't even have to take it out to read it. She knew it by heart.

MEMO

From: Peter E. Tranden, Superintendent, Redburn State Facility,
       Department of Corrections
To: Catherine Pierson AKA Candace Peters
Re: Parole Hearing
       The parole board of the State Correctional Facility at Redburn
       requires your presence at a probation hearing, Tuesday, November
       10, in the board room. The board will begin meeting at 1:00 PM.
       Failure to attend will mean forfeit of early consideration status.

SONYA

Walking down the hall on her way up to the art room, Sonya smelled something sweet and burnt and somehow familiar. Turning, she saw the sign 'Beauty Parlor' on the door and recognized the smell of cooking hair. She heard Ruth's voice in there, and another voice. So Ruth was back at work, had gotten her note, but had not come to look for her.

As she climbed the stairs she was back in that old brick dormitory in Mississipi, with all the little girls lined up by the one electric outlet in the hot, breathless hall at night, straightening their hair and singing the latest Mo-town hits. She and Harriet had gone down to teach in a six week Freedom school. They had only known each other a few months then, everything was still sweet between them. At night they went around together, tucking in the little girls and telling them stories. Harriet was the one who told them, really, making them up as she went along. In the morning Sonya would do art with them, and then the story creatures, the people and animals and ghosts and witches, would emerge on paper or in clay. The two of them had made a good team. After the children were in bed it would still be much too hot to sleep, and they'd sit on the steps in the hot night, telling each other the stories of their lives. The bugs had been enormous and fuzzy. They made loud, plopping noises when they landed against windows or on the pavement, and seemed almost like creatures from outer space to their northern, city-bred eyes. Sometimes they could hear the high tinny sound of someone picking a guitar, carried for miles in the still air.

Sonya usually tried not to think about Harriet. Or Jenny, whom she'd almost succeeded in forgetting. Then there was Mira. And now Ruth. Although the situations were not really comparable, since she'd only slept with Ruth that one time, and that under duress. You could hardly call it walking out on someone when you'd never really been with her in the first place. Sonya wondered if Ruth would speak to her at all at the meeting this afternoon.

Usually only those women who didn't have to work came to the art room in the morning, but today there was a large group. Donny explained that work assignments had been cancelled.

'They're having a big meeting,' she explained, 'to find out what happened to Loraine. Who really kilt her, you know.'

Sonya was struck with the insistent images of death and burning, enclosed inside the grids and fences all the women but Gladdy surrounded their work with. She circulated quietly, helping and listening to the flow of talk.

'You never know.'

'What could happen in here.'

'That's right, for all you know they got plans to burn us all up, one by one.'

'That's right.'

'They could burn up a whole lot of us and no one would ever know!' Alice's voice was gleeful, and Sonya got ready to intervene.

At noon the group left for lunch, but Donny hung around to talk.

'I like this room,' she approved. 'People can scream and yell in here and get it off their chest, but everyone knows you wouldn't really let no one get hurt.' Sonya blushed with pleasure at this, and tried not to think about having brought in the feathers. Donny surprised her then, by coming over to her and leaning all of her lank, tough-butch self against her like a small child.

'When I was little,' she said, 'my Mom went in the hospital and died. No one ever said of what. You think they could of killed her?'

In the middle of Sonya's response the phone rang. It was an irate Mrs Hanson, demanding her immediate presence at the meeting, which she'd somehow managed to forget.

Five minutes later she slipped, with a sinking feeling, into the only remaining vacant chair directly across from Ruth, who immediately looked away. She'd fixed up her hair, and now looked more beautiful than ever, though a little emaciated. Sonya noticed Tranden, whom she hadn't seen since her initial meeting with him, at the head of the table, flanked on either side by Dave and Hanson. He was smaller than she'd remembered, and appeared cowed by the proceedings. She recognized Proudy and Moody, Riley and Delaney, and the ineffectual young man who'd been assigned to Telecea.

'I had tried,' began Hanson, 'to emphasize the importance of this meeting to each of you. Apparently I was insufficiently clear for at least one of you, who had to be issued a personal invitation and kept the rest of us waiting. . . .'

Sonya's face burned. Was it possible that the whole point of the meeting was to fire her? If so, surely all these people wouldn't be required.

'I'm very sorry I had to keep all of you waiting,' she apologized. 'I had a client in crisis whom I couldn't leave.' She decided that since this was all some sort of theater, she might as well give a good performance. 'In light of recent events, I thought it better to be over-cautious.'

Hanson smiled in triumph, as if Sonya had unwittingly given herself away. 'It is unfortunate, my dear Miss Lehrman,' she said smoothly, 'that such commendable caution on your part had to wait until after these unfortunate events had already occurred. I feel sure that if this had happened a little sooner, it might have prevented your giving Telecea Jones, without consent from any of your supervisors, may I add, the, shall we say, props, which certainly contributed a great deal to her mental state that evening.'

So they had found out about the feathers and were going to blame it all on her! Sonya tried to hold back angry tears, horrified at being trapped.

'This is ridiculous!' Ruth's voice raged out of control. 'You're making her the scapegoat and I won't allow it.' All of them who had been staring at Sonya, full of relief that it was her and not them, now turned to Ruth with surprise and interest. Hanson was the only one who remained unperturbed.

'Perhaps you feel, Miss Foster, as Telecea's long term therapist, that *you* should shoulder the blame?' Sonya could tell that Ruth was about to agree that yes, it *was* all her fault. Hanson must have picked this up too, because she passed quickly on to the next one in line. 'Or you, Mrs Riley, you were on duty that evening. Naturally you wish to assume responsibility for any events transpiring during your shift? Or you, Mrs Proudy, who saw Telecea's behavior in Max, but failed to notify the authorities? Or you, Miss Wiggins, actually approached in the cottage by the two women who would later be burned, in an appeal for help which you ignored? Or you, Mr White, assigned to one-to-one coverage of Telecea at all times when she was not confined to Max. Where were you that evening? Or perhaps you, Miss Putnam, as the nurse on duty in the hospital that evening, perhaps you feel that in failing to ascertain Loraine Bradley's condition before sending her to City Hospital, that *you* ought by rights to shoulder the blame?' She had mentioned almost everyone in the room except for Tranden, who sat yawning with a vacant expression, and Dave, who had the grace to look slightly embarrassed. Sonya, still breathless from what felt like her own narrow escape, couldn't help admiring Hanson's strategy, repulsive as the woman was. She'd done a great deal of research in a very short time. If the matter of Loraine's death *should* come up in a court, which appeared not unlikely, it seemed clear that the staff of Redburn, with the possible exceptions of Ruth and herself, would present a highly united front.

'I'm asking each one of you here to make an appointment to speak privately with me during the coming week,' Hanson finished smoothly. 'Thank you all for your cooperation, and for your contributions to the floral tribute which has been sent to the Bradley family. I know that many of you would have liked to attend services, but they will be held in Wisconsin, where Loraine's family lives. I am sure that we, both as individuals and as a group, will be able to use this unfortunate tragedy constructively, to increase our efforts here at Redburn to function even more effectively as a unified rehabilitative team.' She looked around the table now, fixing each of them with her penetrating smile. Sonya shuddered when her turn came. She could imagine this woman in a few years, not as commissioner, since she was, after all, female, but somewhere up there at the top. The meeting broke up slowly. Ruth, who had left before anyone else, stood by the door, seemingly waiting for her, and Sonya went to meet her. As she got closer she saw that Ruth was crying helplessly. She could hear Dave, Hanson, and Tranden behind her and she moved instinctively, putting out a hand to guide Ruth away from them. But Ruth flinched and drew in her breath sharply.

'No,' she said so loudly that all of their eyes followed her as she turned, still weeping, and almost ran to the front door.

FRIDAY, NOVEMBER 6

RUTH

'Sure we'll take her,' Ann Butler agreed. 'We've got the opening, and if you say she's ready, I'll go with it, Ruth. The only thing is we usually don't have good luck with women who just came out. We try taking one every year or so, and it never works. After at least a year on the outside, that's when a woman's most likely to make it with us. Once she's made the decision to stay out herself.'

'But how is she supposed to make that decision if she doesn't have anything to support her on the outside?' Ruth stopped, took a deep breath, and tried to sound less involved. 'Don't you see, if Candy doesn't have a job, some kind of alternative community out there, she has to choose between total isolation and heading back to the streets. It's like plunging someone who's never learned how to swim into the middle of the ocean and hoping they'll make it to shore.'

'Slow down, Ruth.' Ann's voice was warm and steady, a kind of anchor. 'I told you we'll take her. I still think she'd have a better chance after at least a few months, but if both you and she want it that way we'll take her right away. After two weeks, I mean. Believe me, there's no way she's gonna be able to handle work and school the day she gets out.'

'Thanks, Ann.' Ruth succeeded in lighting a cigarette, and inhaled deeply. Her hand on the phone hurt from gripping it too hard. 'I don't mean to be pushy about this. It's just that Candy's very special to me. And I don't know if you heard, but we had a death here, and the woman who died was a good friend of Candy's.'

'Yeah, I heard. Was she a client of yours too, Ruth?'

Ruth paused, suspicious. Did she sound that upset, that out of control? 'Yes, she was.'

'What are you doing for yourself around it, Ruth?'

'What do you mean? I'm OK.'

'Listen,' Ann went on. 'I lost a client a year back. Suicide. And it was a major thing for me. I was a member of a really supportive peer supervision group, but that wasn't even enough. I had to get myself back in therapy for a while.'

Ruth thought longingly of laying her head on Ann's chest and telling her all about Loraine and Candy and Telecea and Sonya and Victor, and how everything had ended or died or gone away. 'Do you . . . would you have any time to get together and talk about it with me?' She knew her voice was a mess now, but it didn't matter as much.

There was a long pause. Ann's voice was different when she finally answered, strained and far away. 'I'd like to say yes, Ruth, but I think I'm not the right person. You and I never talked about the way our friendship sort of died out when you met Victor and I guess I still have some feelings about it. I was pretty hurt is what I mean. I don't think I could be there for you the way you need someone to be right now.'

'Oh. Well, thanks for arranging it about Candy. I'll send the papers in today. And I'll be fine.' As Ruth hung up, she was crying again, this time with shame and disgust at herself. She'd never thought about Ann's feelings back then, never even considered her. She blew her nose and lit another cigarette. After so many years of hardly crying at all, now she couldn't seem to stop. She had to meet with Dave, Hanson, and Tranden in a few minutes to review Candy's papers for the parole hearing on Tuesday. Then she could finally go home and collapse again for the weekend.

When she got to Tranden's office, the three of them were sitting there, smiling at her in a sympathetic, ominous way, and her stomach turned over. Clearly, this was not the formality she had anticipated but something terrible, like Wednesday's meeting only worse because now she was alone with them.

Hanson started. 'We'd like to begin by letting you know we're not here to judge you in any way, dear. I'd like you to think of us as people who understand, who are on your side. Who would like to help you through this.' The two men were nodding solemnly.

'Thank you for your concern.' Ruth aimed for the pleasant, a little surprised. 'Of course I was most disturbed about Loraine's death. I imagine we all were. Other than that, I'm not sure what you're talking about.'

Hanson cleared her throat with annoyance. 'For your sake, I'd prefer not to go into detail, dear. Why don't we just put it that you haven't been quite yourself for a while now. You've been with us a long time, Ruth, and we all know how deeply you care for the girls. But overinvolvement is a trap we all have to take care to avoid, isn't it, dear? That's why we're suggesting a leave of absence right now.

For you to concentrate just on you.' She patted Ruth's shoulder. 'Dave was warning me just the other day of the very same thing. "Sheila," he told me, "be careful you don't get so busy taking care of everyone else that you forget about yourself!" It's a real danger in our profession!' She poked Ruth again, around the stomach. 'There's a you in there that needs some babying too!'

Ruth was finding it hard to breathe. 'I'm afraid I don't understand what you're talking about,' she finally got out. The three of them exchanged glances, clearing their throats.

After looks from the other two, Tranden spoke up. 'Your behavior at the meeting Wednesday, Miss Foster. Quite inappropriate.' He seemed to have run through the extent of his speech and Dave took over, giving Ruth a sorrowful look.

'This isn't any easier for me than it is for you, Ruth. I've been trying to let you know for weeks that I've found your behavior with our . . . mutual colleague, no need to name names here . . . well, let's say not strictly professional. And unfortunately, with both of you working with Telecea, this situation did develop. I remember sitting in your office not more than two, three weeks ago, warning you that Telecea was heading for trouble. You responded with a great deal of anger at the time. Accused me of meddling in your personal life. I think as events turned out you'll have to agree that that response was uncalled for.'

'In view of the tragedy,' Tranden put in importantly.

The voices in Ruth's head were getting louder, reproaching and accusing her, agreeing with everying the three of them said. She tried desperately to keep them out.

'I had no idea they'd let Telecea go to the party that night,' she tried, wildly. 'The only reason I didn't forbid it specifically was because it never occurred to me that anyone would let her. I'm not on duty at night, you know that. I didn't know that Loraine was taking drugs, I couldn't help it that they didn't give her a urine at the hospital when they admitted her.'

'Ruth, try to calm down.' Dave reached out his hand and she flinched. 'Obviously it was no one person's negligence. We're trying to do what's best for you in this situation. Dr Allen at the hospital told us that you were quite insistent in your questioning of him about the events of that night. What we'd like to suggest right now is that you trust us to take care of the details. Take a paid leave of absence for a few weeks and don't even think of this place. By the time you come back all this will have blown over.'

'Let that nice young man of yours pamper you a little,' Hanson put in.

They were all smiling now, congratulating themselves. 'Mr Tranden was just giving me a few statistics,' Hanson cooed. 'Before you came in, dear. Redburn has the highest safety records of any institution across the country. We're head and shoulders above the men's institutions, as I'm sure you know. We serve as a kind of model, don't we, Dave, I'd call it a model of institutional caring. Now there's no point in allowing an isolated incident like this, which certainly won't happen again. . . .'

Ruth had given up trying to control her voice. 'How do we know it *won't* happen again,' she interrupted. 'If we don't even bother to try to find out what really happened, if we just cover it up.'

'Ruth dear, this is no place for hysterics!' Hanson stood up. 'I'm afraid our suggestion for a leave of absence, to start on Monday and to extend for an *indefinite* period may have to be a little more than a suggestion.'

Ruth remembered with a sickening jolt that Candy's parole hearing was Tuesday afternoon. No matter what they did to her after that, she had to be here on Tuesday to see Candy safely out.

'I'll take a week off as you suggested,' she agreed. 'I have more than a week's sick leave coming anyway. But I'm afraid I'll have to be here this Tuesday for Candy Peter's parole hearing. I'm not willing to break that commitment.'

'My dear Miss Foster, you have no choice in the matter,' Hanson began, but Tranden had roused himself to an unusual degree.

'Young lady, contrary to your fears, no one has anything to hide,' he murmured. 'As you must be aware by now, the parole board meetings are more or less a formality. Our decisions are made well before this meeting, based on the inmate's entire experience at the institution. In this case, unless something unforeseen occurs between now and Tuesday, Miss Peters should be heading home late next week. But if it will reassure you to sit in on the meeting, that's agreeable to me. On the condition that you do go home immediately afterwards. And I'd like to strongly suggest that you seek professional help before you consider returning to work.'

'Legal help first,' Ruth wanted to shout, but she was afraid that now that they knew her weak point they'd blackmail her by doing something to Candy. Maybe she was being paranoid, but she decided to keep her mouth shut until Candy was out.

At home, there was Victor's familiar smell of damp wool and tobacco, and a note from him on the kitchen table.

> Ruth—
> I came to get my guitar. Lisa called when I was here, says to please call her. I'll be at Bill's for the next few days if you need me, or you can call me at work. Will let you know if I'm someplace else. Vic.

Ruth tried to imagine the two betrayed husbands, sitting around playing songs on their guitars, commiserating together and making each other cups of tea. Were she and Lisa supposed to get together now? It made her want to avoid Lisa, not that she had much of an urge to see her anyway.

She wandered around the apartment, trying to feel his absence. It was hard, because he'd only taken a few clothes and his guitar. She wondered if that meant he'd be back. It was strange how little it seemed to matter to her. It should matter, after six years, shouldn't it? But he felt vague and blurred already, a little unreal.

Ruth pressed her forehead onto the cold hard surface of the kitchen table. Sonya, who still hadn't called, felt real to her, but in that aching, terrible way. Candy had felt real when she was cutting her hair. Except for that it was mostly just the voices. Now there were new ones, Hanson's and Dave's and Tranden's voices, tearing at her. Loraine's parents' voices. And Telecea's voice, asking again and again in Ruth's head. 'You gone kill me? You gone kill me now?'

CANDY

It was a cold gray early afternoon. Candy sat at one of the benches at Four Corners, looking out at the freezing wind in the yard, and trying to imagine what would it be like once she got out. It felt like a different dimension, like one of them science fiction outer-space movies on TV, just a big fucking empty place it was impossible to think about or make plans for, really. And being in here now was another weird dimension in itself, like there wasn't no more regular time, like as if all the clocks in the world had speeded up and stopped dead at once. And today it had skipped all of a sudden to winter, so even the goddamn weather was off.

Donny came by and said hello. She was one of the only ones to even speak to her lately, but even she got all embarrassed around Candy, like the way people act around someone that's dying of a disease or something.

The next one to come along was Gladdy, walking in from the yard in her tore-up pink summer dress without no coat or nothing. 'Aint you cold in this wind, Gladdy?' Candy asked her, but Gladdy shook her head no and asked her for a cigarette, which at least was treating her the same old way, so Candy gave her two.

'Gladdy aint got no time to worry bout no fur coat,' she said. 'She gots to deliver this important message. Then she gots to go on up the art room and paint her picture.' She smiled at Candy. 'How come Candy Cane don't come up and paint with Gladdy?'

Candy shook her head in disgust. 'Cause I can't stand that doggish teacher you all got up there,' she said. Gladdy got down on her hands and knees, right there at Four Corners and started barking like a dog.

'Stop that shit, girl,' Candy snapped at her. 'What you trying to do, bring the police down here and take you up to Max for playing the fool?' But Gladdy just went right on barking. Candy had noticed that some of the nuts like Gladdy and Alice had started behaving more like Telecea now she was gone. It was almost like someone had to be doing that particular number, so they was filling in for her, until wherever it was they sent Telecea to this time got sick of her and sent her on back. Although Candy had heard it was this computer-run joint, where you never got to see no other human being, not even no screw, but just had to do whatever the computer voice told you or else you got a electric shock. Even Telecea couldn't drive no machine crazy, so maybe she'd stay gone, this time.

'You almost made Gladdy forget her important message.' Gladdy had got up off the ground and was dusting her front off. 'Ginzer say come back the cottage cause they's a letter for you.'

Candy's fingers went down in her pocket and touched Billy's letter. Maybe this was another one from her, saying the first one was all a mistake. But when she got back to the cottage it wasn't no letter from Billy. Candy's heart started beating fast as soon as she saw the writing on the envelope, that looked so much like her own writing that she couldn't ever forget it even after so long. She used to get cards from her Mom on Christmas and sometimes her birthday, but that had stopped about five years ago. Candy figured she'd let her Dad find out about it. She was always like that. When she used to be drinking she'd leave the empties somewhere where he'd have to just about trip on them, or if she was doing something he didn't approve of she always had to go and drop some kind of hint about it. It would be just like her to leave the cards around for him to find. Candy used to think she was either real dumb or she liked to get beat up on.

She took the letter in her room to read it in private. She wished it would say he died, maybe that her Mom had got fed up and croaked him, but Candy knew she never would. She rather get beat on every week. It was a long letter, this time, not no card. 'My own dear daughter Cathy:' it started.

Well I hope this letter finds you fine and in good health. Well Cathy I have been thinking of you, remembering the good times we used to have when you were 'Home'. I am sure you knew you were always in my thoughts and prayers even tho your father had forbid me to write or visit knowing how much it hurt me. I guess you must be a "grown up lady" now and last time I saw you just a "Teen-Ager". It hurt me so much to be seperated from you Cathy, you are my youngest and I guess its alright to tell you now always my favrite, that I spoiled more so then the other to. Well your sister Sally lives in Savanannah Georgia now and sent me pictures of her kids but I have never seen them. And Stan and his family are right here in town but I'm afraid not to much comfort. Well I know you must be wandering how come I am writing now after all these years, well he left me. They retired him tho beween you and me it was really "Fired" him from the force, well he said it was because he told them to their face how "Corupt" they was, but I think it was really because he couldn't keep up with the times and called the "Colored" policemen 'Nigger' which they had told him not to any more. Well, he was "home" with me a few months that was very hard and then I had to go in the hospital for some female trouble and had a hysterectamy, (excuse my spelling, Cathy!) any way my health hasn't been good since. And I believe his pride just couldn't stand not working so he left. And I must say I feel very low and sick and miss you Cathy dear and sometimes wonder why I was put on this earth which is just a "vale of tears" as they call it, but now I have joined AA and put my trust in God and feel better and the drinking problem I had when he left and because of my pain (what I mean is "an alcaholic" but now I am sober) and so you see He is helping me after all. And I am writing in the hopes that maybe now your sentence must be almost over you could come home again like when you were a little girl Cathy and all was well and we could forget the past and start afresh like they say in AA one day at a time and I would enjoy giving you some little partys or "Social gatherings" saying that you had came back from "College," I have met some very nice young men through AA and who knows maybe my dream of knowing my own grandchildren might come true after all. Well write and tell me what you think of my "plan", my hand is tired from this long letter, well I hope it makes up for the time I couldn't write to you, so hoping to hear from you and that this finds you in the best of spirits and health and with God.

Love, Mom

Candy threw the letter to the floor. She hated the way it fluttered down, all soft and stupid, just like her Mom. She picked it up, balled it in her fist, and threw it down again, and then she picked it up and smoothed it out again.

She remembered how when she ran, she used to always have in mind making a whole lot of money and then sending for her Mom to come and live with her. Which didn't even make no sense, seeing that her Mom had never put herself out or taken no flack to save Candy's ass when her Dad was out to get her.

She remembered how that first time she ran when they caught her she made a real ass of herself when he showed up at the station in his uniform. She'd been with this sick dude, Gene, that specialized in young girls he used to sell to perverts that couldn't make it with no full-size women. By the time they caught up to her she was scared silly and fucked till she was good and sick, and when she saw her Dad she'd already started to run up to him when she heard him say to the other cops, 'This little tramp aint no kid of mine. You can send her up and throw away the key, as far as I'm concerned.'

At first when she was in the state school he'd come up to visit her with her Mom, probly just to make sure Mom didn't bring her nothing or talk to her. The other kids would get visits that brought them food and money and it was the worst shame she could think of, the two of them sitting there staring like she was a dog they had to visit twice a year. After a while she used to try to aggravate him cause she knew he wouldn't hit her out where anyone could see it.

'You must think you're fucking God,' she'd scream at him. 'That you can have a kid and treat her like shit and won't nothing happen to you. Well, you're gonna get yours.' And cause the matrons was right there watching he'd have to walk out of there without laying a hand on her, and then after a while they both stopped coming.

When he was getting ready to kick ass at home you could always tell cause he'd start pulling the curtains and turn on the radio. Most of the time they wasn't no music in the house so she got so as soon as she heard that country-western shit she'd start running. At least she'd never sat back and took it the way her Mom did.

So now he'd left, her Mom wanted her back. Candy took and read the letter again to see was it really true. The crazy thing about it was how much she wanted to go back in a way herself, just like she'd kept on believing her Mom would come and live with her, even though she knew she never would. What would probly happen if she did move back, her Dad would walk in the next day and take out his belt, and this time Candy wouldn't say a word, just kill his ass. And spend the rest of her life in the joint. And her Mom would cry a little when she got took away and maybe send her a card five years later.

What her Mom always did to her was make her feel this giant scream inside her that felt like it might kill her if she couldn't get it out, but there wasn't no way to, except maybe by hurting someone. Some of the worst beefs she'd gotten herself into in here had happened right after she used to get them damn cards.

Candy lay down on the bed now and tried to let the scream out in the pillow but it wouldn't. Maybe she would show the letter to Foster on Tuesday before her hearing, which was the next time she was sposed to see her. Some of the girls was saying Foster had really had a nervous breakdown this time, that she had got sent away someplace and they had gave her electric shocks so she wouldn't remember nothing that happened the night of the fire. That she wouldn't never come back. But Candy knew it couldn't be true cause Foster had said she'd be at the hearing Tuesday. At least she didn't think it could be true.

Sometimes Foster used to tell her pretend like the person was right there and say just what she would say to them. Candy decided to do it in a letter, like she'd did with Billy a few days back, just write what she really felt and then not send it unless she wanted to. 'Dear Mom,' she wrote, in her writing that was so much like her mother's.

I was glad to recieve your letter, well I guess they say better late than never but I'm not so sure. I would of liked to get it before when I was still in a lot of ways a kid that needed her mother. I am a woman now, and one that knows how to get along on my own, because I had to. I know he didn't want you to see me in here but why couldn't you of just sent me letters or called when he wasn't home. I didn't expect no visits or nothing and I know I did screw up bad, but it seemed like you could of sent a few letters. And if I had a daughter I would of never just left her like you did, no matter how much trouble she got in or what someone told me to. You said I was your favorite, then why did you do that to me?

Candy stopped right there. She had wrote a lie. Cause she *did* have a daughter, or had had, anyway. And she had did just exactly what she said she wouldn't do – gone oft and left her. And that poor kid hadn't did nothing but get her ass born. In her case at least she had been a real bad girl, that kept on fucking up after she'd been gave one more chance quite a few times. Candy was crying now. She started another letter.

Dear Mom:
I wish you knew how much I wish I could come and live with you and things could be the way they used to only I don't remember it exactly the way you do but thats all right. I missed you and missed you all this time and every visiting day I kept thinking you might come. I'm not saying its you'r fault but you didn't and now I can't come. I'm sorry your sick and that he left you if your really sorry about that but he'll probly come back and anyway maybe your better off without him and can start a new life like I have to do now to. I'm glad your in AA, from what I have seen its a good organisation that helps a lot of people. I'm going into a program where you go to college and work at the same time, I will be a counseler for young girls that got in trouble like I was. Maybe I could come see you or Vise Verser later when I get settled and my head together it isn't that I don't want to see you cause I do. I will write again when I know my adress.

She signed it, 'Love, Cathy,' then added:

PS. You mentioned female trouble well I didn't really have any but they told me I did and took out my womb, anyways I had a hysterectomy just like you so I can't have no more kids. So you won't have no grandchildren from me, so maybe you could get to know Stans if he had some and is in

town or maybe get in touch with Sal. Could you send me her adress please? If you send it right away I will still get it here.
> Love, Candy
> (what they call me now.)

SONYA

'Now, I appreciate your loyalty, dear, but you mustn't forget the loyalty you owe to the girls you work with either.' Mrs Hanson leaned forward and patted Sonya's knee. It was their private meeting and Hanson seemed intent on getting her to say that Ruth was crazy. 'Dave tells me he's seen a lot of anxiety in them this week and I don't think it's surprising. An adult they have looked to as a model of acceptable behavior suddenly begins to act quite irrationally.'

Sonya smiled blandly, realizing that wanting to be fired gave her a definite advantage in this situation. 'I think it's more likely that they're anxious because Loraine got killed and they're afraid it might happen to them,' she said.

Hanson was still trying. 'I'd like you to remember when you were a schoolgirl, dear. That isn't that long ago, is it! Let's say you had a friend who had problems with a particular subject. Would it really help her to give her your own examination to copy from?' Because Sonya didn't answer, she supplied the answer herself. 'Of course not. It would only cover up a deficiency which would surface sooner or later anyway. Sometimes it's important to think hard about what will really help your friend the most in the long run.'

Sonya felt a sudden rush of understanding for the masks of blank, hostile stupidity which most of the women wore when they faced any staff. Such a mask was forming on her own face right now. More and more, she realized that to leave as soon as humanly possible was the right decision.

TUESDAY, NOVEMBER 10

RUTH

Murph gave Ruth a funny look when she came in on Tuesday morning.

'They know you're here?' she asked, as if she knew better.

'May I have my mail, please?' Ruth spoke coldly, and Murph gave her a long look.

'Lost a lot of weight, didn't ya? What's the matter, you been sick? I sent your mail on down to Mrs Hanson, the way she told me to.' Ruth told herself not to waste her anger.

'Will you buzz me in, please.'

'Gotta check.' And Murph sauntered slowly over to the phone, stopping to arrange something on her desk on the way. It was just like a royal court, Ruth thought, word got around quickly as to who was in disfavor. She was startled to hear a voice at her elbow, belonging to the yellowish, rat-faced man she'd often seen outside on the compound.

'You better take it easy, lady,' he said. 'You get a lot of hep in here, catch it from the terlets. Then you get a relapse just like that.' He snapped his fingers, revealing dead white palms and long yellow nails. 'Had it four, five times, never would take care of myself right. Now I got a chronic case.'

Ruth had felt slightly sick all weekend and her stomach heaved dangerously.

'Come on back, Jim,' Murph told the man. 'We'll search you now.' Jim vanished behind the desk and Murph reluctantly buzzed Ruth in. When she got to her office she saw a typed notice on her door. 'Miss Foster will be out indefinitely due to illness. See Miss Wisen, Mental Health Secretary, for reassignment.' Rage exploding inside her, she ripped the notice off and threw it on the floor. Hanson had done her work well. As far as everyone on the compound was concerned, she was already gone. Inside, her office was dirty, cluttered with crumbs and coffee cups full of floating butts. There was a chewed piece of gum fixed squarely on the desk. Almost blinded with anger, she began to clean up. So she was supposed to pack her things up quietly, after the parole-board meeting, and leave for good. If they thought for one minute that they could keep her quiet by labeling her as crazy, they had a big surprise coming. She had already decided to make public whatever information she knew, and now she swore to herself that she wouldn't leave without dragging them with her in a nice big court battle.

She thought of staying in the office until Candy came in, to repossess it, but it felt violated to her, the air thick and nauseating. Instead she decided to take a walk outside. She sat on a bench in the yard, pulling her coat around her and shivering. The harsh smell of marijuana floated sickeningly toward her, and she looked up to see two women huddled together smoking reefer. She pointedly looked away.

'Hey girl, want a toke?' There was nobody else out here in the wind, so they had to mean her. Was it some kind of joke, or could they really not know who she was?

'No thanks.' She got up to go back in, but she was too late. One of them was approaching her.

'You sick, huh?' the stranger asked in a friendly way, smiling to reveal a gap between her front teeth. She was a stocky, handsome woman whom Ruth had never seen before, so she must be new. Ruth smiled awkwardly, trying to get away.

'Yes, I'm not feeling that well. . . .'

'Wait a minute, sister.' The woman grabbed her arm and held on. 'I seen you shivering and turning colors. Been through it myself. No wonder you didn't want no reefer, huh? When I'm coming off, the smell makes me wanna puke too. Aint they giving you nothing for it? You want me to walk you down the hospital, raise up a little fuss? Shit, they sposed to give you something, honey, aint sposed to let you do it cold! By the way, the name's Rae. Just got in Sunday. How bout you?'

Rae's other hand had moved to Ruth's neck and Ruth took a quick step back. 'Ruth,' she said. 'But listen . . . I'm not. . . .'

'Well fuck you then, baby! They lots more where you come from, cracker cunt! Hey, I don't want no one don't want me!'

Ruth, even more shaken, went back into the building. She'd sat outside a lot before, and no one had ever mistaken her for an inmate. She wondered what the next step in her acquaintance with Rae would be if she were really an inmate, and was glad that she didn't have to find out.

Sonya would have enjoyed the encounter, she thought. She'd have been pleased to be mistaken, and would have told the story for weeks afterwards. Probably she would have thought of a way to deal with it so that she and Rae ended up laughing together. She wondered how much longer Sonya would last here after she herself had left, and overwhelmingly, against her better judgment, she ached to see her.

CANDY

'Good luck this afternoon, Candy,' Dickface Thorne had the balls to say to her. 'As pretty as you look today, I'm sure they won't deny you a thing.' The bastard was on the board his damn self, so he already knew what they was or wasn't gonna deny her. She smiled in his face, thinking of the things she had took from his office.

Then it was like she'd hoped for but been scared wouldn't happen. Foster's door was open and she sat there behind the desk, looking skinny and pale but pretty much like her old self.

'Hi, Candy,' she called out. 'Come on in.' Candy came in and sat down in her place, and then she couldn't look right at Foster so she looked at, not the blue mug, cause she had broke that, but the black and speckled one.

'We got the board meeting in two hours,' she reminded Foster. 'You get them papers in for me?'

Foster nodded. 'Everything's set.'

She was talking in her old voice, and before she could stop herself, Candy blurted it all out. 'Miss Foster, everyone's been saying stuff about you. Alice Anderson said you went crazy and got locked up and she said they was gonna do something to you, cut your brain up or something so you wouldn't tell any one what happened to Loraine. She said they already did that to Telecea. And Wiggins told me she heard Hanson tell Dr. Thorne you had a breakdown and wasn't coming back.' First Foster's face went all white like Candy had slapped her, and Candy could of kicked herself, but then those two red spots came in on her cheeks and she got mad.

'I'm sorry you had to hear all that crap. I guess they figure that if they tell everyone I'm crazy my word won't be worth anything and I'll keep away.'

Candy liked the steady angry sound of Foster's voice. Her own words came fast now. She told Foster how ever since Loraine got burnt she hadn't had her burning dream no more, and did Foster think maybe the dream had been a warning that if she'd listened to maybe Loraine wouldn't of had to get killed. She told her she was freaked out about the parole hearing cause of that feeling of they could just grab you up and do any damn thing to you, like they done to Telecea, and what if they only said they was letting her out and really took and put her in that place where you didn't get to talk to no one but computers?

Foster said she thought the dream was about Candy's past and wasn't a warning, and that Candy had done everything she could of to help Billy and then Loraine, and instead of blaming herself she ought to feel proud. And that it was natural to feel upset about Loraine's death. She said Candy would probably feel upset about it for a long time, but she didn't need to blame herself. Then she said she could understand why Candy was worried about the board meeting but she was sure nothing like that would happen and she would be right there, making sure it didn't. The way she said that Candy could tell Foster had thought of the same thing herself, and didn't think Candy was weird or paranoid or something for being scared. Then they both realized it was eleven o'clock.

'Shit,' Candy said. 'I didn't even get to show you all these letters I been carrying around for you to see.' Foster thought a second. Then she said she didn't mind skipping lunch if Candy didn't so if she wanted to they could just go on talking until the hearing.

'I'm already dressed for it,' Candy agreed. For a moment it was too hard to look right at Foster and she went down in her purse to find the letters. When she got to them she saw they was all worn at the edges, and she remembered that postcard Loraine had pulled out to show her, the one with the fucking bride and groom on it. 'It's one from my mother and one from Billy,' she told Foster, but then she had started crying and she wanted to tell Foster it was about Loraine's card but she couldn't talk.

'Never mind,' Foster said. 'You can tell me in a minute. I'll read these.' She did, and by then Candy could talk again.

'It's not that she died that's getting to me so bad,' she said. 'It's that damn card.'

'You mean you were crying about her life as much as her death?' Foster asked. 'And that she never got the chance to really get past that postcard?'

'Yeah!' It was a relief to have Foster say it like that. 'And see, when I read Billy's letter I got scared for me that way. Like if I stay hooked up with her what if *I* never get past that shit either?' Foster nodded. 'I got to see her when I get out,' Candy went on. 'I got to at least give it a chance or else I'd always be regretting it. But I aint counting on it no more. On her.' It was like saying it out loud made it even more true.

Then, like she knew it wasn't quite real to Candy, Foster started talking about the school program and what the courses would be like and the work, and this woman she had went to school with, that was a teacher there. And then they could hear them getting ready to go to lunch out in the hall, cause it was twelve o'clock.

All of a sudden Candy got a sinking feeling. She had been so busy worrying about everything else, she hadn't really thought about how, if everything went right, this would be her last time seeing Foster. She looked at Foster and thought *she* was thinking it, too. She looked sad, and almost transparent, and for the first time she really saw how much weight Foster had lost.

'Shit, girl,' she said. 'You better start eating!'

Foster smiled at her. 'Shit girl yourself,' she said. 'You better keep in touch, after you get out of here!' Candy felt a little better.

'Do you think you're still gonna be here?' she asked.

Foster tried to smile. 'Not for a while,' she said. 'I just don't know. But if I'm not working here anymore, I'll be working somewhere, and I'd like to keep seeing you, if you want to continue therapy. I'll always have an office.' Then she looked at Candy's expression and laughed. 'Or if you've had enough therapy for a while we could still stay in touch,' she said. She wrote down something on a piece of paper and gave it to Candy. 'Here's my home phone. Maybe we'll both be around for a while longer, but just in case we're not, call me and we'll have a cup of coffee.'

'Yeah,' Candy said. 'I think I'd like that better. We could be like two people talking.'

Candy could tell Foster was sad just like she was. 'One thing,' she said. 'If we're going to be two people talking, you better call me Ruth.'

'OK,' Candy said. 'Ruth.' It felt funny to say. Right then there was a knock on the door and without even waiting for Foster to answer it, Hanson came busting in, looking at them all suspicious like she expected them to be fucking or something.

'I'm sorry to interrupt,' she said, but not like she was really sorry. 'Dr. Thorne told me that this little tete-a-tete has been in progress for at least two and a half hours now, and you and I have an appointment, Miss Foster.' She gave Foster a weird look, and Candy could tell she'd just now made up this appointment. Foster got all tight-assed the way she used to be.

'I'll be with you when Miss Peters and I have finished our meeting,' she said in a voice like ice. Then she raised up her eyebrows and stared hard at the door until the old bitch had to leave. But when the door closed, she was shaking.

'Old Fuck-face,' said Candy. 'That bitch better watch her back starting now. I still got me some friends in here.'

Foster shook her head. 'I'm not even gonna pay any attention to what you just said. I can't stand the woman myself. But you know it aint about attacking her!'

Candy laughed. 'Maybe it is time for you to leave, girl.' She couldn't quite say Ruth yet. 'This place must be really getting to you if you're starting to talk like us. But you're right, I'm not about to mess myself up like that.'

'Good,' said Foster. Then she got quiet and serious. 'Just in case this is the last time we get to talk for a while,' she said, 'there's something I want you to know. We've been working together for two years now, Candy, and I've watched the way you handled the last weeks. I have so much respect for you, Candy. You're a very strong woman.' Candy nodded, afraid to breathe.

'It's going to be hard out there,' Foster went on. 'It's going to be hard and lonely and crazy a whole lot of the time. You're going to want to give up sometimes and get sent back here. But I think you can make it. I have this deep feeling that you can make it.' Then it was almost one o'clock, and time to go to the hearing.

Afterwards, when Candy thought about getting out, she always tried to remember her talk with Foster instead of the board cause it was even more of a joke than usual. At the end it was on Tranden and he said in view of her progress they'd decided to give her a special early release, that is, just as soon as her papers, which was being processed right now, came in, with three years probation of course. Then they were all looking at her, waiting for her next line which was 'Thank you,' but she just couldn't get it out, even by telling herself over and over wasn't nothing for sure until you held those papers in your hand and even then it was better to wait till you was out the door before you told them about themself. Cause once she said 'thank you,' she knew what words would have to come after. 'Thank you, you motherfuckers. Thanks for letting me out a month early cause you were so chickenshit about me spreading the word how you killed my friend. Thanks for teaching me more than I ever knew about how to hate. And a special little thanks for stealing my womb. I hope every one of you gets the thanks you deserve.'

She held all that in. Then she thought of something she did want to say. She looked right at Ruth. 'Without Miss Foster's help, I'd still be back where I was. She's the best thing this place got going for it, and I sure hope she stays a long time so she can help other girls like she helped me.' Hanson and Thorne and Tranden's faces all went sour, but Candy knew they couldn't keep her back for that. She and Foster gave each other a real smile, and then Candy walked out, wiping her wet hands on her skirt.

SONYA

On the subway to the train station, Sonya was determined not to feel guilty about Ruth. She turned her thoughts deliberately away, trying to picture the loft on the Bowery that Barb had told her about, and mentally arranging her pieces for the sculpture contest. If the loft was right, she could get a U-Haul for her clothes and sculptures and be living in New York by the weekend. She'd just have to leave her furniture and get Barb and some other friends to go back for it with her in a week or two. Right now she knew she had to get out of this damn town as soon as possible.

'But Sonya, you can't!' Ruth's voice returned to plague her. 'You can't just tell them today and leave tomorrow. At least have the common decency to give them a month to terminate!' But according to Ruth's friend Lisa, who'd woken Sonya up with her call this morning, Ruth might not be in any shape to scold anyone right now. Lisa had called because she was worried. Apparently, Ruth had been officially fired from Redburn at the same time as Victor had picked up and gone. Unsure how much Lisa knew about the whole mess, Sonya had told her that she'd been out of touch with Ruth and was heading out of town for a couple of days, but that she'd call Ruth as soon as she got back. If it turned out she didn't have time she'd just have to call from New York. Ruth had done OK without her all these years. She'd manage. And there probably wouldn't be time. She didn't see how she was going to get any sleep in the next few days as it was.

Now she wondered why Victor had left. Things had to have been building up between the two of them for years. She hoped it didn't have anything to do with her. Anyway, even if Victor had used that abortive night she and Ruth had spent together as an excuse to walk out, it wasn't her fault.

If only they'd fired *her* instead of Ruth. For some strange reason they weren't bothering about her, almost as if they'd found out she was leaving on her own, which was impossible because she hadn't told anyone. They hadn't even questioned her when she asked for these two days off. Shit, she'd still have to deal with Redburn on

Thursday and Friday. But after that she'd never have to see Ruth or Redburn or any of them again.

She wondered if she could make her own departure a protest against Ruth's having been fired. But the women probably wouldn't understand no matter how she did it.

'Termination's a word in a textbook,' she argued with Ruth in her head, as she'd been doing all week long. 'If I'm leaving I'm leaving.' What the hell difference would a month of misery for everyone make? As far as she was concerned, a clean break was as good a way of ending as any other. It was her way, anyway. Ruth would be horrible about it, but that was because she'd feel abandoned herself, not because of anything intrinsically wrong in what Sonya was doing. Not that she was really abandoning Ruth either. A person was allowed to move.

Sonya got off the subway and went into the train station to buy her ticket. Just ahead of her in the line, a drunk was arguing with the woman behind the window. 'Listen, I got to get to Wisconsin, my old lady . . .' Sonya remembered Loraine and shivered. The sooner she got out the better.

Anyway, it wasn't as if she'd been at Redburn for years and years, like Ruth. If some of the women had grown attached to her in such a short period it wasn't her fault, was it?

The ticket to New York felt good in her hand, a guarantee that she was getting out. If only it wasn't round trip. And saying goodbye to Ruth would be the worst of all. Maybe she could just write her a letter and mail it the day she left for good. She could say what Barb had pointed out to her on the phone, that there was nothing strong about sticking doggedly to a place that was neither nurturing nor growth producing. Not to speak of a job which forced you, no matter what your politics or how much you genuinely cared for the women, to ally against them with an administration that was as corrupt as they come. Ruth's recent experience ought to make her understand that part anyway. She could say that Ruth's having been fired had been the last straw, that when she'd heard that, she'd given in her own resignation.

'Yeah, sure.' Ruth would laugh in her brittle way. 'Tell it to Telecea.' But Telecea was gone. She'd just end the letter by saying that knowing Ruth had been the best part of the whole fall, she hoped Ruth wasn't angry, and she'd stay in touch. It didn't feel great, but it was the best she could do. Maybe she'd send Ruth one of the Redburn sculptures, after the competition was over.

'New York City,' announced the loudspeaker. 'Leaving at Gate Five.'

THURSDAY, NOVEMBER 12

RUTH

Used to interminable delays on all papers involving inmates, Ruth was surprised to receive a certified envelope Thursday morning. Inside was the official notification of her termination, signed by Tranden and by someone in the main office, and dated the tenth, the day of Candy's hearing. 'Poor Judgment and Mental Instability Resulting in Danger to Inmate Population' were listed under 'Reasons for Action.' There was also a separate letter from Hanson, barring Ruth from the institution as of today and requiring her to pick up her things out front within the week.

Ruth smashed her fist against the table, hurting herself. She pictured hiding out in the parking lot with a baseball bat, waiting for Hanson to come out, then hitting her with it again and again. When Dave and Tranden came out she'd do the same thing to them.

Her rage disappeared too quickly, leaving an emptiness in its place. She picked up the phone without letting herself think about it, and dialed Sonya's number. As it rang and rang she remembered. Of course. Sonya was at work, up in the art room. Everything was going on there as usual. Redburn Prison wasn't going to close down just because Ruth Foster had been fired. But it was terrible to think of the mental health wing, of *her* office taken over by someone else. It was unreal, a nightmare, as if she'd come home one day to find that her key didn't fit in the lock anymore, that new people had moved in while she'd been gone, that her things had been removed and no one knew who she was. Only this was even worse in a way, scarier. Because Redburn had been the place where she had been on her own, away from Victor, where she did work she believed in, where she could recognize herself. It was more her home than this apartment, more her home than anywhere else, and now it was gone and Ruth felt as if she was gone too.

They disappeared me, Telecea used to say, and Ruth whispered it to herself, understanding for the first time what she'd meant. 'They disappeared me.'

She thought of Candy, who was gone from there just like she was, who had to be feeling strange and homesick and unreal too. Because even though you were locked up it still became, maybe not your home, but still what you were used to, what you knew. And when that was taken away there wasn't anything there, just emptiness. Candy should be at the Y by this afternoon if they hadn't decided to fuck her over somehow at the last minute, and Ruth wanted badly to go there and see her. But she knew that she couldn't, that it would be a crazy thing to do, that she had to let Candy go.

And anyway it was Sonya and not Candy she really wanted, Sonya who could fill her terrible emptiness. How was it possible that she hadn't called, even after she'd found out that Ruth had been fired? Then it came to her that Sonya wasn't there anymore, that she'd disappeared somehow too. She would never see Loraine again, no matter what she did, and maybe it was the same with Sonya.

Ruth went into the cold empty bedroom and curled up in the bed and after a while she started to cry and then she couldn't stop. It went on and on, agonizing wrenching sobs that seemed to have nothing to do with her and then the phone was ringing and she ran, blind, towards Sonya's voice.

'Ruth! I finally got you. You don't sound so good.' It was Lisa and Ruth wanted to fling the phone against the wall, to crack it into a million pieces, but she kept the receiver there at her ear. Lisa was saying that she had a good friend who was a feminist lawyer, that she'd already talked to her about Ruth's case, that she'd said Ruth should definitely appeal. 'Shall I give you her number?' she asked.

'No.' Ruth got the words out with an effort. 'Can I get it later?'

'Sure,' Lisa agreed, 'or I could bring it by for you after work. You shouldn't be alone too much right now, Ruth. You should be with friends.'

'Thank you.' Ruth heard Lisa's voice, her warmth, but it was somewhere far away, at the other end of a long tunnel. 'Not today, but soon. Why don't you visit soon.' After she hung up, she paced the apartment. Victor had come by to pick up more of his things yesterday, so now there were bare spots, especially in the living room.

'I'm seeing someone,' he'd said. 'I'm getting my life together.' She hadn't known if he'd meant a lover or a therapist, but it had been too much trouble to ask. The whole time he was there all she'd wanted was for him to get it over with, to take his things and go. What if Sonya called right then with him in the house. Then she'd never believe he was really gone.

CANDY

At the last minute they got together and gave her a party, which Candy didn't expect at all, cause of the weird way they'd all treated her since Loraine got killed, and cause of how it all happened so quick at the end – the hearing Tuesday, and then her papers coming in Wednesday saying she could leave out by noon on Thursday.

Her little bit of stuff was packed by Wednesday night, so on Thursday morning she didn't have nothing to do, and she went out in the ice cold yard and walked around. She stopped for a minute under the window at Max where they used to keep Telecea, remembering the time she'd stood right under here and yelled up that message Norma had gave her, and how at first Telecea had started to sort of believe her but after that she always said Candy had stole Norma's voice. There was a rumor Telecea was gonna be shipped back, and Candy wondered if it was true. They was saying they had done a operation on her out there and Candy hoped they wouldn't send her back turnt into no vegetable. When she really thought about it, what happened to Loraine was more Telecea's fault than anyone else's, but for some reason, Candy couldn't look at it that way. She walked around shivering and trying to say some kinda goodbye to both of them, Loraine and Telecea, and to her tree, that was all bare and lonely looking now, and to this yard that was the same place where her and Billy had been walking that time in the snow when Billy first said she loved her.

And then Lou came flying over, pulling on her saying come quick they was an important phone call for her in the cottage and her hopes went flying up cause she thought it was Billy saying she'd got her message through the grapevine and was on her way out to pick her up. But it wasn't. It was the party. It was Norma and Lou, Donny and Linda, Fran, Frankie and her new woman Pat, Edie and Avis, Jodie, with her new woman Grace Powers of all people, and Gladdy. Norma had baked this big fat chocolate cake that someone had wrote 'Good Luck Candy Cane' on, and what got to Candy most was how they had all went and dressed up. Here was Norma in her blue-black church dress and Lou all dolled up with her hair corn-rolled, and even Gladdy dressed decent and looking almost like a normal person. And for a while Candy felt bad, like these were her only true friends, the only people that knew what she was really about, and she'd never find anyone like them on the outside. The call came in saying she could go, and then Norma hugged her tight against the rustling blue-black and said, 'I'll be out soon, too, and you know I'm a look you right up, girl, and you remember you are someone, and don't let no one tell you different.' And then Candy hugged them all and Gladdy told her, 'God gone protect you, Candy Cane, cause Gladdy told Him watch out for you.' And they all went with her to the front and no one acted like they thought any less of her cause it was just that state car waiting with her shit in it, and even if they did all start talking about it when she was gone, she wasn't gonna be there to hear it anyway.

When she was out the door walking to the car was when it hit her the hardest that Billy wasn't there, and wasn't gonna be there, the way she'd kept on hoping she would show up right up to the last minute. At least it wasn't Moody driving, but instead that little dude they used to have watching Telecea, that they must of put in there cause she wasn't no kind of security risk no more. So she asked him would he please meet her down by the road in ten minutes cause she wanted to walk out on her feet, and he shrugged and said alright but don't go near the fence or it was his job.

And so Candy walked down the grassy slope across the street and over the cement parking lot and it was really happening the way she planned it. She went in the field and then she looked back and saw the big fence, only she was on the other side of it now and she wondered was there anybody watching her through the hole. And then there was a noise and when she turnt around the white horse was coming right up to her. She picked up some grass and he nosed it right out of her hand and she reached out and touched him on the nose and it was a real horse, warm and breathing in and out. She closed her eyes and smelled the air and opened them and everything was still there, the horse and the green field with woods behind it smelling of almost winter now, and she thought it was alright in a way to be alone without Billy, because she had done what she wanted to do. And then she started to walk back slowly, to the state car that would take her into the city.

She was glad she had took the time to say goodbye in her own way cause the nightmare started up right off, when the dude left her on the busy street in front of the Y, with all her shit piled up on the sidewalk. He didn't offer to help and she wasn't gonna ask no screw for nothing even on her way out, so there she was. It was a neighborhood she remembered, just a few blocks from where she used to hussle, but she felt like she'd forgot everything she used to know. Even the hard pavement under her feet and the cars speeding by felt strange. She stood there, with her four suitcases and three paper bags, knowing she must look like she had just got put out, and waited for someone to come along and help her with her bags. Didn't nobody stop, though, and she started to feel like she had brought the being invisible out here with her. Some broads gave her a dirty look, like who does this bitch think she is standing out here blocking the sidewalk. And a few tricks licked their lips or whistled or something but that was it.

Finally someone did stop, a fucked up little dude with a torn windbreaker and a process. She wished if it had to be a mack at least it could of been a fine one, but she didn't have no choice in the situation, so she gave him a little smile and when he helped her carry the bags up to the lobby she told him her name was Telecea Jones and gave him a bogus address for where he could find her as of tomorrow. All the time she was trying to get rid of him, these two old bitches had been sitting staring at them from behind the desk that had the mailboxes and phones and shit. The minute he left, the nastier looking one, that had lipstick smeared all over her horse-face and pink powder in the ugly old creases, spoke up.

'Candace Peters? From Redburn?' Candy just nodded, and the bitch went on. 'I warn you right now young lady, you are not allowed to have guests in here, you will have to ask your friend to meet you elsewhere from now on.' Candy just stood there with her mouth open at first, cause shit, this wasn't no different from in there. Then she remembered she was out, where there wasn't no more D reports for cussing.

'How the fuck am I sposed to get my shit in here?' she asked, nasty and streety as she could be. 'I know you-all seen me standing out there, but I didn't see no one getting off they ass to help.' This, with knowing she was fresh out of jail, must of scared the bitch, cause she shut her horse jaws with a click. Candy managed to get her shit to the elevator by herself by making a few trips, keeping her eye on one piece while she dragged the other and knowing she'd croak anyone that touched it with her goddamn teeth if she didn't have nothing else to do the job with. Then she realized she didn't have no key.

Horse-face gave it up real slow, with, 'We have a full house up on the fifth floor and I expect you to respect the other girls' rights. Any complaints and you can find someplace else.' Candy kept one eye on her stuff and came right up in her face.

'You treat everyone this way or just girls new out of jail?' she asked. Then she went back to the elevator. By the time she got herself and all of it up to the room they had gave her on the fifth floor all the energy she had used to get the dude to help her and make him leave and to tell horse-face off had drained away. She fell out on the bed in the room with its green walls that was too too much like her room at Redburn, and closed her eyes.

After a while of just laying there she looked out the window and there was all the people, still speeding by. All of a sudden her chest felt so tight she couldn't hardly breathe, and she was dizzy too, like she was on one of them fun-house rides where they whirl you round. They had told her it was gonna be hard when you got out, but nobody hadn't told her about this shit! She closed her eyes again and tried to breathe real slow and to think of something that would make the ride stop. What she was looking for was Billy, but the ride was going round too fast and she couldn't get off and she started thinking that Billy wasn't real after all. And she didn't even have her phone number. And then she got the thought in her head that if she did get the number and called, Billy would say, 'Candy Peters? I don't remember no Candy Peters,' and hang up the phone. Now she felt like the only thing that would save her was if she did find a way to call Billy and Billy did know her. She thought maybe Mabe would know, and she had Mabe's number. But the only pay phone she'd seen was way the hell down the lobby, right in front of them two at the desk and she just couldn't do it. But she had to get in touch with someone fast, cause she didn't have shit on her, not even one lousy joint. Like a damn fool, she had got all paranoid at the end and thought they might do an internal on her and ship her to that computer joint if they found anything, so she had left out clean. And of course they hadn't searched her, and now here she was, going some kind of crazy in here, and knowing if she even had a little bit of reefer, there wouldn't be nothing to it, she'd just walk straight past that bitch to the lobby and make her call and go on about her business. But she couldn't. She just couldn't do it. It wasn't even dark yet, probably around five o'clock or something, but she took off the little pants suit that she had wore to leave in style, that she had seen after five minutes out there wasn't in style no more after all, threw it on the floor with the rest of her shit, and crawled in the bed.

SONYA

As if to rub things in, the empty art room was radiant today, as beautiful as it had appeared to Sonya on that day of celebration when Ruth had come in bearing flowers. The sun flowing through the windows shone on the room's strange, pleasing angles, made Ruth's white wall glow, and cast striped shadows on the white oilcloth of the long central table. It warmed the rich brown of Gladdy's easel standing in its corner near the door, and tarnished the silver frame of the mirror which Telecea always turned to the wall. Today it was Sonya who couldn't look into it. She took out her camera and looked at the walls, which she realized, now that it had all ended, were truly unique. The monsters, with their variegated colors and shapes, danced on Telecea's wall, their long feathered tails trailing. Gladdy's wall, with its flowing river and invitingly smoking chimney, could have hung in some museum, alongside other American primitives. Even Alice's structured box had its own grace. She photographed the walls painstakingly, recording every inch in both close-ups and long shots, almost as if she were doing a criminal investigation. After she left, they'd almost certainly come in and paint it over, but at least now there would be a record. And the photos, blown up, would make a good back-drop to her sculpture entry. She avoided photographing her own wall, although she rather liked the mural, with its bright colors and earnest, almost photographic realism. It made her uncomfortable with the promise she saw in it, an assurance that the group she had painted, or at least one like it, would sit at this table for a long time. Just as Sonya took her last photograph, Gladdy came in, the top of her pink dress unbuttoned, her shoelaces trailing. Someone had begun to braid her hair, but had apparently stopped halfway. Ordinarily Sonya might have finished the job, or would at least have buttoned her up, but she couldn't bear to do either today. There were still a few pictures left in the camera, and she laid it on the table in front of her. Questions about its presence might provide a good lead-in to the explanation she had to make, and the taking of a few group pictures, with copies promised to everyone, might serve as an appropriate ending ceremony. But Gladdy didn't notice the camera. She was upset, jerked out of her usual state of slightly manic serenity.

'Now aint it a dirty shame what they doing downstairs!' She stood, swaying as if in church, 'Done strip that sweet Ruth Foster office, Lord! Take whatever they lay their dirty hands on. Why you let them do it? Why?' Sonya wondered uncomfortably whether this last was directed to her or to the deity.

'Aint enough to lock us up,' Gladdy went on. 'Strip us of all we gots, Lord. Now they gots to come get them that try and helps. Strip that poor girl right down to the bone, that what they done. Cut off her pretty hair, now they done took her office from her. Send her out in the cold wif no flesh to her bones. Let that wind git her, Lord.' Gladdy rocked on her feet and moaned. Tears ran down her cheeks. 'You done put old Gladdy in the harness, Lord. Strip her of all her kids. Now you gone take the only friend she got. What gone come next, Lord? Tell me what come next!'

Sonya sat, helpless. She'd known that Ruth had been Gladdy's therapist for a while and still spent some time with her, but she hadn't realized that this much attachment still existed. She had no idea what Gladdy might do when faced with a second parting, and she was feeling more and more unwilling to find out. But maybe Gladdy had sensed it herself, with her usual intuition, and was lamenting for both losses at once? If only this were true and Gladdy would break it to the others as they came in, saving Sonya from having to do it herself!

'Least I still gots my painting.' Gladdy spoke more cheerfully now. 'Gone make me a picture, Lord. Picture of Ruth Foster so I remembers her always.' She began carting out the jars of paint and brushes, preparing to go to work. Always before, Gladdy had stuck to pleasant scenes from the past, never once bringing her present reality and distress into her art, and never referring to herself in the first person. She'd had to pick today, of all days, to make this tremendous progress. Sonya couldn't stand it. She wanted to run out of the building right now, without telling anyone anything, and never come back.

Now Donny and Linda walked in, swinging hands. 'Hey Sonny!' Donny beamed at her. 'Got a good idea today, alright!' She, too, went to the cupboard for paints. Alice was next, then Jody, then Avis and Edie, and finally Grace. Several of them got started on their own. The others waited for direction, talking together meanwhile, a friendly and cohesive group. The dismemberment of Ruth's office was the hot item of the day, with Candy's departure that morning

413

running second. Everyone spoke of Candy with respect, and a kind of hope. 'She's gonna make it,' decided Donny. 'You aint gonna see her ass back here no more.' The group feeling about Ruth, in contrast, was much more tumultuous. Alice, Edie, Donny, and Gladdy, the ones who'd worked with Ruth, were the most upset, but Ruth seemed to mean something to all of them.

'I aint surprised!' Edie snorted. 'She cared, dint she? Old tight-ass and all, but at least everyone knowed she cared. Course they getting rid of her!'

Enviously, Sonya realized that she was doing it all wrong. She should have waited for Ruth to be officially fired, then sent in a letter of protest so outrageous it left them with no alternative but to fire her too, posted somewhere the women could see it. That way nothing would be her fault. They'd talk about her as warmly as they were talking about Ruth. But her decision had its own momentum now. She'd already made her plans. It was too late to put it off, but at least she could tell them she'd been fired too. Maybe she could even get Hanson to fire her later in the day.

'What are we doing now?' Alice, Linda, and Grace were getting anxious. 'What we sposed to do today?' She couldn't answer them and Gladdy belatedly gave the alarm.

'Art teacher gonna cry. Something else bad happenin'. What now, Lord?' They all turned to Sonya, suddenly more quiet than she'd ever seen them. Donny left her seat and came over to her.

'What's wrong, Sonya?' Her voice was panicky and her fore-head beneath the swept-back black hair was sweating. She seemed childlike, as she often had before, and Sonya realized for the first time that Donny genuinely cared about her. Somehow she hadn't believed that her leaving would actually hurt anyone.

If this were a movie, she thought, the inevitable ending would suddenly be reversed. At her realization of Donny's love, a look of quiet peace would spread over her face. 'Nothing is wrong,' she'd tell Donny, very gently. 'Nothing except that I realize how much I care.' The curtain would go down on that note, and they would all live happily ever after, or, anyway, as happily as it was possible to live in prison.

But that wasn't the way it worked for her, in real life. This new knowledge only increased her guilt, and the terrible pressure. 'You're not going to like this.' She said it harshly, in a different voice than she'd ever used to any of them, and saw Linda, who cared deeply

414

only for Donny, and so was less personally involved than the others, guess the truth. Linda reached for Donny to warn her, to protect her somehow, but she was pushed away. Donny, like Alice and Gladdy, needed it not to be true.

They were forcing her to say it aloud. And so she did. 'You've all been talking about how they made Ruth Foster leave. Well, I have to leave too. The same thing's happened to me. They fired me too. This is my last day.'

'You fuckin' liar!' They all froze, because it was Donny screaming, Donny the just, Donny the art room's voice of reason. 'They are *not* making you leave. You're bored with us! You got what you wanted. You're following your bitch, that's all. You never cared. I wish you never came here! I wish I never talked to you, you dirty cunt!'

Donny picked up the camera from where it sat on the table. She threw it, with her strong pitching arm, as hard as she could against the mirror. Both the mirror and camera shattered, loudly. Glass and metal fell. Then, without pause, Donny picked up the first of the full quart jars of paint on the table and threw it against Ruth's blank wall. She threw a second jar against Telecea's wall. Laughing harshly, Edie ran to get the rest of the jars of paint from the cupboard. She and Avis began throwing them against the walls too. Jody and Linda joined in, and finally Grace and Alice. Only Gladdy stood, loudly mourning the destruction of the wall that was her memory. As if wounded, the ceiling rained color. Ruth's white wall was covered now, with red, blue, yellow, and green paint, sloshing together in a brown mess halfway down. Telecea's wall, along with the others, was obliterated. The paint covered Sonya herself, dripped in her hair, and ran down her front. She tasted it, with her tears, on her lips. There would be no record, no witness, after all.

FRIDAY, NOVEMBER 13

RUTH

Ruth rang Sonya's bell, willing her to be there. If she wasn't, Ruth had decided to wait, for hours if she had to, until Sonya came home. Because she had to come home eventually, she couldn't have moved, not that fast. But she hadn't answered her phone all week, and when Ruth had called Redburn this morning they'd said she wasn't there either. All Ruth wanted was to see her. Just to see her and touch her and know she hadn't disappeared. She knew she was being crazy but it felt like something she couldn't do anything about, like having to eat or drink or breathe.

As it turned out, she didn't have to wait long. She heard steps on the stairs, and then Sonya opened the door. She wore overalls. Her hair was pinned up on her head and she was covered with dust. Inside the doorway Ruth clung to her, taking in the feel of her face and the solidity of her body. She hadn't disappeared at all, or even changed.

'I was afraid you were gone,' she said. 'I was afraid I'd never find you again.' Sonya's body stiffened. Too quickly, sighing, she pulled away and led Ruth up the stairs.

At the top Ruth saw cartons and boxes, everything piled together and torn up. The sculptures were packed away out of sight and she knew that Sonya was leaving.

'When?' she whispered, sitting on one of the boxes.

'Tonight.' Sonya stood awkwardly at the door. 'But just to New York. It's not that far.'

'You left Redburn?'

Sonya nodded, not looking at her. 'I had to. I was going to call you to say goodbye before I left.'

'No you weren't.' Ruth looked at her and she knew perfectly clearly that Sonya had intended to leave her as quietly and as ruthlessly as she'd probably already left the women at Redburn. This knowledge did nothing to take away her terrible loss. She stood perfectly still, holding her mouth closed against the moan she wanted to make.

'No. You can't.' She reached out to hold Sonya back, and then she felt another part of her stir, a hungry determined part that didn't

416

care about anything except what she needed so badly. She looked over at the stripped bed.

'Leave tonight then,' she said to Sonya, 'I don't care. But come here now.' Sonya came, and Ruth fumbled at her clothes until Sonya took them off herself. Then she took off her own clothes and Sonya came to her on the bed and Ruth's tremendous thirst found the great brown nipples, the answering heat of Sonya's body, and she pressed as close as she could, drinking her in.

CANDY

Candy was burned real bad, with her whole arm on fire. Off in the distance Billy and Dina and that Lehrman and some other girls from the joint was passing one syringe back and forth. And then she saw it was Foster in there doing it too. Candy wanted some bad. She wanted to stop the pain and she kept on begging, 'Please, please, pass it over here.' All of them was in it together, and acting like they couldn't hear her, but finally someone did give it to her, and she grabbed it and stuck it right in a vein in her arm and then she heard a voice screaming and screaming, 'There aint nothing in it, you fool, there aint nothing in it!' but it was too late. She had shot herself up with air and now she was dying.

She woke up alone in the green room sweating and panting. It was morning, with sun coming through the little window. She jumped out of the bed and started looking through the suitcase she'd packed to live out of the first week, and now she didn't even care what she put on cause she just had to have some dope. She pulled out her old jeans and a pink nylon blouse and got dressed, and was on her way out when she remembered about carrying a purse out here and went back for it. But when she looked in the mirror, she knew wasn't no way she could let Billy see her like this – a skinny scarey looking girl with long stringy different colored hair with the roots gone dark and a pale face with big shadows under the eyes.

She thought what she'd do, she'd go to this club, Tops, where she used to hang. Because she needed some dope bad.

She tried to hold her purse like she wasn't expecting some screw to come up to her and ask her what the hell was she doing with money, and made it to the elevator. Another girl was standing there, waiting for it, too. Candy was trying to act all relaxed and not even look at her, so she jumped a foot when the girl started talking to her with this weird accent. 'You haf stay here long?' She must of been a Puerto Rican or something, but she didn't talk like the other Puerto Ricans Candy knew from the joint.

'No, I just got here today,' Candy said. 'From California.' And then she got all paranoid cause what if the girl had just came from

California herself and would expect her to know about it. But she didn't seem like she was from no California. She was kind of cute in her own way, but dressed real weird, with this black fingernail polish and shoes with them real high cork bottoms that used to be in a few years back. Her hair was dyed a funny red, almost purple color.

'I just now haf walk from the airplane,' she said, having all this trouble figuring out what words to say. 'I am still seeks hours after, it ees still night with me, ees like a dream, you understand?' Candy laughed, cause she sure did, but for a different reason.

'That's true, huh?' she asked. 'It was a whole different time where you came from?' This was something she remembered learning in school, about different time zones or some shit but she never had believed it before. 'What country are you from?' she asked.

'La Fronze,' said the girl. 'Pa-ry,' and a thrill went through Candy once she'd realized what she meant, cause she hadn't never known no one from Paris, France before, and here she was, meeting one on the very first day she was out. 'I haf come to be oh pear,' said the girl. They had got out the elevator and was standing talking in the lobby. The two old bitches wasn't around. At first Candy didn't know what oh pear was but the girl went on talking about how she had always wanted to come to America and her family told her it was 'just dream' and then this rich American family came to eat in her mother's restaurant that had some friends that needed a girl to take care of their kids, and they had hired her without even seeing her. Candy had thought that anyone from Paris, France, would be rich and stuck-up and shit, but this girl seemed alright. She said she had came three days early to look around for herself, and that she was gonna stay with this family just long enough to get some money and then, 'New York, Los Angeoleez. Sand-fran-cees-co,' she said. She was talking real big about these places, but she stood in the lobby like she was afraid to go out.

'You hungry?' Candy asked her. 'You want to get some breakfast?' The girl looked all relieved.

'Ah yes, I haf be afraid to go to the restaurant because I do not yet comprehend the money!' she said. Sure enough, she held a bunch of bills and change in her hand like it was play money or something. So it was true what they said about how every country had different looking money.

'Don't worry,' Candy told the girl. 'I'll explain the money to you.' The girl smiled at her.

'It is good for me we meet,' she said. 'I was a small afraid, you comprehend. Only because I haf just come.' Then she held out her hand, all formal, and introduced herself. Her name was Cuttee. But when she wrote it out, Candy had to laugh, cause it was the same as hers, CATHERINE. So Cuttee must be French for Cathy. She was a kind of dizzy naive bitch, that didn't seem like she'd seen too much of life, but Candy was glad she'd met her. Walking down the street, Candy tensed up again cause even early like it was, the men started right in.

'Hey Mama, how much for that nice little piece of ass?' one called, and another, more serious one, came up close, and whispered, 'Twenty?' It made her sick, but she started thinking that here was her dope money she needed, seeing how she already had the name. But Cathy didn't know it was just Candy they was calling to, and she pulled on her bad arm. Candy winced with pain.

'It is true, what they say?' Cathy asked. 'The men in America, they will to kill we in the street to make sex? We shall go back? I do not want to die, this my one day!'

Candy had to laugh. 'Me neither,' she said. 'I got me some living to do. Hey, don't worry about it. Long as you ignore them, they'll leave you alone.' And then they walked down the street just like two straight girls, paying no attention at all.

They went into a coffee shop, Candy going first, like she was used to doing it every day. She explained to Cathy what the different stuff on the menu was, and wished that Ruth Foster would come along right now. 'Hi Ruth. This is my friend from Paris, France,' she'd say. 'I'm showing her the city.' It was rush hour now, with everybody out, and cars and people was speeding by.

'So fast,' said Cathy. Candy smiled.

'You get used to it,' she said. Tops could wait, she decided. Her and Billy could drop in there sometime, when they was back in contact. Which could wait until she had her hair done and some nice clothes. Until she was good and ready.

SONYA

The U-Haul van was packed with everything Sonya had been able to carry by herself. She took the sculptures down last of all, placing the package containing Telecea's frozen, fragmented face on top of the bulky one in which the figures of Candy and Billy swung together on the subway pole. She put the well-wrapped limp form of Rubber Woman next to the box which held Ruth and herself balancing together on the black velvet see-saw.

Suddenly she had the same sickening feeling she'd had when she left Vermont. She remembered her frantic packing then and she knew moving was pointless. She'd carry it all with her, just as she'd carry the expression on Donny's face and the way Ruth had looked at her when they lay together this afternoon. It would make more sense to drive the heavy van with its burden straight into the harbor.

She could see the headlines. 'Lesbian sculptor destroys self and work in protest against prison conditions.' It was already dark, and she turned on the headlights. As she pulled carefully out, she imagined Ruth reading it and weeping, saw the movie camera fade on a last shot of the water closing over the whole mess.

Sonya smiled to herself. She liked the image. She turned the van onto the freeway, heading North.

SUNDAY, NOVEMBER 15

CANDY

Sunday afternoon Candy walked Cathy to the Greyhound station, and said goodbye to her outside the door, cause the bus station was one of the places she'd worked on her escape, and it had real bad vibes for her. They was one or two ho's hanging outside too, looking as down and sick as she must of then, but luckily it wasn't nobody she knew. She'd only lived here a few months before she got busted so at least it wasn't like being in certain cities where every hussler on the street would of remembered her face. Cathy kissed her once on each cheek like a real French person on TV, and cried, and said Candy was her first American friend and she would never forget her and would telephone her as soon as she could. Candy was much too used to see people leave to cry herself, so she just waved goodbye and turned to walk back to the Y.

Yesterday, the two of them had went in this classy little place where the cute faggoty hairdresser took one look at her and said, 'Let's take off that face and see what's underneath.' He wiped off all her make-up, so she was just sitting there with her bare, lined face and dripping wet hair but he didn't seem to think she looked too bad.

'With those cheekbones you don't need all that,' he told her. 'You could look very classy with just a little lipstick and eyeshadow and oh my dear what have you been doing to your hair?' Then he started cutting and it fell on the floor, red and silver and blond, Candy's old dead hair. The girl that looked back at her in the mirror had short fine light brown hair around a sharp pale little face. At first it didn't look a bit like her, but then she remembered her eighth grade graduation picture, which was the last time she had her hair like that, and was also the last time she went by the name Catherine. 'That's more like it,' the hairdresser said. 'You should never hide a face like that.' And he gave her a real smile.

After getting their haircuts, her and Cathy had went back to a certain little store they'd kept on passing, and Candy bought herself a wine-colored pressed-velvet jump suit, with them baggy legs that was tapered at the ankle and a short pleated jacket to go over, cause that's what the style was now, simple and just a little butch. She found a pair of fine suede shoes to go with the outfit in the same store, and felt a little funny, paying one hundred and fifty cash which was more than half of what she had saved out of all those hours in the goddamn flag room for shit she could of easily walked out with, but it was cool. It was what she'd planned, sitting under her tree, and now she'd did it, which already made her different from all the girls that used to talk and talk about their hot shit plans, but the second night out would find them decorating some street corner.

Plus, she needed a good, classy outfit like this, so the first time Billy saw her she'd take one look and know she wasn't about no more streets. She'd called Mabe's number but the phone was disconnected, and the only address she had was the project where Billy's mother lived. It was just possible that Billy hadn't talked to no one and didn't know she was out here. What was more likely she was holed up somewhere, too fucked up to call. Or maybe she'd found another woman and was through with Candy. No matter what, she needed to hear it from Billy's own mouth. And if she had to go to Billy's mother's place to find her then she was ready to do that too.

When she got back to the Y, on her own again, the old bitch told her someone dropped off a package for her. She got all excited, but it wasn't from Billy after all. What it was was a letter from Ruth Foster and the mug she'd bought to replace the one Candy had took that time. The card, that had a picture of two girls talking on the front, said that Foster had already left Redburn and when she was taking apart her office, she'd found the mug and wanted Candy to have it. It said she was fine, and it was probably time for her to leave Redburn anyway, and she was thinking about Candy and hoping things were going well for her and not to worry too much if she felt strange at the beginning. That *she* felt strange, and she hadn't even been inside, just worked there, so bad as it was, it must be a hard place to leave in some ways. She said she'd be out of town for about a week, visiting an old friend in California, the one who made the first cup, and here was her phone number there just in case Candy wanted to call and after that she could call her at home any time and she would love to see her soon. The card was signed, 'Affectionately, Ruth.' Candy held the mug tight in her hand and walked fast to the elevator so the horse-faced bitch wouldn't see her cry. Cause for some reason the note did that to her, just like seeing Foster sometimes used to. It made her feel like a little girl that wanted its mother. She sat down in the bare green room and cried a while, and then just sat and thought. Then she wrote Foster a letter back.

Dear Ruth:
How are you doing? Fine I hope. I hope you had a good time in
California and got some sun. You deserve it!! Thank you for the
cup and note. The card is very pretty too. I was sorry to hear your
not at Redburn anymore, and hope that bitch (excuse my
language) Mrs Hanson didn't fire you. Your probably right there
are better places to work where they won't give you so much shit
(smile). It meant a lot to me to get the note and package, I cryed. I
hope you understand when I say I need to find my own feet more
before I call you. I want to know I can make it on my own. I would
like to call you in awhile when I already started school and work
and have my own place and everything. Cause you are the one
person that in a way was almost like a mother to me, what I mean
is you always lissened to me and cared and helped me to get in the
program and everything. But when your a kid you have to leave
home. Today I got my hair cut back to it's original color and I
have a appointment to talk to your friend Ann at that school Monday. She
sounds nice. Really I will be in touch pretty soon. Yes it is strange out here
but I am handeling it fine so far. Thanks for every thing.
    With Affection your friend
    Catherine Pierson
(the former Candy Peters)
P.S I met a girl from Paris France and showed her around.

424

WEDNESDAY, NOVEMBER 18

CANDY

First thing about these projects was the smell. Candy thought it smelled poor, and stopped to ask herself what did that mean. It was the smell of piss, she answered herself, piss and spilt booze, and most of all, the smell of garbage. Redburn, with all its roaches and bugs, always smelt like a hospital or something, probly cause of the shit they washed the floors with, and Candy's room at the Y had the same smell. Some little kids was following behind her, so she guessed they wasn't used to seeing a whole lot of white people here, except for maybe the welfare and the police. This was a big motherfucker, not the kind of project she'd pictured where everybody knew each other and neighbors hung out of windows gossiping, but just blocks and blocks of these big dirty-yellow buildings that looked like they was closed up tight, like the windows didn't even open, and outside there wasn't nothing but cement with garbage on it. She could see now that it wasn't going to be as easy as she thought to find Billy here, and she realized that Billy, proud as she was, might not have gave her the address cause she didn't want her to see it. But Candy didn't know no other way to find her, except for hanging at Tops and putting out the word that she didn't know where Billy was, which was one shame she could do without. 'Hey,' she called to the group of little kids in back of her. 'Any of you-all know a lady named Billy Morris? Live with her mother, Miz Morris? Little boy about your size call Timmy? Girl they call Teeny?' The kids acted like they was deaf, staring at her all blank. Then one little girl with wild nappy hair whispered something to the others and run off. Candy stood against a ugly yellow wall, waiting.

A half-grown boy came out the nearest building. 'What you want, baby?' he asked her. 'Who you come here looking for?'

'I'm waiting for my friend that lives here,' she told him. 'Billy Morris.'

'Yeah, well, look like he aint coming.'

A woman's sharp voice suddenly screamed from the window. 'Don't be talking to no welfare, Butch. Lady lost, let her find her own way home.' Candy was beginning to wish she hadn't cut her hair and wore her new suit. No one had ever took her for no welfare before.

'You see a briefcase, papers on me?' she asked, talking street and black as she could to the boy and loud enough so the woman could hear too. 'I'm looking for a girlfriend of mine, name Billy Morris. Live with her mother, Miz Morris. Little boy name Timmy.' The woman's voice said something about cracker shit and the window came slamming down.

'Aint never heard of no people like that round here,' the kid said. 'But I do know a real nice place you and me could go. You get high?' Just then the little girl came running back with Timmy. It took Candy a minute to recognize him because he looked so different, not all clean and dressed up like he used to be at Redburn, but just another one of these wild little street kids with a dirt streak in his face and his sneaker-laces dragging. He gave her the same blank stare the others had, though she could of swore he knew her. She got down next to him.

'Hey Timmy,' she said. 'You remember me from going to visit your mama, don't you? She home with Grandma now?' Timmy nodded. A sly look was on his face. 'I want you to take me to where you-all live,' she told him, firm as she could.

Timmy stepped back. 'Mama say don't talk to nobody I don't know,' he said. The little girl that had went to get him was poking him, whispering something. 'I show you if you gimme a dollar,' he said. Candy reached in her purse and gave him the dollar, and the whole band of kids started leading the way. She followed, with the half grown boy behind. It was a regular parade. They stopped in front of a building and Timmy stared up at her.

'You go on upstairs and tell your Mama I'm here,' she told him. 'Tell your Mama, not your Grandma, hear?' He went running up the stairs, and Candy waited. She kept telling herself she was about to see Billy, but it didn't seem real cause it was so different from the way she planned it, with the two of them coming toward each other like in the movies. After waiting a while she started up the dark pissy stairs herself, hoping there wasn't no junky with a knife waiting for her halfway. On the fifth floor she heard a kid screaming like he'd just got hit, and she knocked on that door. No one came, but she kept banging, sure it was the right place, and determined as hell, now she'd got this far.

Finally Mrs Morris opened the door a crack, with the chain still on. She had rollers in her hair, but otherwise she looked like she did at Redburn. Candy could see a piece of the apartment inside, all clean and stiff, and the smell of ammonia came out at her strong. Mrs Morris talked to her real soft, so Billy and whoever else was in there with her wouldn't hear, but like she wanted to kill her.

'You go on now,' she said. 'Go on and leave my girl alone! She got enough trouble without the likes of you coming messing in. Go on now, git back to from where you came from, wherever that is, and don't come bothering us no more. Aint nobody ever taught you don't come in where you aint wanted?' The bitch closed the door in her face. Now Candy was sure Billy was in there.

'Billy, it's Candy,' she shouted as loud as she could at the closed door.

Mrs Morris was back. 'You git right now or I'm a call the police on you, girl.' Candy could tell it was costing her a lot not to shout. She got ready to book fast in case the bitch tried to hurt her with something.

'Go ahead and call them. I aint done nothing wrong,' she yelled. Then there was a big commotion, screaming and yelling, and she heard Billy's voice, telling her mother get out the way. Then it was Billy, out in the pissy hall with her.

'Look, baby,' she said real quick. 'I can't deal with you here. I'll meet you at the Dome, right across the street, in fifteen minutes.' Billy ducked back inside and the door slammed, locked, and double-locked. Candy heard Mrs Morris, who wasn't holding her voice back no more.

'I'm telling you this one time, Louisa Ann,' she screamed. 'You let that little honky ho' anywhere in my eyesight again, you can git out my house. Don't care if you do go right back in there. You know that little cunt nothing but trouble. If they find her outside here her throat cut who you think they gonna blame?'

Downstairs, the little kids was all gone, and the teenager was lounging on a stoop. She walked on by him, and out of there. Across the street was the Dome, a nasty-ass place if she'd ever seen one, but fairly quiet now cause it was still early afternoon, with just a few old drunks and junkies that wouldn't give her no trouble. Candy sat in a corner with a beer, and tried not to think about how Billy had looked, with her hair all flat on her head, her eyes glued half shut, and her skin dull and ashy. Still beautiful cause there wasn't nothing she could do to herself that would turn her ugly, but shit, it was early in the day to be fucked up.

She scrunched up in her corner and pretended it was happening different, the way she'd planned it. That it was somewhere else, even her room at the Y would do, and Billy had came to see her, dressed up and straight, to tell her she'd been waiting for her, that she'd found a place for them.

Then Billy was coming in the door and Candy held out her arms and just breathed her in, her smell and the taste of her lips that she'd been so thirsty for, and for a minute it seemed like it didn't matter that it was here, in this dirty-ass bar instead of the way she planned it.

'I love you, I missed you so much,' she breathed into Billy's ear. But Billy pulled back, restless and speedy.

'Why you wanna come over my mother's like that, girl? Shit, baby, I would of gave you the address if I wanted you coming round, now wouldn't I? Well, you better not get no attitude bout how she spoke to you. Coming like you did.'

'I don't have no attitude.' Candy felt suddenly, terribly, tired. 'I just came because I wanted to find you and I didn't know no other way. I didn't know if you even knew I was out or where to find me. I been out since Thursday.'

'Yeah, I knew you was out,' Billy mumbled. 'Just waiting to get myself situated, you know. They went and set me up, I told you that. That school shit fell through, plus I had a place arranged for us, two bedroom place, you know, but they screwed me outa that, too. Looks like someone got to the landlord before I did, you know, filled him in on my background a little. Dude said it was all a misunderstanding, that apartment was rented since last week, you know the kind of bullshit they hand you.'

'Yeah, I know.' Candy started telling Billy bout *her* first day out, how the two broads had tried to humiliate her and how she told them off, when she saw Billy was half in a nod, somewheres too far away to hear her.

'Yeah, yeah, that shit sucks,' she broke in, before the story was half over. 'Any time you start trusting them motherfuckers and their bullshit plans you know you in trouble. That's what I always used to try and tell you bout that goddamn shrink you used to tell our business to.' Finished with her rap, Billy nodded off again. A pimp and his two girls had came in the bar and was looking Candy over. The pimp caught Billy's eyes and the two of them smiled out the corners of their mouths. The beer tasted old and sour in Candy's mouth.

'Billy, we got to talk, but this aint the place,' she said. 'I got me a room at the Y, you want to come back there with me?'

Billy looked at her like she was nuts. 'What you don't seem to understand is I aint got no cash to go no where,' she said. 'Why you think I'm staying up here in the first place? Before you and me talk, we gotta make us some money some kind of way, girl.'

Candy felt a chill go right through her. She could of started to cry, right there in that place, but she heard her voice come out hard and cold instead.

'Yeah? And how we gonna do that? You got something in mind?'

Billy grabbed her bad arm, hard. 'Don't start,' she said in a low voice, but full of hate. The other people in the bar was staring at them, but she knew that Billy could leave her under a table in here and wouldn't nobody blink an eye.

'You come in here with your hot shit hairdo. College girl clothes. Come to my mama's house where aint nobody asked you in the first place. What you come for anyway? You want something from me? Well, nobody take from Billy Morris and don't give back.'

The tears were on Candy's face now, and it wasn't about how her arm was hurting, either. 'I came here cause I wanted to see you,' she tried once more, but she knew there wasn't no point to it. Billy knew she wasn't gonna get no dope money from her, and the way she was now that was all she wanted. Now it was about punishing, and she knew enough not to stay around and take it.

'Get up ho'.' Billy jerked her by the burnt arm again. Then she let go and slapped her hard across the face. And all of a sudden Candy didn't care if she did get hurt.

'I aint your ho' and don't you ever call me that again,' she screamed, and then she hit Billy and kept hitting her. Not like she'd slapped her back that time at Redburn, but the way she hadn't fought since she was thirteen and new at the reform school, before she was anybody's fem or anybody's anything, except just a little animal trying to survive.

Billy was shouting and trying to grab hold of her. Candy tasted blood in her mouth, and it was the taste of her bitterness. From believing in Billy and getting this in return, and the fence always in her line of vision, and the dirty streets out here that wasn't no different from the fence after all, and the looks they gave her in the street, and in the Y, and the new clothes she'd spent her money on to

429

see Billy, that was bloody and dirty now, and everymotherfuckin' thing, and next thing she knew she was standing over Billy with a broken beer bottle in her hand and that dude was coming up in back of her when something stopped inside her and she froze. She looked at Billy's face, wet with blood and tears and dirt, and at her eyes, all empty and gone. And then she did what was the hardest thing of all, which was to pick up her purse and back out of that place, still holding the bottle, part of her wanting so bad to drop it and cry and say she was sorry and hold Billy but she knew if she did, it would all start up again only now Billy would have to keep hurting her for what she'd done.

Out on the street she was crying and she knew if Billy or the mac or anyone else wanted to come after her they could do what they wanted cause they wasn't no fight left in her. But like a miracle a cab came by and like another miracle, the dude stopped for her when she screamed out. She got in, first dropping her bottle outside, told him the Y downtown, and prayed. And thank God he didn't tell her forget it but just started driving, and then after a while a gentle West Indian voice said, 'Lady, none of my business sure, but you bleeding, you want I take you direct to the hospital, maybe?' She felt her nose and it wasn't broken, so she told him no thanks, she was OK.

And she made it somehow past the bitches at the desk, keeping her face turnt away, and up in the elevator, and in the bathroom to wash off the blood. And then she was in the little green room with the door locked, thinking at first about how would she make it to the interview at the school place, with her face messed up and her new clothes ruined. And then she curled up small on the hard bed, shivering cause she always called Billy her people and now she didn't have no people. Now she was out here alone.

AFTERWORD, FRIDAY, DECEMBER 4

RUTH

When Ruth came out of work it wasn't dark enough to be dangerous yet, so she walked to the subway through the park, where the Christmas lights had just been turned on. They were all icy blue this year, and she shivered in the cold, feeling alone among the streams of other people going home from work. She didn't want to go straight home herself, so she walked up the hill lined with old brick houses, their windows yellow with light. She could see dark silhouettes of people moving behind each window talking or eating, in groups of two. Part of her yearned to be inside, with someone else, safe and warm, but another part was glad of her fierce aloneness, glad there was nobody waiting for her at home, nobody counting on her. She felt with her gloved hand for the notebook and pen in her briefcase.

She'd started writing again at Martha's, and lately she'd been writing in her journal a lot and working on some of the entries afterwards. They were short, not quite stories because they didn't really have plots, but not poems either. 'Yellow windows,' she said out loud as she wrote. 'Windows yellow with warm and unknown lives.'

'The warmth of unknown lives,' she tried out, liking the sound of that better. There was a woman coming down the sidewalk toward her, and she shut up, knowing she must sound like a crazy person, but not much caring. Then she saw that it was Candy.

She stopped still, her heart lurching crazily. It was like meeting a part of herself she'd stuffed away, and she wanted to take Candy in her arms. 'Candy, it's good to see you,' she said instead, glad that her voice came out steady and clear. 'How are you?'

'Alright.' Candy's hair was darker than Ruth's now, cut short and stylish. She wore tight jeans, a brown jacket with a fur collar, and brown high-heeled soft leather boots with matching fur tops. She shrugged and wouldn't meet Ruth's eyes, stamping her feet in the cold. 'I'm doing pretty good. Keeping it together. How bout you?'

'Pretty good, too. I got a new job, in a clinic near here.' It was too cold to stand there making small talk, but Ruth couldn't bear to let Candy go just like that.

432

'There's a place down the block, do you have time for a cup of coffee?' she asked.

Candy looked embarrassed. 'I'd really like to . . . Ruth,' she managed. 'But I'm on my way to meet someone. From the program you know, we're studying for this test.'

'That's OK.' Ruth had found her work voice again, smooth and reassuring. 'Call me when you're ready.'

'I will.' Now that the encounter was almost over, Candy looked her in the eyes for the first time. 'Don't think I forgot you or something,' she said passionately. 'I'm gonna call soon as I get it together a little more. It's hard out here at first you know. It's a bitch.' They reached out briefly, touching gloved hands. Then Candy took off, walking rapidly on her brittle high heels. Ruth watched her stop, look back at her, and then vanish.

CANDY

Candy walked up and down in the cold, freezing her ass and all jumpy cause she was sposed to meet this dude and he was already twenty minutes late and she didn't like standing on no corner like some damn hooker. She looked down the hill and saw the park, all lighted up with these cold blue lights, and she wished he would get the fuck here so she could get it over with. Just enough cash to get her own place, that was all she needed, it wasn't like she was really dealing or nothing. She would sell what he had for her, put a security deposit down on her apartment and leave it right there.

Sometimes she wondered how the fuck Foster had thought she was gonna make it on the stipend they called pay in that goddamn program. Probly she never gave it a thought. The program was getting to her anyway, the way they always hung over you like they was just waiting for you to fuck up, and then didn't pay you enough to cover your food bill, let alone the $500 down the landlords wanted before they'd rent you nothing. Sometimes she caught herself explaining shit to Foster in her head. 'Look,' she told her now, 'you may not approve of my doing this, but what would you suggest, really? Keep on staying with Lee until I give in one of these days and start taking on her extra tricks?' She missed Foster sometimes, but wasn't no way she was going to call her now, the way she'd made it to the program only about half the time in the past couple of weeks. Ann had probly called her and told her about it, and Candy could just picture Foster's face when she heard, all screwed up and disapproving, thinking how she'd wasted her time arranging it.

Candy walked up a block and then turnt around and started walking back. She decided if the dude wasn't there by the time she got back she'd forget it. There was a broad coming her way talking to herself, and then all of a sudden it turned into Foster, the real Foster, coming toward her and smiling, and her heart jumped and she wanted to run to her as fast as she could or run as fast as she could in the other direction both at once, but it was too late for either one.

When Foster spoke to her it was like the loneliness of the past months rose up in her all at once. Foster looked ready to cry or to hold out her arms, and for a crazy minute Candy wanted to run into

434

them and tell her everything. About the Y, and walking past horseface every day till she couldn't take it no more and moved in with Lee. And what happened with Billy and how she still thought about her constantly. And about the time she went out with Lee and Donny, who was out on her furlough, and shot a lot of dope and knew she didn't want that life no more but was scared she was gonna do it anyway. And how she had to find her a place soon cause or else it was gonna be too late. About how she was thinking of dropping out the goddamn program if they didn't kick her out first, and about the dream she had every single night that she was back inside and a couple times that she was Telecea and they had locked her in a cage and cut up her head.

But that dude was due to show up with his blow any minute, now Candy didn't want him to, and wasn't no way she could pass him off for someone else. And anyways Candy knew this wasn't the right time to talk to Foster, not when her life was still fucked up like this, and so she told Foster goodbye and walked away as fast as she could.

Walking down the street she wished she asked Foster more about herself and how she was doing. She planned how she would call her up sometime soon in the future, and ask her that kind of shit, like a real friend. By then she'd be able to tell Foster she'd had to drop out the program, cause all in all it was nothing but a set up. And about how she'd pulled it together and made it anyway, all on her own.

SONYA

Because of the overwhelming response to her winning entry in the 'Women's Art as Social Consciousness' show, Sonya's first class at the new institute was so over-enrolled that sixty women had to be turned down. She was calling the class, which included some discussion and some experiential work, 'The Artist and the World.' This was only her second time, but she already knew she'd love teaching. The twenty women in the class, with their trendy, carefully selected second-hand clothes, their paint-stained hands, and their rapt faces, drank in every word she said. It was a little like having the movie camera on her constantly.

'If you're really serious about what you're doing,' she concluded this morning's lecture, 'you'll have to come to terms with a certain kind of loneliness. I'm not talking about total isolation, but rather a separateness, a refusal to merge your identity with any particular person, place, or group.'

She approached the blackboard, gesturing with the chalk. 'What I think you'll find, if you haven't already found it, is that most people inhabit a small tightly structured world, which on some level they believe to be the only world which really exists. As an artist, you're outside of this.' She drew numerous small dots on the board, connecting them with spider-web-like threads of lines. Then she made another, larger dot, with no entangling lines. 'This one is you, the artist,' she told them. 'Lots of systems will try their best to draw you in, and it won't be easy to resist these efforts, it never is. They'll include the assurance of love, comfort, belonging, roots, and family. How many of you are willing, as part of your job as an artist, to resist these things?'

A dark haired young woman raised her hand. 'What you're saying sounds sort of male and elitist to me,' she argued. 'How can you portray anything, except superficially, if you're not intimately involved? Think of women's folk art.'

Sonya nodded, smiling. 'That's a good question,' she agreed. 'It's not an easy line to draw. It's true that in order to understand you must enter to some extent. You assume the customs around you. You wear the costume. Sometimes you find that it fits you, that you feel at home in it. That's fine. The danger comes only when you forget that it's a costume, and think of it as your skin. When you forget that other people wear other things, in other places. That there are other places. It's when you become so encircled that you can't see out that you can no longer function as an artist.'

An older woman with a crackly voice and long grey hair was waving her arm. 'Is your point that as artists we're always outsiders?' she asked.

Sonya nodded yes. 'We are always outsiders to some degree, which can be hard. But don't forget the advantages. When most people's concrete world collapses around them, as worlds tend to do, they're crushed, they break down in some way. You, the artist, don't need to do that. As long as you're still alive you can make a sculpture, a painting, write a poem about the collapse. And then move on.' This last sounded too cold, so she decided to get more personal.

'It's a way of survival,' she explained. 'I had a student once at the prison I worked in who believed she was possessed. When I met her, she was at the mercy of occult and Godly powers. She felt herself to be a passive victim, condemned to carry out God's violent commands. I taught her to express her feelings of possession through her art. She began to paint demons. She learned to take some control of her own life in that way.' Somehow this calm story felt so far from Telecea that Sonya was afraid someone might challenge it. 'I'm not saying she's out in the world making money as an artist now,' she added. 'She's still in prison, still deeply troubled. But at least wherever she is now, wherever she may be sent, she has a tool of control and survival that no one can take from her. I couldn't stay with her as her teacher. Instead, I hope I gave her something she could keep.' The students loved her prison stories. She decided to tell another, even more revealing.

'Let me tell you about how I used this survival mechanism, myself,' she said, 'when I was fired from the prison, for activism. My students there couldn't understand this, of course. They believed I was leaving because I didn't love them, because I didn't care. On my last day they destroyed the art room. My year's work went down the drain. The room was entirely torn up. I didn't know if *I* might not be torn up next. I stood there, with paint streaming down my face, down my hair . . .' She heard the class draw in their collective breath. 'At the same time,' she concluded, 'there was a part of me which watched the event as it happened, and saw it as an incredibly

437

colorful, vivid happening, full of power. My artist-self was recording it, and that was what saved me.' The students all nodded, in satisfied admiration, as she continued.

'If you hallucinate, watch the images, paint them, sculpt them, write them down. If your lover leaves you, make a loss piece, a grief piece, an anger piece. If you're obsessed with someone, do study after study of her or him. If you're a compulsive eater,' she smiled here in gentle self-mockery, 'do a food piece, an eating piece. If guilt about something is bothering you, think of the tremendous piece you can make out of that.'

She looked around at her starry eyed students, knowing she could take any one of them home with her after class. 'I'm not saying that your lives will become easier as you claim yourselves as artists,' she finished. 'Your objective experience, like that of my prisoner student's, may not change at all. But your experience of your experience will change.' She smiled warmly at each of them. 'I recommend it highly as an identity,' she told them. 'It's a way of life in which you never really lose.'

TELECEA

Make them send me back. Back to this place. Think they can take and use me up. Think that metal box can eat my brain. Eat my dreams. Think they can do me so I can't make no more sculptures. So I don't know where I am. I know alright. This place call Max. Been here before. Will be here again. Make them send me back.

All them evil ones with they unclean ways. Change they costume, change they voice. Grow a dick, take it off. Say, Send her to the empty place. She know too much, got to take her mind out. Send her to the place aint got no color. No smell, nothing to see. No peoples.

Nothing to hear, just the voice in the metal box. Please get out of bed now. Thank you. Now you may make the bed and take the tray.

Send her there, see what happen to her dreams. But He been protecting me all the time. Send me my visions in my sleep no matter what poison they puts in my food. And when they try and torment me with the box, He send me His own voice out that box. And my teacher Sonya voice. Right out that metal box.

All the time He keep talking to me. Tell me I am His child. His good sweet child that never hurt no one. One time He speak in Norma voice. Tell me they the ones born bad wif the devil in they soul not me. Tell me be patient and He bring me back. Just wait and lissen don't eat no food. So I aint ate nothing. Get weaker and weaker. And after a while they has to move me out. To they hospital where they got real nurses not no metal box. But I keep on doing what He tell me and after a while all them nurses be going off on each other. Get so sick they can't eat they own selfs. I aint done nothing to them, just lissen and wait and tell them what I knows. But one day they all say, Get her out of here, or we quitting.

So they brung me back. Back to this place. And I still got my sculpture picture in my head. And I still knows how to wait. Wait for my teacher to come back.

She coming closer. Almost here right now. Talk to me all the time and He do too. Tell me, You the one, Telecea. The artist. The one He pick. Tell me, You be they ghosts. Get in they heads when they sleep. Be they Venger for what they done. They black-white

devil in they dreams. They beasties. Be they crazy girl. They trick
with a gun up they cunt. They dick curl up inside them. They ho'
Jezebel. Tell me, You be wherever they be. Lissen and watch. Up in
Max or wherever they puts you. She talk to me every day. Tell me,
You be the witness.

THE END